June's March

In Millbrook, love's a little wild—and so is grandma.

By Heather Jane Hill

<u>What's been said about *June's March*...</u>

From Aussie Readers...

'Enjoyable and easy read as June discovers love and a love of country life by baptism of fire,' Helen, S.A.

'The best read I've had in a long time,' Carl, Qld.

'Loved it, H,' Cass, Qld.

'Really impressed. Why can't I meet a "Dave"? Can't wait to read the next book,' Jenny, S.A.

'You made me cry, H,' Denise, Qld.

'You may have written about real life, H. But unfortunately, it's not MY life, lol. But I wish...' Michael, Qld.

'I really enjoyed it and can't wait to read your next novel,' Amanda, S.A.

'I read it in one day and laughed out loud many times. And about Dave...I want one,' Karen, SA.

From Overseas Readers...

'I highly recommend the novel, *June's March* by Heather Jane Hill. This story takes place in Australia with the main characters, June Hall and Dave Andersen coming from very different parts of the country. The author's descriptions of this unlikely relationship drew me in as if I was part of the story. Once I started reading it I finished it in 2 nights. The author's writing technique makes this an easy read!' Sharon, Ohio, USA.

'You made me laugh, H,' Dr. Kendra—American roaming locum.

'I loved it! You made me cry!' Margaret—pensioner, Adelaide.

For Veronica

Who taught me:
You're never too old to make new friends,
And you're never too young to lose them.
Oh… and a little about "Bunnings Boys," too…

RIP, my beautiful friend.

Chapters

Chapters—Cont.

* Canoodling without delivering the goods!

Chapter 1

__The Closest Neighbour__
Week 1—Sunday Afternoon

'Lord—love a duck!' June Hall sat as stiff as a week-old corpse in the driver's seat of her suddenly stationary hire car and took stock of what had happened. Reflexes had made her brake hard, swerve left, and bring the nifty white vehicle to a standstill on the road verge. She'd been driving cautiously. Slowly. She always did in unfamiliar places or on unfamiliar roads, and this situation was both—Tropical North Queensland on an unsealed road!

Adrenaline surged through her veins, and her heart pounded heavily inside her chest. As a nurse, she understood how adrenaline worked on the body, so she drew in and released slow, deep, purposeful breaths to regain her composure. She was fine, and the car appeared to be so, too.

Two-metre-tall grass stood sandwiched against the front and passenger side of the car. She didn't know grass could grow so tall, and despite the inconvenience of blocking her view, she was grateful for it. Without it enveloping the car, she may not have been so lucky.

'That was too close,' she sighed. The engine idled flawlessly, its sound washing her with a wave of calm. She directed her eyes to the rearview mirror to watch the white utility with a trailer in tow that had forced her off the road disappear into the distance. Why anyone would drive over a crest while hugging the middle of the road was beyond her.

'Note to self…' she said, pulling her sweaty palms from the steering wheel and wiping them down her sundress. 'When in the sticks, stay well left on crests!'

The car remained in drive, her foot firmly on the brake. She shifted the automatic gear selector to reverse, moved her right foot to the accelerator, and pressed it down gingerly. The wheels spun on the flattened grass. *Please don't get bogged.* Then, as if answering her silent plea, the tyres gripped, and with a hefty rev, the car shot backwards onto the firm road.

Over the crest and down the hill – just as explained in the email she'd received - a red letterbox came into view. She slowed and stopped. A rustic, handmade sign on an equally rustic gate read Barrine Views, L & M Woodward, Lot 56, Arthur Willis Road. She noted the property opposite bore no name despite the stately brick pillars that framed its entrance. She jumped out of the car, stood at the gate, and stretched. After her morning flight from Adelaide to Cairns, her drive up the winding Gillies Highway, and a brief stop for groceries in Yungaburra, she'd finally reached her destination.

To open the gate, she had to detangle an old octopus strap that secured it—this tested both her fingers and her patience. She drove the car through, closed and secured it again.

'Where would this country be without good ol' Occy Straps!' she chuckled. In her eyes, the strap was well past its use-by date. Frayed, elastic strands poked through or hung limply from the faded, split casing, and the metal hooks were rusted, stripped of most of their plastic coatings. She wondered how many years this one had been on the gate.

She'd never been anywhere tropical before, and despite the stifling heat and humidity, "thick enough to cut with a knife," she was in awe of the undulating scenery around her. The vivid greens of rainforest pockets and the lushness of grass paddocks impressed her, but she'd enjoy the view later. A shower was calling. She'd never experienced true humidity and doubted she'd enjoy it during her stay—it was physically sticky.

The Woodwards' driveway was long and neat. It comprised two crushed stone tyre strips framed by freshly mowed grass. As she made her way uphill toward the house, she grinned widely. Every cow within cooee appeared interested in her arrival, even if only fleetingly between grassy mouthfuls. This was just as she imagined the beautiful Atherton Tablelands to be.

An open bay in a three-bay shed drew her attention. *This must be where the Woodwards park when they're home.* She drove into it. In the next bay was a ride-on mower sign-written, The Beast. She guessed she'd have to tackle that at some stage and hoped it came with step-by-step instructions—she'd need them!

Dr. Woodward and his wife had left for a UK holiday that morning. As they would not meet June in person, they'd thoughtfully emailed her with a subject line, "Everything you need to know about our property and our surgery". She had printed the many pages, read the first few paragraphs, and then placed the information in her suitcase. She'd read it in full when time allowed.

She turned off the car's engine to a short-lived silence. Four barking dogs of varying sizes rushed from the direction of the house to stop outside her car door. She had at least read that the dogs were friendly and hoped it was true. She'd never had a dog—she just wasn't an animal person. Besides, pets and a shared city apartment weren't a match in her eyes.

She struggled out of the car to their chorus, and each dog of undeterminable breed pushed forth for its share of attention. She made as much of a fuss as she could. Three of them appeared lean and healthy. The fourth, black in colour, was round and overweight.

'You like your tucker mate, don't you,' she acknowledged with a giggle. Her collar read, Daisy. She'd nickname her Tank— round like a South Aussie rainwater tank. She rubbed its broad head. This dog, she recognised, was a Staffy. The dogs, happy with a brief introduction, promptly headed back to the house. They'd been patted, introduced to the newcomer, and were consequently uninterested. Their destination was the sizeable deck off the front of the house. June imagined they'd spend most of their day lazing on it and watching the world go by, and why wouldn't they, she surmised.

She opened the boot and retrieved her luggage, then half-carried, half-dragged the cases across the grass to the deck, and up its stairs. There was a chain across the top step. She stared at it, unhooked it, and pushed it to one side, wondering if it was some kind of theft deterrent. *Do you need a theft deterrent with all these dogs?* She headed for the front door, and just as advised, it wasn't locked. Logically, this was a long way for any thief to come.

The Woodwards' house was far from what June had envisioned. Like the gate and the sign, it too appeared rustic. Doctors in Adelaide, in her experience, generally had splendid, modern homes that reflected their income and the hours of work they put into their careers. She had seen the inside of many city homes and surgeries through her job as a locum practice nurse and until now, had never worked or travelled rurally. She'd expected a few differences but never envisaged sharing her life with four dogs and a menagerie of other creatures she had yet to meet or read about. The only reason she was here was as a favour to her agency. The nurse who had been booked for the locum had fallen ill, and they'd been unable to replace her at short notice. In addition, the money on offer was unrefusable. The Woodwards would get their money's worth. She'd make sure of that. She always did.

What lay beyond the glass sliding door was a pleasant surprise. An immaculate and huge, country-style kitchen built of pine and Mini Orb greeted her. She dragged her bags through the door, keen to check it out further. Pots and pans hung in no real order from an old timber ladder suspended above the stove.

'Quaint *and* creative!' she admitted. She wasn't tall, but she would reach the pans she needed. She could see herself spending time in this kitchen!

On her way back to the car, June noticed a tiny home beyond the shed. She wondered—was it a guest house? Perhaps a She Shed? She'd find out in time. Opening the boot, she unloaded her bags of groceries. In the kitchen, she unpacked them and filled the fridge. She glanced at a bottle of red wine in her hand. It was too hot for room-temperature red, so she placed it in the fridge with a couple of other bottles she'd bought with her, not knowing what shops were available locally. *Sacrilege.*

The kitchen clock read 5:00 p.m.. 'Five o'clock already!' she voiced, surprised. 'No wonder my stomach's rumbling.' She wheeled her bags down the passage, peeking into each room. Adjacent to the bathroom, she found what had to be the guest room. There were towels, plus a soap, folded lovingly on the bed. *Oh, it's just like a hotel.* She began to unpack. She was here for the entire month of March, so she wanted to be comfortable. March, she'd been told, was a wet season month in the tropics—this was evident by the greenery and not by the sky, which was clear and blue for her arrival.

She set out her clothes in an orderly fashion—organisation was her favourite thing. If things weren't organised, she couldn't function at her best. She used the coat hangers and hung her dresses and work scrubs in the wardrobe, and as usual, the hangers all faced the same way. She finished the task with a yawn. Dinner, she decided, would be a simple sandwich washed down with one glass of barely chilled red. She'd hit the sack early too, she had work in the morning. She made her way back to the kitchen.

The Woodwards' kitchen exuded both practicality and style. June imagined that with a cooking space like this, they were probably both excellent cooks. She also figured that if they were as dedicated to their work as they appeared to be to their home, the practice would run like a well-oiled machine. It was Mrs. Woodward she would replace during her locum.

Hungrily, she took a plate out of the cupboard and placed it on the bench. Before she could take anything from the fridge, a chorus of dog barking drew her attention. She made her way onto the deck. A white ute with a trailer in tow came barrelling up the driveway. *Is this the same one that forced me off the road earlier?* If she were certain she'd give them what for, but she wasn't.

She headed down the stairs and out to meet her unexpected visitor, a visitor who wouldn't be for her—only the doctor's surgery knew she'd be here. The ute pulled up, its engine stopped, and a man wearing a well-worn, cowboy-style hat on his head jumped out of the cab. He was alone, and she could see he was on a mission. He hesitated before her, glanced at her hire car in the shed and then back at her.

'You the house-sitter!' he remarked. It was more of a statement than a question.

'Yes,' she replied warily. 'June—June Hall.' He tipped his hat, nodded, and proceeded to the rear of his trailer. She watched him curiously. The trailer held captive a large steer. He opened a gate that doubled as a ramp, then jumped up alongside the animal. She hoped for his sake; the beast was friendly. Without a rope or harness, he encouraged the bovine to walk backwards out of the trailer. With four hooves on terra firma, he rubbed its head—as if it were a dog—slapped it on the rump and sent it on its way.

'Off you go, Winston,' he insisted. 'You've got a reason to stay home now—a sharp-looking house-sitter!' She heard the man clearly; his voice was strong and travelled through the silence of the block. She blushed in response to the comment. She'd never been called "sharp" before. Sharp was a word she related to needles and their disposal—aka her sharps bin. This man was not using the word in a medical context. As he lifted and closed the ramp, the steer made a beeline toward her with a trot and flick of its tail.

'Oh,' she voiced and promptly backed up to the stairs. At this point, she forgot about both her accident and being sharp! The approaching man roared with laughter.

'He just wants a cuddle,' he reassured her. 'Seriously,' he added. 'He won't hurt you—crush you maybe, but not with intent. Make sure you never get between him and a fence or let him corner you while you're here.' June's eyes widened.

'A cuddle? What on earth are you doing bringing that thing here?' she asked.

'He belongs to the Woodwards.' The man looked surprised. 'Didn't they tell you about Winston? I'm returning the blighter for you to look after—it's the third time this week I might add!' She glared at him momentarily.

'I thought,' she started. 'It was small—like, like, well like a little calf or something!' She now wished she'd read the Woodwards' email in full.

'To be honest,' he continued. 'This is Winston's postal address. He much prefers residing at my place—*unfortunately*! If I catch him one more time pushing down my fence and grazing in my paddock, it'll be a beef banquet at mine.'

'Oh?' June studied the man with curiosity. He had an attitude, she thought. The term "Bunnings Boy" came to mind—that's what they called them back home, men who always dressed down like they worked 24/7. Men who lived and breathed DIY and outdoor life.

The man hesitated at the door of his vehicle.

'Tell Doc I'll be billing him for the fencing wire for the umpteenth time,' he said. *Is he seriously asking me to do his dirty work for him?* 'I told him he was mad taking on a poddy calf as a pet, and that was two years ago.' He opened the ute door as if to get in but instead reached inside and fetched something. He stepped toward June and handed her a business card. 'I'm Dave. Best put my number in your phone—I'm your closest neighbour.' She glanced at the card and read it: David Andersen, Third Creek Beef, Paddock-to-Plate. 'That's if you get stuck,' he continued. 'Or need anything while you're here?' She nodded to show her appreciation for his gesture.

'Thanks,' she said. Dave stood in front of her and adjusted his hat. She noted his eyes and found herself staring. They were blue—a deep blue like the ocean. Did he hold secrets, just as the ocean did? No, she decided. He would not. This Bunnings Boy would be nothing but transparent. She blinked and saw clearer— the eyes that stared back at her were indeed a transparent blue, a brilliant blue. They were like sapphires. Yes—sapphire blue, she concluded. Dave broke the silence between them.

'Mind you, you might have to run around the block to find phone reception. It comes and it goes.'

'I'll keep that in mind,' She smiled. She studied him briefly. While he appeared rugged, he was jovial, showed confidence, and had an aura of calm about him.

'Seriously,' his tone changed with the nature of his advice. 'We always carry our phones with us out here for safety: in case of snake bites, accidents and things.' *Snake bites?* June's face contorted in horror.

'Well, best be getting back to it.' Dave Andersen turned, jumped into the driver seat and started the engine. Through his already wound-down window, he gave a hearty wave, turned the ute one-handed on a fifty-cent piece and headed back down the driveway, this time somewhat slower. She watched him before exchanging glances with the large, fawn-coloured steer that stood before her. He busily chewed his cud, then turned and meandered away. He had the lush green grass of the block in his sights.

Chapter 2

June returned to the kitchen, made her sandwich, poured herself a glass of wine, and then placed them on the table. From the bedroom, she grabbed the lengthy, printed email she'd brought with her. She'd read it thoroughly while she ate.

On the second page titled, The Dogs, she skimmed over two paragraphs of instructions. She learnt what time their dinner was and the procedure to be followed. She made every effort to concentrate and take it all in, but her travel fatigue had other plans. She looked up and over her paperwork, spying four hungry faces silently studying her through the door.

'Well, team, I guess it's your dinner time,' she said, popping the last piece of sandwich into her mouth. She chased it down with the last drop of wine, left the email on the table and took the plate and glass to the sink. Four tails wagged eagerly, making her smile. Tank appeared the hungriest, making noises that sounded like an attempt to talk—or hurry her up. *It might just be okay having your company for the next month.*

She took the dog bowls and biscuit from the cupboard and the kangaroo mince from the fridge and dished out the suggested serving size to each bowl. She'd feed the dogs, have a long, cool shower and hit the sack.

Like a professional, she balanced four dog bowls full of food and kicked the sliding screen door open with her foot. Her days of emptying bedpans had helped her develop great balancing skills. *Once one drops a full bedpan, one never does it again!* She placed the bowls before each dog.

'There we go, you lot. Gourmet a-la-kangaroo.' She watched each dog scoff its food as though they hadn't eaten for a month, and as they ate, she thought of something she never would back home: food—hers, theirs, the ham in her sandwich… and Dave the Farmer.

She'd never given much thought to where the meat she ate came from. Sure, she knew that ham came from pigs and beef came from cows and so on… but having to physically kill an animal—she just couldn't do it.

'That's why we have blood-thirsty farmers,' she resolved and purposely changed her thinking. If she thought too much about the evils of farming, she wouldn't be able to stomach meat.

While the dogs made short work of their food, June made her way around the deck. She took note of what she guessed was an outdoor breakfast bar—or was it a wine-o-clock bar? *This could serve as both.* There were two stools tucked neatly underneath an impressive, thick slab of timber mounted on strong, metal legs. It was inviting. *Beautiful.* She ran her hand across the well-waxed surface wondering what sort of timber it was—teak, mahogany, pine? She had no idea. She realised she knew nothing about timber. Her home state of South Australia didn't have a thriving timber industry. Momentarily, she considered her grandparents' modest, Adelaide home.

They have a lot of antique furniture—all made of timber. But what sort? She should know. She didn't know. She made a mental note to pay attention when she returned home, and to ask about it. She considered going antiquing with them—they did that sometimes, and she knew they'd be delighted to share their interest with their granddaughter.

She pulled one of the stools out and sat on it. Her eyes flicked back and forth between the scenery around her and a carving on the timber top. The carving looked as though it had been done professionally, and recently. It consisted of arrows pointing to landmarks. Her eyes followed each one.

The mowed hilltop that surrounded the Woodwards' house gave way to undulating grassy paddocks—home to cattle. To the east, was the Andersen property—the one with brick pillars but no name. Beyond the paddocks, to the north, was a flat-topped hill of rainforest. She studied the arrow that pointed to it—Lake Barrine. She could walk around the lake according to an article she'd read on the plane, and if time allowed she would. Other arrows pointed south toward Millaa Millaa, Townsville and Brisbane. North toward Cairns, Cooktown and Weipa. And west toward Yungaburra—her grocery stop—Atherton, Herberton and Mount Surprise. She thought they all sounded intriguing.

With sunlight fading early as it did in a state that rejected daylight-saving time, and mosquitoes that resembled flying venesection needles homing in on her soft, inviting legs, June ventured back inside, closing the screen door behind her. The dogs were happy. *They must be immune*. Two were in their beds and the other two were sniffing around out on the grass. *What goes in, must come out*. She locked the screen door for the night. Sleeping with an unlocked door was just too foreign to her.

She glanced at the few dishes on the sink. *They can wait till morning.* A comfy-looking couch in the lounge beckoned, but she knew if she sat on it, she wouldn't get up for the rest of the night. Through the windows that overlooked the garden, she saw no sign of the steer. She hoped it hadn't broken through Bunnings Boy's fence again. She went to the bathroom, showered, set her alarm for 6:00 a.m., and jumped into bed. She forgot about her goal of reading the email—it stayed on the table where she'd left it. She hit the sack and went out like a light.

Chapter 3

Grey Custard
Week 1—Monday Morning

A noise rang out. June woke with a start and looked at her phone. It was 4:01 a.m. Roused now, she heard the noise again—*cock-a-doodle-doo*.

'Bloody Rooster!' she groaned and pulled her pillow over her head. She'd not seen the hen house yet and planned to do rounds after 6:00 a.m.

'*Cock-a-doodle-doo!*' the bird repeated, annoyingly. There was no going back to sleep, and it was still pitch dark!

Now wide awake, she decided it was the perfect time to read the emailed instructions. She climbed out of bed, headed for the kitchen and made a steaming hot cup of tea. She took the tea and the printed email from the table back to bed.

Between sips of tea, she tackled the email one page at a time. There was a lot to absorb, but the Woodwards' instructions were clear and precise. Under the heading, Winston, it stated, "Ensure you put the chain across the stairs of an evening or Winston will spend the night on the deck!"

On the deck? She wondered what they meant. She hadn't heard anything. A feeling of dread overcame her. She *had* unhooked the chain and left it that way. She dropped the papers on the bed, placed her half-finished tea on her bedside cupboard, and in her knickers and t-shirt, made a beeline for the sliding door. It took a moment to find the deck light switch in the dark and when she did, she wished she hadn't. The dogs were on their beds sleeping comfortably and there, standing in the middle of the deck, was Winston. Reality struck. She smelled it before she saw it. *Where there's a steer, there's dung.* She sighed. And dung there was—steaming piles of it, splattered like large bowls of grey custard spilled from a great height. For a moment, all she could do was stare in disbelief. *You can wake from your nightmare now, June Hall.* The urgency to act became very real. Winston shuffled toward her voice, his hooves scraping through the mess, spreading it further and grinding it into the crevices and grain of the timber deck. She flung open the screen door and threw up her arms.

'Kshh, kshh,' she called out, baffling the beast. She wanted to shoo him off the deck and as far away from the chaos as possible before he made it worse. 'Kshh, kshh,' she repeated until the baffled steer turned, headed down the stairs, and retreated to the lawn. June surveyed the mess, the overwhelming stench of manure making her gag.

She contemplated. As soon as the hot, tropical sun rose, it would shine on the deck and bake the manure like concrete. She had to remove it sooner rather than later. She picked up an old pair of gumboots that sat in the corner by the sliding door.

'These things are huge,' she said of the boots. 'Doc Woodward's no doubt. She checked them for spiders and then pulled them on. 'Better than no boots at all.'

Clomping around the splatters gingerly, she headed down the stairs. In the pre-dawn light, she found a shovel and a rake. Back up the stairs, she scraped the piles up one at a time. Up and down the stairs she went, placing each steaming pile on the garden. With the last shovel-full removed, she took the garden hose and dragged it up onto the deck. The dogs watched on, intrigued, but refused to move from their beds. *Hmm, immune to both mosquitoes and the smell of dung!* June glared at them.

'Great that some of us get to sleep,' she said sarcastically. With the worn, old deck broom in one hand and the hose in the other, she got to work. She hosed and scrubbed, then hosed and scrubbed again, until all signs of Winston's manure were washed away between the slats. She cleaned the boots and what was left of the broom—most of the bristles had fallen off and been washed away with the manure—then returned the hose to its hanger.

'You will *not* set foot on this deck again while I'm in charge, Winston Woodward!' she grumbled, clipping the chain back across the top step of the stairs. She needed a shower. She had the scent of manure fixed in her nostrils and specks of splash-back stuck to her legs. She'd take dogs over bovines any day!

Chapter 4

The Menagerie
Week 1—Monday Afternoon

By 5.30 a.m., June had not only cleaned up after Winston but had also finally finished reading the Woodwards' notes. She had no idea there were so many animals on their property. She was to check the chickens and ensure their food and water containers were full. They were free-range but housed securely overnight. She'd read that the chook house had a dedicated solar panel to power an automatic door—she couldn't wait to see how that worked. She was to collect the eggs daily, in the evening where possible.

There were turkeys at the rear of the block. They slept high in a tall fig tree but required a bucket of feed in the mornings. They too were free-range to a certain extent. There was a blind pig in a pen as well.

'Hoo boy' she voiced. 'I'm going to be busier here than at work!'

With the morning sun already blazing and the temperature rising, she threw on old clothes, slipped into the oversized deck boots, and headed outside to do the chores. She needed to be in Millbrook by 8:00 a.m. to start work.

First up, she found the chicken coop. The chickens were up, about, and scattered all over the block. Some scratched through leaf litter in search of bugs. Those who either weren't hungry or had already eaten fluffed their feathers in dirt baths. June watched their antics and some watched June with equal interest. Whether or not she had food was on their minds. A few came running, just in case.

'So… you're the culprit that woke me this morning, huh?' she grumbled at the stately, multicoloured rooster that took no notice of her. 'I'm keeping my eye on you, young man. I'm sure there's a chopping block in the woodshed.' She noted several roosters, though the others looked young.

The chook house was outstanding and amused her no end. It sat on stumps, the floor approximately one metre off the ground. From the noise within, and the toing and froing of busy chickens up and down the access ramp, she figured the nest boxes were located inside. A closer inspection confirmed this—there were human-accessible lift-up doors on the side for collecting the eggs.

The ramp to the doorway was covered in synthetic grass for grip. Above the doorway was a sign—The Penthouse, and a penthouse it was indeed. The floor consisted of form ply designed to slide out in sections. The ply scraped and cleaned easily, allowing manure that fell during the night roost to be collected for the garden. There were notes on a garden too—a vegetable patch beyond the car shed. She was welcome to use anything from it and looked forward to fresh produce. Fortunately, they'd added, "We don't expect you to maintain the garden, you'll be busy enough".

So that's the solar panel. She took note of it fixed to the coop roof. The automatic door closed after roosting time and opened bright and early each morning, creating a haven at night. She considered foxes. She couldn't imagine what other dangers there'd be. The chook house was far from your average coop; it was outstanding. *An architectural marvel.*

Her second stop was at blind pig, Wilbur's pen. She smiled at his name.

'You know, Wilbur,' she said calmly as she approached the waist-high fence. 'I bet your chicken buddies have names just as quaint as yours!' The pig, while unable to see her, appeared happy to hear her voice and followed it. She had never been close to a pig before—not even one *with* vision. Humming a tune to make her position known to the mammal, she lifted the lid on an old metal rubbish bin next to his gate and peered inside. The pig snorted, making her jump. He knew the noise and what it meant—*breakfast!* 'Oh,' she hesitated. 'That… um… sure looks scrumptious.' She hoped she sounded more convincing to the pig than she sounded to herself. She took the jug from on top of the feed and as instructed, scooped up the required amount and then poured it over the fence and into his feed trough.

'Reee-reee-reee,' Wilbur headbutted the trough and searched with his snout until he located the food, then ate hungrily. Fixated on his eating—or rather, scoffing, she dropped the jug. Fortunately, it fell into the trough where she could reach it. Had it landed on the ground, it would have stayed there. She didn't have time to enter the pen, and she'd need time—time to work up the courage to do it. She put the jug back into the feed bin and secured the lid. She had a lot to learn—not just about the Woodwards' animals, but about animals in general. She watched the pig for a moment as he devoured his breakfast. He had the manners of a… well… a pig! A glance at the water trough told her she didn't need to change or fill his water, so she moved on. Besides, she was struggling physically. As well as her time restraints, she had lost the ability to control her gag reflex. The smell of Winston's manure lingered in her nose like an unwelcome visitor. She didn't need Wilbur's adding to it.

Under a large fig tree, a rafter of turkeys waited for breakfast. June estimated 30 and approached them cautiously.

'Would they attack her?' she wondered. According to the Woodwards, the birds roosted in the tree nightly, returning to the ground at sunrise, but each morning they faced a dilemma. They landed outside the fenced-off papaya plantation where they preferred to spend their day. On the plantation, they could wander freely, feast on bugs, and fertilise the soil to their heart's content. This was nature's organic pest control and fertiliser all in one.

The turkeys ran to the plantation gate, their excitement visible. They too, knew food was on its way and lined up like eager schoolchildren outside a classroom. She noted those at the back were impatient and shoved and squabbled with those in front. It reminded her of her school days, where unruly bullies pestered well-behaved children in front of them in a manner that would avoid the teacher's eyes.

The papaya plantation was around 2000 square metres in size. The ground itself was steep, particularly where it dropped off beyond the fig tree and fence line. June edged past the turkeys, trying not to look nervous.

'Out of the way you lot,' she insisted. A few gobbled in response, more a hurry-up than an acknowledgement of her authority over them. At the gate, she took the lid off a bucket of dried, cracked corn that had been soaked overnight. The turkeys moved in tight around her. The Woodwards had thankfully prepared the mix the day prior. According to her list of instructions, she was supposed to soak six cups of the dry feed in water every night and give it to them every morning. That didn't seem hard.

'Back off,' she warned. 'Or open this ruddy gate for me!' With the bucket over her arm and the turkeys pushing at her feet, she removed the Occy Strap that secured the gate and opened it. She took two steps into the plantation yard, leant forward, and hung the bucket onto a hook fastened to a post. It sat right at the top of a steep slope.

'Looks like you guys have scratched or pecked away every blade of grass on this poor little slope,' she said. 'That can't be good!' She moved back and left the hungry birds to it. One by one, they entered the yard, the sloping soil no challenge to their anisodactyl feet. Some gathered around the corn bucket and either persistently argued or patiently waited for their fill of the corn. Others were disinterested, instead happy to wander down among the papayas and roam. June Hall had to admit that turkeys were indeed fascinating creatures and being close to them, for her, was a first. She could have stood there all day watching them, but work called. She made her way back to the house.

Dressed and with her bag and lunch packed, she ran her eyes back over her lists of instructions, double-checking she'd done everything that was expected of her regarding the property. She glanced at Dave's card on the bench and wondered—should she put his number in her phone? *One never knows when one might need a local.* She added him to her contacts.

With the door locked, she stepped over the Winston chain. Doing this every time she took the deck stairs would be a hassle, but she'd tolerate it. It was far easier than cleaning up piles of steer manure. She walked to her car. The sky was clear, and the sun shone on her back. How anyone lived in this environment was beyond her. She was freshly showered and already her skin was tacky to the touch from humidity. A bead of sweat trickled down her back. *This weather isn't fit for humans or animals.* She opened the car door, hopped in, started the engine, and turned the air-conditioner to high. She directed the jets to her face and body and soaked up the relief it offered.

Down the lengthy driveway and through the gate, she indicated automatically to turn right onto Aurthur Willis Road. She didn't know why she did that with no one behind her. There, also turning out of his driveway, was Dave. He smiled broadly at her and waved out of his window. She noted it had been wound down.

Seriously, do you not use your air-conditioner? No sense, no feeling! He waved her forward and she headed out onto the unsealed road that would take her into Millbrook and to the surgery. She'd heard it was a small town with a big heart and hoped the rumour had it right. As she drove, she watched Dave follow her in his ute. Her imagination wandered—what would he look like in smart clothes? In clean clothes? Clothes that made those broad shoulders and biceps even more noticeable. A warm sensation passed through her—hard to say if it was from her thoughts… or the air-conditioner struggling to keep up in the humidity.

Chapter 5

Self-Made Man
Week 1—Monday Morning

DAVE followed June until he reached his bottom paddock. He had to check a section of fence, attend to the troughs, and administer antibiotics to a wounded steer he'd yarded. When those jobs were finished, he faced the clean-up from yesterday's customers visiting his new paddock-to-plate venture. As he reflected on the turnout, a smile tugged at his lips. Setting up a barbeque-style attraction in a slaughterhouse had been a mammoth task, but he was no stranger to hard work or commitment.

It had been over a year since his wife had left. Survival meant moving forward. At the time, he'd felt hurt beyond repair. He'd married for life—or so he thought. There had even been talk of kids, but in hindsight, he should have realised from the get-go—there'd been signs.

Living rurally didn't suit everyone. Plenty of men and women in agricultural settings had their relationships fall apart, be it through distance or other reasons—he wasn't the first farmer to face heartbreak, and he wouldn't be the last.

Dave was born and bred on the land but attended boarding school in the city. Travelling during his gap year, both domestically and abroad, only reinforced that city life—big or small—wasn't for him. He'd felt lonelier in a crowd than he ever had with just stock and stars for company. Oh, how he'd missed the stars—the city lights stole their brilliance.

Ending up separated and alone on a new property hadn't been in Dave Andersen's life plan. He'd bought the house, the land, and had the debt and a wife—then, suddenly, it was just him to manage it all.

The old slaughterhouse in one of his paddocks caught his eye at the time. He'd stood there, thinking, *why not?* What he hadn't expected when he decided to renovate was becoming his grandmother's full-time caregiver, but on the upside, both challenges cured his loneliness and gave him no time to dwell—just things to do and someone to talk to at night.

Opening a paddock-to-plate venue had been a steep learning curve, but through it, he'd discovered two passions he never realised he had—cooking and educating. From the outset, he wanted his business to be more than just a place to eat beef. He wanted people to learn and appreciate the effort behind breeding cattle and understand sustainability.

He designed flyers, planned how to host and educate visitors, and curated the menu. He even spent time with an old schoolmate-turned-winemaker, ensuring he stocked the best wines to pair with beef. Local where possible.

Dave was an owner-builder, designer, renovator, and marketer—plus chef, retailer, educator, carer, and farmer. Not to mention—housekeeper. Running a paddock-to-plate, a home, and keeping up with his meddlesome gran meant there was always work to do.

But above all, Dave was an animal man. His cattle were cared for to the highest standard while they lived. Slaughter days weren't easy, but they were part of farm life—something he'd grown up with, accepted, and moved on from.

Dave was a proactive, self-made man, turning setbacks into stepping stones and dreams into reality.

Chapter 6

Always Running

Week 1—Monday, Dave and Alice

Alice Andersen collected her handbag from the lounge room and popped it in the basket on her wheeled walker. She'd been to the bathroom and was ready for her trip to Millbrook Surgery. She turned to make her way toward the passage—she would *not* keep her grandson waiting. He was the apple of her eye.

Dave's ute tore up the driveway, tyres crunching on the gravel as it arced into a half-circle and came to an abrupt stop—passenger side perfectly aligned with the front garden path. A moment's silence followed, then the vehicle door slammed. Alice glanced at her watch, worried, as the thudding sound of work boots running on concrete grew louder—thud—thud—thud—thud.

She knew what would come next: two deep grunts, one for each boot wrenched off hot, sweaty feet. Two familiar thuds—one after each grunt—signalled the boots hitting the veranda. She waited for the leathery, shuffling sound, and there it was. He never let her down and always kicked his boots away from the door; never would they be a trip hazard for *his* grandmother. *That's my boy. Best grandson ever.*

As the squeaking screen door banged shut, Dave appeared in the lounge room doorway, panting but grinning—a smile that, as his grandmother knew, should have been melting hearts!

'Always running,' she grumbled. She moved forward and stood face-to-face with him. 'You need to stop, listen, and truly see the beautiful things in front of you every single day. We all cross the finish line, you know—so walk, don't run. Time goes quickly enough.'

'I don't have time for your words of wisdom today, Gran. Are you ready to go?' he asked, with perfect composure.

'Yes, dear…' she replied, her caring eyes looking him up and down. 'You've been doing too much—*again!*'

'That's Mondays… plus the clean-up took much longer than I anticipated,' he admitted. 'Yesterday was a busy one.' He stepped aside to let her into the passageway. 'Let's go,' he insisted. Alice hesitated, noting he looked hot.

'You don't want to shower before our appointments?' She looked concerned.

'Yes, of course…' his smile straightened. 'But if I do, we'll be late. Don't fuss. It's fine. I'm sure Doc Flint will forgive a fellow man for working hard. I'll change my shirt and grab a clean pair of boots—*that okay*?'

'A boot and shirt change will suffice,' she agreed. 'You *do* work hard—*too damn hard, David!*' She nodded. She pushed her wheeled walker past him.

'So, you keep telling me—*Graaandmother!*' he replied with a smirk. She called him David during her philosophical or meddlesome moments—the latter always worrisome.

'I'll wait by the car,' she insisted and picked up her pace. 'I don't want you driving too fast,' she mumbled. 'As we know, accidents can happen.'

'Sure, Gran. Be right there,' Dave answered. In his bedroom, he pulled on a shirt—one he didn't have to button. There wasn't time for buttons. He ignored his sweaty socks, took a clean pair of boots from his wardrobe, and made a beeline back to his ute—screen door slamming behind him. Running, he arrived simultaneously with Alice, helped her in the car and then threw her wheeled walker—The Silver Stallion—into the back.

Dave drove down his long, country driveway, stopping momentarily at the road to give way. There were rarely cars on Arthur Willis Road.

'Doc and Mrs. left yet?' Alice asked.

'Yesterday morning, Gran. There's a house-sitter there now.' He glanced left and right—no traffic either way—and then subconsciously, across and upward toward Barrine Views. Alice noted his glance and was inquisitive.

'Oh… what sex?'

'A woman. 'Bout 30.' Dave rolled his eyes and pulled out onto the road.

'Your age, then?' Alice asked, needing more information. 'Is she pretty?'

'Very,' he said poker-faced and without thinking. He accelerated at a fast but cautious speed. With luck, they should arrive just in time.

'Perhaps you can invite her for dinner, dear?' Alice threw him a look as best she could with her osteoarthritic neck.

'Gran. Really?' He shook his head. 'You know I don't have time for that.'

'You should make time,' Alice insisted. 'All work and no play make Dave a dull grandson. Besides, I might like the company.'

'Well, you might meet her, yet…' Dave explained. 'Rumour has it, she's working at the surgery—a nurse. Filling in for Mrs. W, I hear.' Alice said nothing—just looked away at passing paddocks, though she didn't see them, her mind busy scheming behind a mischievous smirk.

Dave focused on driving and the task ahead. He'd become a regular at the surgery since taking on the role of Alice's carer. It was just the two of them these days—grandmother and grandson—and that was all he had time for.

Chapter 7

Beyond Carrot Cake
Week 1—Monday, June

It took less than an hour for June to feel at home in Millbrook Surgery. The computer system was one she was proficient with and that made all the difference, as did the staff who welcomed her with open arms. The cupboards in the treatment room were labelled, making finding what she needed a breeze. Coral, the surgery's practice manager, had even prepared her morning tea—a flat white and homemade carrot cake—perfectly timed between patients. The ten minutes it took her to devour it, was just the boost she needed to soldier on.

During June's morning orientation, she'd spied the carrot cake in the staff room—it was her favourite. Alongside the cake, on an old wooden table, were mangoes, avocados, an extra-large block of chocolate, and other fruits she'd never seen before.

'Our patients bring in all sorts of goodies for the staff,' Coral had explained. 'If they're on the old table, they're anyone's—go for it.' That sounded great to June. It appeared that country patients were most thoughtful. She'd also warned, 'Working here, dear June, you'll soon put curves on that lean body of yours.' June agreed she just might.

The morning's patients had presented with ailments quite different to what she was used to. She'd removed a scrub tick from a patient's back and dressed the fresh wounds of an old farmer; his rusty ute tray had fallen off its hinges, scraping the skin from his shins as it fell to the ground. There'd been the usual ECGs and the taking of vital signs for several patients. She'd immunized a six-month-old baby, dressed a sprained ankle, and noted that she was soon to see a patient whose pet python had mistaken their hand for a rat!

She glanced at the computer and noted the name of her next patient—Mrs. Andersen. She headed to the waiting room to collect her. *Mrs. Andersen of Arthur Willis Road—could she be Dave's wife?* June scanned the room full of waiting patients.

'Mrs. Andersen,' she called. An elderly lady sitting in the corner stood up slowly and unsteadily. She fumbled with her wheeled walker. June approached her.

'Hello. Are you Mrs. Andersen?' Alice nodded. 'I'm June, the locum nurse. I'll be looking after you today. Are you able to walk okay or shall I fetch the wheelchair?'

'No dear. I can walk. I'm just a bit slow, that's all.' June escorted her to the treatment room, weighed her as they passed the scales, and then showed her to a seat in her office. She took Alice's blood pressure. 'So, you're the Woodwards' house-sitter, dear, is that right?' Alice looked her up and down.

'Yes, that's right. I'm here for March while they're in the UK,' she explained.

'Well, it's lovely they can take a whole month's break— Goodness knows they earn it running this show… and it's even lovelier that *you* can take care of their property and the menagerie. They've such a stunning home.' The elderly woman had an infectious smile; however, June wouldn't label the Woodwards' home stunning—unique or eccentric perhaps? Rustic-bordering-on-charming for sure. 'My grandson is right. You *are* very pretty.' June felt the warmth in her cheeks as she blushed.

'Your grandson is Dave?' she asked.

'Yes… that's right. Dave Andersen. You've met him, then?' Alice straightened in her chair with positive excitement.

'Yes.' June recalled last night's Winston delivery. 'Briefly,' she said.

'Excuse me, Nurse June,' Dr. Flint said politely. Flinty, as he was known by the staff, was not unlike the character of the

Professor, in the Back to the Future movies—tall, with wild white hair and a face full of wisdom and character.

'Yes, Doctor,' she answered politely, her swivel chair now facing away from her computer and toward the office doorway where he stood.

'Have you finished with our dear Alice?' he asked. 'If you are, I can see her now.'

'Yes,' June replied. 'Observations done—all in normal range. I checked Mrs. Andersen's vaccination status on the Australian Immunisation Register and it's all up to date. However, I did notice her weight has dropped a little since her last visit with us.' Alice was a tiny woman as it was. Dr. Flint raised his eyebrows, and his gaze fell upon Alice.

'Good work, June. Thank you. We'll chat about that in my room, won't we, Mrs. Andersen,' he nodded, and Alice returned his nod. June noted the unspoken language between them.

'Can I help you up, Mrs. Andersen?' June asked.

'No, I've got this, dear.' Alice stood using her wheeled walker for support.

'June,' Dr. Flint continued. 'I have Mr. Andersen with me. He has an appointment—it's for his annual health check—after Alice. Would you mind doing an ECG on him? When you're done, send him to my room. He needs to be part of Alice's visit too. I'll chat with her in the meantime. Sorry...' he quickly looked apologetic. 'Oh... do you have time?' June glanced at the screen and then back to the doctor. She nodded.

'Sure... I can fit him in,' she said. At that, Dave's head poked around the corner, and he smiled.

'We meet again,' he said.

'Is he okay Doctor?' Alice piped up. 'Are you alright, Dave?' his grandmother asked. Dave nodded.

'He's fine, Alice,' Dr. Flint insisted. 'It's just part of his health check.' June noted he never stopped smiling.

'Bunnings Boy!' she sighed, under her breath.

Dr. Flint escorted Alice to his consult room. June led Dave to a narrow bed in the treatment room that sat beside a machine. She drew the curtains around them.

'Shirt off please, then lay down for me—on your back. Head to the window end.' Dave blushed.

'Oh… I apologise, though. I didn't have time to shower before I came in. Time wasn't on my side,' he explained in an embarrassed tone. June walked outside the curtain.

'Call me when you're ready,' she asked and gave him a minute.

Geez Dave, he reflected. He wanted to run. He had no idea he'd be put on the spot like this. *Not your day, Andersen!* His inner voice had a scolding tone.

Didn't have time to shower? The man lives with his grandmother and can't find time for a lick and a promise. I bet she still does his washing, cooking and everything else for him!

'Ready,' Dave called out nervously. June entered the space behind the curtain, took down a box from the top cupboard and pulled out a sheet of ECG electrode stickers. She studied his chest. There was hair across it, but not too much. It wasn't growing where she needed to stick her electrodes, so no shaving was required—a time saver. Then a naughty thought overcame her. *You, Dave Andersen, delivered Winston my problematic steer.* This was a chance for revenge. *Bugger being professional, June—do it!*

'Have you had an ECG before?' she asked. 'An electrocardiogram?'

'No… No, I haven't,' he replied nervously.

'I'm going to have to shave some of your chest. My stickers won't stick otherwise. And use alcohol wipes to remove any body oil.'

'Do what you have to,' Dave replied. June reached for a disposable razor that wasn't your everyday Bic.

'This is a surgical razor,' she told him. He watched her twirl it in her fingers like a tiny baton. 'It works a treat.'

'Oh yeah,' was all Dave could say. Not only was he nervous taking his shirt off in front of the confident, beautiful blonde nurse before him, but he hoped like hell he didn't smell like the rear end of a cow.

June felt the spaces between his ribs and shaved the spots she needed to—only she shaved them somewhat larger than was necessary and wasn't gentle about it. Her thoughts kept flitting between Winston's early morning "grey custard artwork" and the possibility of it being his ute that had run her off the road. By the time she'd finished, Dave looked like he had a skin condition—the type where hair grew in patches. She wiped the alcohol swabs across the shaved areas, paused while the skin dried, and then placed the stickers where she needed them, and attached the leads.

'This will only take a minute. You need to lie perfectly still for me and just breathe normally. It only hurts momentarily,' she fibbed. Dave's body language was one of concern, but he put on a brave face. June watched the computer screen as the ECG played out and then saved a copy. All was fine. As she turned toward him to remove the clips from his chest, she found him staring at her.

'Is there anything wrong?' she asked. Dave looked away, embarrassed.

'No… No, not at all. I was just thinking what unusual green eyes you have. They remind me of… of…' *Here we go—the green of a Makita Drill?* 'Your eyes are like the emerald in my grandmother's eternity ring—gracious and deep. She always says the eyes are the windows to your soul.'

'Oh… she does?' June replied, noting he wore no wedding ring, nor was there a sign he ever did. 'My grandmother used to say the same thing when she was alive.' *And your eyes, Dave Andersen, are the blue of sapphires.*

'Finished?' Dave asked, as she pulled off the last sticker with satisfaction. She felt good now—this was revenge for Winston's artwork.

'Yes. All done. Best head to Dr. Flint's room with Mrs. Andersen. He'll be waiting for you. He'll see the ECG in your file. Do you know which room is his?'

'Yes. Too familiar. Oh, and I didn't feel a thing—the ECGC—gram-thing, I mean. Great job!' he smiled. June kept a straight face—one didn't feel an ECG. As she wiped the leads over with a disinfectant wipe, she couldn't help but notice Dave's abdomen flexing as he sat up. He was defined—*very* defined! June swallowed so hard she hoped it wasn't audible. He didn't have a six-pack—he had the whole darn carton!

He pulled on his shirt. She had mixed feelings about this Bunnings Boy. Her inside voice should have the giggles right now, laughing at the hairless patches she'd revenge-inflicted upon him, but all she could feel was guilt.

'Be seeing you I guess,' Dave nodded as he made his way out of the curtain booth.

'Probably,' June answered. She'd avoid him. She wasn't here to make friends or socialise; just to work and then go home—sooner rather than later. After only 24 hours, she knew life in the steamy, unforgiving tropics was not for her.

Chapter 8

An Unguarded Bucket in a Pig Pen
Week 1—Monday Afternoon into Night

June drove her car back to Barrine Views after her first day as a locum nurse in Millbrook. She was physically tired. So much had happened that day—so many things she wouldn't usually deal with in a city practice—and her mind was racing. She relived each situation, wondering if she'd handled things as they should've been handled. She felt she had, mostly.

With things to unload, she skipped parking in the shed and pulled up on the Woodwards' front lawn instead, under a shady tree. She had her work bag, handbag, a bucket of scraps for Wilbur, and a small box of fruit for herself to carry into the house. The latter were compliments of the old wooden table in the staff room. Later, she'd park her car in the shed. She killed the engine to yet another chorus of dog welcomes—could this ever get old?

Carrying her first load, she made her way up the stairs, unhooking and dropping Winston's chain at the top. She put her work bag and handbag in the kitchen then headed back out to get the box of fruit and bucket of scraps. As she reached the top step, she noticed something bright green on the banister that surrounded the deck—it was on the underside. She bent down to further investigate. It looked like a frog, but it was lifeless and looked plastic. *Is it plastic?* She poked it gently. It moved, but ever so slightly, most unhappy to be woken from its slumber. It was the biggest frog she'd ever seen, and it had white lips.

'Sorry mate,' she said. Then she noticed there were several of them. The more she looked around, the more frogs she saw. How had she missed them last night and even this morning? She wondered what noise they made if any at all. She'd take note. 'Why does everything like this deck so much?' she said, laughing. She retrieved the box and bucket from her car and ensured the chain was hooked back up on her return. Winston was not welcome. He was under a tree, busy drinking from a trough—a vertically-cut half-drum fixed to a horizontal stand. She watched for a moment. She'd have to keep an eye on it—it could be his main source of water. Doc hadn't mentioned whether she had to keep it filled up or even whether she was expected to shovel up his manure from the grass. She'd keep an eye on both.

In the kitchen, she poured herself an icy glass of water from the fridge. She was so very grateful for the air-conditioning at the surgery—a luxury she thought she'd never have to consider or enquire about when accepting a locum. She would in the future. The Woodwards' house didn't have air conditioning—just fans—and she wondered how they survived the heat, and how she would last a whole month in their home without it. She had sweated and dried so many times during the day, that her clothes felt stiff and as if they were glued to her. She was looking forward to a cold shower, a dinner of fresh eggs she'd yet to collect, and a glass of wine—refrigerated red—after she'd seen to the animals.

Donning the oversized boots, June headed off, making a plod-clomp noise as she walked. She started with Wilbur—who made short work of scraps tipped over the fence into his food trough—before moving on to the turkeys.

At the fig tree, she opened the plantation gate, leant forward, and collected the empty bucket from the hook on the timber post at the top of the slope. She shut the gate, securing it once more with the Occy Strap. It struck her as funny that, come roosting time, the turkeys could fly from inside the plantation, over the fence and high up into their massive roosting tree. Yet in the morning, they could only manage to land at the base of the tree—never back inside the plantation, where they preferred to spend their day. It made no sense to her that they needed a human to open the gate for them. Now, she truly understood why they were called turkeys. But she still didn't understand why the gate had to stay shut. The Woodwards hadn't mentioned why. She considered Winston as the reason.

She lifted the lid off the large drum that housed the dried cracked corn, took the cup that sat inside it and scooped up six cups—as per directions—placing them into the smaller bucket; the one that hung on the hook. She covered the feed with water. The lid to the small bucket remained on the ground where she'd dropped it in the morning—flustered trying not to become turkey food herself, if that was even a thing. She picked it up and brushed it off. It had been trampled somewhat but not damaged. Tomorrow, she'd be smarter and put it up and out of the way— on top of the large bin. *That makes sense.*

'And tomorrow's breakfast is good to go… ta da!' she said as she walked away, but no turkeys were in earshot.

From the rear of the yard, she could see for kilometres. Lush green paddocks, hills and valleys stretched out around her, with rainforest pockets and breathtaking views in every direction. The sky was afternoon blue and cloudless, except for a dark grey cluster of clouds forming in the distance, to the west. *Build-up Clouds.* They looked like scoops of ice cream piled on top of one another—*too far away for any rain action*.

The chickens were scattered around the property but appeared to be heading closer to the Penthouse, scratching and pecking to their heart's content. June headed to their pen to check it out further—this morning had been rushed. It was indeed state-of-the-art. Doc Woodward had written that he'd both designed and built it himself; it was his pride and joy. The structure looked similar in style to the high-and-low-set Queenslander houses she'd noticed while driving through Millbrook. They were all on stumps of varying heights, and she wondered if it had something to do with flooding or keeping cool.

The Penthouse was clad in horizontal timber slats and painted a bright shade of pink. Meshed panels allowed for a much-needed breeze and came with shutters—perhaps closed during storms for protection. She assumed as much. She took a moment to inspect the solar panel more closely. Wires ran down from it, weaving their way inside. One set led to the automatic door, which she already knew opened and closed at preset times—sunrise and sunset. Curious, she peered inside.

'Boy oh boy, it's real,' she muttered with a giggle. Another set of wires powered a fan, which was spinning and oscillating. Next to it was a speaker. She wasn't expected to do it during her stay, but the Woodwards played relaxation music to the chickens daily—it supposedly produced better eggs, according to their notes. June smiled at the couple of chickens already inside. 'This is awesome, girls… you sure do live a good life here!' Doc had also noted the building was snake-proof. She had shuddered upon reading that. She was terrified of snakes.

On closer inspection, she saw more wires inside the house. They disappeared through the floor. She stepped back and bent over to look underneath. Just as Doc had explained, they continued down the side of a support post and into the ground. She heard it before she saw it—a discreet buzzing every 30 seconds.

'Oh, my,' she said, smiling. A metal thermos—three-quarters buried and holding ball bearings—vibrated softly, sending tremors into the ground to ward off snakes. *Bloody snakes.*

On the base of each Penthouse post was a feeder or waterer. She topped them all up, then walked around to the side where the nests were located. She lifted each of the four lids and found eggs in three of them—eight in all.

'Farm fresh eggs for dinner!' she stated, cheering. She was thrilled but wondered. *Should I even say that? Do they know I will eat them?* Gathering them carefully, she placed them in Wilbur's now-empty scrap bucket. She had one more chore—ensuring Wilbur's trough was full of water. She'd been putting off the job knowing she had to enter his pen. She made her way there, nervously.

'C'mon, Wilbur-son… let me in,' she demanded, pushing open the gate. He pushed back, his blindness leaving him with only one alternative to find her—headbutting toward her voice. She reached down and patted his head. He calmed then sniffed and snorted. She relaxed, her nerves giving way to a giggle. 'You ridiculous pig. You scare me but you're a real softy, aren't you.' She popped the bucket down and he followed her footsteps to his water trough. Attending to the trough turned out easier than expected. A tap hung over it so all she had to do was pull on a chain which pulled up a plug.

'That's a good idea,' she voiced to nobody but Wilbur. 'Much better than putting your hand in murky water. Goodness knows what could be in there, hey buddy!' The old water ran out and the pig revelled in the mushy ground it created. With the tap running over the now-empty trough, she splashed water around it to clean the sides then replaced the plug and waited for the trough to refill. At that moment, the clouds drew her attention—they seemed to be growing bigger and blacker by the minute. With the water trough full, she turned the tap off and made her way to the gate. 'Oh… you rotten so and so!' she cried out, glaring at the pig. Wilbur couldn't see her face but picked up the expression in her voice. He sheepishly rubbed up against her. 'So… pigs like eggs, hey!' She rubbed his head with affection—she couldn't be mad. 'There goes my egg dinner,' she sighed. *And another note to self, don't leave an unguarded bucket in a pig pen!*

With the animals cared for and the scrap bucket rinsed and left at the bottom of the deck stairs—a reminder to take it to the surgery in the morning, she felt utterly drained. It had been a big day. The staff at the surgery mentioned that a sports drink would help replace the salts she was sweating out and therefore her energy levels—she'd get some on her next shopping trip and try it.

She fed the dogs, made a beeline to the shower, and followed it up with an easy—eggless—dinner of salad and tinned tuna. She enjoyed it in the company of the dogs, out on the deck, and washed it down with cold water. She skipped the glass of red she'd been dreaming of—much too tired for that. As daylight faded and before vampire-like giant mosquitoes homed in on her, she headed inside, rinsed her dishes, and went to bed. As she lay in bed, her thoughts were of Dave Andersen. He seemed a nice man and was ruggedly good-looking. Had she been too hard on him? She scolded herself for her lack of professionalism regarding the razor but refused to dwell on it. She fell asleep, her thoughts of Dave pushing away the one thing she'd meant to do before retiring—move the car into the shed!

Chapter 9

Never Park Under a Fruiting Tree
Week 1—Tuesday Morning

Dave wanted to catch June before she left for work and hoped he hadn't left it too late. He headed down his driveway, crossed Arthur Willis Road and continued through the gate and up the driveway opposite. As he neared the top, he could see her—bag in one hand, Wilbur's scrap bucket in the other—heading across the lawn and toward her car. He noted the shed parking space was empty and thought nothing of it. By the time he pulled up next to her, she'd stopped dead in her tracks.

Curious, Dave jumped out of his ute. He felt good today—full of energy, even though the heat was stifling. He cleared his throat, but her eyes didn't meet his. It was as if he wasn't there. They were fixed upon her car, staring with a look of horror etched on her face. One glance at her car told him why.

'Ah… fruit bats,' he said. 'Unwritten rule number one: never park under a fruiting tree—especially overnight—when you're in bat country.' She didn't respond. Dave tried desperately not to laugh, but her expression was priceless. He couldn't help it—he burst out laughing. She turned to him, her eyes blazing with fury.

'I'm glad you find it funny…' she growled, holding back tears. 'I need to leave for work. I won't be able to see out the windscreen safely.' Fruit bat droppings had landed all over her car—there wasn't a panel or window unaffected. It looked like someone had tipped a can of paint over it in an artistic way.

'You need to wash it straight off. It's pretty acidic stuff—won't do the paintwork much good,' he explained.

'I can't,' she said, tears welling. 'I haven't got time—I should have left five minutes ago.' Dave watched a tear escape and run down her cheek. She dropped the bucket and wiped the tear with the back of her hand. She felt both stupid and embarrassed and Dave felt for her. *City girls!* He stepped toward her and picked up the bucket.

'How about I give you a hand?' he offered. 'Grab the hose—that one by the stairs. We've got a bucket, and I've got rags in my ute box.' While Dave fetched the rags, June threw her bag in the car and went to the hose. She unravelled it from its hanger—the same hose she'd cleaned up Winston's mess with—turned on the tap and dragged it to the car, careful not to get wet in her scrubs and work shoes. Dave held out the bucket, and she filled it with water. 'I'll scrub… you hose as I go.'

'Okay,' she sniffled. Like a machine, Dave went around the car with his bucket and rag, working methodically from the roof down. He rubbed and scrubbed at the fruit bat droppings then stood back after each section of the car was done to let her hose off the muck. June—angry at herself for not putting the car into the shed overnight—soon calmed. The movements of Dave's shoulders and muscular arms as he worked diligently, along with the swaying back and forth of his denim-clad buttocks, turned out to be surprisingly therapeutic. *Who'd have thought, June Hall.* She smirked. *Bunnings Boy therapy… pity it can't be bottled—that'd put Big Pharma out of business!* Before she knew it, her car looked like new.

'Thank you so much, Dave. I owe you.'

'You get going,' he insisted. 'I'll put the hose back.' June hopped in her car and started the engine before winding down the window and calling out.

'Again, thank you.' She smiled before driving away. Dave replaced the hose, the task at hand causing him to forget why he was there.

Chapter 10

June's second day in the surgery treatment room was just as eventful as the morning that began with the soiled car. Two separate ambulances had been called to escort patients to Atherton Hospital, three cases of urinary tract infections and four hour-long medicals for long-haul truck drivers. She gathered that they hadn't seen a woman in some time—three had asked her to dinner.

Five o'clock came around in a flash and the working day was over. She only had time to reflect on the morning's events after parking her car in the shed. *Why had Dave come to Barrine Views?* She couldn't guess and brushed the recollection from her mind. Noticing an odd smell inside her car, she left the windows partially down to air it out overnight. She wasn't sure what she smelled, but she'd noted the Woodwards' house, the surgery— everything, seemed to have the same smell. She considered mustiness. She was used to dry air and the scent of dust back home.

After unloading her bags, she showered, changed into an old t-shirt and shorts, threw in a load of washing, and then grabbed the bucket of scraps she had brought home for Wilbur. She ventured out—plod-clomp—to do her rounds with the animals. At the pace her first two days had gone, she'd be back home in Adelaide before she knew it.

She went to Wilbur's pen first and offloaded the bucket of scraps—certain she had seen a grin of appreciation as he swallowed the last morsel. She topped up Winston's water trough, then attended to the chicken feeders and waterers. There were seven eggs in the nests. She placed them gently into

Wilbur's empty bucket. She wondered how the Woodwards went through so many eggs. Cooking? Sharing them at the surgery? Selling them? She made a mental note to either share or eat them—eggs were definitely on the menu tonight.

At the turkey gate, she stopped to take in the view. Dark grey clouds—more than yesterday—continued to build up. Surely, a good downpour would cool things down. She hoped for one. She prepared the turkey's corn for the next morning then returned to the house, bucket with eggs in hand.

As she replaced Winston's chain on the top step, a massive bolt of lightning lit up the late afternoon sky, streaking across the horizon. Ten seconds later, a clap of thunder exploded in the distance; it was so loud it made her jump. A gust of wind whipped through the trees, sending leaves scattering noisily. More rolling and rumbling followed as the clouds continued to build and draw closer by the minute. The activity around her was intensifying. She considered that it just might rain. *I feel cooler already.*

The animals were fed and watered—she didn't have to worry about them if it rained. However, she spared a thought for the turkeys and wondered how they coped in a downpour, high up in their fig tree. She checked the house windows. They were open but screened, and she was confident they wouldn't let water in. They wound outward from the bottom—possibly designed for that very reason. She'd feed the dogs, whip up eggs on toast with a glass of wine on the side, sit on the deck in the company of canines, and enjoy her first tropical storm—and she did just that. But this time, she didn't feed the vampiric mosquitoes—she'd found a stash of insect repellent coils in the pantry.

The rain was torrential, yet the temperature remained hot, an unusual phenomenon for June Hall from South Australia—almost the driest state on the driest continent. And while she enjoyed the light show and the croaking of now-active giant, green tree frogs, she grew weary and went to bed. No doubt the rooster would not let her down come 4: 01 a.m..

But sleep does not come easily in a storm. Above her head, the ceiling fan—on high speed as a necessity—whirled and clunked, while strange noises in the roof space rolled and bumped. Tropical rain slammed down on the tin roof, persistent explosions of thunder overhead shook the timber house, croaking frogs refused to retire, and a fireworks display borne by lightning continued to light up her room like an 80s disco—even through closed curtains!

Chapter 11

One Stylish Dash Mat
Week 1—Wednesday Morning

4:01 a.m. and the rooster was at his finest. June opened her eyes certain they'd only just closed. She listened. Between each crow, she could hear the faintest drizzle. Finally. It had hammered down all night! Along with the rain petering off, it appeared the frogs had called it a night too. She was grateful.

After a cup of tea and a laze in bed until five, she remembered the washing she'd put on the evening prior. She collected it from the machine and hung it on the clothes horse in the laundry. There wasn't much—mostly underwear.

'Morning all,' she called to the dogs. They looked up with their eyes—not their heads—then continued their slumber.

Dawn saw the rain stop but it was still cloudy and most likely, not over. June jumped at the opportunity to do her animal rounds and not get wet.

To say the ground was sloshy was an understatement and although oversized, she was grateful for the gumboots once again. When finished, she decided to head to work early—she had an entry key and the alarm code and could catch up on some paperwork before the surgery opened.

Readied for the day, scrub pants rolled up, work shoes and bags in hand, she stepped over the Winston chain and then carefully made her way toward her car. This time she wore her thongs—they were lighter than boots and water-friendly. She squelched across sodden grass and splish-sploshed through wide puddles—like she was a kid again. She opened the back door, tossed her things onto the seat, shut the door, stepped forward and then slid into the driver seat—only to leap straight back out. She went white and felt as if she might faint. She lowered her head, took a few calming breaths, then slowly stood and glanced back into the car. There on the dashboard was the biggest snake she'd ever seen. It lay dead still, even after she'd most likely frightened it. Its length was far longer than the dashboard and it wasn't about to move.

'Fuck.' No other word fit the situation. How was she going to get the thing off the dash and out the door? She thought about it. If she tried shooing it with a stick, she might anger it. It could slide down and hide out under one of the seats, then she'd never get it out. There was only one thing to do, and she knew she had to do it—-ring her closest neighbour.

'This is Dave,' he answered in a sprightly tone. She was never that sprightly, that early. It was 7:00 a.m. *Thank goodness, he's up. He must have a rooster too!*

'Um…' She paused to breathe. 'Dave, it's June Hall—the Woodwards' house-sitter.'

'Oh—hi June. Is everything okay?' he asked. *He's thinking my car is covered in bat shit again.*

'Um…' she breathed. 'Not *entiiiirely*.'

'What's up? Anything I can help with?' She kicked herself that she had to ask for help and screwed her face up as if in pain.

'Dave… it seems I have a visitor in my car—on my dashboard,' she said.

'Oh,' he replied. His tone changed to a serious one. 'Okay—what is it?' he asked, unphased. She hesitated before answering.

'It's… err… the biggest snake I've… well… ever seen.' He could hear the fear and apprehension in her voice.

'Oh. Righto. What colour is it?' Dave guessed what it might be, he just needed clarification of which species. She studied it through the windscreen. Dave was not prepared for the description he got.

'Um… its background is ecru—no, fawn perhaps tan. It has blotches all over it—they're coffee—yes coffee in colour. It looks as if someone has outlined every blotch perfectly with a permanent marker—a dark chocolate one!' she explained. He was taken aback. He took a breath, pulled his phone away from his ear momentarily and stared at it. He'd never heard a carpet python described in such feminine detail before.

'Okay,' he managed to say before she continued talking nervously, cutting him off after just one word. She'd moved gingerly around the front of the car to the passenger side to get a look at the creature's head.

'It has a fat head for a snake,' she continued. 'Its eyes are wide apart and more to the side—like a fish but not really like a fish.' His eyebrows raised. 'Oh, and Dave...'

'Yes, June,' he replied.

'It's frowning and does *not* look happy!' she added. With the phone to his ear, he took his keys from the kitchen bench and made a beeline to his ute, smiling broadly—she'd just described the head of his bank manager.

'Pythonidae—Morelia Spilota', he said, in the calmest of voices. She could tell by his breathing that he was walking fast. In the background, his ute door slammed shut—then the call transferred to Bluetooth.

'A what?' she enquired. Did she hear him wrong?

'It's a carpet python,' he explained, the noise of the ute travelling now audible to her. 'Harmless, but they still give a nasty bite. I'm on my way...' Before she could reply, he hung up.

She slipped her phone into her pocket—her eyes fixed on the beast. *A carpet python?* She wondered—was it searching for food or shelter? Where would it have ended up if it had not been able to access her car? On the deck? In the house roof space? Was it already inside the car, hiding? She shuddered. *June, stop it—or you'll never sleep again!*

Dave arrived in under two minutes—it had felt like fifteen to June. He pulled up right behind her car, just outside the shed. She heard his footsteps scrunch-squelching, but did not move her eyes. If the python moved, she needed to see where it was going. She could *not* drive a car with a huge slithering creature hiding under one of the seats or curled up in the dashboard somewhere—she knew it could fit. One of her patients had mentioned pulling a three-metre python from a watering can on his front veranda—a small space for a big creature!

'Morning,' he called out. She heard him lift the squeaky lid of the toolbox on the back of his ute and then close it. It was a sound she recognised from him fetching rags just yesterday. He walked up and stopped beside her; he was carrying a bag. 'Snake bag,' he said, holding it up. From the bag, he withdrew a pair of gloves and a metal object. 'That's one stylish dash mat!' he said, smiling—he was always smiling. How he could be humorous in this serious situation was beyond her, but at least now he was here, and she could safely glance away from the giant. She looked at him, a wave of calm washing over her.

'Thanks so much for coming, Dave. How will you get it out?' she asked.

'Without making him angry, hopefully,' he answered. 'We have a few of these beauties around here.' *Now I find this out.* She sighed. He waved the gloves in front of her. 'These are so I don't get my hands bitten,' he said, pulling them on. 'These fellas can wield a mighty painful bite… An extendable hook,' he continued, extending the telescopic metal rod with hooked end out as far as it would go. 'To keep his head where it needs to be… And a bag to rehome him in—unless, of course, you do want to make a dash mat out of him.' She shook her head vehemently.

'That's a pass,' she said. He handed her the bag and she took it without knowing why. It was stiff like a feed bag.

Dave, without hesitation, walked from the passenger side to the driver's side of the car. June followed him closely and curiously—she was not leaving his side. He leant in and she considered she just might faint. Like an expert, he grabbed hold of the python's tail end with one hand and placed the extended hook under its head with the other. He lifted it from the dash and backed up.

'Hold the bag upright and open and rest it on the ground—these fellas weigh as much as a dog,' he insisted. 'And try not to let go of it!' She did exactly that, but closed her eyes nervously, taking short peeks out of one eye. She didn't want to experience it any closer than she'd been and could feel herself trembling.

He steered the creature's head into the bag, removed the hook and at the same time, swiftly shoved its body inside. He pulled the bundle from her and in a heartbeat, closed it and tied it up with a short piece of rope he pulled from his pocket. Her eyes were now wide open. She had to check herself, to make sure she hadn't peed in fear. Relief overcame her—the dampness she could feel was head-to-toe sweat from the experience. She wanted to cry but held back. *For goodness's sake, June Hall. Don't embarrass yourself any further.*

'You alright?' he asked as their glances met. 'You're a bit pale.' She nodded and looked away. The damsel in distress thing was foreign to her and she didn't like it. She'd always been and always was, in control. She considered she'd made a mistake coming here. She hoped her locum experience would pass swiftly and focused once again, on her breathing. She had to slow her heart rate and regain her composure.

'I'll survive,' she said, forcing a smile. 'You make a terrifying situation look easy,' she added. As she breathed, she noted that he wore a blue singlet—tight-fitting and torn. He sure dressed like a Bunnings Boy. She fantasised about what might be—if anything—beyond the Bunnings Boy tag she'd given him. He picked up the bag—weighty, judging by the way his bicep flexed. He made everything he wore look good, everything he did look easy—and it was getting to her.

'He's a heavy fellow,' Dave said. June noted he wasn't even breathless from his efforts. She swallowed. A strange sensation washed over her. She didn't know whether it was a feeling of gratitude or something else—most likely the weather, she considered.

'What will you do with it?' she asked, standing well out of the way.

'I'll take it down near the lake and let him go in the rainforest.'

'You're not going to kill it, are you?'

'Hell no. They're gentle giants and take out rats and stuff—important fellows in the ecosystem.'

'Oh. Right.' she agreed. *Rats and stuff?* She wondered what other disgusting things surrounded her here.

'You're leaving early today,' he commented, the heavy bag hanging from his hand as if it were full of fairy floss.

'Paperwork,' she replied. She was feeling lightheaded.

'You okay to drive? You don't look too good.' He looked her up and down.

'Oh, I'm fine,' she insisted. 'Just a bit of shock, I guess. I'll give it a few minutes before I leave and maybe have some water from my water bottle.'

'Good idea, and before I forget again. I popped over yesterday to ask you to dinner but with the bat poop and all—it slipped my mind.' *Oh no. Is he asking me on a date?* She was speechless. 'Gran fell in love with you at the surgery and insisted she—we show you some local hospitality.' He didn't wait for a reply. 'Tonight. Seven, okay? My place. Bring nothing.' She was taken aback.

'Um… sure…. Alice, wasn't it—your grandmother?'

'That's right—Andersen. Same name of course.'

'Right. Okay. I suppose. Tell her thanks—a lot. I'll pop over at seven then.' Dave turned his back and took a few steps to his ute. He lifted the contained python into the back.

'Tell me…' she said. 'I've learnt not to park under fruiting trees—especially at night, and not to leave my car windows down. Is there anything else I should know or prepare myself for in advance?' He thought, then grinned.

'Yeah, maybe. Don't walk outside after dark without a torch—the garden orb spiders in the trees are the size of dinner plates. Even I don't like those buggers.'

'Awesome,' she replied and watched him jump in his ute, reverse and drive away with a smile and a wave. Her whole body tingled but what was affecting her—the python experience, the idea of plate-sized spiders, or Bunnings Boy himself?

Chapter 12

It's Fingers in Pies

Week 1—Wednesday Afternoon, June

June was in the treatment room cleaning up after her final patient of the day. She was in good spirits. The day had gone well, and it had been mostly calm. A calm day with no unexpected drama or injury was rare in general practice, and in her experience, was always followed by a day of complete chaos. She'd wear her running shoes tomorrow.

'Need a hand with anything?' Coral asked, as she entered the treatment room. June turned to acknowledge her.

'Nope, all good here, thanks.'

'I'm sorry I haven't had time to catch up with you,' Coral said, apologetically.

'That's private practice,' June remarked, with a smile.

'Have you settled in okay? Has reception given you enough time between patients? Have you found everything you need?' Coral asked, then stretched her back and June noted it. That was the problem with spending eight hours chained to a desk—stiffness and soreness. At least she got to move around, and she liked that.

'Yes, to all of the above.' June smiled. 'I've just about finished then I'm headed home.'

'How's life going at the Woodward menagerie?' Since her first moments at the surgery, June had noted Coral's interactions with staff, patients and doctors alike. She was both a thoughtful and genuine soul—a good trait for a manager.

'You know about that then—the menagerie.' June started folding a pile of towels, the last job of her day, and Coral jumped in to help her.

'Oh yes,' she chuckled. 'Doc W always has a funny story to share about his "other family" as he calls them. He keeps us both entertained and well-fed with a constant supply of eggs and papayas—sometimes veggies from his garden, too. We all love him to bits, and Mrs. Woodward too—they're both kind-hearted, giving, and pillars in our community.' This was good news to hear. June had hoped this very unusual locum was for the greater good.

'Yes. Shame I won't get to meet them,' she said. She really would have liked to.

'Plans for dinner?' Coral asked and added, 'A couple of us are hitting the pub for a counter'y if you wanna join us.' June looked blank, so Coral added an explanation. 'Counter'y— counter meal.'

'Of course,' June said, trying to look as if she'd understood the word "counter'y". She wondered if it was a North Queensland thing—she hadn't heard the term back home which of course meant nothing. It was probably said, just not in her small circle of friends. June's eyes portrayed what she was thinking as she glanced out of the window and back at Coral.

'Yes, I know,' Coral laughed. 'It hasn't stopped raining all day but that doesn't stop us up here—only cyclones do that. We love our wet season—if it doesn't last for eight months like last year; that gave us all cabin fever.'

'Thanks for the offer,' June said and put the folded towels in the cupboard. She was finished here but now had to drive home, see to the menagerie, and get herself ready—all by 7:00 p.m.. Together, they walked toward the staff room. A couple of patients were behind closed doors with the doctors—their last consults for the day—so the building was quiet. 'I appreciate being included and absolutely would have come, but I have a dinner appointment tonight.' She wondered if it would still be on, considering the increasing thunder and deluge that wasn't stopping for a breath. June loved rain—but in winter when you could snuggle up in bed with a hot chocolate and a good book!

The feeling of being hot and sweaty while it hammered down outside was just so foreign.

'Junie? Good on you,' Coral said with a knowing grin. 'Anyone we know?'

'Just the neighbour,' she commented, matter-of-factly.

'Not Dave Andersen?' Coral looked surprised.

'Yes, Dave and his grandmother, Alice.'

'Well, it's about time Dave started dating again.' June was quick to defend herself.

'It's no date—Alice asked me over. She said she'd love some company.'

'Of course, she did.' Coral grinned like a Cheshire cat. 'She's wanted to set him up since his wife flew the coop, and he won't have a bar of it.'

'His wife "flew the coop"?' June said, surprised.

'Yeah, he married a city girl—Loopy Linda. Mind you, we don't call her that in earshot of him or Alice. Strange one, though. Perhaps she couldn't handle the quiet life. Mind you, Dave's not quiet. He has his hands in plenty of pies—just not mine,' she laughed and noted the confused look on June's face.

'Fingers,' June corrected. 'It's fingers in pies.'

'Well, he has all his fingers in all the pies—busiest man I know. There isn't a woman around here that would refuse a come-on from Dave Andersen.'

'Oh.' June went quiet for a few moments and let Coral's description and opinion of Dave sink in. She considered the Dave she knew so far. He seemed a jovial character, even when it came to cleaning bat poop and wrangling pythons. He had good manners, both over the phone and face-to-face. He always smiled—annoyingly so, given his rugged looks. He was obliging, helping her at a moment's notice, and he wasn't shy about introducing himself and offering neighbourly services from day one. She acknowledged that perhaps she should be making dinner—as a thank you for services rendered. Maybe later. But Coral's comment still baffled her; she didn't know, nor could she imagine—besides cattle—what "pies" a Bunnings Boy like him would have his fingers in. Not that she needed to know where his fingers went—only that they weren't going anywhere near her knickers! If he thought that possible, he had another think coming. She was a city girl—not his type—and here for work. That was all.

June swapped her shoes for her thongs, rolled the bottom of her scrub pants up once more in preparation for the sodden ground, collected her bag and Wilbur's scrap bucket and readied to leave.

'See you tomorrow, Coral—enjoy your counter'y tonight.' She smiled and made her way to the back door.

'Thanks,' Coral called after her. 'Hey, keep some civvies packed in your car—all of us that live out of town do—that way we can go out on a whim after work. And you enjoy your dinner also—with *Daaave*.' June shook her head, reminded of schoolyard days and being teased about boys.

Without intending to, she slammed the door behind her. Holding her bags above her head—the Woodwards' umbrella left in the kitchen at Barrine Views—she made a dash to her car, but the rain was heavy, and she got half-soaked. Tropical North Queensland raindrops appeared ten times bigger than the ones back home. How funny it was—she was just as wet from rain as she was from perspiration. *Ah, the tropics.*

Chapter 13

Caring For Alice

Week 1—Wednesday Afternoon, Dave

Dave spent the day—as always—outdoors. He liked life that way; busy with no time to overthink. He drove one paddock of cattle into a fresh paddock, mended a punctured tyre on his ATV, serviced his ute, paid some bills, ensured the order was in place for Sunday's Paddock-to-Plate BBQ session, and took two steers in the trailer to the Millbrook Butchery.

While in town, he picked up some groceries. Pushing the trolley to his ute, he caught his reflection in the window. *Geez, Andersen, you need shearing.* Trolley and all, he made a beeline across the road to the barber. With no appointment and only a short wait, he was home by 4.00 p.m.—still plenty of time to cook a dinner fit for a guest.

'You there, Gran?' he called out. He placed the shopping bags on the kitchen bench and started unpacking them. His grandmother came into the kitchen, pushing her wheeled walker.

'How was your day, darling?' she asked.

'Oh, you know—never a dull moment,' he replied. He noted the basket on the table. 'You brought the washing in…?' he growled. 'I told you not to—not until I get time to fix the path. You'll trip and break your hip.'

'Blah, Blah, Blah,' she replied. Dave shook his head at her. As much as he loved her, she could be frustrating.

'I mean it. What don't you understand about "osteoporosis"?' He asked, frowning.

'Supercalifragilisticexpialidocious,' she replied, lifting a hand off of her wheeled walker and waving it in the air as if she were waving a magic wand at him.' She let out an evil chuckle and Dave couldn't help but smile.

'I'm serious...' he insisted. 'Now... are you ready for your shower? I have to cook dinner.'

'Yes, that would be nice. I'll get ready and meet you in the bathroom,' she said. Dave just nodded, busy putting the last of the cold items in the fridge. Alice made her way to the bathroom, stopping to collect a clean dress on the way. Usually after her afternoon shower, she got into her nighty, but tonight they'd have a visitor.

Alice was unsteady on her feet a lot of the time and Dr. Flint had banned her from showering alone. Dave was her official carer. He'd taken on the role after his grandfather—Alice's husband—passed away. Pop Andersen had been gone for over a year now.

Having lived on the land most of her life, she needed no persuasion to rent out her retirement home in Millbrook and live with Dave on his property full-time. After Pop's death, she was at a loose end; at Dave's place, she had the quiet of the land and peace of mind too, for no matter how busy Dave got, he was only ever minutes away.

Alice was a character—a stubborn one at that. She did everything in her power to remain as independent as possible, refusing to be a burden on anyone, especially Dave. Cooking dinner for one extra, assisting with her daily shower, and escorting her to the odd doctor's visit were not big deals in Dave's eyes. However, if he interfered outside her basic needs, she swiftly put him in his place.

Alice kept herself busy knitting squares for the CWA who in turn, stitched them together to make blankets for the Millbrook Nursing Home. One afternoon per week, she was picked up by the RSL bus and taken to bingo. She cherished the opportunity to catch up with old friends, eat something besides Dave's foreign muck, and feel a part of the community for a few hours.

Dave hadn't minded Alice moving in. She did what she could and wasn't a bother. Besides, it had been lonely in his house since his wife left. Marrying a city girl wasn't the smartest thing he'd done, but his situation wasn't rare. The loneliness of country life didn't suit everyone, especially young women who were used to more company and excitement than rural life offered. Dave and Linda had remained acquaintances and kept in touch, calling each other on special occasions, but love was no longer there. Linda had been Dave's first serious love. They say time heals wounds, but Dave wasn't about to find out, and if Cupid's arrow did strike again, she'd be a country woman—through and through.

'How's the temperature?' Dave asked as he adjusted the shower.

'Perfect Love.' Alice soaped up her face washer and began scrubbing herself all over. 'Is that pretty nurse still coming for dinner tonight?'

'I think so. We agreed on 7:00 p.m..'

'Do you like her?'

'Gran, honestly. Stop trying to set me up,' he insisted, with a sigh. 'You know she's from Adelaide and that's a bloody long way from here and might I remind you, it was your idea for her to come, so *you* could have a chat—remember! That's all there is to it, and I mean it.' Alice gave a sly smile.

'What are you making for dinner?'

'Chilli con carne.'

'You know I don't like spicy stuff. That foreign muck gives me gas.'

'It's a very mild version,' he informed her. Dave rinsed Alice's back and handed her the shower head. She rinsed the rest of her body, then Dave turned off the taps. He handed her a towel, took another off the rack and dried her back for her.

'You know you don't have to do this for me, Love,' she said. 'We can get the blue ladies in.'

'We go through this every night, Gran. It's not a drama, just a five-minute job. Besides, getting them out here for five minutes' work makes no sense—especially in the rain.'

'Yes, but it's bloody awful that you have to see all my wrinkly bits and creases—I feel bad for your eyes, not for me. Must make you want to get the iron out!' Alice busied herself with the towel.

'To be honest, Gran, my head is always elsewhere—generally on tomorrow and planning the day so I can get everything I have to do done,' he explained.

'Alright, alright,' she agreed. 'Help me to the dry chair, then you can get back to your bloody carne'y chilli dish.' Dave smiled. His grandmother had been a meat and three-veg woman all her life and didn't like change.

Dave tidied up the bathroom as best he could and then got to work in the kitchen. He'd prep the meal and clean himself up before 7:00 p.m.. He was excited for Alice to have someone else to talk to.

Showered and in his room, he pulled out multiple shirts and struggled with which one to wear. A glance at the clock read 6:50 p.m.. He realised he was fussing and wondered why. He didn't have time to fuss. *Just pick a damn shirt, Dave Andersen. You're hosting a house-sitter, not the bloody queen.* He wondered what was going on in his head. He was six-foot-three and nothing fazed him—nothing except pretty women!

Chapter 14

And The Rain Kept Falling
Week 1—Afternoon into Night

June drove slowly and cautiously, her wipers on top speed. When she left the bitumen and hit unsealed Arthur Willis Road, the car lost traction, so she slowed down even more. The tall grass on the roadside had been somewhat flattened and she considered that the rain had done it. *Holy cow, that's heavy rain and a lot of it!*

She reached the Woodwards' driveway and looked towards Dave's house—not that she could see far. The usual cattle that loitered near the roadside fence were nowhere to be seen. *Even they've ducked for cover from this weather.* She couldn't fathom why they spent their days leaning through the wire fence to eat from the grassy verge. Their paddocks were just as lush, and the fence wire looked like it would cut them or at least hurt them.

Drenched from opening and closing the gate, she drove carefully up the sloping driveway and parked in the shed. She would keep the windows up tonight and deal with the musty smell.

Four wet dogs came running to greet her, each one demanding a pat.

'You guys don't smell pretty,' she told them. She brushed her dog-hair-covered hands across her scrubs. 'Seriously, why do you insist on shaking off your wetness right next to me? Do I *not* look wet enough?' She rolled her eyes. She could do with the umbrella that was in the kitchen right now, even if only for show. She hesitated at the edge of the shed and looked out. *This rain is so warm and so heavy, with a bar of soap I could shower outdoors.* It sounded like a romantic idea in theory, but with her luck,

Bunnings Boy would come up the driveway as she put it into practice. With that thought, she sprinted to the house—bag and scrap bucket in hand—and tried not to slip over. The dogs ran close behind her.

She reached the deck and climbed the stairs, avoiding the mud the dogs had tracked up and down.

'Oh, this bloody deck,' she cursed. She unhooked Winston's chain, stepped up the last step, and replaced it securely. Now undercover, she looked around—the grounds were sodden. *If this is what happens after 24 hours of rain, what would one week of it be like?* She glanced down the hill and toward Dave's property, but it was futile. Visibility was limited. *I guess it's safe to drive that far tonight.* She had not received any messages to say dinner was cancelled, so she dropped her bags inside the door and got straight onto her chores with the animals.

First, she fed the dogs. Then she pulled on Doc's gumboots and since she was already wet, stayed in her scrubs—this time bringing the umbrella although she wasn't sure why.

Wilbur, happily playing in the mud, got his scraps. The chooks, huddled in the dry either inside or under the Penthouse, had their feeders topped up. Winston, whose trough was overflowing, got ignored.

June zig-zagged across the yard—plod-clomp, splish-splosh—ending up at the turkey yard. She carefully placed Wilbur's empty bucket holding six eggs, onto the ground next to the gate. The turkeys, unfazed by the weather, stood around in scattered little groups—some across the muddy slope below the gate and others in groups beneath the fig tree. She stared at them, and they stared back.

'Don't tell me you haven't seen an umbrella before,' she said, smiling at their expressions. 'In this climate, that can't be possible.'

'Gobble, gobble, gobble,' one responded. She loved the noises they made. Balancing the umbrella on her head, she used both hands to unravel the Occy Strap from the gate.

'You could at least be up in your tree, not making that muddy slope worse,' she told the group on the slope. The fig-tree dwellers looked at Wilbur's bucket, hopeful for food. 'Don't get your hopes up,' she advised. 'They're chook eggs and they're *not* for you—that's a definite!' She would take the eggs with her tonight for Dave and Alice—Dave hadn't said anything about having chooks himself.

Opening the gate, she stepped forward, leant over and reached out to unhook the turkey feed bucket from its hanger. She hadn't expected it to be heavy as she lifted it, but it was—full of water. It sent her off balance. In an instant, she toppled over and slid down the slope—head first. She hit a lone papaya tree and grabbed hold of it. It would prevent her from sliding further down and into the rest of the trees.

Shit. She blinked through raindrops to look up at the gate. *Shit, shit and double shit. I must be six metres down.* Four more and she'd be at the base of the slope and into the thick of the papaya trees. A few turkeys that had jumped out of the way moved closer out of interest.

'What are you lot looking at?' she asked, spitting out a mixture of water, mud, and quite likely poop. *Ptuh...* 'If you didn't eat all the grass and churn the hillside with your stiletto feet, I wouldn't be in this predicament.' A large tom defecated just above and in front of her. The gobbler plop began a downhill slide—softened and propelled by the rain—and headed straight toward her. 'Oh... don't mind me!' she said sarcastically. *Ptuh...*

'Gobble, gobble, gobble,' he replied. He puffed his chest out proudly and his tail feathers fanned out in a show of dominance. She feared it may attack her, being that it stood over her. She raised herself as much as she could. She needed to be big and loud to scare it away.

'I hope you like it hot, buddy...' she bellowed, waving her hand. 'Oven hot—I'm going to cook you!' *Ptuh... If I can remember which one you are.* He strutted off and the others followed. They headed down to where the bucket had tumbled to see if it contained food. She reflected on Dave's advice. *What terrible listening skills you have, June Hall. Where's your phone and torch now—your phone to call for help, and your torch to see the bloody "plate-sized" spiders after dark?* She groaned in frustration.

Daylight was dwindling—it was darker than normal thanks to the rain and clouds. She considered the time would be sometime after 6:00 p.m.. Previous days had been dark by 7:00 p.m.. *What kind of state doesn't do daylight saving? Honestly—it'd be handy right about now! Ptuh…*

She considered her choices. She could climb up a six-metre mudslide to the gate or slide four metres down into the plantation. If she chose to slide, she'd be in the thick of the papaya trees. She'd likely have to wander around blindly—there were no streetlights out here and any hope of moonlight had been washed away by the weather. She'd be forced to wade through the thick mulch around the trees—mulch made up of fallen leaves over time—and try to find somewhere to jump over the tall, barbed-wire fence that kept the cattle out of the plantation. If she managed to do that, she'd then have to trek back up to the house through the cow paddock and the tall grass that filled it. That would be hard enough to do in broad daylight, let alone post-sundown. Not to mention there was a very large bull lurking out there somewhere.

'Poo—bum—bugger—shit!' she voiced in frustration. *Venomous snakes, ticks, pythons, plate-size spiders, vampiric mozzies, bulls, and who knows what else is out there waiting to get you in the dark, June Hall.* 'Fuck that—I'll climb!' In her last moments of light, she kicked off the gumboots that were now full of water and watched them slide away. She readied to use her toes to grip the mud. *Ptuh…*

The umbrella had tumbled with her, the tip of the rib stabbing into the mud—its resting place between her and the gate. If only she could reach it, she might be able to use the rib tips and stick them in the ground, just like a turkey uses its hallux.

"Ah… eh… ew… argh…' She grunted and she groaned, using her fingers and her toes as best she could to dig in and grip. The mud smelt horrid and it didn't taste great either. *Ptuh…* What had she gotten herself into? Turkeys passed her by, leaving the plantation to fly upward and overhead into their tree to roost. *Bloody turkeys! Bloody rain!*

Bit by bit, over and over, she clawed at the mud with all her might—she'd never spat so much in her life. *Fingernails would be handy right now.* The turkeys had nails on their feet, and they had no problem climbing. She never could grow her nails; they were always soft, being washed 100 times per day at work. *Seriously? Are you thinking about nails—at a time like this?* Nails may have assisted, but they'd surely have broken. *Ptuh…*

With each attempt she'd climb a short distance—a metre or so—only to slip straight back down again, the same papaya tree stopping her each time. Rain heavier than she thought possible surged down the slope, past her and over her, making her efforts futile. Exhausted, and now in an environment as dark as the devil's soul, she admitted defeat. *Ptuh…*

Against her will, June Hall broke down and sobbed. She couldn't wipe her tears nor blow her nose—her fingernails jammed with mud and poop and her hands and body covered in the same. She let the rain flush the tears from her eyes and the mucous from her nose, occasionally spitting and firing off the odd snot rocket to keep her airways clear.

She heard a stray turkey flap above her head, on its way to roost. *Arsehole!* She couldn't see and she wondered, could it? She'd Google it one day—whether turkeys could see in the dark— that's if she ever got out of this mess. *This mess.* Reality hit—she was alone in the dark, in the deluge, and she would be all night. She hoped her failure to arrive at work would lead to her being found but that was 13 hours away. No—at sunrise she'd slide down and walk out through the cow paddock. Then she'd shower, go to work, and act like nothing had happened—put it down to experience. *If I survive? Ptuh…* It was going to be a long, wet, night. She hugged the lone papaya tree and wished she'd never laid eyes on Barrine Views.

And the rain kept falling…

Chapter 15

A Soft Cry for Help
Week 1—Wednesday Night, Dave

It was 8:00 p.m.. Dave turned off the oven and dished up his grandmother's dinner—she looked disappointed that June hadn't come over. Dave wondered why she hadn't. He hoped she didn't feel he was coming on to her. Was she still at work? Perhaps there was an emergency? Emergencies were regular at the surgery. Had she made it home safely in this rain? He didn't mind being let down, but he was more surprised than anything. June didn't seem the type to let anyone down. After all, look at everything she was doing for the Woodwards. He called her mobile. There was no answer. Could she have had an accident? He knew Arthur Willis Road could be challenging in wet weather. He needed to investigate.

'Gran, I'm just going to check on June—to make sure she got home okay in this weather.'

'Sure, sweetheart. That's a good idea,' Alice agreed. 'Be careful—it's raining cats, dogs, *and* sheep out there!'

Dave put his phone in his jeans pocket, picked up his keys, threw on his Driza-bone coat, snapped the buttons closed, and walked swiftly to his ute. In the cab, he checked the trusty all-weather torch that always sat beside him on the passenger seat; it was charged and bright. He drove down his driveway. At the bottom, he hesitated. Should he check the road first? No, he'd start his search at Barrine Views.

At the Woodwards' gate, as the rain poured down on the ute, he pulled up his collar and placed his hat on his head—his normal wet-weather procedure. Not only did his hat keep the rain off his face, but it ensured water that hit it, ran outside his coat and not down his neck and inside it.

Beyond the gate, he drove slowly up the driveway, stopping outside the house. He let his engine idle for a moment while he looked around. Her car was in the shed—she had made it home—but there was no sign of life or any lights on anywhere and there weren't any power outages as far as he was aware.

He turned the engine off, grabbed the torch, and made his way up the stairs to the deck two steps at a time. He jumped over Winston's chain and called out. The dogs acknowledged him but remained happy in their baskets.

'June,' he called out. 'June, are you there?' Dave could be loud when he wanted to be. She surely would have heard him if she was around the house—unless she was in a deep sleep. He didn't know her, after all—perhaps she was in an alcohol-induced sleep. He brushed that thought aside. Surely not. She didn't seem the type for that. He slid the unlocked door partially open, turned on an inside light, and called out again. She wasn't asleep on the couch—he could see that; however, her bags lay dumped on the floor just inside the door. Nothing looked unpacked. She must have gone straight out to feed the animals, he figured. Had something happened? He turned around and headed for the garden, splish-sploshing as his boots made their way across soggy ground and through puddles.

He shone his torch in every direction, calling her name as he went. Wilbur was alone, happy in his muddy element. Winston was utilising the protection of a broad poinciana tree. The chicken door was closed, so the chickens were in the Penthouse for the night. *She wouldn't fit in there.* Dave had no idea why that thought even crossed his mind. He'd checked the animal pens—where else could she be? He made his way toward the large fig tree at the rear of the house block. Then, over the sound of the rain, he heard it—a soft cry for help.

Chapter 16

The Lengths Some People Go To
Week 1—Wednesday Night

Shivering, June curled up as tightly as she could against the papaya tree that supported her. It didn't stop the heavy rain that washed over her, but its broad-lobed leaves—singular on the end of short, sparse branches—buffered it slightly. It wasn't South Australian winter cold, but the constant deluge steadily lowered her body temperature. She called out every few minutes. It was futile with only roosting turkeys close enough to hear, but it kept her alert—and maybe even scared off creepy crawlies she couldn't see in the darkness.

How had she gotten into such a predicament? She wondered if the turkeys felt as exposed as she did. And then she heard something over the rain. *Wishful thinking?* She listened and heard it again. Someone was either calling her name or she was hallucinating. Looking up, she could see liquid sparks flicker through the air. *Is that… light?* The downpour cut through the beam as if trying to wash it away, but there was no hiding it—it was indeed torchlight.

She had to get their attention; they'd never find her down the slope. Blinking water from her eyes and spitting between words, she called out at the top of her voice.

'Hello… is anyone there?' she spat. 'Please help me. Help… help…' *Ptuh…* 'I'm down the slope.' Before she could call out again, the beam shot down from the gate above and cut through the darkness, illuminating her and forcing her to squint and turn away, momentarily blinded.

'The lengths some people will go to just to avoid dinner with my grandmother!' Dave called down. As distraught as she was, she smiled at his comment and replied.

'Help me, Dave. I took a tumble, and I can't climb up. I've tried and tried… it's just so darn muddy and slippery and…' she paused to spit again.

'… well fertilised!' Dave finished her sentence with a grin, not that she could see it. She dropped her head sheepishly.

'Yes…' she agreed. *Very well fertilised. Ptuh…* She took a few deep breaths through her nose; she'd live to see another day. *Look on the bright side, June Hall. At least you're not starkers, with a cake of soap in your hand.*

'Stay where you are,' Dave insisted. 'I'll get a rope from my ute and be straight back.' She watched as the light disappeared.

'Stay where you are,' she muttered. *Ptuh… And where did he think I was about to go?* Was there anything that man didn't have in his bloody ute? She focused on nasal breathing to stop herself from thinking about "plate-sized" spiders.

To June, Dave's absence felt like an eternity, though in reality, it was only a few minutes. He returned and threw the lifeline down to her.

'Can you reach the rope?' he asked, his strong voice perfectly audible despite the weather.

'I think so,' she replied. She reached out using the papaya trunk for leverage. *Ptuh…* She wondered whether she'd have done better with the gumboots on; she'd retrieve them from the bottom of the slope when things dried out. She called back. 'Too far left.'

'I'll try again,' Dave yelled, pulled the rope back up, then threw it toward her a second time.

'Got it,' she hollered, water entering her mouth again. *Ptuh…*

'Tie it around your waist,' he explained. 'Let me know when you're ready and I'll pull you up.' She tied the rope as tightly as she could, though it was only a double granny knot.

'Ready,' she advised. She was naturally soft-spoken and found it difficult to project her voice at any time, let alone the incessant torrential downpour. Dave propped his torch against a post to give himself free hands and the best light possible.

'Here we go,' he hollered, and began pulling at the rope, bit by bit. He had to stand a fair way back from the gate for traction.

On her stomach, June tried to help by digging her toes in, but it was fruitless. As Dave grunted and hauled from above, she clung to the rope—arms stretched high, legs dangling—and did her best to keep her face out of the mud. He gave it his all—or at least what remained after a solid day's work. She wasn't heavy; he'd lifted calves that weighed more.

With every yank, more mud clung to June's already-soiled scrubs. She could feel the cold seep through and knew, just as much was collecting on the inside as it was on the outside. *Oh, my favourite scrubs... they'll never look the same again.*

'Ah… grr… eh…' she could hear Dave grunting. *How do I not hear him spitting rain? Ptuh…* As she was dragged past the umbrella she'd lost during her tumble, she reached out with one hand, grabbed it and pulled it from its resting place in the mud. The slippery move flipped her onto her back. If she didn't already have mud caked through her ponytail, she sure did now. She automatically held the umbrella above herself, thrilled that the rain was no longer in her face. Swiftly, both June and the umbrella reached the top and made it through the gate—but Dave kept pulling. She was dragged until she was well away from the slope's edge. She'd never been more relieved to feel level ground beneath her and lay there catching her breath. Dave dropped the rope, stepped to her side, bent over and peered under the umbrella.

'Hi,' she said, looking up at him, straight-faced.

'Hi yourself,' he replied with a grin. He reached down for her hand and hoisted her up. She stood with the umbrella above her. 'You, okay?' he asked, stepping back to retrieve his torch. He appeared genuinely concerned. She nodded. Only her pride was hurt.

'I'm okay, but I feel like such a duffer,' she said. He shone the torch toward her and ran the beam up and down, checking for any obvious signs of an injury. As he did, her eyes fixed on him. Framed by the dark of the night and reflected by the gentle gleam of his torch, he looked like the hero in a rom-com—especially in his Akubra hat and long oilskin coat. And then he stepped up next to her.

'Oh,' he remarked, his nose curling up. He'd gotten too close and quickly stepped back. She could smell herself too now—the umbrella preventing the rain from washing away the radiating scent of turkey poop. Embarrassed, she dropped her head.

'I…' she started, but her voice caught as she choked back a sob. Dave struggled with what to say next.

'Well, look on the bright side…' he said, grinning from under his hat. 'It could've been pig poop! We have plenty of those feral buggers around here.' June nodded. *Yes—pig poop. That would've been worse.* 'Lucky for you…' he continued. 'Doc's papayas are well-fenced.' *Yes, lucky indeed.* The corner of her mouth lifted ever so slightly, but he didn't notice. She appreciated his banter. Dave Andersen's go-to in an awkward situation was always humour. He considered her silence—in this situation, it may not have been appropriate. 'Don't mind me,' he babbled. 'Sorry… you must be feeling pretty shitty right now.' And there it was—his foot in his mouth. *Jeez, you're a mug, Andersen—you said pretty shitty!* He stepped forward, reached out and put his already-soiled hand on her muddy shoulder.

'You've had a frightening ordeal. Are you sure you're not hurt?' he asked, and she nodded again. Only her pride was hurt, but it was healing, safe in his presence.

'Hey—you hungry?' he asked, his own stomach growling.

'Um… not right now, to be honest,' she replied softly, still spitting muck from her mouth. Even with a nurse's tough stomach, the stench was too much for her. Dave, on the other hand, could eat anytime. He quickly realized the timing of his question wasn't brilliant given her current condition. He stepped forward, untied the rope from her waist, and then secured it to a fence post above the slope. He threw the unattached end down toward the papayas.

'I'm donating this to the cause,' he said. 'If you tumble again—and I'm sure you won't—the rope will be here as a safeguard. I'll talk to Doc when he gets back—suggest revegetating with something turkey-proof. Now, let's get you back to the house. We'll clean you up, then I'll fetch dinner. Do you like chilli con carne—mild?'

'Sounds good,' she smiled, her white teeth bright against her muddied face. 'It might take me a while to clean up, though.'

'I imagine it will,' Dave agreed, with a caring smile. He noted the bucket of water on the ground, glanced in and saw the eggs. He knew they'd be no good after their soaking, so he drained off the water, placed the eggs in Wilbur's trough, and carried the bucket. Together, they made their way to the house, Dave's boots splish-sploshing and June's bare feet slip-slapping across the wet ground.

At the base of the deck stairs, Dave put the bucket down then unravelled the hose and turned on the tap. He took the umbrella from her, hosed it clean, and threw it up over the railing and out of the way. It would dry in time.

'Now, let's clean you up before you go inside,' he offered. She agreed and stood—arms outstretched—while he hosed her front and back, top to bottom. The water temperature through the hose was far from cold and she was grateful. She stopped shivering. 'Your turn.' He passed her the hose so she could flush inside her scrubs.

'Thanks,' she said. While she hosed, he went up the stairs, dropped the Winston chain, and turned the deck lights on wondering why he hadn't turned them on earlier. He yelled down over the deck railing.

'Tell you what... I'll head off so you can strip down outside—keep the house clean. I'll be back in half an hour with dinner.' And with that, Dave took his torch, jumped in his ute and drove away.

June stripped in the garden and between the rain and the hose, rinsed off her scrubs, hair and underwear ensuring nothing either physically or in her imagination remained. Hanging the hose up, she rolled the clothing into a ball and squeezed out as much water as she could. She ascended the stairs naked, the bundle of washing held respectfully in front of her and replaced Winston's chain—she'd had enough of poop for one day. Inside, she threw her scrubs into the washing machine on a quick, hot wash, then jumped into the shower and scrubbed until the water ran clean. And when it did, she scrubbed again.

After two rounds of brushing, she tossed her toothbrush in the bin. She gargled mouthwash three times yet still tasted turkey poop. Or was that just trauma?

'Can't wait for tomorrow,' she muttered to her reflection. And yet, somehow, she already knew—things wouldn't be any less eventful.

Chapter 17

Foreign Muck
Week 1—Wednesday Night

June was in her bedroom when she heard Dave's perfectly tuned ute return. It idled momentarily—thrum, thrum, thrum—before he cut the engine. She'd changed into a light summer dress, pottered, and felt fresher and calmer. She'd also ensured she sprayed on a hefty dose of perfume—in case the scent of the slide wasn't just fixed in her nostrils.

Dave gave each of the Woodwards' dogs a pat before reaching the sliding door. He was free of his coat and hat and had freshened up. He noted clean scrubs hanging over a clothes horse under the sheltered part of the deck. *That was quick—* she'd already washed her scrubs and hung them out. He considered the time. He'd meant to be back in half an hour but had taken much longer. Alice had insisted on hearing every little detail of June's mishap—she'd only gotten half the story. When it came to women—any woman within cooee of Dave, whether personal or professional—Alice was one meddlesome Gran, and she was getting worse by the day.

At the door, he dropped his umbrella and kicked off his thongs, pushing them both out of harm's way.

'You decent?' he called out and waited.

'Come in,' she called back, her voice distant. As he slid the door open, he saw her walking down the passage toward him. He stepped inside carrying a picnic-style basket and closed the door.

'You look a bit different,' he smiled and thought she looked as fresh as the morning sun; her short, fitted dress had a delicate floral pattern and her wet, neatly combed hair trailed over her shoulders. Instinctively, he drew in a deep breath. He liked what he saw. *Focus on the food, numbnuts.* He dragged his attention to the basket and put it down on the wide bench-cum-breakfast bar that separated the kitchen from the dining room. He remained on the kitchen side while June stayed on the dining side.

'Mmm—smells wonderful,' she said, waiting for him to open it.

'It's not flash,' he said of dinner. 'But you need something warming.'

'Warming,' she laughed. 'When are you *not* warm up here?' She pulled out a stool and sat down, her nose level with the basket.

'Mid-year, usually,' he added.

'Seriously?' she asked. 'It gets cold?'

'Sure. We're over seven hundred metres above sea level,' he said. 'We have the odd cold day, but mostly cold nights—good for snuggling up with a book.' June smiled. That was exactly what she liked to do in the cold.

'You read then?' she asked.

'Yes of course.' He stood straight, gave her a serious look and added, 'Do you think that because I work the land, I can't read?'

'Oh no, not at all,' she explained. She hadn't meant to insult him. Then he cracked a broad smile that stopped just short of a laugh—he was stirring. She relaxed and smiled back.

'As well as being able to read, I can cook—pretty darn well, actually!' he boasted. 'But you can make up your own mind about that.' He opened the basket and started unpacking it. She watched his every move.

'I didn't know your hair was so long,' he commented. 'It's always tied up.'

'Yes, well my line of work requires it,' she explained. 'You don't want strands of hair hanging in an open wound.' Dave screwed his face up at the thought.

'I guess not,' he laughed. She thought what a happy man he was to be around.

'Are you sure you didn't hurt yourself out there?' he enquired again. June eyed the interesting things coming out of the basket. 'No cuts or anything?'

'No cuts. No anything—Doctor. I am fine,' she insisted.

'Just making sure. Got some good anti-biotic cream in the ute,' he said. *I bet you have, Dave Andersen—you have everything but the kitchen sink in that thing.* 'Works great on cattle wounds,' he added. She raised her eyebrows and grinned. He lifted the lid off a glass dish and her eyes lit up.

'Oh, that looks divine,' she praised him, eagerly. 'I love chilli con carne.'

'Great! I'm glad to hear it,' he said, relieved. 'Gran calls it "foreign muck". She's pretty set in her ways—a meat and three veg connoisseur—but she eats it all the same. I love experimenting with foods from different cultures, but there's only Gran and I to eat it.'

He pushed an empty plate toward her, followed by a knife and fork then placed a serving spoon into the dish of chilli con carne. He'd brought everything they needed.

'Help yourself,' he insisted. June dished herself up several spoonfuls of the chilli dish. 'Spuds,' he offered, taking the lid off a blue plastic container and popping a pair of tongs into it. June took two, noting they'd already been partially cut and buttered with a fresh sprig of parsley on each one.

'Thanks,' she said and sampled a mouthful of the chilli. 'Delicious… Hey, do you like wine?' she asked, remembering she had some. 'I've got a nice Barossa Shiraz. It's bold and peppery and would pair beautifully with this. Would you like a glass? It's refrigerated if that's okay.'

'Sure,' Dave replied, dishing food onto his plate. 'Sounds superb, but I'll grab it—I'm up.' He turned around in search of glasses and she read his mind.

'Right corner cupboard—opener too,' she instructed. He opened the cupboard, took out two red wine glasses and the bottle opener, and then took the bottle from the fridge.

'This the one,' he asked, holding it up. She nodded.

He set the glasses down and opened the bottle.

'Do you like to air it?' he asked, straight-faced. She smirked.

'In another life, maybe,' she laughed. 'This life doesn't allow time to "air" wine—not for me anyway.'

'Then we have a lot in common,' Dave chuckled and poured them each a glass. Still standing, he took a mouthful of his chilli.

June found it hard not to stare at him. She'd noted, more than once, that he had a physique worthy of a calendar. Her mind jumped back to him washing the car, wrangling the python and hauling the rope. The memory made her feel warm inside. It was obvious he worked physically hard on the land, but the fact he'd said he liked to read made her wonder if there could be more to this Bunnings Boy.

'You don't have to stand and eat, you know,' she said, pointing to the stool next to her. He nodded and smiled, put his fork down, walked around next to her, picked up the stool and returned to the kitchen side of the bench. As he sat down, an odd look fell across her face and Dave noticed.

'I'd rather look at you while we chat, not sit next to you and stare at my old picnic basket,' he explained.

'Oh. Of course,' she nodded. That made sense. She smiled and began to relax. She didn't want to stare at him, so she focused on eating and although she hadn't felt it earlier, she was very hungry.

'Beaut drop this,' Dave agreed. He held his glass up and June responded, lifting and clinking her glass against his. 'To turkeys,' he quipped, his grin devilishly naughty. She burst out laughing and he joined in with a belly laugh so loud it made her laugh even harder.

'To bloody turkeys,' she finally agreed, regaining her breath. It was the release she needed to feel totally at ease after her ridiculous ordeal. They ate their way through the meal making small talk between mouthfuls. June groaned several times in awe of the dish and repeatedly complimented him on it.

'I shit you not, this really is—hands down—the best chilli con carne I have ever had!' she insisted and figured he was either a very good cook indeed, or it was a top-quality supermarket dish stripped of its packaging.

'Thank you,' he said, puffing out his chest with pride. In the light-heartedness of the moment, she made the mistake of looking into his stunning blue eyes—they appeared to sparkle, completely captivating her. *Sapphires indeed.* Dave's eyes locked on to hers, and for a moment, they studied each other. Feeling herself flush, she pulled her eyes away, looked toward the window and took a slow, deep breath. She could see him still smiling out of the corner of her eye. He was always smiling, and it was a smile—she imagined—that would break many hearts. He scrubbed up well. *Please stop smiling—just stop it.*

'I can't believe it's still raining,' she said, keeping her eyes on anything that wasn't him. 'Will it flood?'

'No. This is just a few showers. When we get a monsoon trough or a cyclone, it can last for days—sometimes weeks—and then it floods, particularly on the coast. The rivers and creeks up here swell, but water runs downhill, so it's short-lived. That's when it's good to be on top of the mountains and not at the base of them.'

'I can't imagine it,' she said, picking up the wine bottle and topping up their wine.

'It's also pretty darn humid then, too,' he said, stressing the word "darn". 'So much so, that if you stand still long enough, mould grows on you.' Her forehead lines creased thinking about it.

'I remember seeing the news,' she said, 'When you had Cyclone Jasper… It looked unimaginable.'

'Yeah, that one dumped a lot of rain—over a metre in a week I believe.' He took a sip of wine. 'A lot of damage and heartache—especially for those who live near the beaches and the mouth of the Barron River. Scary stuff!' June was quiet trying to process his words. He changed the topic. 'How's the job going?' he asked.

'Oh—good. Everyone has been so helpful. It's a plus that the computer program is one I know well. It's always hard when you have to learn a new program,' she explained.

'Thought they'd all be the same in a doctor's surgery,' Dave remarked, surprised.

'Nope. Lots of different programmes out there,' she said. 'All the patients have been great too—very welcoming and supportive.' She held back a smirk, suddenly remembering his ECG and wondering if the bald patches on his chest had started to grow back at all.

'That's great,' he said, stacking their empty plates and piling the cutlery on top. 'Well, I'm sure the Woodwards are more than happy that you could come. They don't get much downtime.'

'I can imagine.' She stood and pulled the plates away from him and toward her. She smiled at the empty dishes. 'Well… we made short work of your masterpiece.'

'That's what it's for—eating,' he touched her hand accidentally as they both reached for the chilli dish. He quickly pulled back, a tingle running through them both.

'I'll give them a quick wash for you,' she insisted, busying herself. 'You cooked and that's fair in my books.' She walked around the bench and into the kitchen. He stood intending to help. 'No, sit,' she insisted. 'I've got this. I'm sure your day has been even bigger than mine.' She placed the plates, cutlery, and glass dish that held the chilli into the sink and filled it, adding a generous squirt of dishwashing liquid. She then collected the other few dishes from the bench.

Dave sat on the stool, his back now to the bench, and waited. While she washed up, he said nothing, just sat quietly and studied her from behind. The long, blonde hair that fell down her back was now mostly dry and swayed ever so gently with her movements, as did the curve-hugging dress that fell perfectly over her bottom, stopping well above her knees. He caught himself wondering what sort of underwear she wore, the thought sending a jolt through him. Then, an unexpected reaction happened in his own underwear bringing him swiftly back to the present. *Oh no... Hell no!* He stood abruptly, nearly knocking over the stool. He grabbed his picnic basket, stepped up to the dish drainer and hurriedly started putting the dishes into it. She looked at him sideways.

'Wait... they're not dry yet,' she said, surprised. 'I can dry them.'

'Oh, they'll dry,' he insisted. 'Sorry... it's just that... well I remembered what a big morning I have tomorrow.' He forced a casual shrug but fumbled the basket closed. 'Best we both get some shut-eye, eh?' June couldn't get a word in. 'You'll have a big day too, no doubt.' With the basket on his arm, he stepped back to the bench, spun around, picked up his glass and skulled the last bit of wine in it. Then, he set the glass back down with a clumsy bang—almost knocking it over. 'Oopsy,' he said, catching it.

She turned toward him, taken aback by his suddenness.

'Oh... okay,' she said, and glanced at the clock. 'I guess it is getting on a bit.' Dave nodded. 'Well, thank you for dinner, and again, for coming to my rescue tonight. I guess that sort of thing is why you say to always carry your phone.'

'Exactly!' he said. 'Always carry your phone.' He made his way to the sliding door and flung it open. 'Well, have a good night,' he called back with a glance over his shoulder. He stepped through the door, closing it behind him with the same force he opened it with. He slipped on his thongs and collected his umbrella. 'Bye,' he called out and left before she had a chance to repeat the same.

That was weird. She watched from the doorway as Dave Andersen jumped over the Winston chain, descended the stairs taking two at a time, and hurried to his ute—not even bothering to lift the umbrella over his head in the rain. June remained there until the ute disappeared into the weather. Had she done something wrong? She sniffed her skin, just in case she was still giving off turkey fumes, but it was only the lingering fragrance of soap and perfume she could smell. She closed her eyes and rested her head on the screen. Probably a good thing he left, she thought. She'd either felt or imagined him watching her as she stood at the sink. Had he been watching her the way she had watched him—more than once? With a sigh, she remembered why she was there—to work and nothing more. She carried the clothes horse in from the deck; her scrubs would dry overnight under her bedroom fan. She'd want them tomorrow—her other two pairs were still in the dirty wash basket.

Lying awake in bed, staring at the ceiling, June Hall recalled her tears on the slope. *Stupid girl.* She scalded herself. She was a fiercely independent and talented professional. She didn't need a hero, she just needed to think about what she was doing a little more, especially on foreign ground.

Dave Andersen pulled up in his garage and killed the engine. He sat in the dark momentarily. He shouldn't have gone over there but if he hadn't, she'd have been stuck on the slope all night. He had to avoid her at any cost. While his body told him she could be more than a friend, his head was reminding him she was a city girl and always would be—he wasn't going down that path again! He hit the steering wheel hard with the palms of his hands. He would not get involved with the Woodwards' house sitter and that was that. He would throw himself into his work as he always did.

Chapter 18

The Green Monster
Week 1—Thursday Morning

AT exactly 4:01 a.m., the rooster crowed. June lay in bed, listening, wondering how much energy was spent with each crow. Did it impress the chickens, or were they thinking the same as her—*shut the fuck up?* The crowing had to be deafeningly loud inside the Penthouse. She imagined the ladies pushing and shoving—feathers flying, just to be the first one through the automatic door to escape the ruckus. They'd never get a lay-in.

In between the rooster's crows, she noted it had stopped raining. *Thank goodness—a reprieve!* She smiled and stretched. It may be a temporary break in this wet season, but she'd take it happily.

She needed to find a decent broom—one that had more than six bristles. Cleaning the deck after Winston was bad enough; now that it was covered in muddy paw prints, she needed to be able to scrub. If she didn't find one, she'd buy one sometime. There was no rush.

She climbed out of bed at 5:00 a.m., well-rested. The gumboots were in the papaya plantation, but she had her rubber thongs and made her way—splish-splosh—to check the animals. Wilbur got grain and the chooks some seed. Winston was hiding—*please don't let him be in Dave's paddock again.* The turkeys went without for the morning. Last night hadn't afforded the time to soak cracked corn. She imagined the rain would bring out plenty of bugs for them to feed on. They'd be fine. The gate had been left open last night after her ordeal—she thought of Winston. *Oh no…* Perhaps that's where he was but there were no hoof marks to be seen near or down the slide. She closed the gate and secured it with the Occy Strap, happy he was either in the house yard or had absconded.

After straightforward rounds with no dramas, she had a shower and returned to her room to dress. She took her scrub pants from the clothes horse and put her left leg through. In an instant, she let out an almighty squeal—something wet and cold had latched around her calf. She withdrew her leg shaking both her leg and her scrub pants violently. She fell backward and landed on her unmade bed. Amid the chaos, something green shot across the room—bang-splat. It stuck to the wardrobe mirror. She sat up and quickly regained her composure—*a giant green tree frog.*

"Oh, my giddy aunt! You nearly frightened the life out of me,' she gasped. The frog didn't move. She hopped up off the bed, checked her clothes and dressed, keeping an eye, all the while, on the green monster. Gingerly, she approached it and bent down in front of it. It had to have been either in or on her clothes when she brought the clothes horse in last night. Suddenly, she felt sorry for it—it was now out of its environment. She wondered: Was it scared of her? Had she hurt it? She'd come to know they were physically harmless, but the fright it had given her could be fatal to a very frail person.

June Hall shook her head at what was happening to her, day in and day out, in this hostile environment. She had to be on guard every minute of every day... almost. It seemed like creature after creature was out to get her—both the adrenaline and the thought of it caused her to laugh out loud. She felt as if she were in a movie, but this was the kind of stuff you just couldn't make up.

Cupping her hands and holding her breath, she took the frog from the mirror and returned it to the deck. She then placed the clothes horse back into the laundry. In the corner was a long-handled, nylon-bristled, scrubbing broom. *Just what the doctor ordered.* She picked it up, unsure of how she hadn't noticed it before, and carried it to the deck. She'd leave it in the corner—a reminder to scrub the deck when things dried up a little.

Chapter 19

Were You Riding a Horse?
Week 1—Thursday Morning

'So, how was dinner with "you know who"?' Coral asked, ducking into the treatment room between June's patients. June smiled at her and replied.

'That's for me to know and you to find out,' June said with a playful smile.

'That's what I'm trying to do—find out!' Coral had a look of frustration on her face. June gave in.

'It was fine,' she told her.

'Just fine?' Coral said, wanting to hear more.

'Yes fine. We ate food and we talked a little. That's all. He's good company... jovial.' June continued restocking needles while she had a few minutes spare.

'Any kissing?' Coral pried.

'That nosy question doesn't deserve an answer,' June said firmly. Coral knew she'd overstepped the locum nurse's boundaries.

'Oh, I'm sorry. Take no notice of me. I'm just teasing. Do you want, or need anything for the treatment room? I'm headed to the shops.' Coral waited while June gave it some thought.

'No.... I think I'm good. Mrs. Woodward seems to have stocked up for the entire time she's away—and the six months after she returns,' she chuckled. 'Seriously, I've appreciated how thorough she is, though.'

The treatment room office phone rang. June walked to it and answered it.

'Treatment room. This is June,' she said in a friendly—yet professional—voice.

'June, it's Lisa in reception.' June hadn't had much time to chat with the receptionists, but when she had, they'd all been more than helpful. She detected a tone of urgency in Lisa's voice.

'What's up?' she asked, getting straight to the point. Lisa replied.

'Dave Andersen just called.' June froze on hearing his name so soon. 'It seems his grandmother's had a fall. He's bringing her in for a check-up. I believe she has some skin off on her shins.'

'Oh, no… thank you, Lisa. Let me know when she arrives.' June hung up the phone and ensured the area around the ECG bed was clear. She lowered the bed ready for her patient, fetched her dressing trolley, and partially pulled the curtains around. She would assess Alice here, as it was protocol to take a heart reading for elderly patients who had fallen, to ensure the fall wasn't due to an underlying heart condition.

'Can I do anything to help?' Coral asked.

'I'll need a wheelchair.'

'Sure,' the office manager was happy to help. 'I'll get it for you.' She retrieved it from the storeroom. When she returned, she parked it ready, brakes on for safety.

Fifteen minutes went by, and the treatment room phone rang again.

'Hello,' June answered.

'I can see that Mr. Andersen has just pulled up outside.'

'Okay, thanks, Tina… I'll be there in a moment.' She hung up the phone, flicked the chair brakes off, and wheeled it along the corridor and out the front doors. Dave was standing on the passenger side of his ute, door open, talking to Alice calmly. June wondered if he was expecting the wheelchair. *Tina would have advised him.*

The surgery had one park at the front designated for patient drop-offs, pick-ups, and emergencies. The main car park was at the rear. Dave's eyes followed Alice's, and he looked around to see June approach. She glanced at him, smiled, and nodded hello. He returned her smile and stepped out of the way.

Looking into the cabin of the ute, June noted it was very clean for a work vehicle. She leant in and glanced down at Alice's shins.

'Oh dear, Mrs. Andersen. You've been on the trampoline again.' Alice let out a single chuckle at June's attempt at humour.

'Yes, dear. It was the triple backflip that got me. I won't be doing that again, anytime soon.' June touched her shoulder.

'Yes, those doubles and triples can be a real party-stopper.' She looked her in the eye and gave the tiny woman a warm and genuine smile. Alice smiled back, she knew she was in good hands. 'Can you get into the wheelchair, Alice?' she asked.

'Yes, of course,' Alice insisted. 'It's only torn skin.' June pushed the wheelchair as close to Alice as she could get it and put the brakes on. Alice continued, 'Dave wanted to treat it with his magic cattle cream and patch it with duct tape, but I wouldn't have it.' Dave, who stood behind June, scowled at his grandmother. Alice returned a sweet smile, but he knew that behind it, she was really saying—*Gotcha sonny boy!* Oh, how she loved to have the upper hand. June turned and looked at Dave in horror, but he was quick—his scowl had already flipped into a smile. She glared at him.

'Cattle cream? Duct tape?' she asked, her top lip curling up subconsciously in disbelief at what she was hearing. Dave had to turn Alice's words into humour—he'd growl at her at home for telling untruths.

'Works fine on cattle,' he said. 'Cheaper too!' June turned back to Alice.

'Probably best then that we do check you out—duct tape or no duct tape.' Alice patted June's hand.

'You're such a kind girl,' she told her. She was now her favourite nurse and number one target.

'Besides,' June continued. 'We have our own cattle cream here.' Dave laughed to himself; he could see June had a good sense of humour and imagined that's what got her through her day, doing the stuff she did. And besides, cattle wounds and human wounds were all the same in his eyes—blood, guts and drama.

While Alice shuffled herself to the edge of the passenger seat and then swung her legs around, June—having surveyed the situation—pulled a pair of nitrile gloves out of her pocket and put them on. Blood was oozing through the dressings Dave had placed over the wounds—face washers tacked on roughly with micropore tape. *Well, at least Bunnings boy hasn't used duct tape!*

Generally, June knew from experience, that grazes and skin tears weren't as bad as they first appeared. She hoped this was the case for Alice. She steered the elderly woman's hand to the far side arm of the wheelchair and assisted her into it. Once seated, she released the brakes, pulled the chair back enough to allow herself to reach the footrests, then placed each of Alice's feet onto the rests.

'I'll have Alice in the treatment room with me if you want to find her once your car's parked,' she told Dave. She turned the chair toward the still-open double doors of the surgery.

'Great, thanks a bunch,' he said and moved to relocate his ute. June pushed Alice past reception and the waiting room where she gave onlookers a smile and a wave fit for a queen. She stopped in the treatment room next to the ECG bed—brakes on—and helped her patient onto the bed.

When Dave arrived, he could hear his grandmother chatting away jovially behind a curtain. He stood outside of it and waited, hoping his beloved Gran would be kind to him and not discuss his private business.

June heard Dave's footsteps, but her concentration was on removing Alice's dressings without taking off any more skin than had already been lost.

'So, how did you fall, Mrs. Andersen?' she asked.

'The Silver Stallion got away from me on the garden path.' June stopped what she was doing and glanced up at Alice.

'You were riding a horse!' she blurted in surprise. Alice laughed, as did Dave.

'That's what she calls her wheeled walker,' he explained. 'Because it's silver.'

'Oh... well,' June smirked. She'd never heard a wheeled walker given such a name. 'You've got to watch those walkers, especially the ones with wheels,' she agreed. 'Some do have attitude.'

Alice had four wounds, three on one shin and one on the other. 'I need to leave your wounds uncovered for a moment, so Dr. Flint can see them,' she said. 'I'll fetch him.' She began to make her way out from behind the privacy curtain.

'So... how was the delivery of foreign muck last night?' Alice asked, stopping June in her tracks. June glanced over her shoulder and back at her. 'He's a wonderful cook, my grandson. He'll make the right woman a good husband one day.' Dave cringed at his grandmother's words.

'It was delicious, Alice. There was nothing left over.' June tried again to leave, but the grandmother pried further.

'You couldn't make it over to our place then?' she asked. 'Something come up, did it, dear?'

'I got caught up with the animals,' June explained, giving nothing away, and walked outside the curtain before Alice could ask another question. She glanced at Dave and offered a gentle grin. It seemed he hadn't shared her misfortune on the turkey slope, and she was grateful. Before she could move into the corridor to fetch Dr. Flint, he appeared in the doorway and stood next to them both.

'Dave,' he nodded, acknowledging him.

'Doc,' Dave responded.

'Alice in there?' he asked, nodding toward the curtain.

'Yes,' June replied. 'She's taken skin off both shins.' Dr. Flint pulled the curtain back slightly and the three of them gathered around Alice on the ECG bed.

'Can I have a look at your wounds there, Alice?' the doctor asked politely.

'You won't fix them if you don't, Doc,' the elderly woman replied. They gave each other a mutual smile. He studied each wound as June and Dave looked on.

'Well Alice, what time do you shower?' he asked.

'What's that got to do with the price of eggs, Doc?' Alice said, confused. Dave and June remained composed.

'I usually help her around four-ish,' Dave explained.

'Goodo, then. Keep them covered and dry at all times. I'd like them dressed daily.' He turned to June. 'June, as Alice is your neighbour, what's say you finish early each day and dress them on your way home—after her shower? The timing should work out well.' June thought about it momentarily.

'Well, I suppose I can do that,' she agreed. Dave remained poker-faced.

'I don't want to put you out, dear,' Alice said, looking at June with thoughtful eyes. 'But that would be wonderful. I think that's exactly what I need.' Alice was not about to let her say no.

'You wouldn't be putting me out, Mrs. Andersen. I'd be happy to do that.'

'As long as you don't mind then dear—it's a done deal. You're such a good girl. You'll make someone a lovely wife one day—you're not already married, are you?' she asked, looking for signs of a wedding ring. Dave cleared his throat and June almost choked on a sharp breath, then Alice turned to Dave. 'Won't she Dave—make someone a good wife?' There was nowhere to run or hide because if there was, Dave would have been out of there. Dr. Flint came to the rescue.

'Excellent… then it's all sorted. Can you give them a good flush—make sure there's no dirt in there—then put the skin flaps back where they came from? Bit of wound gel and paraffin gauze on the open areas, and a dry dressing then bandage—that you beaut stretchy stuff. What do you think?' He looked at June for confirmation.

'I think that'll work well,' she agreed. It was pretty much her go-to for most skin tears.

'Can you dress them firmly now, then redress them a little looser tonight?' he asked.

'Sure,' she nodded in agreement.

'Oh,' Doc continued. 'And we won't require an ECG in this instance.' June's eyebrows lifted—she thought that unusual, but

Alice was his patient and it was his call. Dr. Flint headed out from behind the curtain, calling back, 'I'll see you in a week, Alice.'

'Got that,' Dave voiced. He'd heard the instructions clearly and would bring her to the surgery in one week.

While Dave watched on, June opened a dressing pack like an expert. She flushed and cleaned the wounds with saline to remove debris and as Alice's fall was outdoors, she took great care. Ever-so-gently, she pulled skin that had been torn and returned it to its original position. She then cut pieces of paraffin gauze and placed them over wound gel on the uncovered raw sections of flesh. Next, she covered each wound with a non-stick dressing, then bandaged both legs to keep the dressings in place.

'You need to stay off your legs today and keep them well elevated, Mrs. Andersen—can you do that for me?'

'Of course, dear. Anything for you.' She turned to Dave. 'And since dear June couldn't make it over last night and she's coming over tonight, perhaps you can whip up something for tea that we can all eat together. Show her we appreciate her work.' Alice shot them both a knowing grin. Dave squirmed. His grandmother was matchmaking at her finest. He gave a nod and forced a smile.

'I'll be there just after 5:00 p.m., if that isn't too early.'

'Not at all, dear. It'll give us time to chat,' she turned to Dave. 'Won't it David?'

'Okay Gran, we've taken up enough of these good people's time. Let's leave them in peace.' June lowered the bed and Alice slipped into the wheelchair. June went to push her.

'Please... let me,' Dave said firmly. 'I'll take her out to the car then bring back your chair.' June nodded a thank you and got on with cleaning up the treatment room.

Chapter 20

June and Dr. Flint were headed toward the back door. It was 5:00 p.m.. So much for finishing early, June thought.

'Friday tomorrow, June. Thank you for all your help this week. It's been lovely having you fill in for Mrs. W,' the Dr. remarked jovially.

'My pleasure,' June replied. 'The week's flown by. Between animal sitting and learning all about the patients, I've hardly had time to scratch myself.'

'Ha, just as well,' he laughed. 'Scratch yourself around here and Lee-Anne will have a script in your hand before you can say "prickly heat".' June giggled.

'She's very sweet, and I've enjoyed working with her,' June said of Dr. Lee-Anne Burt, the youngest of the doctors on staff. 'She hasn't asked for much. I feel I should be doing more to help her.'

'You're doing just fine, June. We know you're as busy as we are—we won't put unnecessary demands on you. Between you and me,' he said. 'Mrs. W is a wonderful nurse, but she does too much. I think you'll agree, we could easily have two nurses in our treatment room.'

'She's very organised,' June said gratefully. 'That's probably the only reason I've managed as well as I have, and yes, I can see enough work here for two nurses—especially when all five consult rooms are in use.' Dr. Flint opened the door.

'After you,' he said, gesturing and following her outside. Together, they walked to their cars at the rear of the car park.

'Plans for the weekend, June? You're young, you need to get out and explore.'

'Well, I have Mrs. Andersen's wounds to dress each afternoon, and…' Before June could finish, Dr. Flint spoke out.

'You must go for lunch at Third Creek on Sunday,' he insisted excitedly. 'Dave's reclaimed an old slaughterhouse—in a paddock town-side of Barrine Views—and renovated it charmingly. He does a barbeque lunch. He has everything beef you can imagine—well, not quite, no beef wine, perhaps.' June's eyebrows lifted at the thought of beef wine. *I hope you're joking about that!* 'It's all his beef—tender beyond words. You won't get a better steak for kilometres.'

June cringed. There was something unappetising about raising beef and then killing them off. To her, it was not unlike eating your pets! She could *never* be a farmer.

'Yes,' she said, reflecting for a moment. 'I think I passed it—I saw the sign.' She recalled the business card Dave had given her: Third Creek Paddock-to-Plate.

'See you tomorrow then,' Dr. Flint waved as he reached the driver's side door of his car and opened it. 'Let's see what Friday brings us, eh?'

'Yes, let's see.' June smiled, and they both jumped in their cars. Tomorrow was indeed Friday—and the end of her first working week at Millbrook Surgery. She considered the weekend and imagined time on the Woodwards' deck, views, a good book, and canine companionship. *Yes, that's what you'll do, June Hall—relax.* This would be her Saturday and Sunday. She did *not* dream about eating beef.

Pulling up outside Dave's house, she sighed. Could Alice be pushier about her grandson? She'd have to ignore her silly comments during visits—make small talk, not Dave talk. She'd get through this. She was not here for love and Bunnings Boy. After all, every time they'd been together—other than the Winston drop-off—it had been solely because of her ridiculous need to be saved. Then there was Alice's dinner invitation which he forgot about—thanks to bat shit. And, of course, the ECG event at work. She wondered how he put up with his meddlesome grandmother. *He must be used to her.* Men were blessed with the ability to switch off. And besides, it was obvious *he* wasn't interested in anything more than chit-chat—he'd made that crystal clear when he'd dashed out, picnic basket and wet dishes in hand. The end of March couldn't come fast enough—*there's no place like home.*

***

'They're lovely-looking wounds, Alice,' June said, pleased with how the skin had settled underneath the dressing. 'I can see you've kept off your feet this afternoon—no swelling. That's great. Thank you.'

'Don't thank me, Lovie, you did all the work. I just fell,' Alice remarked with a smile. June nodded.

'You did a good job keeping them dry in the shower.'

'Oh, I just had a bird bath tonight—bit hard otherwise.' Alice adjusted herself in her chair.

'Whatever Dave is cooking smells amazing. You get well looked after, don't you?' June concentrated on re-dressing the wounds.

'Oh, you betcha I do. World's best grandson, that one.'

'Do you have other family, Alice?' June was making small talk but was also curious.

'Yes dear—couple o' hundred clicks west. My son and daughter-in-law run our family's station. We gave the kids the reins a few years back, when we retired in Millbrook—I was born there, you know—in little ol' Millbrook. David's older brother is out on the station, too.'

'Older brother?' June enquired.

'Yes. Justin—tall, skinny drink of water, that one. A good bum-raspberry'd blow him over, not like Dave. Dave's shorter but built like a brick shithouse.'

'Oh,' June prompted. *A bum-raspberry?*

'Justin works on the station. Dave's his own man,' she explained. 'One day, out o' the blue, he sees this place—Dave, that is—and buys it. Pop and I were tickled pink to have him move so close to us.'

'It's always nice to have family nearby,' June added.

'Oh, yes indeed. My granddaughter is at boarding school. I don't get to see her or the station these days. I miss the Outback terribly.' Alice looked away, silent for a moment. June allowed her space to gather her thoughts. 'Anyhow,' she continued. 'With Dave buying this place, I am close to town and have farm life too. Winner winner, chook'n dinner for me.'

June noticed Dave from the corner of her eye. He stood in the doorway, hands in his pockets. How long had he been listening?

'Excuse me, ladies. I hate to interrupt, but there's a quiche and some salad on the table when you're ready.' Both women smiled at him.

'I'll just finish off bandaging and clean up,' June said. Dave returned to the kitchen.

'He's a wonderful man, you know,' Alice said gently. June met the old woman's gaze, gave her hand a gentle squeeze and followed it with a soft but genuine smile.

'I'm sure he is Alice, but if you're expecting us to develop some sort of relationship—which I'm getting the hint you are—it can't happen,' she insisted. Alice's face dropped. 'I live in Adelaide, Alice. I don't belong here. One week at the Woodwards' has shown me that, and I'm sure the next three weeks will only make it clearer.' Alice leant forward.

'Love conquers all,' she whispered, and gave the nurse a wink. *You're one persistent lady, Alice Andersen. Are all country women as tenacious as you?*

Alice made her way to the dining room, pushing the Silver Stallion. June packed up her gear, disposed of the removed dressings, washed her hands in the bathroom and joined her. Dave put a glass of water with lemon, mint and ice on the table in front of each of their place settings, then sat down.

'This looks as divine as it smells,' June said wide-eyed. As she savoured her first mouthful, she realised how hungry she was.

'I'm glad you're here,' Alice grinned. 'No foreign muck!' Both Dave and June held their laughter.

They enjoyed dinner, making small talk throughout. June was the first to finish. She placed her knife and fork across the plate, took a deep breath, and released a soft sigh.

'That was the best quiche I have ever tasted,' she said. 'Compliments to the chef.'

'As was my chilli con carne,' he reminded her. He smiled and she wished for the umpteenth time that he wouldn't. It had a profound effect on her. 'One pot wonder,' he said. 'Anything you can cook in one pot or dish is my go-to on weekdays. Fewer dishes, more time. Dessert is a cheesecake, compliments of the IGA freezer section. Would you like a piece?'

'Sounds great.' June was familiar with the frozen section herself. She stacked their plates, but Dave jumped up, leant across the table and took them from her.

'They can go in the dishwasher later,' he insisted. He spun around and placed them on the bench behind him. Then he took the thawed cheesecake from the fridge, a knife and spoons from the drawer, and dessert plates from the cupboard. June unknowingly watched him move around the kitchen, and Alice knowingly watched her. He delivered three generously cut pieces of cheesecake to the table. When Alice finished hers, she asked to be excused.

'I'm feeling a little tired. I think I'll go to my room—put my legs up. Night, all.' She stood and took hold of her wheeled walker. 'C'mon, my Silver Stallion… to the bedroom we go.'

'Goodnight Alice,' June said. 'I'll see you tomorrow.' Alice nodded but did not look back.

''night Gran,' Dave stood and pecked her on the cheek before sitting back down. When Alice had left the room, Dave turned to June. 'Coffee or seconds?' he asked.

'No thanks,' she replied swiftly. 'I really must go. I have the menagerie to feed before the sun goes down completely.'

'Keep your phone on...' he said, but June finished his sentence.

'...me at all times. Yes, be assured I won't forget again—that's a promise,' she declared. Dave held back a chuckle; he had a turkey poop-covered June still fresh in his mind.

'It's very kind of you to come to the house and look after Gran,' he mentioned.

'All in a day's work,' she replied. 'Alice is a lovely lady, you're lucky to have her still around. She really cares for you. I lost my paternal grandparents some time ago now, but I still have my maternals, and I love them dearly.'

'Oh, I'm sorry to hear that—you can have Alice anytime you like,' he laughed. 'She might be small, but there's plenty of her to go around.' June had known Dave barely a week—Alice even less, but she could already see where he got his quick-witted sense of humour. She stood, took her dish and spoon to the sink, and placed them beside it.

'Sorry to leave you with the mess, but Winston, Wilbur and the crew won't wait.'

'I understand that more than you know,' he added, following her. As he approached, June turned around. They stood face to face in the middle of the kitchen, June empty-handed, Dave with a plate in his left hand. Their gazes caught and held, a fleeting moment stretching between them. Instinctively, he reached out to touch her. Reactively, she clasped his hand in a firm, old-fashioned handshake.

'Um… thanks again for dinner,' she said, surprised, her face blank with confusion. They shook several times before Dave dragged his hand away from hers. He took a step back. She was dumbfounded. *You shook my hand? Is this a Queensland thing? A farmer thing? A Bunnings Boy thing?* She had no idea why he would do such a thing. Dave just felt embarrassed.

'Um… I'll walk you...' was all he could say. The word "out" had disappeared from his vocabulary. He scraped his fingers through his hair, gripping it at the roots in frustration. *Dave, you buffoon, you shook her hand! If brains were dynamite, you wouldn't have enough to blow your nose right now!* Her touch had made his skin tingle. He lowered his arms and shoved his hands into his pockets, both to stop himself from doing something stupid again and to hide their slight tremor. He felt hot and struggled to focus.

'Ahem,' he cleared his throat awkwardly. *What the hell is wrong with you, Andersen?* Sure, she was a stunning woman—even in baggy, grey, scrub top and pants, but he'd been around stunning women before without this reaction. He took a deep breath and released it slowly, hoping it would help him focus, but it didn't work—his mind was a whirlwind. Her baggy clothes only encouraged his imagination—his inner Neanderthal was officially awake.

'Ah, eh,' he couldn't clear his throat. They exchanged an awkward glance. *Do you even know how alluring your emerald-green winkers are?* The faster March passed, the better—then she'd be gone and out of his head. *City woman, Dave Andersen—don't dream about it and don't go there!*

While Dave stood motionless, June collected her bags from beside the dining table.

'I'll see myself out,' she said hurriedly. She gripped her bags tightly; afraid they'd slip from her suddenly clammy hands. *They weren't clammy or shaking before that stupid handshake.* She had to get back to the Woodwards—her haven. His sapphire-blue eyes were baiting her. *You're a threat, Mr. Andersen—my fight-or-flight response is screaming it.* She headed toward the front door. 'Bye,' she called, but didn't wait for an answer. She went directly to her car and straight back to Barrine Views.

Seated in the idling car, in the shed, she realised she was deep in thought about tomorrow afternoon's visit with Alice. But it wasn't Alice she was thinking of?

Bloody fight-or-flight response—you know his type better than I do, don't you? And you're ready to fight against the lure of that infuriating Dave Andersen with his stupidly good looks and his ridiculously nice grandmother and his annoyingly good cooking skills and those damn blue eyes—bloody rotten Bunnings Boy!

Chapter 21

The Other Brother
Week 1—Friday

June stepped out onto the deck. Giving the dogs their breakfast was her last morning chore before leaving for work—she was dressed and ready for whatever Friday threw at her.

'You've got to be the easiest dogs I've ever had the pleasure of looking after,' she said, and poured a cup of biscuits into each of their bowls. 'You greet me with a wag, follow me around the yard, rarely bark—you're just awesome.' She watched them eat for a moment, noting that black staffy, Daisy aka Tank, was getting fatter by the minute. *Am I over-feeding her?* She turned to walk back inside, but something caught her eye: beautiful pink hibiscus flowers on a bush in the garden. Her memory was jogged.

'I almost forgot,' she said out loud. Only the dogs were in earshot, but she didn't care. 'It's Tropical Friday. I'm supposed to wear something bright. Why didn't you lot remind me?' They ignored her tone and refused to look up from their biscuits. 'Care factor zero, huh?'

Back in her room, she swapped her grey scrub top for a hot-pink t-shirt; it was the brightest thing she had that looked passable with scrub pants. She also threw a pair of flat shoes and a dress that wouldn't crease into a plastic bag, remembering what Coral had said about keeping civvies in her car—she'd throw them in the boot. On her way to the shed, she picked one of the hibiscus flowers and placed it behind her ear. *Now I'm tropical!* It wouldn't last long, but she'd made the effort. She drove to work happy to have reached Friday unscathed—well, workwise anyway.

'You look great,' Coral remarked, as June placed her bag into the staff room cupboard. Everyone looked tropical, and the whole surgery had an upbeat vibe. Today would be a fun day.

June's first patient was already in the waiting room.

'Don't worry about Tom,' Coral said. 'He's always early and happy to wait. His appointments with us are an excuse for him to get out. He hasn't fared well since becoming a widower.'

'Oh, I understand. Many don't, and fair enough.' June prepped and then fetched Tom in for his vitamin B injection. She made light-hearted conversation with him and observed his mood discreetly. Losing a lifelong partner was never easy. If she had concerns, she'd pass them on to his doctor, but she didn't. He appeared upbeat, was getting out, and mentioned a future travel plan. They were all positive signs.

Her second patient required an intravenous iron infusion to treat anaemia—the procedure took just over an hour. It was often given to women cursed with menorrhagia, teenagers not eating well, and those who didn't absorb iron for whatever reason. Today's infusion was for a woman with Crohn's disease.

June went on to perform an ECG on an elderly man with chest pain, a wound check post hip-replacement in Cairns, suture removal post BCC excision by Dr. Burt seven days prior, and an asthma management plan. Next up was an aviation medical. *An aviation medical?* She hadn't done one of those before. Grabbing the procedure manual, she found the index and looked up "Aviation Medical". She glanced over it and was happy with what she saw.

'Piece of cake,' she mused. 'You got this by the balls, June Hall!' Ready to call her patient in, she glanced at the screen for his name—Justin Andersen. *Justin Andersen?* It had to be Dave's brother. She made her way to the waiting room, aware she was looking for a tall man.

'Justin… Justin Andersen,' she called. Justin looked up from his phone, his eyes lighting up as they met June's. He was expecting Mrs. Woodward, not the attractive, young, blonde nurse who stood before him. His phone disappeared into his pocket—almost by itself—and he stood eagerly.

'That's me,' he said. He had an air of confidence about him. June had to crane her neck to look up—he towered over her. Alice was right, he was a "tall, skinny drink of water". He had to be 195 centimetres tall, she thought.

'Hello, I'm June, the locum nurse. I'll be doing all the things we need to do for your aviation medical before Dr. Burt sees you to finalise it all.'

'Justin,' he gave a single nod and held out his hand. *Handshaking must be a Bunnings Boy thing.* She did not shake it, but she did brush his fingers lightly with hers in a half-hearted effort. He looked at his hand, confused, and dropped it to his side. She did not need another handshake from an Andersen man. The last one had left her dishevelled.

'Righto,' she said. 'Follow me, please.' Like Dave, he was ruggedly handsome. She turned, and he followed her as requested, into the treatment room, his smile never wavering.

'Mrs. W. away?' he asked.

'Yes,' June kept it short, sweet, and avoided eye contact with him. She noted his features were similar to Dave's, but he lacked his brother's striking blue eyes.

'We'll start with your ECG, if that's okay?' she explained. 'Remove your shirt and lie down on the bed, your head toward the window—facing up!' Justin removed his shirt hastily and with confidence—unlike Dave, who had removed his sheepishly.

'Do whatever you have to,' he said. 'Always happy to please a lady.' He was full of conversation and questions, so June ensured she had control of the dialogue.

'What do you fly, Justin?' she asked.

'Helicopters,' he replied.

'Oh wow,' June said, surprised. 'Where do you fly?'

'Over the station mostly—to round cattle up, check on things, usual stuff.' June performed the ECG and then printed out the reading. She left the curtained privacy cubicle.

'You can pop your shirt on now,' she called back. 'Then I need you in my office to check your lung health.'

As she set up the spirometry, Coral came into the room, aiming to catch June before Justin walked in.

'June…' she said, softly. 'Us girls are going to the pub for tea tonight. They have great meals and live entertainment on Fridays. I've booked a table for six thirty and included you on it. Is that okay? If you knock off at four thirty, you'll have time to visit Alice, feed the menagerie, change and drive back to town.' June felt exhausted just absorbing her words, let alone doing it all. However, she was put on the spot—she'd already booked.

'Um,' she hesitated. 'Ok… I guess… I don't have a better offer, so yeah, dinner with the girls will be great.'

'Awesome, I'll go book it now.' Coral turned to leave. *Book it now?* June knew she'd been outmanoeuvred. She sighed. She was going out, like it or not. She'd put a dress in the car for exactly this reason, but she still had the animals to tend to and Alice to visit. Her outfit in the boot would stay there for another time, she'd wear something from her wardrobe for tonight.

'Where and how do you want me, ladies?' Justin asked, a playful twinkle in his eye. He blocked Coral's exit and leant against the door frame, shirt dangling from one hand. He nodded first toward June and then at Coral. June had already noted that, like his brother, he also had a body fit for a calendar.

'Shirt on, thanks,' she reiterated, being the professional nurse she was.

'You sure?' I don't mind leaving my shirt off—you want to study my lungs, don't you?' June's eyebrows lifted at the comment, then he flexed his pecs and abdominal muscles and pointed to them. 'Good lungs, hey?'

'Shirt on,' June repeated, calmly. 'Your lungs are internal!' Coral stepped forward and pretended to poke his flexing abs.

'Put that six-pack away, Justin Andersen,' she insisted, shaking her head. 'You know this is a beer-free zone.' She stepped to the side of him, wanting to get past.

'Good one, Coral,' he laughed.

'You *really* are impossible, Andersen,' she insisted. 'You were in school, and you are today.' She tried to remain straight-faced and play the serious office manager, but his devilish, one-sided smirk and flirtatious eyebrows were too much. She giggled like a schoolgirl.

'You're thinking about my bullwhip,' Justin gloated. 'And what I can do with it, aren't you, Coral?'

'You wish,' Coral said, and turned to June, who looked on most confused. 'He skips with it—his bullwhip. Local jump-rope and rodeo bullwhip-cracking legend.' June looked impressed. 'Now out of my way,' she insisted. She had managerial work to do.

'See you 'round, Coral.'

'Not if I see you first, Justin.'

Justin put his shirt back on with a playful shrug.

'Sounds like a date to me,' he said. June looked at him, confused. 'The pub tonight...' he explained. 'Girls' night.' *Big ears*—he'd overheard them. 'I'll be there. Stayin' in town tonight. Buy you a drink?' He had a smile much like Dave's that would melt hearts. June ignored him and dove straight into revisiting the technique for his biennial spirometry, something he enjoyed way too much. As she wrapped her lips around the cylindrical mouthpiece on her demonstration device, his eyebrows shot up, and a mischievous grin spread across his face. Unfortunately, she'd seen this reaction from male patients more times than she cared to count, but she knew how to handle it—by ignoring it entirely.

After the spirometry, she tested his hearing—beyond eavesdropping. It was fine. She performed a drug urinalysis that included watching him void—for legal reasons. He turned that into a performance piece. Then she tested his eyes, took his vital signs, measured and weighed him. The rest was up to the doctor.

When Dr. Burt finished the medical, Justin Andersen strode out of her consult room and down the passage like a man who was sure of himself. As he passed the treatment room, he stuck his head in the doorway, surprising June.

'See you tonight, Junie,' he said. June just smiled. *I don't think so.* This brother was overconfident and nothing like the other.

The afternoon moved slowly. With her first working week behind her, June Hall felt she'd gained a good understanding of how both the treatment room and the surgery ran. She'd made one billing mistake and struggled to find one or two items early on, but thanks to Mrs. Woodward's meticulous organisation and some help from Coral and the others in reception, she'd survived.

She looked at the clock—4:30 p.m.. All patients had either been seen or were still in their consults, and there was nothing booked in for the treatment room. She knocked off, gathered her things, and headed to the Andersen house. *It's going to be a long night.* Tomorrow was Saturday. She hoped the rooster would let her sleep beyond 4:01 a.m.

***

'Where's Dave this afternoon?' June asked, unwrapping Alice's bandages.

'Who would know... he could be anywhere,' she replied. 'Honestly, that boy—he's been busier than a one-armed taxi driver with crabs!'

'Oh,' June said, surprised. She now had to concentrate even harder on what she was doing, for Alice's description had etched an unwelcome picture in her head.

'He's mighty thoughtful, though—my Dave,' Alice added. June ignored her and kept working. Meddlesome Gran was at it again, trying to sell her grandson. 'Busy as he is, he made a sandwich and left it in the fridge for my dinner—just in case he gets caught up. Doesn't want me to starve, I guess. Must think I'm as useless as tits on a bull. I can still make a sandwich, you know.'

'I'm sure you can, Alice, and that *is* very thoughtful of him,' June agreed, recalling the weight loss she'd noted at the surgery. She watched a concerned look suddenly fall across Alice's face.

'I sure hope it's not a crab sandwich,' she declared. 'I don't like them in *or* on me.' June did *not* want to get into a lengthy discussion about crabs, full stop. She had to keep moving, she had a six-thirty dinner date.

'Your wounds look great. No sign of infection. They're healing up nicely.'

'Praise the Lord...' she said with a smile. June hadn't thought of Alice as a religious woman. 'I'm a leg model in my spare time, so just as well!' she joked.

'Well, if it makes you feel better, Alice, I'm not a leg model. My father gave me kankles, not ankles.' Alice disagreed.

'Not at all, dear. You have lovely legs and a lovely smile too.' *But you haven't seen my ankles—I always wear scrub pants.* June finished bandaging Alice's legs and tidied up around her.

'I'm sorry, but I can't stay and chat, Alice. I'm going out for dinner.' She kept moving, packed up her bag, and readied to leave.

'Oh, how lovely... where?' she asked, secretly hoping it was with Dave.

'The pub—with the girls from work.'

'Sounds more appetising than a sandwich. They do a good snitty there,' Alice remarked. 'Ridiculously big—hang over the plate. Half of one will quiet the worms for a week.' And now June had a new picture etched in her head. 'Their mushroom sauce is to die for.'

'I'll keep all that in mind.' June remembered meeting Justin. 'Alice, I met your other grandson today.'

'Justin?' she enquired. *Does she have other grandsons she hasn't told me about? Grandsons who are even larger, both in size and personality!*

'Yes, Justin, and he's as tall as you said.'

'He's a hard worker and a good boy to me, but he can be a bit of a lad sometimes if you know what I mean.' June had an inkling. She nodded and smiled.

'Well, I'll be off if that's okay? Got to tend the Woodward menagerie before I can even think about going out.'

'You work too hard, my dear. Enjoy your night and drive safely. Watch out for those darn roos and pythons too, they're all out after dark—eating and fornicating—bit like Justin, really.' June shuddered at the thought of all three. Alice, wheeling the Silver Stallion, walked her to the door, frustrated that Dave hadn't been home. *Alice, you need to do better. Time is of the essence.*

As June drove down the Andersens' driveway, Dave was on his way up. He waved out of the window. She wanted to stop and say hi—to have a casual conversation in passing—but he appeared to be in a hurry. He didn't slow, so she didn't either.

Back at Barrine Views, the menagerie was as hungry as ever. The grounds had begun to dry out a little, making her rounds easier. She'd yet to retrieve Dr. Woodward's boots from the papaya plantation and had been managing in thongs—the only suitable footwear she had for soggy ground. Having her toes exposed made her nervous; she was wary of them being pecked at by the birds, or trodden on by Wilbur or Winston.

Her round saw her collect eight eggs. She considered taking them to the surgery on Monday, along with any others she collected over the weekend. Perhaps she'd make herself an omelette too—or maybe a quiche like Dave had made.

With her chores all done, she showered and headed to her room to dress. As she sorted out what she'd wear, something made multiple loud bangs in the ceiling above her. She ignored it and put it down to the wind, then it happened again. She looked up. *It must be the wind—what else could it be?* She glanced out the window. The air was still. *Perhaps something's loose up there?* She'd worry about it tomorrow.

Holding the dresses she'd packed in front of her one at a time, she paraded before the mirror. It was yet another hot night, so she chose the dress that would be the coolest—it was emerald green and complemented her eyes. It had tiny white polka dots all over and shoestring straps. She threw it over a chair and hung the other dresses back in the wardrobe. She put on her knickers—she'd go braless with the shoestring straps—then towel-dried her hair before styling it with the hairdryer. Her long, blonde locks looked bouncy and sassy, and her hair felt amazing, but she knew once she put her dress on and stepped away from the fans, she'd be sticky again. The constant humidity just did that to you. She brushed her teeth, applied some subtle lipstick, slipped into her heels and finally, put her dress on. She picked up her phone, slipped it inside her small crossbody evening bag along with her credit card, lipstick and keys, and headed out the door. She was quite looking forward to getting to know the girls beyond a quick hello over the internal phone system or a passing nod in the corridor. She hesitated. Did she need a torch to avoid "plate-sized spiders"? No, she had one on her phone.

As she left the Woodwards and turned onto Arthur Willis Road, she glanced toward Dave's house. His ute was there; he was probably home for the night, she thought. Alice would have his company. She wished momentarily that it was Dave she was having dinner with again—he was such a great conversationalist. She brushed the thought aside. *Bring on a snitty big enough to quiet the worms!*

Chapter 22

Best Take This Outside
Week 1—Friday Night

When June walked into the old, two-story timber pub a few minutes late, it was rocking. The celebratory atmosphere was thick—the perfect end to a big week. Excitement bubbled inside her, and her feet itched to be free of their heeled prison and dance the night away.

A three-piece band played in the corner of the large, bar-and-dining room—one man played the guitar, another played the drums, and a woman sang. To June, her voice was slightly hoarse, but it suited the country genre.

She pushed through the crowd, peering between shoulders, but nobody was dancing. They were all rooting for one person who took up the entire dance floor—a very tall shirtless man wearing a cowboy hat, jeans and boots. He was skipping at a speed she'd never seen before and in ways she'd never seen before.

'Boy-oh-boy… it's Magic Mike Millbrook-style,' she said, her soft voice inaudible. When the song came to an end, the crowd's noise grew tenfold with roars, whistles and cheers. She saw the man bow like a true showman, then step back and crack a bullwhip. The almighty crack made her jump. Nobody else seemed to mind; they just became more vocal. *They've seen and heard this before.* As the man turned to face her direction, she recognised him. *Justin Andersen—I should've guessed.* She spun around on her heels—she did not want to be seen by him—and then a hand grabbed hers.

'There you are,' a voice yelled over the noise. It was Coral. June felt relieved. 'Follow me.' She dragged June to their table. They sat down and joined receptionists, Lisa and Angelica and doctors, Lee-Anne and Anna. Lisa poured a glass of water from the jug on the table and placed it down in front of June.

'Thanks,' she said appreciatively, and took a sip. She'd been rushing all afternoon and hadn't had nearly enough to drink.

The music continued. June automatically tapped her foot to the beat. It was loud, but conversation could still be heard. Patrons now filled the dance floor; it seemed Justin had disappeared. June was relaxed now, she'd enjoy herself tonight—eat, have a drink, and dance!

After a light get-to-know-each-other-better conversation and a discussion on work and career paths, all six women went up and ordered their dinner at the servery. June's stomach was rumbling.

'Schnitzel—with mushroom sauce, please,' she said, taking Alice's advice.

'Chips and salad or veg?' the woman taking the order asked.

'Chips and salad, thanks,' June replied. Returning to the table, she did a quick turnaround—her small crossbody evening bag swinging with the momentum. She'd have a bourbon and Coke with lots of ice—just one.

After a brief wait at the bar, she ordered her drink—half-strength—and emphasised extra ice. Fixed on watching the bartender, she was taken aback when a large, hot hand pressed against her lower back. She stilled. It was too low to be acceptable if it were a stranger's hand. She looked to her left as the male figure came around her—his hand not moving from where he'd placed it.

'Hey there, Junie.' Justin stood close to her, shirtless, with sweat beads still visible from his bullwhip theatrics. His cowboy hat made him look even taller than he was. 'Had a feelin' I'd see you here tonight, *Daaarlin'.* Let me buy you a drink.' June could smell the alcohol on his breath as he slurred his words. He placed his expertly coiled bullwhip on the bar to free up his left hand. 'Beaut night, hey? Music, atmosphere—I miss this livin' outback.' The bartender put the drink June had ordered in front of her. She reached for her wallet. 'Put it on my tab, mate,' Justin told him. The bartender nodded, but June shoved a ten-dollar note toward him.

'I'll pay for my drink, thank you,' she insisted in no uncertain terms. He looked sideways at Justin. Justin gave a stern nod.

'On my tab, *maaate,*' he insisted. The lady's seen me with my shirt off more than once. She can have a drink with me.' The bartender looked at June and then at Justin.

'No trouble tonight, Andersen,' he said sternly, his eyes fixed on Justin. 'The lady's drink is on the house.' He turned and served another patron. *Great, thanks. Now I get to listen to him waffle on—drunk as a skunk.*

'You're new 'round here, Junie,' he mumbled. June noted he was swaying and wondered how on earth he managed the bullwhip theatrics he had done, under the influence of alcohol.

'It's June, and yes, I'm here for a few weeks only,' she said, wishing he'd take his hand off her and that her colleagues would come and drag her away. She glanced across at their table—*empty.* They were all up dancing. Her heart sank.

'Got a property out west of 'ere. You should come visit.'

'I won't have time for that,' she said firmly. 'I'm working most days.' *Get your hand off my back!*

'Well, hell. That ain't a problem. I'm stayin' here the night. Got a nice little room out back with a comfy bed and a bathtub. You wanna come do a thorough medical on me—there's things ya missed today, you know—big things!'

June cringed. He had the wrong idea, and his inebriation was exacerbating it. He pressed hard up against her. Her heart pounded—her fight or flight response in overdrive. His hand slipped down, and he squeezed her butt cheek. She jumped—not from pleasure—it was a mighty painful squeeze. With the crowd thick around her, she was pinned between the bar, Justin, and other patrons behind her.

'Please, remove your hand,' she demanded softly and firmly. Justin just grinned as if it were a game and slapped her backside as if she were a bovine. For the first time in her life, she felt scared and physically unable to move—her feet were rooted to the spot. She knew nobody around her, and everyone's backs were to her. Her breathing grew fast and shallow, and sweat formed on the back of her neck. Abruptly, someone pushed between them, separating them.

'Little bro,' Justin hissed, trying to keep his balance. He was less than happy with Dave's timing. Justin looked down on Dave by four or five centimetres, but his hat made the older brother appear much taller.

'Justin,' Dave nodded.

'You tryin' to move in on my action?'

'No,' Dave said calmly. 'The lady's not free tonight.' He glanced at June with sympathy in his eyes. He'd noted her uneasiness.

'They're all *freeee,*' Justin slurred. He leant in toward June and flicked the strap off her shoulder. 'Aren't you *daaarlin'?*' June grabbed at her dress. She couldn't move backward—someone was sandwiched up against her. Dave could see June's distress growing. He pushed Justin back a little and out of her reach.

'You been on the piss—been here all arvo?' Dave asked calmly.

'What's it to you?' Justin snapped, anger welling inside him. '*Rack off,* Dave,' he roared. 'Go find your own piece of fluff!' June could see Dave take a calming breath.

'You know how you are when you drink, mate. Apologise to the lady,' Dave demanded.

'Or what?' Justin slurred. The bartender removed the bullwhip and June's glass from in front of them—Justin didn't notice. Ignoring Dave, he moved toward June, but Dave stepped directly in front of him, separating them. Justin stepped back and threw his hands up in disbelief. Frustrated beyond words, his hands grabbed the back of his head, he turned his back on Dave, bent slightly forward and drew a breath.

Dave turned to June.

'You, okay?' he asked her. 'Has he hurt you?' June quickly nodded, no.

'He's very drunk and…' she replied, but before she could finish her sentence, Dave saw her eyes shoot up over his left shoulder. He knew what was coming and moved to block it, but before he could, Justin grabbed his shirt, spun him around and hit him with a left hook, sending him flying backwards into the crowd. The crowd parted in response, some glaring at Dave lying there clutching his face, others glaring at Justin standing over him, seething in anger.

'Oh my…' June cried out, unsure of what to do. Dave got back up slowly. Blood oozed from his mouth and trickled between his fingers. He shook his head and then eyed his brother.

'Best take this outside,' Dave insisted.

'After you, bro,' Justin asserted and followed him out the side door and into the car park. Some patrons were unaware of what the men were about to do and continued dancing, eating and drinking. Those who knew the brothers followed them to see how it played out. June felt scared for Dave—she didn't want to see him hurt, for while Dave was a solid man, Justin had a long reach.

In the car park, June watched on with the other bystanders as the brothers went punch for punch. Some punches connected; others missed altogether. Both men had blood splattered over them. Finally, Dave charged into Justin much like a bull would charge and sent him flying backward and onto the ground. He did not get up—knocked out cold. Dave stood over him sucking in deep, desperate breaths of air. June ran to Dave.

'Oh my… Dave… are you alright?' she cried. Dave cleared his throat.

'Better than he is,' he replied, panting.

'I'm going home,' June insisted. 'This is too much. I was just after a quiet dinner with the girls.' As June spoke her words, Dr. Lee-Anne walked over to them. She glanced down at Justin.

'I've got an ambulance on the way for him, Dave,' she said.

'Thanks, Doc,' Dave noted appreciatively. She took a close look at Dave.

'Are you okay?' she asked. Dave replied with a smile, his breath almost back to normal.

'Never better, Doc. Never better,' he insisted, but June disagreed.

'You need me to look at those wounds, Dave Andersen,' she said, studying his face. 'And you could be concussed.'

'I'm fine, really.' He wiped the blood from his mouth and touched his eyebrow. 'I'm sorry you had to go through that,' he explained. 'He's not what he seems.'

'Thank goodness you showed up, Dave. I didn't know what to do,' June admitted. 'He scared me.'

'The pub called me—they have my number on speed dial,' he explained. June wasn't sure what he meant. *The pub has you on speed dial?*

The ambulance arrived within minutes—the station was just around the corner, situated midway between the pub and the surgery. June considered this a fitting location. *They probably get business from both.* It drove into the driveway, and the paramedics got out. Justin was conscious now but somewhat dazed.

'Don't get up, Justin Andersen,' Dr. Lee-anne insisted. She stood over him, hands on her hips. Groaning, Justin gave a nod in agreement. June considered he'd be in pain from the punches Dave threw. He didn't look very comfortable either—flat on his back and shirtless on the hard bitumen surface of the car park. He rolled to his side and vomited. Fortunately, most of the patrons had made their way back inside thanks to Dr. Lee-Anne's insistence. 'Stand out here any longer,' she'd said. 'And I'll have to sell you a ticket.' June could see that Justin and Lee-Anne's doctor-patient relationship was an interesting one.

'Night in hospital for you, Justin,' Dr. Lee-Anne told him sternly as the ambulance officers attended to him. 'You were knocked out this time. Best sober up a bit too. If all's well, Dave can collect you in the morning.' Justin knew better than to argue.

'Yeah, Doc. You're the boss. Whatever you reckon,' he mumbled with a polite tone and in between post vomit spitting. Justin happily let the paramedics attend to him. 'Thanks, guys. I love you all,' he repeated. He appeared to have punched away all aggression displayed both before and during the fight. June was intrigued. His behaviour left her with unanswered questions. She hoped he'd be okay—he was more a likeable character than an unlikeable one. However, she felt much more at ease with him on the ground than with him in her face. *Bunnings Boy to your rescue, girl—again.*

As the ambulance drove slowly out of the driveway—no lights and sirens required—Dr. Lee-Anne turned to June.

'Would you like to rejoin us inside, June?' she asked.

'I think not, Doc. I want to see to Dave's wounds.' She turned to Dave. 'Will you come back to Barrine Views so I can dress your wounds?'

'I'm fine, seriously.' He didn't want to be a bother, he just wanted to sleep. He was hurting both physically and for his brother.

'I insist.' June asserted and used the only card she had. 'If you refuse, I won't do Alice's wounds at your house. You'll have to bring her into the surgery every day, instead.' Dave knew how much time that would use up in his day.

'Alright, but only because you insist,' he replied. 'I really am fine.' He stopped to think for a moment. 'To be honest, I'd love a cup of tea,' he added.

'Done,' June agreed.

During the chaos, the counter meals had arrived at the table. Coral had taken the liberty of getting June's dinner put into a take-away container—she'd figured she might choose to go after all the chaos. Management had put an extra box in the carry bag. "Thanks again, Dave" was scribbled on top of the foam lid. She brought the bag out to the car park and handed it to June.

'I figured you'd want out of here after this fiasco,' she said. 'But you're still welcome to come back and eat it at the table.' She glanced at Dave. 'Your usual is in there too.' He nodded.

'Cheers,' he said, gratefully.

'Thank you so much.' June took it from her and then turned to Dave. 'You can follow me home.' And with that, June jumped into her car, started the engine, and waited for Dave to do the same. She drove off with Dave following close behind.

Chapter 23

He's Not a Bad Brother
Week 1—Friday Night Continues

As Dave drove behind June along Arthur Willis Road, he reflected on his fight with Justin. Every ache he felt was a reminder of each punch he'd either thrown or received. He wriggled and stretched his fingers as best he could while still gripping the steering wheel. If his hands hurt this badly, Justin would feel pretty rough in the morning.

They arrived at Barrine Views. It wasn't far to travel—a five-minute journey. June got out of her car, opened the gate, and then drove up the driveway to her parking spot. She made sure all the car's windows were closed before getting out and locking it. Dave closed the gate behind him, drove up to the house and parked on the lawn, close to the deck. He did not park under the fruiting tree. She took the phone from her bag, turned on the torch, picked up the carry bag containing their dinner and made her way to the house. They met on the deck stairs.

'Come on, you,' she said in a caring tone. 'Let's get you cleaned up.' She noticed he walked with a slight limp. 'Leave your face alone. You'll get an infection if you keep touching it with dirty hands.' He pulled his hand away.

'Are you always this bossy?' he asked.

'Are you always this badly behaved?' she replied. They both stepped over the Winston chain and crossed the deck in the low light. June slipped the strap of her heels down and kicked them off, leaving them buckled. Dave pulled at his boots, hopping on each leg in turn as he prised them off. He nearly lost his balance several times. He hadn't even been drinking. June opened the door and felt for the light switch. She located it, turned it on, and they stepped inside. June put both the package and her bag on the bench.

'Take a seat,' she insisted, pulling out a stool at the breakfast bar. 'The light is best here.' June's instructions were clear, and Dave followed them. She dabbed his wounds with saline-soaked gauze, cleaning them one by one. He had a cut above his eye—right on the brow, a developing black eye, and a split lip, and that was just the start. 'Is the blood on your shirt from Justin or your mouth? Or do you have injuries on your body?' She asked. Dave shrugged. 'Well, if you don't know, you'd better take your shirt off so I can see.' Dave unbuttoned his blood-stained, blue-checked shirt, took it off, bunched it up and placed it on his lap. 'You'll want to soak that,' she told him.

'Yeah, I know,' he answered, touching his lip once more.

'Stop touching it,' she scalded.

'It's okay. I *can* wash clothes. It's not like I haven't had a fat lip, cuts, and blood stains before.'

'Well, pardon me for caring,' she scoffed. 'Tell me, do you make a habit of fighting, Mr. Andersen? Or is it just your brother who brings out the best in you?' June dabbed Dave's eyebrow dry and placed three wound closure strips across it to hold it together. It was just short of needing sutures. 'Don't get these wet or take them off for a couple of days if you can help it.' With a cotton bud, she ran a smear of pawpaw ointment along the wound line—between the closure strips—to seal it. Then she covered it with a trimmed-to-shape, non-stick dressing and fixation tape to secure it.

'One more thing while I'm up close and personal,' she said, and retrieved a penlight from her bag. 'Close your eyes and then open them each time I say.' She used the penlight to check his pupil reactions and repeated the test several times. She was happy—he did not appear concussed.

'I'm not in the habit of starting a fight or fighting as such,' Dave explained. 'But when Justin comes to town, it seems to end up that way.'

'Why, for goodness' sake? You're brothers. Why do you fight?'

'Well, it…' Dave started.

'Shh. Let me check your lip,' June insisted. Dave stayed quiet while she pulled at it and studied it using her pen light. 'It doesn't need sutures. You're lucky. They bleed a lot—lips—but they heal quickly. It might bleed again if you stretch or knock it. Just apply pressure if it does—with something clean!' She put the penlight down, stepped back, folded her arms and looked at him straight-faced. 'Ok, now tell me why you fight with him.'

'June…' he started. 'Justin… well… he's not a bad brother. He's a good brother and a hard worker. He had bad luck some two years ago and he hasn't been the same since.'

'Bad luck?' she asked, prompting him to continue.

'He went rabbiting with mates. There were two in the ute cab and three on the back tray—Justin was on the tray. The paddock had ruts in it from the wet season, and the ute hit a big one—the driver didn't see it. It rolled. Justin and another bloke were thrown free, but the third—his best mate—wasn't. He was crushed—died at the scene.'

'That's awful, Dave,' June sighed.

'There's more. The driver took his life weeks later—couldn't handle the guilt, I guess. Shot himself. Justin hasn't been the same since. He's continually looking for answers as to why his mate died and he lived. It had been his idea to go rabbiting. He feels guilty, but it wasn't his fault.'

'Did that make him hit the bottle?' June asked.

'Not at first. Initially, he became withdrawn, then after a time, he started drinking. My parents have banned alcohol from their property to try and help him.'

'But he was drinking tonight?' June was confused.

'None of us can stop what he does outside the property. Occasionally, when he needs a few things, he makes his way to Cairns, does his running around then has a night or two here at the hotel. He wipes himself out and visits Alice—not in that order, of course—then heads home. I'm amazed he hasn't been banned from the pub altogether. I think they feel sorry for him. Most locals know what he went through and how he struggles. It's usually me who gets in a punch-up with him. It saves some other poor bugger copping a flogging and the police laying charges.'

'You think that fighting is a way to help him with his grief?' June was dumbfounded.

'No. He's seeing a psychologist and mostly is pretty good. We've been having fisticuffs of some sort since we were kids—doesn't mean we don't love one another.' June watched a genuine smile begin to appear on Dave's face as he talked about his older brother, but it straightened instantly as his split and now fat lip pulled.

'What does Alice think when she sees you all banged up?'

'She knows what's going on and keeps her thoughts to herself. We've offered him the spare room, but he won't take it—I think he's embarrassed. He needs to blow off steam. He'll settle in time, I'm sure. He has a lot of pent-up anger.'

'Does the pub *really* have your number on speed dial?'

'Yep.... They call and I come and sort him out, and if I can't, they have my permission to call the police. They haven't had to do that yet—fortunately. They don't serve him alcohol. He gets shit-faced in his room. Probably buys it in Cairns while he's down there.' June stopped and thought. She'd never have guessed Justin was a man in pain. He'd seemed so sure of himself. *As they say, never judge a book by its cover.*

'I saw him doing his bullwhip performance,' June said. Dave laughed.

'The women seem to love it—bloody show pony,' he said. 'He's been doing that since we were kids—well, we did have to amuse ourselves for hours on end around the station and the cattle.'

'Do you partake?' June grinned, her eyes wide.

'*Mayyybe,*' Dave's baby blues weren't capable of lying.

'Well, Mr. Andersen. Be sure to let me know when and where you're performing—I'll bring the Millbrook Surgery cheer squad!'

'Not happenin',' Dave clarified. June nodded; she hadn't for a moment considered him as a showman but enjoyed the banter.

'Reheated dinner? Tea? Or a cup of hot chocolate—it's my specialty?' she asked.

'No food. Hot chocolate sounds great—haven't had one of those in years,' he replied. She put the carry bag containing their meals into the fridge. She wasn't hungry anymore either.

'Give me your shirt, first. I'll throw it in the wash.' Before Dave could refuse, June snatched it from him. She took it to the laundry, sprayed it with stain remover, then threw it in the machine for a quick wash. On the way back from the laundry, she stopped behind him. She ran her finger lightly from the bottom of his spine to the top. He shuddered, but she didn't notice. 'I think you'll have a bruise on your back. It's very red where you landed on it—multiple times.'

'Yeah, I can feel it.'

'What about the front of you?' Dave moved his hands, and June ran her eyes over his chest. Red marks had already started forming where the punches landed. 'I think I should take you to the hospital to get checked out. You could have internal injuries.' Dave laughed.

'If I went to the hospital every time I had a punch-up or hurt myself working, I'd never get anything done.'

'Men,' June muttered, and busied herself. She took out a small saucepan, added milk, cocoa, and a large chunk of chocolate, and stirred it over a low flame on the gas stove. When the chocolate melted and the milk was heated through, she swapped her wooden spoon for a whisk and mixed it into a drinkable delight. She poured it into two mugs.

'Sugar?' she asked.

'Yes,' he replied. She smirked.

'Do you want sugar in your hot chocolate?' she clarified.

'No, thank you. I'm sweet enough.' *I'm sure you are.* She popped two marshmallows into each cup and stirred them vigorously until they started melting into the drink. She put each cup onto a saucer, placed a teaspoon next to it and set them both on the breakfast bar. She walked around Dave, pulled out the stool next to him and sat down.

'Thanks,' he said and went to smile but winced. His lip had stiffened, and he started it bleeding again. June grabbed a tissue from the box on the bench and went to dab his lip. He took it from her.

'Sit, please. It's fine—Just don't make me laugh.'

'You probably shouldn't drink that while it's so hot.'

'I'll give it a few minutes,' he agreed. One hand pressed the tissue on his lip, and the other stirred his hot chocolate. In the silence, a banging in the ceiling drew his attention, and he looked up.

'I think something's loose up there,' June explained. 'It bangs most nights.' Dave recognised the sound instantly.

'Sounds to me like you've got a visitor.'

'A visitor?' June's face turned pale. 'What sort of visitor?' She asked. Dave knew he'd said the wrong thing. If he explained it was a python—and possibly one with a friend, she'd never sleep.

'Rat,' he said, convincingly. 'White-tailed rat. They're common around here. Won't hurt you. I'll come and trap him in the morning. You can't kill them. They're protected now. I'll take him down to the lake to feed the python I took there the other day.'

'Wonderful,' June rolled her eyes. As she sipped her drink, she watched Dave discreetly. His chest was broad, his lats defined, and his arms and biceps were strong. *Chiselled, they'd call you in a romance novel.* He was the epitome of strength and masculinity. June felt herself flush and forcefully dragged her eyes back to the contents of her mug. She watched the last of her marshmallows disappear, certain it was the heat of her gaze that had hurried the process. She cleared her throat.

'Justin really frightened me at the pub,' she admitted. 'I've never felt like that or been in that predicament before. I didn't know what to do.' Dave just listened. 'You have no idea how relieved I felt when you showed up.' He turned to look directly at her, and she turned toward him.

'I'm so sorry he made you feel that way, June. You didn't deserve that—no one deserves that. I'll make sure he's aware of what he did to you. He needs to realise just how much control he loses when he drinks. Alcohol or not, nobody should feel scared of another person. He has some apologizing to do and some serious work to do on himself.'

'Please… don't make a fuss. I didn't know what was tormenting him. Nothing came of it except your cuts and bruises.'

'That's not the point, June. He needs to work harder on his rehabilitation instead of drowning his problems in alcohol. I'll be having a serious talk with him.'

'Don't be too harsh. It sounds like he's had it tough.' Dave gave her a one-sided smile.

'You're too nice, June,' he said, then turned back to his hot chocolate. With his teaspoon, he poked at the last skerrick of marshmallow and watched it disappear. The stirring of his mug distracted him from the feelings she was—yet again—stirring inside him. It was time to go home before his testosterone got the better of him.

Chapter 24

A Harem Inside the Roof
Week 1—Saturday Morning

Saturday morning started at 4:01 a.m., via Barrine Views' rooster alarm clock. June was used to his crowing now and simply accepted it. She had learnt in her first week that placing a pillow over your head didn't dampen the sound, ignoring it was impossible, and threatening the feathered warrior with the axe made him even more fearless.

Dressed in around-the-house attire of shorts, tank top and thongs, she started her animal rounds at sunrise. Wilbur received scraps from Friday's bucket and some of the gourmet mix from his bin. He ate with gusto and appreciation as always. The weekend meant no bucket of scraps from the surgery on Sunday, so she made a mental note to dish out double of his feed tomorrow.

The chicken feeders were still full, but their waterers needed a top-up. She thought how wonderful it was that by free ranging throughout the day, they found enough fresh goodies to keep them happy, and not reliant on the seed in their feeders.

Winston was grazing contentedly in the house yard. She topped up his water trough. June had become an expert at stepping around his giant droppings. Each one she saw made her grateful that cows didn't fly. She took the shovel and the wheelbarrow and collected all the manure she could find. She'd let it stack up, then deliver a full load next to the vegetable garden.

The turkeys were waiting eagerly at the base of their fig tree, and around the bucket of cracked corn that had soaked overnight. While they looked on, June removed the lid from the bucket and strained off the excess water. She pushed past the excited birds and opened the gate. She was comfortable with the process now and didn't fear the turkeys.

Since her fall, she had found a pole with a hook in the shed. She didn't know what it was used for but claimed it anyway. This was her backup hanger-upper in case of more torrential rain. With this gadget, she wouldn't have to step onto a wet slope and risk another fall. She glanced at Doc's boots still lying at the bottom and considered fetching them. Things were still very damp. They could wait a bit longer.

She made her way back to the house with one thing left to do before she could relax for the morning—feed the dogs. She popped half a cup of biscuits into each of the four bowls on the deck. None were interested except Daisy, who devoured two bowls before June hurriedly picked up the other two.

'No wonder you're carrying a few extra kilos, Tank,' she told her.

After a bowl of muesli, she took a cup of coffee and a book she'd been wanting to start, out onto the deck. She dragged a comfortable deck chair to a shaded corner. *Now this is the life.* The humidity was high, but there was a slight breeze. The 180-degree views east were superb of rolling green hills, grassy paddocks, rainforest pockets and thick pine forest. Finally, she had time to simply absorb it. There were two or three clouds in the distance, but they did not look threatening. They were white and flickered across the sky like fine strokes of watercolour on a canvas.

"Chapter One" June began to read. Toward the bottom of the first page, she was interrupted by the dogs barking. She looked up. Dave was driving up the driveway toward her, and he had a passenger. As the ute got closer, she could see it was Justin. They could have been twins in their cowboy hats.

'There goes my peace,' she sighed and closed her book. She put it down alongside her near-full cup of coffee, then stood up and walked over toward the top step. With four dogs by her side, she spoke under her breath. 'Sic 'em, you lot—the one in the passenger seat, I mean.' Dave pulled up, and they both got out—like a mirror image of one another.

'Morning, June,' Dave called.

'Mornin',' Justin called.

'Now here's something you can't make up,' June muttered, as they swaggered closer. They were both a sight for sore eyes; Dave with one black eye and Justin with two. She shook her head, disbelievingly.

Justin didn't wait for Dave; he rounded the car and approached her directly. He pulled a bunch of mixed flowers out from behind his back and stopped at the bottom step. He extended his arm and offered them to her.

'This isn't a very flash peace offering, buddy, but it's the only one I have at the moment. I want to sincerely apologise for being such a dickhead and creep last night.' June stepped over the Winston chain and descended the stairs, stopping on the bottom step to study him. She took in his bruised face before her gaze dropped to the arm that held out the flowers. A light bandage midway down his arm told her he'd had IV therapy overnight. *That's probably why you don't appear hungover—you're rehydrated.* Around his wrist was a white plastic wristband. *You've come straight from the hospital—someone should have cut that off!*

'Thank you, but you didn't have to bring these, Justin,' she said. Her voice was firm, leaving no room for argument, and then she smiled. 'But I'll take them—It's been years since someone gave me flowers.' She took them from him, closed her eyes for a moment and breathed in their scent. 'Beautiful,' she said. Dave's ears had pricked. Why hadn't she received flowers in years? He wondered how that was even possible—she was gorgeous in his eyes and Justin's too, after last night. Justin relaxed—no longer in the bad books. 'How are you feeling, Justin?' she asked with genuine concern for his wellbeing.

'Like a bruised idiot,' he smiled.

'Oh… you really frightened me last night and put me in a very uncomfortable position,' she told him.

'I know. I've spoken with Dave. Again, I'm truly sorry. I'm going to seriously try and stay off the grog—it's no good for my troubles and I never want to put a lady in that predicament again.'

'I'm glad to hear that. I wish you well.' June genuinely felt for him. Losing his friends must have been a terrible ordeal and would play on anyone's mind. Dave cleared his throat, interrupting their conversation.

'You baggin' or catchin',' he said, looking at Justin.

'Catchin',' Justin replied. 'Got a longer reach than you—your black eye should know that.' June recognised the snake kit. While Justin had been apologising to her, Dave had been fetching it.

'What are you doing?' she asked.

'Noise in your roof—not a rat,' Dave explained.

'Let me guess… a python?' she shuddered. Dave smiled sheepishly at her. 'And you let me sleep here with it, last night—*all night!*' she frowned.

'I didn't want to tell you, June. You wouldn't have slept at all.'

'Very true. Thanks for thinking of me.' Her sarcasm humoured both men.

Justin fetched a drill from the toolbox on the back of Dave's ute, then untied a ladder from the roof rack. He carried them to the house. 'Whereabouts, bro?'

'Second window. Above the kitchen. That was last night, anyway. Could be anywhere now,' Dave explained. While Dave turned the mains power off, Justin set the ladder to lean on the gutter and climbed up, drill in hand. On the roof, he began to remove the screws from one of the roof sheets. He placed each screw into the front pocket of his jeans so as not to lose them. Dave followed him up with the snake kit. June placed her flowers onto a step and moved out onto the grass to watch. Justin pulled the roof sheet up, placed it to one side and yelled down.

'Don't stand under here, June. In case the sheet slides off.' She moved away a little. She hadn't considered that as a possibility and certainly didn't fancy being decapitated by a falling sheet of roofing iron.

Justin stood inside the roof space, his bottom half inside the void, his top half above it. He slipped on the old welding gloves and took the extendable hook from Dave. Dave readied a bag as Justin gazed across the insulation.

'Frickin' party in here!' he said loud enough to be heard on the ground. 'There's more than one. They're curled up together, I reckon. Either that, or he's one big mother...,' he explained. June wanted to be horrified, but chuckled instead, as a fearless Justin took a moment to adjust his privates while donning welding gloves—an awkward manoeuvre for any man. *Only another Bunnings Boy would attempt that.* Dave turned to look down at June.

'June,' he called loudly. 'Can you get us a pillowcase or something similar? A bag of some sort. I only have one bag. Maybe, check the shed for an old seed bag.' June made her way to the shed and returned hastily with an old sack. She climbed halfway up the ladder and threw it up to Dave.

'Thanks, good throw,' he said with a nod. He was focused on the job. *You're still struggling to smile with your split lip.*

'Ready, bro?' Justin called out.

'Yep,' Dave replied. Justin ducked down and out of sight. There were several big bangs followed by a bucket-load of muffled swearing, until Justin reappeared through the gap in the roof sheets, holding one enormous python. Dave moved closer to his brother.

'Hold the bag still,' he snapped. The beast did not look light, and Justin appeared to struggle with his balance on the ceiling joists. *Oh my... don't fall... don't let it bite you. This is ridiculous—I've been sleeping and living under that monstrous thing!*

'I am holding it still—you're the one swaying!' Dave shot back, annoyed. June stiffened at the horror of it all. *Ah, brotherly love at its finest.* In one determined move, Justin directed its head into the bag, and with the speed of light, followed with its body. Dave pulled the top of the bag closed and secured it with a cable tie—his moves matching Justin's in speed. Then he dragged the bag a metre or so away from the roof space opening and left it there. The python weighed more than they'd anticipated. June hoped he'd secured it well, she could see movement inside the bag.

'Hurry up with the next bag, Davo—his girlfriend's on the move!' Justin yelled, not taking his eye off the second python.

'Alright, alright,' Dave replied, opening the sack, ready. Justin disappeared back into the roof space. There was another noisy scuffle and more muffled words before he reappeared, holding the python in the air, its head on the hook and its tail in his gloved hand. He bagged the python—headfirst again—and Dave cable-tied it closed.

'They're both heavy buggers,' Justin called out, taking a moment to catch his breath.

'Not a bad effort for someone with a hangover,' Dave joked. 'June,' he called. 'Can you get my torch from the cab of my ute? It's on the seat. We'll make sure he doesn't have a harem inside the roof!'

'A harem?' June thought, cringing. She retrieved the torch and carried it far enough up the ladder for them to reach. Justin took it from her.

'Thanks, buddy,' he said, smiling. He turned and passed it to Dave. 'Here. You're the shortest,' he said. Dave nodded and took it. He disappeared for only minutes, but when he reappeared, he was wetter with sweat than Justin, who had lifted out the heavy beasts. It was hot in the sun at this early hour. June could only imagine how hot it was inside the roof space.

'You can sleep tight tonight, June,' Dave called. 'No harem.' He dropped his torch down carefully for her to catch.

'Thank Goodness,' she sighed. Dave climbed down from the roof, his left hand on the ladder and his right carrying the first bagged python. Standing beside the ute tray, he hoisted it on the back with one almighty grunt, before returning. Justin replaced the roof sheet, passed Dave down the pole, drill, and gloves, then descended the ladder with the second bagged python.

'Thank you both,' June smiled, staying well away from the bag in Justin's hand. He lugged it to the ute and, with equally as large a grunt as Dave had given, heaved it onto the tray, next to its partner. June noted it had taken both men two arms to lift the bags to the height of the tray. *How did they not fall through the ceiling on top of me?*

'Twenty or thirty kilos each, I reckon,' Justin said with a smile as he strolled calmly back from the ute. June felt that the hair standing up on the back of her neck would never go down. *This environment is nuts.*

'At least you know you don't have rats in your roof, June,' Justin said with a laugh.

'Wonderful,' June replied with a roll of her eyes.

'We have one more job,' Dave said. Justin looked unaware but followed his brother toward the turkey run. June left them to it with no idea as to what Dave was planning. She took her flowers inside, put them in water and returned. Within minutes, the men reappeared. Dave, with a half-smile, carried Doc's gumboots. Justin, strolling behind him, caught up and took the boots from him. He hosed them down before handing them to June.

'Thank you, Justin,' she said, taking the boots. 'Thank you so much—both of you. I'll sleep much better without the banging, and now I can retire my thongs for these giant boots,' she said, holding them up.

'Well, we'd better go relocate these beauties,' Dave explained. 'They'll get hot in the bags.' The men made their way to the ute. 'I'll see you at my place around 5:00 p.m.,' he reminded her. June nodded. She had Alice's wounds to dress.

Chapter 25

Blimey, When Did It Get So Hot?
Week 1—Saturday Afternoon into Night

After Dave and Justin left, June's day settled into a quiet kind of bliss. She spent it on the deck, putting a dent in her book and consuming several cups of coffee. The dogs stayed at her feet for most of the day, and Winston and the chickens wandered past occasionally. She decided there was something quite calming about the bok-boking of chickens and the gob-gobbling of turkeys in the distance.

For lunch, she ate custard apple—courtesy of the staff room's communal table. She'd never seen or tasted it before. The texture was jelly-like, and it contained large, black seeds. She didn't mind it, but decided it was a little too sweet for her liking. She wondered whether she'd find them on the shelves back in Adelaide—she doubted she'd even remember its name later. Perhaps Adelaide Central Market sold tropical fruit. She'd take note if she ever visited.

The time on June's phone read 4:00 p.m.. She would head to the Andersens' at 5:00 p.m.. That would give her just enough time to do her animal rounds, shower, and dress. By five minutes to five, she was in her car and making her way across the road. Dave answered the door.

'Hi, June.' It was obvious he had just come out of the shower—he wore nothing but a towel on his hips. June didn't know where to look. Her head tilted toward Dave's black eye, but her eyes were drawn to the trail of dark hair that led from his navel downward, disappearing beneath the towel. *Blimey, when did it get so hot?* She pulled at the collar of her t-shirt. 'Come in,' he said jovially. He stepped back to let her pass.

'Dave,' she couldn't say more than his name. She made her way past him and into the lounge room where Alice sat awaiting her arrival.

'Hello, Alice. How are you feeling today?'

'Oh, I'm a bit tired, Love. Having Justin visit is exhausting.' *And that's the understatement of the week.*

'But I'm sure you enjoyed it anyway,' June said. Alice nodded. June opened her work bag and shuffled through the dressings, tapes, and lotions she carried.

'Yes, I did enjoy it,' Alice admitted. June removed the elderly woman's dressings from her leg wounds.

'I'm just so happy with your wounds, Alice. I think by the time you see Dr. Flint, you'll be able to keep the dressings off.'

'That will make showering a lot easier, that's for sure,' Alice smiled. June re-dressed the wounds while Alice told her stories of her grandsons' childhood.

'All done,' June said, packing up her work bag. She secured the soiled dressings in a plastic bag for disposal, disinfected her hands and stood up ready to leave. 'I'd better check Dave's wounds while I'm here. I'll see you tomorrow, Alice.'

'See you tomorrow, Dear.' Alice gave her a queen-like wave.

June made her way to the kitchen and put the bag of rubbish into the bin under the sink. She called out for Dave.

'Right behind you,' he said, startling her. She spun around to see him standing before her in nothing but a pair of hip-hugging jeans; his still-damp hair freshly combed back. If she could have taken a photo, she would have, but did she really need one? His shirtless physique had imprinted itself on her memory already. *What is it with you Andersen boys and going shirtless?*

'The eyebrow's looking okay, I reckon,' he said. 'I didn't get it wet, like you said.' June looked at his wet hair and raised her eyebrows. 'Well, maybe I did—just a tad. What do you think, Nurse June?' Dave stepped closer and tilted his head, offering his eyebrow for inspection. She moved in to look but spontaneously kissed him. He winced and stepped back instinctively. *Oh no—what have you done, June Hall?*

'Oh... my... I'm so sorry, Dave. I didn't mean to...' But before she could continue, Dave stepped back in toward her, bent down and kissed her passionately—well as passionately as he could manage with a split lip. His tongue teased, his lips caressed, and his bare chest pressed against her—his warmth seeping through the thin material of her t-shirt. Then he pulled away. It took a moment for her to open her eyes. She was both breathless and speechless. He looked down at her, satisfaction in his gaze.

'I'm not going to apologize for *my* kiss, June,' he insisted. 'I've been wanting to do that since the moment I saw you. I know you're from the city and you're leaving, but I really like you. I know nothing can come of us, but it doesn't mean I don't feel attracted to you. I've been trying to stay away from you, but life keeps throwing me at your feet.'

'I'm sorry—I've been such a needy city girl. I'll try not to call on you again.' She found herself blubbering. *He's been wanting to kiss me.* She hadn't been aware of that, but she had been aware of him—all of him. She didn't know what to say or do, so the thing she did best took over.

'Let's check your wounds then, shall we?' She reached up, grabbed the dressing on his eyebrow and ripped it off like you would a Band-Aid.

'Shit!' Dave jumped back. 'That didn't tickle.'

'Well, you can't leave a damp dressing on a wound. It had to come off,' she explained. *What are you doing, June?* 'It looks good. Those wound strips have held up well. Your eye is blacker tonight. How is the rest of your body feeling?'

He moved in closer. She put her palms on his chest to push him back, but they had a mind of their own and stayed there, as if glued. She could feel the stubble that now grew on the patches she'd shaved for the ECG. Her head said, *hands-off—run.* Her hands said, *are you kidding—and let go of this!*

Once again, he moved in close and kissed her, but this time it wasn't gentle, it was long and hard. Her eyes closed, her legs felt weak, and her body lit up in places that hadn't lit up in a very long time. She didn't have to ask how he felt about kissing her; she could feel it! Then he pulled away and stepped back.

'I'll walk you out.' As they turned around, Alice stood in the doorway with the Silver Stallion. Neither of them had heard her. June felt embarrassed.

'Don't stop on my account,' she insisted. June wanted the ground to open and swallow her. Dave was calm—it was his house after all. 'I just need a bottle of water, and I'll leave you both in peace.' Dave opened the fridge, took out a bottle of water and dropped it into the basket on the Silver Stallion. Without batting an eyelid, Alice turned and headed back to the lounge room, a celebratory smirk on her wrinkled face. 'That's the way, my boy,' she thought. 'You won't be lonely for too much longer if you keep that up—not if I can help it.'

June drove down the Andersens' driveway, crossed Arthur Willis Road, and stopped at the gate. After opening and closing it, she continued up the driveway to Barrine Views. She wondered what had just happened. She parked in the shed, caught her breath, and then made her way toward the house. Up the stairs, she dropped the Winston chain, walked across the deck in a daze and headed inside. Had she just kissed a patient? No, she reasoned. Dave wasn't technically her patient—he was a patient's grandson. She didn't think that would breach her code of conduct.

She warmed up her leftover meal from the night before and sat down to watch a movie. Alice was right, the snitty and mushroom sauce she recommended was excellent, even reheated. She needed to not think and not overanalyse. But to just relax and enjoy her Saturday evening. After all, it was a simple kiss, and it meant nothing. *Did it mean anything?* She fell asleep on the couch before the movie finished and stayed there until 4:01 a.m.

Chapter 26

One Outstanding Pavlova
Week 2—Sunday Morning

At first light, June went to the deck door, all set to do her animal rounds. She could hear what sounded like a woman in high-heeled shoes clumping about. When she opened the door, her heart sank. There before her stood Winston, and it looked like he'd been there all night. The deck was—once again—covered in dung. Still flustered from his kiss, she had forgotten to secure Winston's chain when she returned. This time, she had no one to blame but herself. *Here we go again.* She pulled on the gumboots—happy that Justin had retrieved them yesterday—and prepared for action.

She needed to get the steer off the deck. Dave's words rang in her ears: "Make sure you never get between him and a fence or let him corner you while you're here." She had to be cautious. She tried pushing his rear end to encourage him down the stairs, but he just stood his ground. Her strength was futile against the size and strength of Winston. She then decided to shoo him out.

'Kshh… kshh… kshh…' she roared over and over, but he just stared at her. The dogs, however, found her noise disturbing and headed off the deck to somewhere quieter.

'Well, if you're not going to move, you oversized piece of steak, I'll clean up around you,' she threatened. 'Don't forget, there's a slaughterhouse nearby.' If she hosed and banged and crashed around, surely, he'd be disturbed enough to leave of his own accord. Plus, hunger and the sight of green grass calling beyond the stairs had to move him eventually. She would not call Dave.

She ducked down the stairs and returned with her tools—a shovel, a rake, and a hose. She raked—using the side of the rake—each cow pad onto the shovel as best she could, then took them one by one across to the wheelbarrow and added them to the growing load.

'Veggies,' she said aloud. 'You're going to love me.' Then, with the scrubbing broom she'd found in the laundry earlier, she began hosing and scrubbing the deck—in between hosing and roaring at Winston. Finally, annoyed that his peaceful resting spot had become a bovine wash, he made his way down the stairs. June watched him take them gingerly, one at a time. *Whoever built that staircase did a darn good job. How does it not collapse under you? You must weigh a couple of hundred kilos at least.*

With Winston out of the picture and the chain hooked back up, she finished scrubbing. So far in her stay, she'd cleaned the deck three times, twice because of Winston and once because of muddy paw prints—and one week hadn't even passed. *Is this normal hobby farm carry on?* With the deck cleaned, she headed out into the garden—fingers crossed and hopes high—that the rest of the animals had behaved overnight.

As luck would have it, the menagerie had an uneventful night. Grateful, she plodded back to the house—plod-clomp, plod, clomp. She returned to the deck, more eggs in her trusty bucket.

'Ah, you four didn't stay out and about for long,' she said, patting each tail-wagging dog. They appeared to enjoy her company as much as she enjoyed theirs. 'Do you guys eat eggs?' she asked, looking at her collection in the bucket and then at each dog in turn. She thought that might be a way to use up a few. 'You do, I'm guessing, but they might make you gassy.' She had so many eggs in the fridge, she needed to use them, not waste them. She'd try her hand at making a pavlova and take it to Alice and Dave, and she'd double the mixture and make small meringues for work, too. She Googled a recipe, checked the reviews, and began the process.

This was her first attempt at making pavlova and meringues, and it was in an oven foreign to her. For some strange reason, she felt nervous and wondered why. Perhaps because she wanted to gift it, therefore, she wanted it to be perfect.

'What the heck,' she mumbled. 'It's not like I have a deadline, or a dinner party planned. If it doesn't work out, I'll try again another day.'

She beat the egg whites and put the yolks aside for Wilbur. Then, following the recipe step by step and ensuring the ingredients were measured exactly, she baked herself one outstanding pavlova and a baker's dozen of small, nest-shaped meringues ready to fill with cream. The recipe said to cool the pavlova in the oven, so she turned it off and opened the door partially. Her smaller meringues had cooled on the bench. She put them into an air-tight container ready for work in the morning. She was thrilled with the way they all turned out and was excited to share them.

Wiping the last of the dishes, she gazed out of the kitchen window. The day was still young, 11:30 a.m., and it was sunny and bright. *Time to get out and explore.* She had to make the most of her time in Tropical North Queensland as her days off were limited.

She decided to go for a drive, to get to know the lay of the land. After putting the dishes away, she changed into a short summer dress and slipped her runners on for comfort—just in case she decided to go for a walk. She tied her hair up with a scrunchy, perched her sunnies on her head, and tossed her purse, keys, hat and two water bottles into her small backpack. Blasting the air-conditioner, she set off toward Millbrook with no particular plans—open to whatever the day might bring.

Chapter 27

Dave Had the Place Shining
Week 2—Sunday Lunch Time, Dave

Dave had been working at his venture—Third Creek Paddock-to-Plate—since 7:00 a.m. and was already feeling tired. He'd woken several times during the night, reliving the events of yesterday evening. Why had June kissed him so suddenly? Was she feeling what he was—curiosity, sexual attraction, infatuation? Even Justin had agreed, she was stunning in every way.

He asked himself if she hadn't kissed him first, would he have kissed her at all? He didn't think so. He was trying hard to avoid anything that could lead to heartbreak. But her kiss had stirred something inside him—something deep and meaningful—a longing to be with someone again in a way two people should be. But he'd stepped outside his strict boundaries regarding city women and wasn't happy about it.

'You told her you "*really*" liked her, you fool,' he mumbled. 'What were you thinking—that's right, you weren't!' She'd be gone soon, and if he didn't rein in his thoughts about June Hall, he'd only make things harder on himself. He couldn't afford the distraction from his work, not now that things were coming together with his business. Today was Sunday, the only day of the week he opened to the public. He had to get moving.

He had the place shining. Third Creek Paddock-to-Plate looked a million dollars, and at times, he felt it had cost him that. It hadn't. As an owner-builder, he handled everything he could himself and contracted out the rest.

He'd rendered the exterior block walls of the old slaughterhouse with a textured sand finish and painted them a sandstone colour. He had the building re-roofed, adding solar panels for green energy and installing new guttering to direct rainwater into tanks. When Dave discovered the stunning hardwood beams supporting the roof, he knew it would be sacrilege not to make them a showpiece. He brought in ceiling fixers who insulated and lined the underside of the iron, leaving the beams exposed—a striking design feature.

He had plastered the interior of the block walls using a half-circle pattern. This created a Mediterranean feel. He painted them a light shade of sage, and the colour felt as serene as its label on the can—Serenity.

To create atmosphere and semi-separate dining areas, Dave built timber-frame half-walls and fixed them in place. He lined them using the rusty iron that came off the roof and edged them using chunky timber—this created three separate dining areas but still gave the restaurant an open feel.

He hired a company from Cairns to polish the existing concrete floors. To seat guests, he brought in three long timber tables with matching bench-style seating. One setting sat in each of the indoor divided areas. Alongside the rusty iron, serene sage walls, chunky timber trim, and strategically placed potted plants, the venue had a delightful country restaurant feel. For the exterior, there were rain-proof tables and chairs scattered throughout the garden.

Paddock-to-Plate ran on rain, creek and bore water; the toilets out the back utilised recycled water from the kitchen. He'd made every effort to be as environmentally friendly as he could be, and for that reason, installed fans rather than air-conditioning

The kitchen itself boasted modern appliances. Everything Dave had done with the slaughterhouse followed Millbrook Council's rules and regulations, which had caused him numerous headaches through every stage of the build. He'd installed a commercial oven, a cold room, wide benches and abundant cupboard space, creating a roomy, user-friendly workspace suitable for more than one chef. The outdoor barbeque itself had a two-metre-long plate, plus a metre-long grill—he could cook for a coachload if he had to. A drinks fridge and small bar—all on wheels—for wine and beer sat alongside the barbeque.

The landscaped gardens had been strategically created. They boasted a mix of palms and native plants and surrounded both the building and the car park in a way that didn't encroach on the undulating country views. He'd thought of everything—even adding bougainvillea in large terracotta pots that were trellised over archways throughout the garden and across the main doorway. They were a delightful hot pink. The place oozed both a tropical and Mediterranean country-style vibe.

The fact that Paddock-to-Plate sat next to Third Creek was a bonus—it made finding the place easy. Either side of eating, guests could follow a designated pathway along the creek and watch the clear water meander over the rocks. The steers themselves—for those who were interested—grazed the adjacent paddocks and often came to the fence out of curiosity—especially Sergeant, Third Creek's prize bull.

Dave had put much time and effort into building Third Creek Paddock-to-Plate. It had begun as a fleeting idea—something to think about other than his marriage fiasco—and today, he could hardly believe, was his fourth day of operation.

The business offered a barbeque lunch on Sundays only. The main drawcard was the organic beef—grown on site, slaughtered locally, and served fresh off the grill or hot plate. Word-of-mouth was already bringing in tourists and Sunday drivers, keen to also try his home-grown and homemade sweet potato salad with fresh herbs, and his hand-crafted bread rolls.

In the kitchen, Dave pulled his last batch of rolls out of the oven and placed them on cooling racks on the bench; the aroma was mouthwatering. He picked some herbs from the garden and got to making his special salad dressing. After a taste test and some tweaking, he took the cooked and cooled, diced sweet potatoes from the cold room, mixed the dressing through them, and then placed them into decorative bowls. He returned the full bowls to the cold room and, while in there, double-checked the trays of meat which were set out ready for cooking.

With the still-warm rolls arranged in lined wicker baskets and covered with gingham cloth, all he needed now was for his hired help to arrive, and the backpacker was late. Dave hadn't been keen on hiring a backpacker and should've trusted his instincts. If he had to cook and serve lunch all alone, so be it. Besides, the busyness would keep his thoughts from wandering to his beautiful blonde temporary neighbour, June Hall.

Chapter 28

So, You're Not a Pervert Then
Week 2—Lunchtime Continued

June travelled along Arthur Willis Road toward Millbrook. Instead of driving past the sign that read "Third Creek Paddock-to-Plate," she turned in.

'*Mmm,*' she said aloud. 'So, this is Farmer Dave's side gig.'

A portable A-frame sign in the driveway advertised, "Open 12-2 Today". It wasn't quite midday. The car park was empty—all except Dave's ute. She noted he'd parked away from the entrance, so she parked next to his ute. That would make sense—allow guests to park close. She wouldn't be staying long—just enough time for a quick lunch to show her support.

Getting out of her car—small backpack in hand—she felt nervous and hopeful at the same time; nervous about the kiss she'd given him and hopeful they could smooth things over and continue as friends. After all, they couldn't avoid each other while Alice needed her dressings done.

'Ahoy there,' Dave called out. June looked up, saw him, smiled and waved.

'This looks great,' she said, approaching him. Her eyes battled to take in both the building and the gardens. 'Have you *really* done *all* of this yourself? she asked, her hands gesturing wide as if framing the building. Patients of a rural practice love gossip; she'd heard much about Dave and his slaughterhouse. Dave nodded.

'Pretty much,' he said with a proud grin. He was pleased to see her. 'Come,' he waved. 'Quick... let me show you around before the hordes arrive!'

'Oh, I won't hold you up,' she replied, picking up her pace.

'Just kidding,' he said with a laugh. 'I don't know if anyone will come at all, but the last couple of Sundays have been beaut. Anyway, you're here, so there's one customer at least—that's if you're staying?'

'Of course,' she insisted. 'I'm hungry.'

Dave showed her the layout of the building and then looked at the time on his phone.

'I'm officially open now, but there's just one problem,' he said.

'What's that?' June wondered—everything looked organised.

'My hired help—a backpacker—hasn't shown up, so I hope, in a way, that I'm not too busy.'

'I can help you if you need it,' June offered.

'I think today should be okay.' Just as Dave said his words, his phone rang.

'Third Creek Paddock-to-Plate—this is Dave,' he answered. He listened for a few moments and then started nodding. 'Yes… yes… 1:00 p.m.? Okay—see you then.' He ended the call and then looked at June, straight-faced. He thought for a moment before speaking.

'That offer… is it still standing?' he asked, with a pleading grin. His black eye showed only mild bruising now.

'Of course,' she said. 'Why?'

'I have my first coachload coming and they'll be here in an hour—48 plus the driver!' Dave looked petrified.

'Oh, that's easy,' June insisted. 'I worked as a waitress in my Uni days. I'll run around, keep the salads and rolls topped up, collect the dishes and man the bar. You've just shown me around—I can wing-it if I need to. That'll leave you free to cook.' Dave was more than relieved. He gave June a crash course on using his Square Terminal to accept payments.

'Yell if you can't work it out,' he said. 'It's mostly straightforward.' Dave felt awful roping her into work like he was, especially on her day off.

'Will do, Captain,' she saluted. She was pumped—grateful to be thrown in the deep end. She tossed her small backpack into the kitchen and out of the way and donned one of the navy aprons put aside for wait staff. He hadn't mentioned their kiss, and now neither of them had time to think about it. Besides, he had helped her numerous times throughout the week and as far as she was concerned, she owed him this much—and more. She recalled the possibility of spending days on the slope surrounded by turkeys, without his aid. *Bring on the barbeque!*

The first hour was dead, and then 1:00 p.m. arrived. They sold forty-eight tasting plates—one to each passenger on the coach—and they all paid separately. June quickly became an expert on the Square Terminal. Each plate was made up of steak cooked to taste, a skewer of marinated beef, an onion and rosemary-infused meat patty, spicy beef strips, crumbed steak, and a scoop of hearty beef stew—all premade by Dave. June directed them to sit at the indoor benches—to keep them all together and conversing. There, they could help themselves to sweet potato salad and rolls. Many of the guests purchased a glass of wine or three, others went for soft drinks and bottled water.

At 1:30 p.m., as June started collecting empty plates from the group, self-drivers started making their way in. Dave was taken aback.

'Better late than never,' she said with a smile, in passing. She remained upbeat because that's what you did when shit hit the fan. Fortunately, the tables and chairs in the garden were all clean and available.

Each time June had a lull at the bar, she raced around madly collecting empty dishes and topping up sweet potato salad. She wiped down what needed to be wiped down and even checked that the toilets were remaining clean and stocked with toilet rolls. Dave made quick runs in and out of the cold room to collect the necessary cuts of meat. Just as June finished wiping down the benches after the coach drove away at 2:00 p.m., more self-drivers made their way in.

Dave started to panic. Did they have enough meat? Yes, the cold room was full of it, but the salad and rolls had been hammered. June came up with a solution. To stop people from putting food on their plates they couldn't eat, she took the salad and rolls and made room for them next to the barbeque and small bar. Dave then dished up the meat and directed his patrons to June. While June dished them up a reasonable scoop of sweet potato salad and popped a roll on their plates, she also upsold the local wine. Instead of "by the glass," she was selling it "by the bottle". This way, the guests also filled up on drinks, which they paid well for—and not salad. The sweetener was a free soft drink for the designated driver. Her approach also meant a boost in revenue. Occasionally, when Dave had a chance, he'd glance across at her. She seemed to be in her element—a born salesperson. He couldn't believe his luck having her here to help. Next week, he'd have to set up Paddock-to-Plate just as June had.

By closing time—a later-than-expected finish at 2:30 p.m., there was just enough of everything left that Dave and June could eat. They'd both worked up a mighty appetite.

'You cook a mean barbeque, Dave Andersen,' she said as she tucked into her food. They sat at one of the garden tables, too tired to even care about the view.

'Thank you, June. I must say your sales skills are second to none. Where'd you learn how to handle a crowd like that?'

'Well...' she started. 'As I said, I waitressed through my university years. Plus, nursing is very similar in a way. Some days, you have everybody wanting everything yesterday—Joe Bloggs wants his pain medication, Mary Smith wants a bedpan, Johnny Jones wants his shower, and so on. You just need to prioritise and manage people. Those who can, wait. You just distract until you can get the job done. Head down and bum up, as they say.'

'You have the patience of a saint,' Dave insisted.

'Not at all,' June replied between mouthfuls. 'It's just a skill I've learnt, but I didn't learn it all at Uni—experience teaches you. I needed to be on the wards working hands-on, to work that one out.'

'Well, I'd never have gotten through this lunch period without you.' He gave her a thoughtful smile. 'Everyone seemed to leave happy, and you had them laughing a *lot*. What were they laughing so hard about?'

'That's for me to know and you to find out,' she teased.

'Sounds like a challenge?' he said.

'No, not really. The people on the coach are on holiday—that makes them happy to start with. They were also American. Americans like banter, they like to hear us talk and understand our lingo. Mostly it was simple fun things—stirring. When they asked for ketchup, I kept saying, "Catch up?" They thought the fact that I couldn't understand them was hilarious. One woman wanted to "go potty". I told her that meant she was "barmy" in our lingo—she meant the ladies' room, of course.' Dave grinned widely and then glanced at June's empty plate.

'Have you had enough to eat?'

'Plenty. Thank you. I needed that.' Dave stood to take their plates to the kitchen. 'So where do you, um, you know,' June made a gesture by running her pointer finger across her neck.

'Slaughter them?' Dave asked, his face straight.

'Yes… that,' June said, cringing.

'There's a room out the back. It's out of sight. Most of us like to eat these things, but no one likes the thought of killing anything—unless you're a psychopath of course.'

'I just don't know how you…' She hesitated.

'How I do it—kill an animal?' Dave's face gave nothing away—he was used to being asked this question.

'Yes. How do you do it?' June nodded.

'I'm a farmer, June and like any other livestock farmer, I nurture my animals, feed them, watch them grow and treat them respectfully, but being a farmer means I have a job to do, and for me, that's culling beef. For others, it's shearing sheep, culling lambs, harvesting wheat, whatever you do as a farmer, it's your livelihood and you don't take it lightly. My steers out there roam the paddock most happy with their lives, and yes, one day that life ends. City folks want to eat meat, country folks supply it. That's the way things go, June, and if you think I like slaughter days, think again.' June was silent, absorbing what he'd said.

'You're right,' she agreed. All the cows around here do seem mighty happy in their paddocks—especially Winston!'

'When I am too busy, I take them to Millbrook Butchery,' he added. She nodded.

Dave made his way to the kitchen to start cleaning up and June followed him. 'I'll give you a hand,' she said.

'Oh June, you've done enough. Really,' he said, stopping to look her in the eye.

'Nonsense,' she insisted, and continued cleaning up around her. 'This is a lot for one person, and with two, it won't take long at all.'

'Thank you from the bottom of my heart,' he said, gratefully. Together they washed stacks of plates and piles of cutlery. Dave washed, and June dried. Then June wiped down the tables and bar while Dave cleaned the barbeque. Finally, Dave took the cloth from June's hand. 'June Hall, it's time to knock off.'

'I seriously don't mind. I've nothing else to do,' she said.

'Then go for a walk to the creek. It's beautiful. You must see it. I insist.' Dave stood with his hands on his hips.

'Alright,' she agreed.

Her small backpack was still on the bench, so she left it there, headed through the now-empty car park and followed the sign to Third Creek. It wasn't far. She stood in awe on the top of the creek bank and looked down. The water was the clearest she'd ever seen—she had to put her feet in. She made her way down the embankment to the water's edge. Removing her runners and socks, she waded into the water.

'Oh—fish!' she said excitedly. She sat on a smooth, rounded boulder at the creek's edge and revelled in the shade provided by tall rainforest trees. She splashed cold water over her legs, arms and face—pure joy after running around in the heat, caring for Dave's guests. She pulled the scrunchy out of her hair and placed it around her wrist. With her hair falling loose around her shoulders, she ran her fingers through it and then lost her thoughts watching the mountain water trickle over her feet.

Dave completed the essential jobs; the rest he could either do tomorrow or throughout the week. He put a load into the washer-dryer—tea towels, aprons and cleaning clothes—pulled down the roller doors and locked the slaughterhouse. He'd picked up June's small backpack from the kitchen and would take it to her at the creek as a sign of gratitude.

He meandered down the pathway, his head spinning after the whirlwind that had been lunch. When he reached the top of the embankment, he stopped, fixated. There she was, sitting on a rock, feet cooling in the water. The long, blonde hair she had tied up while she worked now cascaded down her back and blew gently in the breeze. She looked a picture and a beautiful one.

He leant against a tree and watched her. His heart rate rose, but he was unaware. He would keep his distance from her, he knew he had to. He could feel himself drawn to her like a bee to pollen. The more he got to know her, the more he was smitten. He yearned to kiss her again. It'd been a long time since he'd held a woman in his arms. He'd had offers—plenty of offers—but none had lured him enough to risk hurt.

June turned around and looked up to see Dave standing at the top of the embankment. She called out.

'Hey, you, have you finished your work?' Dave nodded. 'Come for a swim? The water's lovely, and there's a deep pool right here with our name on it.' *You idiot, June. He would know that.* Dave wanted to—more than anything he wanted to—but he had boundaries, and he needed to adhere to them.

'Sorry—can't,' he called down. 'I need to get back to the house,' he lied.

'Party pooper,' she teased. 'I'll stay here a bit longer. It's just so nice. I can latch the gates when I leave—do what you must, I'll be fine. I'll see you at five.'

'Ok,' he agreed. His desire frustrated him. His body wanted to go to her and make love to her—on the rock, in the water—he didn't care where—he wanted her right or wrong.

'*Ugh,*' he sighed. What he was trying so hard to avoid was happening to him—he was falling for her, for a city girl.

He headed back to his car, his pace quicker than on the way to the creek. He had to get far away. Halfway back to the car park, he realised he was still carrying her small backpack. *Darn it!* He turned and headed back to the creek. When he reached the tree that marked the path's descent, he saw her again, but this time she'd taken off her dress and underwear and was standing naked in the rock pool, waist-deep, facing toward him.

'*Strike me lucky,*' he muttered reactively, blowing his breath out through a pout. His gaze smouldered, and heat crept up his neck. He liked what he saw too much and needed to *not* be there. He was invading her privacy, but at the same time, his eyes were glued to her, just as his feet were rooted to the spot.

June's senses made her look up, and he caught her eye. Instinctively, she crossed her arms to cover herself and then slipped down into the water, leaving only her head above the surface. The cold plunge was a shock to her body and stole her breath for a moment.

'I thought you'd gone,' she yelled up at him. One of his hands flew up to cover his eyes, the other held out her small backpack. She felt her nipples hardened against her forearms, but was it a reaction to the chilly nature of the water or because he'd been watching her? How long had he been there? She felt her cheeks flush and spun around, her back now to him. A shy smile spread across her face. Watching his hand shoot up and cover his eyes had amused her.

'Um... I came back to... your bag... backpack... you might need it...' he explained in a blubbering outburst. June nodded. *Ah, that makes sense—so, you're not a pervert then.*

'Can you leave it there… beside the tree… please?' she asked.

'Yeah… Yep… of course,' he called back. 'Just leaving it now,' he said. He turned his back on her, placed the bag at the tree base, and headed for the car park. *She must think you're a pervert, Andersen.* If he could've reached, he'd have kicked himself in the head—just to knock some sense into his panicking brain.

'Thank you,' June called out, loud enough to carry—but Dave was already out of earshot. He was striding toward his ute. The crunch of boots on gravel, the rev of a diesel engine, and a spray of stones as the wheels spun for traction filled the air.

He was always running.

Chapter 29

Baby Turkeys Are Called Poults
Week 2—Sunday Afternoon into Evening

'I don't know what to do with them,' June said as she unwrapped the bandages on Alice's legs.

'If you were talking about my legs, Dear, I'd be worried.' Alice chuckled. 'Do nothing,' she explained in a supportive fashion. 'The mother will look after them.'

'But there are twelve of them,' June replied. 'I was coming home from helping Dave at Paddock-to-Plate when they stopped me in the driveway. I couldn't believe my eyes. The mother must have been nesting in one of the paddocks. I nearly ran them all over. I got out and followed them. They ended up at the turkey fig tree. The babies are so tiny.'

'Poults, Dear,' Alice said, correcting her. 'Baby turkeys are called poults.'

'They looked as if they'd only just hatched,' June added, concerned.

'They probably had, Dear. That all sounds very normal for a turkey hen. They often disappear from their usual surroundings and lay an egg in a nest each day for about two weeks. Then they'll sit on them for about twenty-eight days until they hatch. They often choose long grass. She's lucky a python didn't take her out in the middle of the night—rats will eat the eggs too, and snakes.' June shuddered at the thought. 'Just make sure the poults have safe access to fresh water—shallow, not deep. They'll drown if they can't get out. They'll huddle under their mother for warmth and protection. They'll be fine.'

'How do you know these things, Alice?'

'It's nature. And I've lived on the land most of my adult life. We grew our chooks, ducks, geese, guinea fowl and turkeys for year-round meat. The guinea fowl were good for eating ticks and keeping snakes away. They'd eat snakes too when they could.'

'You've had an amazing life by the sound of it, Alice.'

'Yes, Dear, I sure have. I was truly blessed with a wonderful husband and an exciting country life. Times were often hard, but we never gave up. I have loving children and grandchildren to show for my efforts, but I feel such a burden on dear Dave these days.' Alice paused, letting her breath catch up with her words.

'I don't think Dave sees you as a burden, Alice—not at all.'

'That's sweet of you to say, Dear.' Alice didn't want to talk any further about her family life. The memories made her sad. She missed her husband every day and felt she had no purpose. She changed the subject to the baking of pavlovas, spurred on by June's delicious gift, and watched what the talented nurse was doing with her wounds.

'The wounds are healing amazingly. Keep doing what you're doing, Alice,' she insisted. 'Elevating them a little through the day is great.' June made small talk, discussing her day at Paddock-to-Plate—skipping the part about her skinny dip—before Alice returned once more, to the subject of pavlovas.

'Your pavlova has got me thinking, June, dear. I've never made one with anything but chook eggs. Talking about your turkeys, I wonder how their eggs would fare in a pav—or even duck eggs.' Alice paused. 'How did I never try that?' June thought about it. She figured the only difference might be the taste, so long as the other ingredients were right.

'I honestly don't know what my pavlova effort will taste like, Alice. But I'm happy that it didn't implode or explode,' she laughed.

'I'm sure it will be delicious, my Dear. Thank you for gifting it to us. I can't wait to taste it, and you've decorated it so lovely with all the strawberries and cream.'

Alice revelled in their conversation. Each of June's visits was a welcome break from the hours of television she watched and the hours of knitting she did. She hadn't been out on the RSL bus—cancelling it due to her injuries—and the chair next to her was piling up with knitted squares.

Soon her wounds were redressed, and June was ready to go.

'Do you like Dave?' Alice asked as June headed toward the lounge room door. June stopped and turned around. The old woman was tenacious in trying to find a wife for her grandson. June hesitated. She was not one to lie.

'Yes, Alice, I do like Dave. I haven't known him for long, but he seems like a wonderful, caring, hardworking man.'

'He's free, you know,' Alice said with the same half-grin she'd seen Dave give. 'You'd make him a great wife. You'd be very welcome here.' June pondered the idea.

'Alice, I know you mean well and care for him deeply, but my life is in Adelaide. It wouldn't work between Dave and me. We'd both just get hurt, and I believe Dave has been down that track before.'

Alice nodded. *Get hurt…?* She'd already thrown herself on the concrete pathway at the front of Dave's house and given herself shin wounds, just so she could get June to call in. She wanted to see the two young people together more than anything, so the more time they had to connect, the more chance Alice had of success. June had three weeks left on her contract. *If it takes a broken bone to keep you and my darling Dave in contact, then so be it—can't be worse than childbirth!* June left the house. Dave was nowhere to be seen—a good thing for June, a disaster for Alice.

Chapter 30

I Brought You a Cage
Week 2—Sunday Evening

June had returned to Barrine Views after her visit with Alice. She'd just finished her animal rounds and was approaching the deck stairs, bucket of eggs in hand, when she heard a vehicle coming up the driveway. As usual, it was Dave's ute, and he had something sizable on the back tray. He pulled up, lowered his driver-side window, and called out.

'I've got something for you.' A grin spread across his face. 'Three things, actually.'

'Oh,' June replied. A smile tugged at the corners of her lips in response. She couldn't help smiling—his boyish grin lit her up. She approached his vehicle and stared at the tray. 'What's the first thing?' She asked curiously.

'Gran was telling me about your poults,' Dave explained.

'She was?' June remarked, unsurprised.

'I brought you a cage. This will give them somewhere to go, come nighttime. Jump in. I'll drive it around near the fig tree. I might need a hand to lift it off.' June walked around the rear of the vehicle, studying the cage. She could see several other items—she ignored them. Her excitement was reserved for the cage alone. She climbed into the passenger seat next to Dave.

Dave drove his ute over the lawn, around the house, and to the rear where the fig tree stood.

'You couldn't have done this a few days ago without getting bogged,' she said.

'True,' Dave agreed. 'You mow the lawn?' he asked.

'No, someone else did. A friend of the Woodwards, I guess. I didn't see them—it was all done when I got back from

Paddock-to-Plate,' she said. 'It was a nice surprise and saves me trying to work out The Beast for another week.'

'Great,' he agreed, glancing at her.

'Truth be told,' she admitted. 'I was keen for the challenge. I've never driven a ride-on mower before.' She paused. 'I can say that now it's done.' She giggled—her giggle warmed Dave's heart.

'I'd say you have enough on your plate,' he remarked.

'You're probably right,' she agreed. When June considered what she had to do in her week, she didn't need that challenge as well.

'Reckon this'll do.' He turned off the engine, and they both got out. Dave untied the rope that held the cage in place—first on the driver-side and then on the passenger-side. He dropped the passenger tray side next to June. She looked on curiously.

'Are you happy if we put it right here? he asked.

'I don't mind. You'd know more about these things than me—you're the farmer. Is this the best place?' Dave looked about to double-check.

'I think so. It's away from long grass and well-shaded.'

'Then here it's going,' she agreed with a nod. Under Dave's direction, they took one side of the cage each and slid it off, until it tipped and hit the ground. Then, after catching their breath, half-lifted, half-dragged it away from the ute until it sat flat on the grass. Dave managed it with ease. June found it awkward and weighty, but she managed. *How on earth did you get this on the tray all by yourself?* June's end had landed with a thud.

'You, okay? You must've had the heavy end,' he winked.

'Exactly!' she laughed. 'That's what I thought. What do we do with it now?' she asked, studying it further. 'Did you make it?' Have you used it yourself? For turkeys, too? Dave smiled, took a deep breath and got set to answer the bombardment of questions she'd thrown at him.

'Now, we set it up. Yes—I made it. Yes—I've used it... for turkey poults, but more so for chicks,' he replied. June stood back, hand on her chin in thought.

'It's an architectural masterpiece indeed, Mr. Andersen.' She was starting to get excited by the prospect of caring for newly hatched poults in Dave's hand-built cage.

The cage was timber framed—square with fine wire mesh on all four walls. It had a gable roof and a solid bottom—the reason it was so heavy. It was relatively high—June guessed it had to be for the mother to fit and stand comfortably. She noted the roof was Colorbond—the same red colour as Dave's house roof. *Now there's a good use for a leftover sheet.*

Dave went to his ute tray, lifted out a bag of sugar cane mulch, opened it with his pocket knife, then got on his hands and knees and spread one-third of the bag throughout the cage. It was a cute little house that now looked quite cosy and comfortable. Returning the bag to the tray, he picked up two fancy-looking containers.

'Are those feeders?' June asked. Dave nodded.

'This one's for water,' he explained, passing it to her. 'You can fill it up and put it in there now if you like.' June walked over to the tap and returned with the waterer full. 'You hook it on the wire, on the inside—so it doesn't get knocked over,' he said. June gingerly secured the waterer inside the cage.

'Perfect,' Dave remarked. When she stood back up, he handed her the other feeder. 'This one's for turkey starter crumble. I've got a small bag you can have.'

'Thank you,' she said. He retrieved it—once again from the tray—and handed it to her. She took it with her free hand.

'This will be enough to get them through their first few weeks or until they learn to fossick for themselves. Don't put it in there with the door open until near sundown or the others will make short work of it.' June listened closely and with interest. 'Get the mother's attention with some—maybe a lean trail—when you want to encourage her into the cage. The poults will follow her. Then shut the door. It'll provide safety for the littlies at night until they're fully feathered and that's at about six or seven weeks—thereabouts. Until they can roost. If you leave the door open through the day, they can come and go, but don't leave the crumble in there with the others around.'

'Got it, Captain,' she said, smiling. Her head was spinning. She felt a pang of sadness that she would not see them get to the roosting stage. *Perhaps the Woodwards will send me some photos.* Dave seemed more enthusiastic than she was. She put the feeder inside the cage. The crumble she'd keep on the deck as a reminder.

'There's a chance that Mum might not be interested in the cage. All you can do is try, but it's their first night back home, so they should be open to it.' June just nodded, trying to take everything in. 'It'll lessen the little ones' chances of being taken at night by a rat or python.' Dave stopped talking, momentarily. 'Oh, I have a second and third thing for you.'

'I thought those were the three things. What are the other two—Valium to help me cope with the menagerie, and another cage?' June said, jovially. 'For Winston?' Dave laughed.

'The other things I have for you are number two, dinner—albeit more leftovers. I figured I owed you that after all the work you did. And number three—this.' He handed her an envelope from his shirt pocket, and she took it.

'What's this?' she asked, staring at it. She was confused.

'Cash for today—wages,' he smiled. 'You worked damn hard. You deserve it.'

'I can't take this,' she said assertively, and handed it back to him. 'It was my pleasure to help *you* out for a change, and it gave me something to do on a Sunday.'

'It's non-negotiable. I had it ready for the backpacker, but you showed up instead. It's not a fortune. Buy yourself a souvenir of the area to remember your stay here—please.' She thought for a moment. *Why not!*

'That's a great idea,' she agreed, and then folded the envelope and put it in her pocket. 'I might just do that!' Her excited smile struck his heart.

Dave moved to the front of his ute tray and tapped on top of an esky.

'Dinner is all in here,' he explained. 'Shall we eat at Winston's favourite spot?' June laughed. *Bloody Winston.* She knew where he meant.

'The deck sounds great as long as Winston doesn't join us.' They both laughed. Dave put the ute side back up, joined June in the cab, and drove around the house to the front.

On the deck, June dropped the bag of crumble by the door, then pulled out the two stools that sat underneath the timber bench. Dave carried the esky behind her; both had stepped over the Winston chain as if by second nature.

'I'll grab some plates and forks,' June said.

'No need. I have everything but the kitchen sink in here.'

'Is that right?' she muttered, teasingly.

'That's right,' he admitted, knowingly.

June peered into the Esky. In containers were cold meat left over from lunch, sweet potato salad, rolls, butter portions, tomato sauce and serviettes.

'Finger food,' Dave explained and set out to demonstrate. 'Do as I do... grab a serviette... bung on a roll—butter and sauce optional... slap on your cold beef of choice—there's only one... whack on salad... and voilà—Dave's gourmet rolls!' June followed his moves, creating her "gourmet roll" just as he did.

'Great idea,' she said. 'You could add this to your menu.' She took a bite.

'Yes, but it's really the same thing—just put together differently and eaten cold.'

'I suppose,' she chuckled. 'Just trying to help.'

'Talking about Winston,' Dave added. 'Have you seen him lately?' June thought about it and felt guilty.

'No... actually. Not since this morning when I put the hose on him to get him off the deck.' Dave had a mischievous look on his face. June glared at him. 'Oh no. Don't tell me he's in your paddock again.' His grin was knowing, and they both laughed. 'That bloody steer!' June grumbled.

'I say that every day of the year and I don't have them pooping on my deck. I tell you what,' he began, then took a bite of his roll, chewed and swallowed it, leaving June chomping at the bit for him to continue. 'I've fixed the fence and I'm happy for him to stay in the paddock with the others. I'll bring him back when the Woodwards' return.'

'Thank you, thank you,' June said. She was ecstatic.

'That'll free you up at least one animal now that you have a dozen more.' Chewing on his next bite, Dave looked at the dogs. 'The black one's getting fatter,' he commented. 'Daisy, isn't it?'

'I know, right—that's why I call her Tank,' June agreed. 'She tries to eat the other dog's biscuits when I put them out in the morning.' Dave called her over.

'Daisy, come here, girl.' Daisy came trotting over, and he gave her a morsel of meat. June watched as he felt around her abdomen, then he grinned.

'Is she okay?' June asked.

'Oh, she's fine,' Dave insisted. 'Has a boyfriend though,' he said. June thought about his comment.

'*Noooooo!* She's not pregnant?' June couldn't believe it. She thought they were all old dogs.

'Sure is.' Dave seemed calm about the situation. June was not.

'But they didn't tell me that—the Woodwards. And they left me notes on absolutely everything.'

'Obviously not. They had to have known,' Dave insisted. 'By the feel of her, she's not far off due.'

'Oh—please. Don't say that. I can't deliver puppies. I have too many animals to keep up with now.' June jumped up, ran into the house, and then returned with the folder of information. She placed it down on the bench, opened it up, then picked up one page at a time and skimmed over it. She got to the last page. 'It only says how much to feed them,' she told Dave, but Dave's view was of the rear of the last page as June held it up.

'Turn it over,' he said. June turned the page over and sure enough, there it was—all about Daisy's pregnancy, care, and pre-booked vet home visits. She was a pure-bred, black Staffordshire Bull Terrier, and they had mated her with a prized male.

'She's fucking pregnant!' June blurted out in disbelief. 'And she's due the week after they get back. What will I do if she comes early?'

'Now you're worrying about things before they happen,' Dave said calmly. 'It's her first litter.' June was almost panicked.

'Oh dash, it all makes sense now. Mid-week, there was a vet card left in the letterbox. It read "All good for this week". I didn't know what it was about. It says here on the notes that they have the vet doing house calls through the week, while they're away. How did I miss this? I mean, I don't see him or her—I'm at work!' June slammed the papers back in their folder, picked up her roll and took a huge bite. 'I need a drink!' she mumbled—her mouth full. She got up and headed back inside. Dave used the opportunity to chuckle to himself. *Is there anything else country that could be thrown at you, June Hall?*

June returned with a bottle of bubbly and handed it to him. Her mouth was now empty.

'Be a gentleman and open the bottle for us...' It was a direction, not a question. Dave pulled off the plastic top, then used his pocketknife to lever the cork out of the bottle. It went off with a bang. He poured the bubbles into the two glasses June had brought in with the bottle. Picking up his glass, he proposed a toast.

'To pavlova, and everything country,' he toasted. June lifted her glass.

'You saw the pav, then?' she said, beaming with pride.

'Saw it—I savoured it. Two pieces before I came over.'

'Two pieces! And you still wanted dinner?' June was surprised. Dave grinned widely.

'Of course,' he nodded.

'Well, good for you, Dave Andersen.' June lifted her glass and clinked it against his. 'To pavlova, and everything country,' she repeated, and they both burst out laughing. It was long, hard, belly-aching laughter and it felt wonderful. June hadn't laughed like that in such a long time. She hadn't laughed naturally and uncontrollably since before her boyfriend ran away with her best friend some two years ago. It felt wonderful. She'd dealt with steer dung, a turkey mudslide, a python in her car, two pythons inside the roof, an unwanted come-on, a pub brawl, a week's worth of country patients, a turkey with poults, and now a pregnant dog. *Can life get any more challenging?* And with that, they finished their "gourmet rolls" and drank the bubbly.

Dave, after food, conversation, and a few good belly laughs, headed home to hit the sack early. Today had been a long day for him, and tomorrow would be just as long. June, after successfully coaxing the mother turkey and her poults into their new home before dark, headed inside, showered, turned on her bedroom fan, and fell onto her bed. She succumbed to sleep as her head hit the pillow; her last thought was of Dave Andersen and how he made her laugh.

Chapter 31

Treats, Emergencies and Toilet Spray
Week 2—Monday Morning

Monday morning started late—the rooster didn't crow until 4:30 a.m. June was thrilled with her extra 29 minutes of sleep. As usual, she did her rounds, this time with the addition of opening the poults' cage.

'You lot are adorable,' she told them. She watched them copy their mother—peck at the crumble, have a drink, and follow her out the door. June laughed at their antics. It reminded her of a schoolyard. *So be it, cage—you are now known as "The Schoolyard".* She was thrilled that the mother turkey had felt comfortable and safe enough to use the Schoolyard overnight.

In the kitchen, she sliced some mango and whipped some cream to decorate her meringues. She placed the cream in one small container and the mango in another and popped them both into a large container alongside the meringues. She covered them all with a tea towel. She didn't want to decorate them until it was time for morning tea for fear they'd go soggy. She hoped the staff at the surgery would eat them. She wanted to get to know them all better, but the lack of time and the pace of their work hadn't allowed it so far. Nor had the disastrous night out at the pub. Today, when she had a moment, she would attempt to have a conversation—albeit brief—with each staff member. She loaded up the car and set off to work.

'Morning all.' June stuck her head around the corner of the staff room, into reception. She was holding the container of meringues. It was nearing opening time, and the doctors were already in their rooms preparing for their day. Coral came out of her office.

'Morning, June,' she said, and then stopped, lifted the tea towel and peered into the container. 'Oh, nurse, what treats do we have here?' Coral's reaction sparked attention from receptionists Lisa and Angelica, and they jumped up and peered into the container, too.

'Well,' June began. 'The Woodwards have so many eggs, I thought I'd whip up some meringues for our morning tea. I made a pavlova too and gave it to Alice Andersen and Dave.'

'I bet you did, June Hall. I bet you did.' Coral gave her a mischievous grin. June rolled her eyes and smiled.

'The meringues just need decorating. I've whipped some cream—enough for a big dollop on each one—and sliced some mango to top it with. That's what's in the small containers,' June explained.

'Oh, I can do that…' Coral said cheerfully and took the container from June. 'At morning tea time… when I make everyone a cuppa. The Docs will love a sweet fix—especially Flinty.'

'I hope so.' June said. She felt nervous about it, and didn't know why. 'I've never made either before—meringues or a pav. They weren't as difficult as I thought they'd be.'

8:00 a.m. struck. The quiet of the surgery gave way to chaos as the phone lines automatically came online.

'That's my cue to work,' Coral acknowledged. 'Thank you so much for the meringues, June. It's appreciated.' Coral headed into the staff room. June continued through to the treatment room. Lisa and Angelica were glued to their phones. Lisa gave a thumbs up and a smile, excited for morning tea.

When June entered the treatment room, she stopped. On the benchtop closest to the door, sat a small box. She picked up the unlabelled box—open at the top—and peered inside. It contained a small speaker. She took it to reception.

'Does anybody know who owns this?' Lisa glanced up. She was still on a phone call and gestured for June to wait. When she finished the call, she smiled widely.

'That's for you, June. I brought it in this morning... Consider it a loan while you're here,' she explained. 'It's a spare Bluetooth speaker I have at home. I figured you could play music while you work. Just in the background, you know. I thought you might like to listen to some country music on our local station while you're here. It doesn't seem fair that reception gets to play music all day and the treatment room doesn't.' June was thrilled that she'd thought of her.

'That's a great idea. Background music will be very therapeutic, not only for me, but for the patients. Thank you, Lisa.'

'If you don't like the local stuff,' Lisa added. 'You can get a playlist through Spotify. I'll come and set it up for you.' Lisa followed June into the treatment room. With the box back on the bench, Lisa took out the small, pink speaker. After a few taps on the computer, the receptionist had country music tunes playing unobtrusively. Work today, June thought, would be most enjoyable. Lisa took a small cord out of the box and handed it to June. 'Use this to plug it into the computer and charge it overnight. I'll leave the box in the staff room.'

'Thanks again...' June said, but before either of them could say another word, Angelica came racing around the corner.

'June! A lady just arrived in the waiting room—something's wrong with her.' June didn't hesitate. She grabbed an emesis bag for the patient and a pair of gloves for herself and walked swiftly into the waiting room. She saw the woman straight away, slumped in a waiting room chair. She looked to be in her eighties.

'What's her name?' June called out. Lisa, who was right behind her, answered first.

'That's Mrs. Laidlaw. Mary Laidlaw!' June gave a nod that she understood, then placed a hand on the woman's shoulder. She called her name and gave her shoulder a gentle squeeze to check for a response—there wasn't one. With her other hand, June stroked the woman's cheek, but still, she did not respond.

'Mary... Mary... Mary... can you hear me? Mary...' June called.

'I need the wheelchair and call one of the doctors—stat!' June directed the receptionists. It was only just after opening, and already several people had entered the waiting room. June could feel them watching on and becoming concerned. Soon they would be distressed—neither June or Mary needed that.

While she waited for the wheelchair and doctor to arrive, June felt Mary's pulse and studied her breathing.

'Where do you want it?' Lisa asked, pulling the wheelchair up behind June.

'Remove the left arm,' June directed. 'And wheel it in backwards, next to Mary's right side. We'll need to slide her onto it. Put the brakes on.' Time did not allow for pleases and thank-yous—every second counted. Dr. Lee-Anne arrived. Mary had been booked in to see her. 'Doc,' June said, acknowledging her arrival. 'Her pulse is bradycardic but regular. Her breathing's shallow. She was unresponsive when I got to her.'

'She seemed fine until she sat down,' a woman seated nearby told them. 'She was puffing a little, like she'd been rushing.' June glanced at the woman momentarily and nodded.

'Thank you,' she said, her focus now back on Mary. Between June and Dr. Lee-Anne, they slid Mary from the waiting room chair, across to the wheelchair. The doctor supported Mary's head while June placed her feet on the footrests, returned the arm of the chair so she wouldn't fall out, and ensured her arms were on her lap and not hanging outside the chair. They wheeled her into the treatment room.

June reversed the chair up against the right side of the electronic ECG bed, put the brakes on and then lowered the bed to wheelchair height using the foot pedals. She removed the left armrest of the chair once more. Dr. Lee-Anne and June took hold of Mary's top half, and Coral and Dr. Flint, who had now come to assist, took her legs. On the count of three, they slid Mary from the wheelchair to the bed and placed her on her back. Coral pushed the wheelchair out of the way while June elevated the bed. Drs. Lee-Anne and Flint examined the patient from her right side and checked her vital signs. Coral pulled the curtains around and then elevated Mary's legs with pillows. June stood to the patient's left, unbuttoned her shirt, and attached ECG leads to her—it showed no obvious cause for alarm. Then she took a blood sugar level reading—the prick to Mary's finger, rousing her.

'Mary,' Dr. Lee-Anne said. 'Can you hear me?'

'Of course,' Mary replied. 'Don't yell—I'm not deaf.' She opened her eyes and smiled at them all. Both doctors smiled back, as did June. 'What are you lot doing to me?' the patient asked. Dr Lee-Anne replied.

'You had a turn, Mary—out in the waiting room. We brought you into the treatment room for care.'

'That's very kind of you all,' Mary said. 'I hope I haven't wet my pants.' Dr. Lee-Anne gave a half grin, as did June. 'It's just that the bladder isn't what it used to be, you know,' she added. 'Can I sit up?' The woman appeared quite spritely now.

'I don't see why not, Mary,' Dr. Lee-Anne said. June put her foot on the bed controls and brought the back of the bed up into a semi-sitting position.

'Were you feeling unwell this morning, Mary?'

'No, Doctor. Just running a little late, so I was rushing.'

'Have you had much to drink this morning?'

'No. Nothing. I didn't have time for anything, I overslept and had to feed the cats.'

'Well, Mary, I think you've had what we call a vasovagal,' Dr. Lee-Anne explained. 'You fainted while sitting in the chair out there. Luckily, you didn't fall off and hit your head. I think we have a combination of too much rushing, a little dehydration, and a blood sugar level on the low side. How about we get you a cup of tea? I'll see my next patient, then I'll pop back and collect you for your consult. That's if you're feeling up to it. Nurse June will monitor you for a while. She can keep me posted on your progress. How does that sound?'

'Sounds like the best consult I've ever had,' Mary said, unable to wipe the smile from her face.

'How do you have your tea?' Coral asked. 'I'll make it.'

'White with one, thank you,' Mary replied. June was grateful Coral had taken it upon herself to get the tea. It freed her up to stay with the patient—she had no intention of leaving her.

June took a second set of observations from Mary. Everything was now in normal range. It was Lisa who walked in carrying a mug in one hand and a plate in the other.

'Here we are, Mary. Tea—white with one. If it's no good, blame Coral—she made it. I've also brought you one of June's meringues at the doctor's request—to help raise your blood sugar level.' Mary's eyes lit up. Lisa set them on the bench, within reach.' June looked concerned.

'Are you a diabetic, Mary?'

'No, Dear—but I might be after that meringue,' she joked.

'Your blood sugar level is low—perhaps you shouldn't skip breakfast anymore, and a glass of water or cup of tea first thing in the morning might be a new habit to get into—before feeding the cats,' June explained. 'I'm sure they won't mind waiting.'

'I can do that,' Mary mumbled as her mouth enveloped the meringue.

Dr. Lee-Anne returned and collected Mary after half an hour. June was finally free to try and get through her morning's work. Patients were waiting in the waiting room for her attention, but as June found out, each one had been told of an emergency, and they were consequently most pleasant throughout their procedures. Not one minded waiting—this didn't happen to her back in Adelaide. It seemed everyone in the city was in a rush.

Coral brought a cup of coffee and a decorated meringue on a plate, for June, mid-morning. June was chomping at the bit!

'I need a bathroom break,' she admitted.

'I'll mind the fort,' Coral offered. 'Oh, I almost forgot. You were so busy before. You have a surprise delivery and it's in the staff room. There's a card, but we couldn't see who it was from.'

'Oh. Okay,' June replied. 'Probably a backorder for the treatment room.' After her bathroom break, she walked back through the staff room. There, in the middle of the main table, was a basket of goodies. On a small card was her name, "Nurse June". June picked up the card, opened it and read it.

Dear June, thank you for looking after Alice at home, for the pavlova, and for helping me at Paddock-to-Plate yesterday. It's truly appreciated. Dave.

June studied the hamper. It was full of chocolates from Gallo Dairyland, cheeses from Mungalli Creek Bio-Dynamic Dairy, and a bottle of something alcoholic from Mt Uncle Distillery. There were crackers and other bits and pieces too. June would study it all at home later. A grin spread across her face. Dave was so thoughtful. She tucked the cold items into the fridge, leaving the rest—crackers, chocolates and booze—on the staff room table. It wasn't the communal table—it'd all be there when she knocked off. The room temperature in the staff room would be fine for the non-perishables.

Angelica entered the staff room.

'Sorry to interrupt your break, June, but there's a couple in reception—holidaymakers from Germany. They asked to see a nurse. They have bites of some sort and look very uncomfortable.'

'Oh, okay. I'll come and see them now. You'd better slot them in with one of the doctors, too. Perhaps Flinty, Lee-Anne has been held up with Mary. June made her way to reception, where the couple were standing. 'Hello, I'm June. I'm the practice nurse. If you'd like to follow me.' The couple followed June down the corridor and into the treatment room. 'The receptionist tells me you have some nasty bites?'

'Ja, we do,' the man explained, his German accent undeniable.

'Do you mind if I take a look, then I can report to the doctor?'

'Ja, Danke,' the man said, directing his wife to sit closest to June.' June pulled the curtains around and then looked briefly at the bites over their bodies, first on the woman and then on the man. She had a good idea of what they were.'

'Where have you been in the last day or two?' she asked. The man's wife spoke, her English somewhat better than her husband's.

'Well,' she started. 'Wir visited some boardwalks down in Cairns. Eins at the Botanic Gardens—oh so beautiful, und eins by the coast—in das mangroves.' June studied their legs closer. The bites were red and blotchy, and it was obvious they'd been scratching at them. They'd made a mess of not only their legs, but their arms and faces as well.

'I think you've had some love from biting midges. They're often called sand flies. Scratching them is not the best thing to do.' June noted the woman's bites were far worse than her husband's—she had long fingernails that were possibly to blame for that.

'Wir don't understand why wir were bitten,' the German woman said. 'Wir used spray to keep insects away, but it did not work, und wir put plenty on.' The man proceeded to get the can of spray from his backpack. He handed it to his wife, who passed it to June. June studied the can.

'Oh… I see your problem,' she said, glancing from the can to the suffering couple in front of her.

'Is this not gut spray?' the man asked. The spray can label boasted a picture of a wooded scene with butterflies in the foreground. June cleared her throat and put her serious face on.

'This spray is not a repellent—one you put on your skin to keep insects away.' She held back laughter; this was not the time for a nurse to laugh at a patient. 'This spray is an air freshener.' The couple looked at each other, confused.

'Air freshener?' they repeated in unison.

'Yes,' June tried to explain. 'This is to make your bathroom smell nice... fresh... pretty... it is not for keeping insects away—not a repellent.' The couple looked perplexed.

'You'll need to visit the pharmacy,' June continued. 'To buy a cream to soothe the itching. Don't scratch them anymore—they can become infected.' On a piece of paper, June jotted down the names of two products.

'Either of these will work, but check with the pharmacist, they may have something better that I don't know about.' She handed the piece of paper to the man, and he tucked it in his pocket. 'I'll just confer with the doctor and see if our diagnosis is the same. I won't be a minute.' She looked at her bookings screen. Dr. Flint had just finished consulting and would be free momentarily. June headed directly to his room, leaving the couple itching to scratch their bites.

'Are you okay, June?' Dr. Flint asked. June had her hand over her mouth, trying desperately not to laugh, but humour got the better of her and a momentary giggle escaped, her hand smothering it. She knew it was unprofessional, but she'd seen the funny side of the tourist's predicament.

'I have two German tourists in the treatment room,' she began. 'It seems they did a mangrove boardwalk and were greeted by biting midges and...' She smothered another giggle before taking a deep breath.

'And—go on,' Dr. Flint said, trying to draw the information from her.

'They couldn't understand why their insect repellent hadn't worked and prevented the bites,' she managed to say.

'They couldn't...' Dr. Flint said. 'And why hadn't it?' he asked. June took another calming breath.

'Well, they showed me the can—they'd covered themselves in air freshener, you know, *toilet* air freshener!' June's lungs felt as if they'd burst if she didn't release the laughter she had bottled inside her.

'Oh my, well that's most unfortunate,' Dr. Flint said straight-faced in his proper English accent. 'I'd better take a look.'

He walked out of his consultation room, and June went to follow him, but couldn't. She shut the door, leant back against it, and laughed until her stomach hurt.

By the time she made it into the treatment room, the German couple had been seen by the doctor and were paying their bill at reception. No doubt, they would make a beeline to the pharmacy. Dr. Flint stared at June.

'Perhaps a strong cup of tea for you, Nurse June?' June nodded her head—she had no breath left to answer. Dr. Flint started out of the treatment room with parting words. 'You know, June, in my years as a doctor, I've never been able to work out a nurse's sense of humour,' he said and disappeared into his room. June took herself to the bathroom, hoping the break would calm her laughter. It worked well, then she spotted the can of air freshener on the windowsill—the same kind. A fresh wave of laughter overtook her. Tears ran down her cheeks, and she gripped her stomach in pain. She considered she might just have a nurse's sense of humour—as mentioned by Dr. Flint—after all.

The day seemed to fly, and before June knew it, she was headed out the back door with the beautiful basket of local goodies Dave had sent her. Nobody had pried, and she was glad of that. The day had been busy for everyone in the practice, and now she had Alice's wounds to clean. She drove out along Arthur Willis Road toward the Andersens', happy and smiling. She'd enjoyed the challenges of her day, the background music compliments of Lisa, and the fact that Mary's turn was no more than a vasovagal episode. Turning into the driveway, she saw Dave. He was on his way out. She sighed. *Dave, my friend, bearer of gifts and accidental hero.*

As their cars drew parallel, both stopped and lowered their windows. June spoke loudly to be heard over the purring of engines.

'Thank you so much, Dave, for the lovely hamper. It was very thoughtful.'

'You earned it,' he said with a smile that touched her heart. 'Alice is waiting for you inside.' He tipped his head in the direction of his house. 'She likes you very much, you know. When her wounds heal, she'll miss your girly chats, I'm sure.'

'I'll miss them too,' she said, returning a smile, but the truth was a bigger picture—what she'd *really* miss was time with him. She hesitated before continuing. 'I can't help thinking she's up to something.'

'Yeah, I get that too,' he agreed. 'She probably is.' He knew his grandmother well.

They remained silent for a few moments, their eyes meeting and locking. He didn't know if it was a reflection off the vivid, wet-season grass in the paddock, but her eyes appeared greener and brighter today. *How do you present so fresh and beautiful at the end of the working day, June Hall?* He pulled his eyes to look forward. Instinctively, he gave a one-sided grin which made his forehead crease under his hat and one eyebrow lift—her presence made him happy. While his appearance was rugged, his smile was downright cute. *Can rugged be cute, Mr. Andersen? Is that even a thing? I'm so hot—the air conditioner can't be working!*

'Ah-hmm,' she cleared her throat. The sound was deep and hoarse; her breath unintentionally catching mid-way—a sign of how hard she was trying to keep it all together around him. *What is wrong with you, June Hall? You've seen him smile before.* He glanced back at her. She returned the smile, but it wasn't a reactive one. She had to force it across her face—her body busy processing a sudden and strange fluttering feeling within. She took a breath to calm herself, but it was too sharp, and she let out a cough. 'Hrkk!'

'You, okay?' he asked. She nodded slowly. His irises drew her attention. Was it the angle of the afternoon sun piercing through the windscreen that made them appear even more sapphire-like today, or something else?

'Well... be seeing you,' Dave said. He put his window up, waved, and coasted down the driveway. June idled for a few

moments and then continued up the driveway, sorry he wasn't
staying home.

Chapter 32

Critters, a Fracture, Stars and Steak After a Morsel
Week 2—Monday Through Thursday Night

Week two of June's locum at the Millbrook Surgery was flying by. Dave brought Alice in for her appointment with Dr. Flint.

'I don't know where time goes, Dear,' Alice said.

'That makes two of us,' June replied. 'I can't believe it's Thursday already. I'll be on the plane back to Adelaide before I know it at this rate.' June removed Alice's dressings in preparation for her consult. Dr. Flint arrived in the treatment room and was pleased with her progress.

'Jolly good, Alice. Your wounds have healed up well. You can leave them uncovered—we've protected them long enough—and let the shower water run over them now. Pat the newly healed areas dry. Don't rub vigorously now—the skin is still somewhat fragile,' he explained.

'C'mon Doc,' Alice replied with a smirk. 'My days of doing anything "vigorously" ended a long time ago.'

'You know what I mean—I don't want to see you back here for a while. Take it easy on that Stallion of yours and try to stay on flat ground. We don't want you breaking a hip! I'll leave you to June to see you out.'

'Thanks, Doc,' Dave said. He'd been sitting on the adjacent bed, taking the weight off. He stood and nodded at Alice, prompting her.

'Yes, thank you, Stephen,' she said. June had noted that some of Dr. Flint's older patients sometimes referred to him by his Christian name.

'Looks like you're off the hook, June,' Dave remarked with a caring smile. 'Got your afternoons back to yourself.' He sounded jovial, but deep down he was sorry her visits to his house were ending.

By 5:00 p.m., June wanted to fall into a chair and stay there. She'd been running all day and felt exhausted, but the treatment room needed tidying before morning. It looked like a cyclone had passed through it—though she'd never experienced one, it was the only comparison that fit. She'd stay behind and get it done rather than start early and do it in the morning.

Being last to leave for the day, she set the alarm and locked the back door. She jumped into her car, eager for home, but when she tried to start it, nothing happened. Several times she turned the key, but each time the engine was dead.

'Bugger,' she snapped, banging the steering wheel with the palms of her hands. It hurt—she rubbed them up and down on her scrub pants for a moment until the wave of pain left her. *Swearing will not start your car, June Hall.* She foraged in her bag, took out her phone, and dialled the RACQ to book a call-out. She was not with the RAA back home but was happy to pay—they were two hours away. June knew it would be dark then. What would she do for two hours? What would the animals do? She had feed to give to Wilbur, and she needed to lock up the baby poults. She also wanted to check on pregnant Daisy. She put her hands on the steering wheel, rested her head and fell asleep until a knock at the window woke her.

Under the bonnet, the man from the RACQ grunted and groaned, then brought his head up and smiled.

'Rats—they've eaten some wiring, Lovie. It'll only take a jiffy to get sorted.' He grabbed his toolbox and within ten minutes, the car was fixed.

'Should be good as gold now, Sweetie,' he said. 'Leave your bonnet up at night, rats don't like that—too open—they prefer to be out of sight.' His smile was genuine and friendly, despite a few missing teeth.

'Thank you so much.' June swiped her card across the man's portable EFTPOS machine and paid her bill.

'Glad to help,' he said and went on his merry way. It was now dark. June had only driven once at night since she'd been in Millbrook—that was the night of Dave and Justin's fight. She had adrenaline coursing through her veins that night. Tonight, as tired as she was, she'd take it easy. *Rats eating the wiring? Seriously? I suppose that's what you get for relocating pythons!* She thought about the balance of nature and whether it was better to have rats around, or pythons! She wasn't a fan of either.

There were very few cars driving around town and absolutely none on Arthur Willis Road. June saw some beady eyes peering at her from the edge of the road and slowed the car. A brown, furry creature ran out in front of her. She stopped suddenly. It continued three-quarters of the way across the road, turned, and then darted back toward the verge. June prepared to drive off, but it ran out in front of her again. This time it stopped in the middle of the road and stared into the car's lights. After some thought, it darted back and forth, quite indecisively. June couldn't help but laugh. She added a commentary to its antics.

'I think I'll go left. Wait… no, right—me thinks right. Hang on… left looks good too,' until finally it ran into the long grass on the opposite side of the road and didn't return. June thought it might be a bandicoot, but she wasn't entirely sure. She saw three all up, on her drive home—each one having no idea if it was coming or going. She wondered how many succumbed to cars and pythons.

Finally, she pulled into Barrine Views and drove straight up the driveway. She enjoyed being able to leave the gate open now that Winston was residing in one of Dave's paddocks. She parked her car in the open bay of the shed and popped the bonnet. With her mobile phone torch, she got out and looked around for signs of rats but didn't see any. She considered that she didn't know what "signs of rats" were. She lifted the car's bonnet to leave it up for the night, just as the RACQ man had advised her to do.

Loaded up with the bucket of Wilbur's scraps, her work bag and her hamper, June thought about the animal rounds she had yet to do. They wouldn't take long, but first, she'd shower. By phone-torch light, she made her way from her car to the house. She went gingerly, Dave's description of "plate-sized spiders" forever in her mind. As she climbed the stairs, *one, two, three, four, five, six, seven,* she smiled. *And no more Winston chain—bloody Winston!* Across the deck and through the sliding door, she dropped everything on the kitchen bench. She turned on the light, then took the cold stuff from the hamper and placed it in the fridge. She stepped back out to the deck and made a quick fuss of the dogs—checking on Daisy—before making a beeline for the shower. Five minutes later and feeling fresher, she threw on a dress and then fed the dogs. She grabbed her phone torch, took the bucket of scraps, slipped on the boots, and headed into the garden—plod-clomp.

Wilbur got his scraps first—not that he minded them being late—then she refreshed the water and crumble in the Schoolyard. She saw no poults—mum was comfortable on the sugar cane mulch—and June figured they'd all be underneath her. If there were any stragglers out there, then that was nature, and so be it. She latched the door, relieved they were utilising Dave's masterpiece for yet another night.

At the turkey slope, she took the bucket from the hook and added cracked corn, water and the lid. The turkeys were all up high roosting in the fig tree next to her. She could hear them moving about, but didn't hang around any longer than was necessary—falling gobbler poop missiles were a certainty. She only had the chooks left to do.

The chooks were securely indoors—all but a white one who lay at the bottom of the entrance ramp.

'Hey, little mate, are you locked out?' June knew she could put her into the Penthouse via the nest boxes on the side. She picked her up and studied her. Something was wrong with her leg. She shone the light to have a look and gasped. Her leg was broken. 'Oh no, how will I fix you—poor, sweet little chook?'

she said, concerned. The chicken didn't appear to be in pain, but June wasn't sure. She carried her back to the house and examined the leg under the kitchen light. It was a closed fracture—the bone wasn't protruding through. She needed help—she needed Dave. She called his number and waited for him to answer.

'This is Dave Andersen. Leave a message…' She hung up before the beep, fearing he could be in bed. She didn't want to wake him. Across the hill to the Andersen house, she could see lights were on. *Perhaps he didn't hear it ring.* Then her phone rang in her hand.

'June—is everything alright?' he asked, sounding a little panicked. 'I was just in the shower.' June remembered the last time she'd seen him in a towel. The thought gave her goosebumps. She glanced down at the chicken in her arms.

'Yes—sort of alright,' she said.

'Meaning?' he asked.

'One of the chickens appears to have broken its leg,' she explained. There was a pause before Dave asked gingerly.

'Do you want me to, um… euthanise it?' he inquired, his voice soft and caring.

'Oh… no… definitely no… would you mind popping over and holding her for me so I can put a splint on her leg?' she asked and waited a few moments for him to reply. *Bad timing, June— he's busy.*

'A splint?' he probed, sounding surprised. 'You want to splint its leg?'

'Well… yes, of course,' she said insistently. 'I can't kill it just because it's broken its leg—but I *can* do a mean splint!' Dave thought about the logistics of it, besides, he wouldn't mind seeing her—he always wanted to see her; that was his problem.

'Give me five to put some clothes on and I'll be over,' he said. June ended the call. *Put some clothes on?* Her eyebrows rose, and then she glanced back down at the chicken.

'Why does the thought of a naked Dave and the sound of his voice conjure inappropriate thoughts in my head that are irrelevant at this very moment?' she asked the chicken. 'Does your rooster have this effect on you?' She thought for a moment. 'I think not! He left you, didn't he,' she continued. 'Stranded… outside for the night in python country… *and* with a broken leg! *Nooo…* Your rooster is nothing like Dave Andersen!'

Holding the chicken firmly, June fetched what looked like an old towel from the Woodwards' laundry and wrapped her feathered patient in it. She held her under one arm and, with the other, poured herself a glass of water. She glanced at the hamper on the bench. She'd share it with Dave one day before she left.

June heard his ute ascend the driveway. She turned on the light that shone over the stairs, so he could see. Dave took the steps two at a time and crossed the deck.

'Thanks for coming,' she said.

'No problem,' he replied. 'It got me out of watching Home and Away with Gran.' June chuckled.

'That show still going?' she asked.

''fraid so,' he replied, and rolled his eyes.

'I'm all ready to go,' June said. 'I have the stuff I need on the bench. Can you hold Mrs. Little, please?' June passed the chicken to Dave.

'You know its name?' he laughed.

'No, I just gave her that. Well, she is little, and she is a chicken.'

'Oh. Righto,' he said, taking the chicken from June, cautiously. 'I remember the book, Chicken Little, but not the storyline. It's probably a movie now.'

June took two wooden barbeque skewers from the kitchen drawer, snapped them to the desired length, then wrapped a small bandage up, down and around each one. The padded skewers made perfect splints. Taking the broken leg and straightening it carefully, she tacked the splints in place with tape. She then bandaged along the length of the leg, from the bottom to the top.

'They're small bandages,' Dave commented.

'Yes, great for digits. I have all sizes in my work bag.'

He studied June as she tended the chicken—her delicate hands worked with quiet precision. He listened to her steady breath as she concentrated, noted the caring sparkle in her green eyes, and marvelled at her soft, soothing words as she chatted and comforted Mrs. Little.

'Have you eaten, Dave?' she asked, glancing up.

'No,' he replied. 'Not yet. Thursday is Cup-A-Soup night for Gran. She insists on making her own dinner to give me a break, and that's it—a Cup-A-Soup—her choice.'

'Oh,' June said, smiling. 'Gourmet!' Dave nodded.

'I have to stick around to pour in the water and carry it to the table—it's boiling-hot soup. Wouldn't fare too well transported on the Silver Stallion!'

'An accident waiting to happen, no doubt,' June added.

'I know, right. She's a kind old soul—but that's why I often leave her a sandwich, so she doesn't play with the kettle. I usually grab whatever. Sometimes I don't eat at all—it's my lazy night, I suppose. It depends on how busy I've been and if I have the energy left to be creative. Occasionally it's takeaway.'

'Well, I haven't eaten, and you haven't eaten,' June said. 'I have a hamper of food, and you don't. I have an open bottle of red too, and you look thirsty. How about you pour us both a glass, while I pop Mrs. Little in a nest for the night?' She dug around and found a small plastic container with a lid. She put some water into the container, placed the lid on, took the chicken back from Dave, and made her way outside and to the chook house, phone-torch to guide her. With Mrs. Little safe and sound in a cosy nest, she took the lid off the container of water and placed it within her reach. She didn't expect she'd stand just yet, but in a few days, she hoped she would. She'd deliver food to her in the morning.

Dave poured two glasses of red from the bottle, noting it had barely been touched. With a glass in both hands, he flung the sliding screen door open with his foot. As he headed through the doorway, he stumbled over his thongs. He looked at the glasses and smiled. He hadn't spilled a drop. He breathed a sigh of relief that June hadn't seen his clumsiness. He kicked his thongs aside—something he usually did out of habit, so he didn't create a trip-hazard for his Gran—and made his way across the deck to stand on the top edge of the stairs. The night was clear, and the stars shone brighter than he'd seen them in a long time. Often, when he couldn't sleep, he'd wander outside and just look at the stars. There was something therapeutic about the universe and the secrets it held. He sat down on the top step holding both glasses of wine and waited for June.

On her return, June threw the old towel she'd wrapped Mrs. Little in over the railing. She climbed the stairs past Dave.

'I'll just wash my hands and grab us a bite,' she said. He nodded. When June came back out, she had a plate of cheese and crackers and a small knife. She sat down, placed the plate on the step between them and took the glass of red he held for her.

'Beautiful night,' she said. They both tucked into the cheese.

'I was just thinking the same thing,' Dave agreed. 'The Southern Cross isn't letting us down tonight.'

'Hmm,' June paused. 'Which one is that, exactly? You don't see the stars this clearly in the city.'

'Yep, been there. That's light pollution; streetlights, building lights, car lights.'

'True,' June agreed. 'I've never given it a thought. It makes sense.'

Dave placed his glass of wine down and shifted closer to her, leaving barely enough room for the cheese plate. Her heart rate quickened. He touched her shoulder with one hand and with the other, pointed toward the night sky.

'See the four bright stars there?' June nodded as he gestured toward each one. 'They mark the Southern Cross. There are five stars, as reflected on the right side of our flag, but four distinct pointers.'

'They're quite distinct, aren't they?' June agreed.

'On the flag, the pointer stars have seven points, and the fifth star has five points.'

'I feel a bit silly, but I've never noticed—perhaps I learnt it in school, but I've forgotten. There's a big one under the Union Jack to the left, my memory tells me,' June said, a look of recall on her face.

'That's right. It, too, has seven points—the Commonwealth Star. It symbolizes our federal system of Government—our six states, plus the seventh point, which was added early last century to represent our territories. Did you know that?'

'I'd have to say no, not really. I haven't thought about stars in years. I recall some called the Saucepan, but I'm not sure which ones they are, either.' Dave pointed up again.

'There's the saucepan and there's the handle. That one's Gran's favourite.'

'Thank you for the lesson, Mr. Andersen.' Dave smiled. 'You're welcome. Life gets in the way, doesn't it? I mean, we get so busy we forget the wonders around us.'

'Too true,' she admitted. *Too true.* She gazed at the stars, taking in their brilliance and wondered why she didn't look at them every night.

'Did you also know that the long line of the Southern Cross points south and can be used for navigation?'

'Well, I guess I'd realize that if I thought about it, but I haven't thought about it, so I'd have to say no. No, I didn't know that either,' she chuckled. 'I'm feeling quite stupid right now.' She looked down at her glass, somewhat embarrassed. Dave clinked his glass against hers.

'I have no idea how to do all those things you do at the surgery. We can't know everything.' June nodded and lifted her glass toward him.

'To learning, then,' she said.

'To learning,' Dave agreed. They both took a sip and stared ahead into the night.

'It's a nice drop, this one,' Dave said, breaking the silence.

'I don't mind a good Cab Sav,' June nodded. They both sat in silence again. Dave felt he should move away from her now that he'd shown her the stars, but he didn't want to—he felt at home, like nothing else in the world mattered right now. And he felt like a school kid on his first date, but this wasn't a first date, nor a second—it wasn't a date at all and never would be. June finished the last mouthful of her wine and jumped up.

'Come on, Mr. Andersen, let's have more from that lovely hamper.' She put her hand down to help him up. He took it but didn't need help. Her hand felt soft and warm, and he held it for as long as he could without appearing odd. Standing, he picked up the empty plate and carried it to the kitchen.

June pulled goodies from the hamper and the fridge and placed them on the timber dining table. Dave topped up their wine glasses. She gathered a cutting board, a cheese knife, a couple of forks, and two small plates—everything they needed was laid out in front of them. They sat down and began grazing. Sitting at an old table, opposite a rugged farmer, surrounded by a menagerie and an unpredictable environment, June Hall had yet to realise how comfortable she had become.

'Do you have anyone special in your life, June?' Dave enquired. June finished her mouthful.

'I did have, once,' she said.

'Once?' Dave prompted.

'I was engaged, but he ran away.' Dave had felt that sting.

'I'm sorry to hear that,' he replied.

'And he took my best friend with him,' she added.

'Ouch, that's not nice,' he stated. He knew how much that hurt—the same thing had happened to him, but he'd only ever shared that with Alice. To everyone else, she'd left to return to the city.

'No, it wasn't nice at all.' She managed a smile. 'I haven't seen anyone since. Trust issues, some say. One day maybe.' She took a sip of her wine. She buried that hurt long ago.

'What about you, Mr. Andersen? Any loves in your life?' *From what Coral says, there had to be.*

'There was once.' His wife—the reason he knew all about trust issues. 'She was from Brisbane. A city girl, through and through. Liked the hustle and bustle. I don't mind the city, but my heart is in the country. Born and bred, I suppose.'

'Makes sense, really,' June said. 'It's where your family is—your roots.'

'We were married for a year,' Dave said, continuing. 'On our first anniversary, she packed up and left—said she couldn't deal with life in the country.' He'd lied through his teeth. The hurt was still too raw to share—even after a year. When your wife runs off with your best mate on your first wedding anniversary, that takes some getting over.

'After my last week here at Barrine Views, I can almost understand why,' June added, sarcastically. Dave gave a small chuckle. He appreciated her humour.

'For me, if you truly love someone, that's where home is,' he said, thoughtfully. June was taken aback at his comment. It stirred something deep inside her. She thought how honest and straightforward a comment it was. If only it were true.

They talked for hours about each other's lives, things they liked and things they didn't. Dave talked about Paddock-to-Plate and plans for his business, and June talked about her career, light-hearted moments, and the many characters she came across each day. Dave looked at the clock.

'Eleven thirty!' he said, surprised. 'Time flies when you're in good company.' June stood up.

'Did you want anything more to eat?'

'No thanks.' He rubbed his stomach. 'I've had plenty—been picking all night,' he replied, shifting his chair out a little to start his move home. June put the leftovers in the fridge and the plates in the sink. 'Can I help you clean up?' he offered.

'No, it's fine. There's only a couple, and they can wait 'til morning,' she said.

Making his way through the sliding door, Dave went to slip on his thongs but hesitated, then turned around. June stood in the doorway in front of him, ready to see him off. He gazed down at her, not wanting to leave. Her green eyes seemed to beckon him, or was it just wishful thinking? She watched him and waited—a statue of yearning—his blue eyes piercing and intoxicating. Or was it the wine?

'Can I kiss you goodnight, June?' His voice was soft and caressing. He knew it might be wrong, and that he'd probably end up regretting it, but he wanted to kiss her so much it hurt.

June swallowed but could not speak. She hesitated and deliberated. *If I go here, there may be no turning back.* There was no doubt she was attracted to him, attracted to everything about him—his honesty, his kind heart, his hard-working nature, his caring soul, and the part of him that was still a mystery. These, she knew, were not the feelings one had for somebody considered just a friend. She succumbed. A peck on the cheek wouldn't hurt—not after all they'd shared tonight. She nodded.

Dave bent down slightly, and June raised her head. Before she could think any further, his lips touched hers and their tongues met. She felt a rush of warmth wash over her and knew the kiss was right.

But Dave desired more—the steak after the morsel. Every part of his body was ready, willing, and aching to be skin to skin with her. To explore her from head to toe. To make love to her. He shuddered, and June stepped back. In his eyes, she could see his dilated pupils, a sign of his need. Spontaneously, she took his hand and led him down the passage. He did not hesitate, nor refuse her offer. As they entered her bedroom, she turned the ceiling fan switch to high. She expected their frolicking would draw a sweat on this balmy night.

Standing alongside the bed, face to face, she unbuttoned his shirt slowly, starting at the top. His breaths grew heavier as her hands lowered. Finally, after the last button was unfastened, she pulled the shirt open. On his broad chest, the patches of hair she'd shaved off to allow the ECG stickers to adhere were

growing back. She pushed her finger into his pectoral muscle—
was it as hard as it looked? Her eyes widened. *Like a rock!* Then
her hands moved upward, clasping the top of his shirt. She
tugged—it slipped over his powerful shoulders. With a little
wiggle on his behalf, it fell to the floor. After a deep breath in and
out to ground himself, he reached behind her, slid the zipper of
her dress down, nervously, and repeated what she'd done to
him—pushed it off her graceful shoulders, and watched it slide
to the floor.

He continued his quest with her bra—his confidence
growing by the second with every hook and eye he conquered.
One, two, three—bingo. He whipped it off and tossed it into the
air without a care. It hit the ceiling fan with a clang, but neither
stopped to investigate.

June stood before Dave wearing nothing more than red,
lacy knickers and a look of temptation. The light filtering in from
the passage highlighted her curves. He took time to admire
them, his smouldering gaze causing her nipples to throb with
eagerness. Appreciatively, he cupped her breasts. She
shuddered. His thumbs massaged her nipples gently, and they
burned under his touch.

With deep-yet-quickening breaths, she undid his belt
buckle, then fumbled her way to unbuttoning his jeans. *One
button—such difficulty, eh....* His heart pounded, his chest
tightening with anticipation. June tugged at his zipper, and he
moved to help her. She placed her hands upon his and moved
them to his sides—she wanted to do it. Slowly, she took hold of
the slider on the zipper and lowered it, one tooth at a time. He
couldn't feel or hear each soft click, but his senses thrummed,
bracing for and picturing each slow notch of the zipper's teeth—
a sensory experience he'd never been privy to, and the enormity
of it shocked him. When the zipper was undone, she gripped his
pants on either side and eagerly slid them off his hips and down.
They bunched around his ankles, leaving him bare from the
calves up. She did the same with her knickers, kicking both them

and her dress aside. He followed suit without a moment's hesitation.

Under the whooshing comfort of the ceiling fan—the snagged bra circling and flapping like a victory flag above their heads—Dave and June gave in to the chemistry and want that had been building since the moment they met. They made love into and through the velvet hours, neither wanting to let their rapture end, until finally, spent, they collapsed together, their pants and gasps yielding to deep, consummated breaths. June's body hummed a tune written just for her. She'd been consumed by Dave's passion, as if every part of her had been seen and touched. Dave's body was played-out, she'd helped him touch the stars. He realised he'd only been existing until now; with her, he felt truly alive.

Dave collapsed beside June and stayed there until the rooster crowed at 4:01 a.m.

***

Dave moaned and stretched—he didn't own a rooster. It was early for him. He rolled over and kissed June on the cheek.

'Morning, beautiful…' he whispered. 'Coffee?' She squinted, opened her eyes, looked at him, and then smiled—the passage light, that had burned all night, provided just enough glow for her to see his ruffled hair and dishevelled morning look.

'Morning, yourself… yes, please.' He stood up, staring lovingly back down at her and then SLAP. June roared with laughter while Dave fought to keep his balance, stumbling backwards and stopping with a thud up against the wardrobe. Her bra—still spinning on high—had given him a wake-up in the form of an unexpected, lacy slap across the head.

'You think that's funny?' He smiled and jumped playfully back into bed.

The coffee could wait until 5:01 a.m.

Chapter 33

She's Dropped a Carving Knife
Week 2—Friday Afternoon

Friday afternoon came around unbelievably fast for June. She was almost halfway through her stay. As she tidied up the treatment room ready for Monday, she heard a commotion at the front door of the surgery. She popped her head around the corner and looked toward the waiting room. Dave was battling his way through the front door, carrying Alice. He headed straight toward her, passed her, and laid Alice on the nearest bed. June was taken aback and glared at a blood-stained towel wrapped around Alice's left foot.

'Oh dear, Alice,' she said as she pulled a pair of nitrile gloves out of the box on the wall. 'Have you had another fall?' she asked.

'I had a little accident, Dear. That's all,' Alice replied.

'She's put a knife through her foot!' Dave explained.

'But I pulled it straight out,' Alice added.

'She was at the fridge,' Dave continued. 'Ready to tackle the last bit of your pavlova and somehow dropped the knife—my *large, sharp* carving knife, I might add. I didn't see it happen, but she said it landed point down, right in the middle of her foot.'

'Oh, no. Are you in pain?' June asked, concerned.

'Not really, Dear. It hurt my pride, mostly,' she admitted. 'We were lucky to catch you before knock-off, weren't we, Dave?'

'Very,' Dave replied, looking over Alice's head toward June. June sensed his eyes upon her and glanced at him. She could see a glint in his eye, then a half-smile tugged at his lip. She knew what fleeting memory had just crossed his mind. She pulled her eyes back to Alice's foot—she needed to concentrate— she did not need Dave Andersen distracting her, as he did so well.

June wheeled a small, round stool over toward Alice's feet, pulled the privacy curtain around them, and sat down. She slipped on the gloves. Slowly, she unwrapped the bloodied towel. She took one look at the top of it and wrapped it back up.

Alice had noted Dave's absence overnight. Discreetly, she observed them—the quiet, telling look that now passed between him and June. *Hmm… you two have played bed tennis—game, set, match!* She fought a satisfied smile; her plans were in motion, and fate was finally doing her bidding. With a steadying breath, she reminded herself of the real reason she was here— beyond matchmaking.

'Is it bad, Dear—too bad for duct tape?' Alice asked.

'It's not pretty, Alice. I don't think duct tape will suffice. I'll fetch Dr. Flint.' June left the treatment room and made a beeline for his consulting room. 'Doc, Alice Andersen is here.' He turned to June.

'Again? I just saw her yesterday. What's up?'

'Well… it seems she's dropped a carving knife, and it's landed—point down—in the top of her left foot.'

'Goodness, gracious—really?' he asked, his eyes wide with surprise. 'Is it still in there?'

'No,' June advised him. 'She said she pulled it out. It's not a small wound, doctor.' Dr. Flint shook his head in disbelief.

'Seems Alice is becoming quite accident-prone,' he said, his hand on his chin in thought. June returned to the treatment room with Dr. Flint following right behind. As they entered the room and pulled back the curtain slightly, he acknowledged his patients. 'Alice… Dave…' he said with a nod. 'I'll just wash my hands.'

While June opened some sterile gloves and placed them on the bench, ready, Dr. Flint scrubbed his hands, waved them dry, and then squeezed into the gloves. He backed in through the curtain and waited for June.

June removed the towel just enough to view the wound, hopped off the stool and allowed Dr. Flint to sit down.

'Does it need stitches, Doc?' Dave asked.

'Let's see,' he mumbled, fixed on the task of examining Alice's wound. He pressed on it and wiggled it, taking in the depth and size of the clean cut. 'It's not pretty, Alice.'

'As you lot keep telling me, but you *can* stitch it here at the surgery—can't you, Stephen?' Alice said. 'June could come and check on it each day—like she did with my shin wounds.'

'I'm afraid not, Alice.' Dr. Flint said. 'You may have cut tendons. It's into an ambulance and off to Atherton Hospital for you. They'll likely take you down the hill to Cairns. You'll need the general surgeons or even plastics for this one.' Alice couldn't believe it; she'd stabbed her foot too hard. *Darn it!* She had imagined a couple of sutures at most, just enough to keep June coming to the house each day for Dave's sake.

'Fiddlesticks!' she mumbled. That wasn't in her plan.

Dr. Flint called the ambulance while June bandaged Alice's foot. She secured the wound firm enough to minimize bleeding, yet simple enough for quick and easy removal. The doctors at Atherton Hospital Emergency Department would need to view the damage as soon as Alice arrived.

'They're not too far away,' Dr. Flint advised on his return to the treatment room. 'Dave, you'll need to pack a bag for Alice. Will you be able to take it to the Hospital?'

'Yeah, Doc. I can do that,' Dave said with a nod.

Alice never envisaged her little prank would land her in hospital. When the ambulance arrived, she was hostile toward the young paramedics. Dr. Flint took them aside and gave them a letter for the ED doctors, as well as a lengthy verbal handover, which included her underlying heart condition and more. On completion, they loaded her onto a stretcher and attached their ECG machine, blood pressure cuff and pulse oximeter. They tried their best to console her, but it seemed the kinder they were to her, the more she grumbled.

'I didn't even get to eat the last piece of pav!' she complained loud enough for June to hear. June sighed. She couldn't believe the pav had lasted six days around Dave! She would make her another one. *What if it happens again—she drops another knife through her other foot.* Meringues, she decided, would be a safer option. She wouldn't have to cut them. June followed the stretcher as the paramedics wheeled their patient down the corridor, through the surgery's rear exit doors and into the car park.

'I'll make you some meringues when you get out of the hospital, Alice,' June said, thoughtfully.

'That would be lovely, Dear,' Alice replied with a sudden smile. *Then you'd have to come to the house to see my Dave.* The paramedics closed the rear doors of the ambulance. 'I'll see you at the house—soon,' Alice yelled from within the vehicle. When the ambulance disappeared around the corner, no lights and sirens required, June closed the doors and headed back toward the treatment room. Dave was at reception settling the account. He waved to her, and she waved back. Then he left for his farm. He had a bag to pack—and deliver.

***

Dave sat next to Alice in the ED.

'Penny for your thoughts, Love?' she asked him. He rubbed his chin and looked at her.

'I'm concerned about you, Gran,' he replied. 'First, you fall on our perfectly flat front path, and now you drop a knife through your foot.'

'Oh, I'm just getting old and clumsy,' she insisted.

'I won't take that as an answer.' Dave's voice was firm— she'd never seen him this way. She sat in silence and avoided eye contact with him until he leant forward and took her hand. 'Why did you take my biggest, sharpest knife—the one I use for meat— to the fridge?'

'To cut the pav,' Alice insisted. 'I told you that!'

'There was only one piece left, Gran—it didn't need cutting.' He patiently waited for an answer.

'Yes, I suppose.' Alice feared he would see through her plan, but before he could ask her another question, the nurse came in. Alice sighed with relief.

'I see you've got your hospital bag ready, Mrs. Andersen,' she said, turning to Dave. 'The ambulance is about ready to take your grandmother down to Cairns,' she advised. Alice was not happy to hear the news. 'You could be down there between one and three days, Alice. It depends on what damage has been done to your foot.' Alice dropped her head. *Bugger.* She hated the city. Dave stood, leant over Alice, and kissed her on the cheek.

'I'll ring you tonight, Gran. Find out what's happening and how long you'll be in the hospital for,' he said.

'Thank you, Sweetheart.' Dave left Alice in the care of the nurses and walked to his car. Something bothered him. She was usually sure-footed with her wheelie walker, and she'd never used his large meat knife before. He kept that knife well out of the way. She would've had to search for it. On the drive back to his farm, he felt a sense of unease. Something didn't add up.

The first thing Dave did when he arrived home was check the footage on the front security camera. He quickly found what he had feared. Alice was meandering without difficulty along the front path, pushing her wheeled walker. She stopped a while and seemed to look around as if expecting something or someone. She waited and didn't move for a few minutes. Then she suddenly threw her wheeled walker out in front of her then threw herself recklessly onto the path. She examined her shins and then hit them a few times with a small rock. Dave's eyes widened and his jaw dropped. Moments after, his ute appeared on the footage, coming up the driveway.

'I knew it!' Dave snapped. He was angry. 'You waited until you could see me nearing the driveway, then you threw yourself down and beat yourself up,' he said aloud. 'You didn't fall. The question is, why? Why are you self-harming?'

Chapter 34

It's Called Dave's Place
Week 2—Saturday Morning

It was Saturday. June woke just before her daily 4:01 a.m. alarm clock rang out. She had a name for him now—Russell Crow. Somehow, it felt far less bothersome to be woken by Russell Crow, than a simple rooster.

After coffee and a lie-in, and with the sun now up, she made her way outdoors. The sky was clear, the air felt less humid than it had been, and she felt alive, like every part of her was smiling.

In the oversized boots, June wandered—plod-clomp, plod-clomp—across the lawn. She was grateful she no longer had to shovel Winston's manure off it, and relieved she didn't have to tackle The Beast and mow it on her day off.

After opening the gate and hanging out the bucket of soaked, cracked corn for the adult turkeys, she slipped her hand into the door of the Schoolyard and delivered the poults their morning crumble. She gave them five minutes to devour it, then released them. Their eagerness to wander with their mother grew daily—almost as much as they did. She admired their brown stripes and laughed at the way they ducked and weaved around each other. She wondered if they were destined for the Woodwards' freezer. There were still 12 living poults—a lot of turkey meat if they all grew to adulthood. The adult turkeys seemed to take no notice of the poults, and why would they, she thought—they had a paddock of papaya trees to fertilise and scratch around in. June was now feeling comfortable in their presence, and they seemed to sense that her confidence had grown—they showed respect and gave her space.

Wilbur raced excitedly to his gate—he did each time he heard her voice—a head rub was now an expectation. He was an affectionate pig, and it was obvious that he'd been hand-raised. She was growing fond of seeing him every day.

With an old bucket and a shovel from the tool shed, she cleaned his pen. Next, she changed the sugar cane mulch in the Schoolyard and wheelbarrowed both the pig manure and the soiled mulch to the vegetable garden, dumping it in a pile. *This is going to be terrific fertiliser.* She explored the garden—weeds were creeping in. *The Woodwards will be busy when they get back.* She didn't have time for weeds.

The dogs had grown increasingly fond of their house sitter. When she first arrived, they showed little interest in what she did or where she went. Now, they left the comfort of their beds each time she ventured out, eager to know what she was doing and whether it involved food. They seemed to enjoy her company, and she enjoyed theirs. When she walked, they walked. When she stopped, they stopped. And when she sat down, they sat down. It appeared they'd become competitive too, vying for pats.

'This glorious day belongs to me,' she said, aloud, and glanced at Daisy. 'So long as you don't go into premature labour, my dear Tank.' She hoped that at some stage, she'd catch up with Dave. They hadn't spoken privately since they'd slept together. She wondered if he regretted his decision. She thought about his body; the reflection gave her goosebumps and drew a naughty smile. Her body was still coming to terms with the way he made her feel—womanly, sexy, and wanted. *Shame—there's never a happy ending.*

The best thing about June's morning was Mrs. Little. Yesterday morning, she had lifted her out of the nest box and placed her underneath the Penthouse—near food and water— for the day. When she arrived home, the chicken hadn't moved. This morning, when she lifted her out and placed her on the ground, she hobbled using her splinted leg—albeit only a short distance. The splint looked a little dirty but was intact, and most importantly, dry. June was chuffed.

'We'll change it each week for you, Mrs. Little,' she said. 'Nurse Woodward can take over when she gets back. That okay with you?' The chicken took no notice.

As June made her way back to the house, she spotted Dave's ute coming up the driveway. It seemed he always caught her with eggs in hand. She headed over to greet him. His timing was excellent, having just finished her rounds. He pulled up, turned off the engine, and got out of the vehicle. Before words could be exchanged, he leant down and kissed her. It wasn't like the passionate kiss he'd given her the other night; it was a greeting kiss. June noted it. She could feel him treading carefully now, unsure of where they stood.

'How's Alice?' she asked.

'Fine,' he started. 'Her foot wasn't too bad, apparently— no sliced tendons. They've stitched it up. I can bring her home this afternoon,' he said, sounding nonchalant. 'However,' a shadow of seriousness crossed his face. 'She's been a naughty girl.'

'Naughty?' June wasn't sure what he meant. 'In what way?'

'Well,' he began. 'I looked back through my security footage to the day she had her fall—it shows the front of the house. It appears she waited until I turned off Arthur Willis Road and into the driveway, then threw both her walker and herself onto the path—very dramatically—and we all know concrete's unforgiving on frail skin.'

'Why on earth would she do that?' June was dumbfounded.

'That's not the half of it—she sits there surveying the damage, which mustn't have been as bad as she'd hoped for, then picks up a garden rock and smashes it on both of her shins… more than once!' June gasped. 'And there's more,' he added.

'There's more?' June repeated. 'What else?'

'The knife wasn't an accident, either.'

'*Nooo!*' June's eyebrows shot up in surprise. 'No one stabs themselves in the foot on purpose.'

'Perhaps they do,' he continued. 'It can't have been an accident, June,' he said, frowning. 'I was wondering about her sudden carelessness, and I'd even considered dementia.'

'That's a possibility,' June said.

'She has *never* used my carving knife. It's a big-arse knife—heavy, too. I couldn't figure out why she'd bypass all the other knives in the drawer to hunt down *my* knife and then carry it to the fridge.' June listened intently. 'There was only one *teeny tiny* piece of pavlova left, June—not enough to warrant cutting at all. Anyway… I confronted her.'

'You did?' June was shocked. 'What are you trying to say?'

'I think she's self-harming, so you're forced to visit each day. She's always trying to play cupid, but this takes it to a whole new level.'

'*Wow?*' June said and thought about it for a few moments. 'But to stab herself in the foot! Surely that's a bit extreme.'

'It is,' Dave agreed. 'But think about it from her angle: get knife… cut pav… drop knife… accident… wounds… dressings… Nurse June's locked into visits again! Her thoughts would've been set on making it all look accidental, she wouldn't have even considered that I might question the knife she used, or the fact that one tiny piece of leftover pav didn't warrant cutting.' Dave's vivid scenario played out in June's mind like a reel of snapshots. It would've been funny—if it hadn't felt so desperate and sad. 'She's well aware I'm onto her meddling ways—that's what makes her clever little heart so cunning!'

'But she knows it can't work out—you and me. I've told her in no uncertain terms,' June said with a sigh. 'I'm in Adelaide and you're up here, but that's the bravest and most desperate thing I've ever heard a grandmother do.' She glanced at the eggs in her hand and then back at Dave. 'She must *really* love you.'

'Yep,' he agreed. 'And she must *really* like you. She's not done anything quite like this before, thank goodness.'

'It *is* extreme behaviour,' June said.

Dave sighed. Extreme behaviour it was, but it was also familiar behaviour. A heartfelt grin broke the serious look on his face—he'd had his rant. He knew deep down that his tenacity—equal parts grit and refusal to give up—had been passed down from his maddeningly persistent, endlessly loveable grandmother. It was her quiet kind of strength, and now it lived in him. Calmer, he remembered why he'd come to see the beautiful house sitter and locum nurse.

'Hey, I'm going down to Cairns to collect her this afternoon. I thought, if you were interested, we could go early. I could show you around?' June smiled widely.

'That sounds wonderful. I'll get myself ready. Give me ten minutes.'

'Ten it is,' Dave agreed. 'I'll run the ute back—swap it for the car. Three won't fit in the ute.' With a spring in his step, he jumped back into his work ute and headed home, while June readied herself. First, she had to hose the pig manure from the gumboots, then put the eggs in the fridge. She ducked in and out of the shower, threw on a set of matching underwear, a purple sundress, and a pair of sandals, and then cleaned her teeth and brushed her hair, securing it in a ponytail. In the kitchen, she filled her water bottle, grabbed her handbag and made her way across the deck, ready for both Dave and the sights of Cairns.

Dave pulled up—his timing always perfect. He knew when a woman needed 10 minutes, you gave them 20. She smiled at him as he approached. He lowered his window, returned a smile, and then raised his eyebrows appreciatively.

'You look as fresh as a daisy,' he commented. June noted he'd changed, too.

'Stop it, Mr. Andersen,' she said playfully. 'Keep that up and I'll think you want to stay over again.'

'Can I?' he grinned, cheekily. *I'd like to!*

'We'll see,' she said. She walked around the car and got into the passenger seat. *I'd like you to.* Dave turned the air-conditioner fan speed up a notch, then turned the car around and drove down the driveway. As they turned onto Arthur Willis Road, she asked a question. 'Why doesn't your place have a name and a sign like the others do around here?'

'It does,' he replied, glancing toward her. 'Have a name, that is.' June looked confused. She hadn't noticed a sign on the gate or on his house, for that matter. Dave accelerated, then looking ahead at the road, he said in a serious tone, 'It's called Dave's Place—*obviously.* Everybody knows I own it. I don't need a sign for that!'

Chapter 35

A Purple Dress with Yellow Gumboots
Week 2—Saturday Afternoon Begins

Dave drove through Millbrook and onto the highway. As he approached the top of the Gillies Range Road, he glanced at June.

'You okay with bends?' he asked.

'Sure,' June replied. 'I drove up this beast of a road the day I arrived.'

'It's the most winding road in Australia…' he explained. 'With an elevation change of around eight hundred metres…. Millbrook is over seven hundred metres above sea level, so we don't get the harsh humid heat of Cairns.'

'Oh,' June said, surprised. 'I'm finding it hot. You mean Cairns is even hotter?'

'Much,' Dave insisted. 'Stifling in summer.'

'I didn't take time to notice,' she said, thinking about the day she arrived. 'I landed, picked up my car, and stayed in front of the air conditioner until I reached Yungaburra, where I stopped for groceries.'

'Living up here in the mountains is nice, but you need to embrace this road if you want to get to the coast. It's the only way to Cairns.' He thought a moment. 'I guess you could travel down the Kuranda Range to the north of us or take the Palmerston to the south—both have fewer bends but are much further to travel.'

'How many bends are there on this road?' she asked.

'Two hundred and sixty-three,' he said. June gave him a sideways glance.

He offered her a mint and she took it.

'Thanks,' she said. 'I might need this.'

'The winding section of this road is nineteen kilometres long—that makes more than thirteen bends per kilometre.'

'Pass me an emesis bag now!' she said with a laugh. 'Seriously, it's all good. I'm usually fine with all that.'

'I'll take it easy—I always do,' he said thoughtfully. 'The views are spectacular—I never want to rush it.' June helped herself to another mint.

On their descent down the mountain and throughout their journey to Cairns, conversation remained mostly one-sided with Dave playing the perfect host and tour guide. He pointed out each surrounding mountain, its name, height, and rainfall, and discussed the early and modern history of both the road and the area. June found it all fascinating.

'You know a lot about this area,' she said.

'I've lived here for a long time,' he admitted. Finally, they reached the heart of Cairns.

'This city is so beautiful—so tropical.' Her eyes were wide, taking everything in. 'Having a progressive city so close to beautiful countryside and amazing drives is just wonderful.' She was in awe.

Dave pulled into an angled parking space—a lucky find, in the busyness of the street. It was nearing lunchtime, and something was going on. There were cars and people everywhere.

'I want to show you a neat little spot,' he said. 'I think you'll like it.' June left her water bottle in the car, taking only her handbag. As they left the car and crossed the road, he instinctively went to hold her hand but stopped himself. She didn't notice. They hadn't discussed the night of their lovemaking, and he didn't want to read more into it than there was.

'Follow me,' he insisted and made his way to a small van selling sugar cane juice. 'Two cups, please?' While they waited, he explained this was Rusty's Markets, a popular destination for both tourists and locals alike. June didn't need his explanation to see it was popular, for the crowd was thick.

With drinks in hand, they wandered about the stalls. 'This is amazing,' she said of the sugar cane juice.

'I get one every time I come here,' he told her, then gave his comment more thought. 'To be honest, I don't come here often at all—but I have had sugar cane juice many times.' June grinned at him. He returned the smile.

Dave explained the variety of tropical fruits on sale, and they tried as many as they could from sampling plates. She fell in love with the vibe. There were stallholders and customers from every corner of the globe.

After they'd seen all the stalls there were to see, Dave got lucky and snagged an empty table out the front of a busy coffee shop. He ordered two coffees at the counter before joining June at the table.

June studied the passers-by. Dave studied her feet.

'What size shoes do you take?' he asked.

'What sort of question is that?' she replied. She looked down at her feet in her sandals.

'Usually, a seven. Sometimes, an eight.' She glanced at him.

'What size are you?' Dave paused and raised his eyebrows. She grinned and shook her head playfully. He laughed.

'What size feet do you have, David Andersen?' she said, clarifying her question.

'Size eleven,' he answered. June thought nothing more of the question. 'I'm going to pop to the teller and get some cash out,' he said and stood up.

'I can pay for the coffee,' June insisted. 'After all, you're showing me around and you got the sugar cane juice.'

'It's fine—the coffees are paid for. I'll be back in two shakes of a lamb's tail.' June nodded. Dave disappeared around the corner while she waited at the table. She didn't mind the time out and focused on the myriad of languages that surrounded her. Finally, their coffees were delivered. The timing was perfect as Dave returned at the same time. He was carrying a white, cotton bag closed with a drawstring. He sat down, took a few sips of his coffee, and then placed his mug down. 'I bought you something.'

'Why?' June said, surprised. *I was thinking, that's a big bag of cash you were carrying!'* She sipped her coffee, then placed it back on the table, alongside her bag.

'Well, firstly, I wanted to, and secondly, it's to help you remember your time at Barrine Views.' He handed her the bag.

'You shouldn't have—what is it?' She loved surprises. She took the gift from him. 'You've already bought me a fabulous hamper, sugar cane juice and…' Dave cut her off.

'And nothing. These, you can use now, then keep them afterwards as a souvenir.' She opened the bag slowly but excitedly, peered in, and then giggled like a schoolgirl. She pulled one of two short gumboots out of the bag to examine it.

'Oh, Dave,' she said, admiring the bright yellow boot and its artwork of cartoon chickens. 'I love them so much!' She jumped up, skipped to his side of the table, bounced on the spot, and threw her arms around him, hugging him tight. He smiled widely, humoured by her enthusiasm and relieved she liked the gift.

'They'll be a lot more comfortable than flopping around in Doc Woodward's oversized ones, as you currently are.' June had forgotten herself in the moment—people on the surrounding tables were looking on with broad smiles. Grinning, she lifted the boot proudly to show it off. Everybody around them clapped, cheered, or gave her the thumbs up. She sat back down, her smile fixed.

'They're your size—well eights, better too big than too small—and the sales lady said they're super lightweight.' June studied them, lifting them up and down.

'They're real light… can I pay you for them, Dave?' she asked. He'd given her too much already.

'Absolutely not!' he exclaimed. 'They're a gift. Consider them to be from both me and Alice. After all, look at what you've done for her. Attending to her wounds every day, and baking a pavlova.' June dropped the boot in her lap and looked at him, gratitude in her eyes.

'Well, I adore them,' she conceded. 'Thank you from the bottom of my heart.' She removed her sandals and tried them on. 'They fit perfectly... can I wear them now?' she asked. Dave laughed.

'Absolutely! Anything goes in Cairns—even purple dresses and yellow gumboots.'

With their coffees finished, they made their way past shops and beyond the hustle and bustle of people to the esplanade. Dave showed off the lagoon swimming pool and the Pier, and they watched on as a group of tourists departed on a helicopter flight. They strolled past the marina—June was amazed by the variety of vessels. There were super-yachts, old boats people lived on permanently, and tourist boats that were, for whatever reason, not out on tour for the day. Finally, they came to the Harbour Hotel's waterfront bar and restaurant.

'Lunch?' Dave offered.

'Yes, but only if we go Dutch,' she insisted.

'Dutch it is,' he agreed. At the counter, June ordered salt and pepper squid and a glass of Moscato, while Dave went for a chicken parmigiana and a schooner of beer. They took the order number stand they'd been given and searched for a table. The restaurant lacked a breeze, so Dave chose a table with an umbrella in the middle of it. He put it up, and both were grateful for the shade. June pulled off her boots. As much as she loved them, her feet were hot. The softness of the grass felt like heaven on her feet.

When their meals arrived, they ate hungrily, sharing titbits from each other's plates, and conversing about all sorts of things. The food was delicious, and the conversation light-hearted. They ordered a second drink from the waiter, which was delivered with haste. By the end of the meal and with two drinks under their belts, both felt very relaxed. Dave poured them a glass of water from the carafe on the table, and they sat in silence, taking in the tropical view. After a few minutes, he cleared his throat.

'Can I ask you a question, June?' His voice was soft, yet direct. June looked at him, surprised.

'Of course,' she replied.

'Anything?' he added. June studied him for a moment. She was curious.

'Okay,' she agreed. 'Sure... anything is fine.' He reached across the table and took her hands in his. His face gave nothing away, but his gaze was penetrating.

'It's about the other night,' he whispered.

'Pardon?' she replied.

Chapter 36

I'd Like to Take You Upstairs
Week 2—Saturday Afternoon Rocks On

June leant in closer. *Did you say it's about the other night? I knew it—you're regretting it.*

Every nerve in Dave's body was on high alert—it had been that way since the night they'd made love. Just being near her, talking to her, left him simmering beneath his calm exterior. But this—being face-to-face with her in a hotel garden, with floors of empty beds above them—was a whole different beast. It made him feel as if his skin had been peeled back, exposing a raw, instinctive layer—a hunger he hadn't known he possessed. He wanted her—openly, and unapologetically—and the desire was no longer something he could ignore.

She waited patiently for him to repeat his question. He swallowed hard, the sound audible.

'I said, it's about the other night,' he repeated. This time his voice was confident and unmistakably clear. She nodded, her heart thudding nervously. 'I know you aren't planning to stay in Millbrook beyond your locum—and I get that. But the other night was special to me, June.'

She studied him. *So… you're not having regrets after all.* His calloused hands could fix fences, wrestle pet steers, and yes—slaughter cattle—but they'd also traced every curve of her body with surprising tenderness. His rugged good looks had probably broken hearts all over Millbrook, and his own heart had been broken along the way; now he was the one making *her* heart flutter—and nobody had ever done that, not even her fiancé. Dave was level-headed. Loyal. A man who'd put his grandmother before himself every time. And he was sharp, quick-witted, insightful, and unexpectedly articulate. He was the type of man who could discuss business and cattle one moment, and make you feel as though you were floating among the stars with him the next. It was everything—*he* was everything… She just wished his sparkling blue eyes didn't make her forget she was here for work and not for a Bunnings Boy.

To appear casual, she took a sip of her water, set the glass down, drew a long, steady breath, and released it slowly. She braced herself to reply. She needed to be in control, but she also needed to be honest. Their eyes met briefly.

'It was a special night for me, too, Dave,' she replied, and pulled her eyes away from his. *Breathe, June, breathe.* Every time she had reflected on their night together—and she had done many times—her thoughts raced, just as they were doing now. She wanted to run, but at the same time, she needed to fall back into his arms. *Stay grounded, June, stay grounded.*

Her eyes searched for a safe space—something to focus on other than his wanting eyes—and locked onto their hands. His thumbs were gently caressing the top of her knuckles. *Are you doing that knowingly, or subconsciously?* Either way, it was affecting her, and it made her shudder. She hoped he hadn't noticed. Even the views and people around them couldn't pull her eyes from his caress. She hoped her infatuation with Dave Andersen would pass, if that's what was happening to her.

Dave cleared his throat again, a habit he had when he was nervous, and that was rarely. Nothing fazed him on any normal day—nothing except the thought of June Hall. And this was not a normal day.

'Making love to you the other night, June, wasn't just casual sex for me.' June nodded. Her body was on high alert, driven by his touch, his deep sensual voice, and the nature of his words.

'Go on,' she prompted. She tensed with anticipation but didn't know why. He hesitated. Her eyes lifted from his hands in response to the pause in his conversation and stopped at his Adam's apple. She watched it move up and down with another nervous swallow. There was something sinfully attractive about the way his throat moved.

Dave hoped what he was about to propose wouldn't jeopardise their friendship. Something untamed stirred inside his stillness—intense feelings, raw desire—and it needed confronting.

'I know this might seem a little forward, June, but I'd very much like to make love to you again.' He watched for her reaction. He didn't want her to be apprehensive. He wanted her to want him just as much as he wanted her.

'Oh...' June replied. Her voice was velvety. She wasn't expecting him to be so forward, or her reaction to be so spontaneous. Her nipples pressed tight against the lacy cups of her bra. 'Do you... um... want to stay over again—tonight?' she asked, her eyes lifting to meet his gaze. 'Or... another night, perhaps?'

'No, June...' he said assertively. *So, you don't want to stay the night?*

'What do you want then?' she asked, not beating around the bush. 'A quick romp in the hay shed? A farewell bang?' Her voice held a mix of confusion and disappointment. She would have liked to be with him—he meant a lot to her now. *Say something.*

She wanted to pull her eyes from his but couldn't. While he sat frustratingly silent, his dilated pupils framed by striking blue irises told another story. He continued.

'June, I don't want to wait until tonight to be with you.' She didn't understand. 'I'd like to take you upstairs and make love to you now, in this very hotel—and not Dutch!' June drew in a long, slow breath then let it out.

'Oh...' She felt her jaw drop and hoped her reaction didn't make her look as shocked as she was. She'd been caught off guard—never had she received an offer like it—and didn't know how to respond. Here she was, in a waterfront restaurant full of lunch-goers, being propositioned. She felt a thrilling mix of excitement and exposure. Excited, anticipating what he'd do to her, and exposed as if she were naked at the table. Had anybody overheard him?

She sat still, body present, but her thoughts had drifted—she was no longer seeing what was in front of her.

...diners surrounding them had overheard Dave's words and were staring at the two of them. She was naked...

'June,' he prompted gently. 'Did you hear what I said?' June blinked. 'I'm dying here,' Dave whispered. He needed a response, and she wasn't giving him one. He prepared himself for rejection.

'What? oh,' she said. She glanced down at herself, then at the nearby tables. She was not naked, nor were the diners staring. *June Hall...* She returned to the here and now—she'd been daydreaming, or was it fantasising? She glared at Dave and noted a concerned look on his face. His proposition had not only affected her thoughts, but it had also sparked a visceral response.

'June,' Dave spoke again, this time he squeezed her hands gently. She'd never had a sexually orientated fantasy before. Now here she was, in a restaurant full of diners, doing just that. She succumbed to the ache in her body and the overwhelming need to be one with him again. She nodded, yes—without hesitation.

Dave jumped up with renewed enthusiasm. He picked up the cotton bag from under the table, pulled her sandals out and dropped them at her feet. Then he jammed the boots into the bag. Holding the bag in front of him, he waited while she fumbled with her sandals, eventually pulling them on. He eyed his glass of water and downed what was left. His throat felt raw and tight, and it had nothing to do with thirst.

June stood, picked up her handbag from the table and knocked her empty wine glass over in the process—it fell onto her empty plate, making a loud "ting" sound. Diners stopped and looked at her. *Shit!* She was flustered. They all turned back to what they were doing. Their frenzy to hurry upstairs was obvious to them, but not to the diners, it seemed. *Thank goodness.* She felt a pang of relief.

Dave took her hand and led her through the lobby. A sharp-dressed man of about forty stood behind the reception desk.

'Good afternoon,' he said. 'A room, Sir?' Dave cleared his throat, swallowed nervously and spoke as best he could, albeit in a husky tone.

'Double, please. King, if possible,' he said, making every effort to appear composed. He pulled his credit card from his wallet and waited.

Frazzled, June stared down at her toes and wiggled them in her sandals. A strap was twisted—they'd be off soon. She ignored it. Dave's toes twitched in his thongs—he was frazzled too.

While they waited, June wondered if the receptionist could sense their urgency, guess their intentions, or even smell the pheromones radiating from their skin. She felt naughty, Dave looked it. Did other people do this sort of thing, she wondered. Eat lunch and then run upstairs and work it off between the sheets? So, while Dave dealt with the receptionist, June studied couples heading in and out of the lift—their faces, their mannerisms—and decided they were not the only ones on a journey of passion.

'Our next available room—a king bed—will be ready in fifteen minutes, Sir.' The receptionist looked up from his computer screen, glanced over the top of his glasses at Dave and then nodded at June. 'Perhaps a cool beverage at the bar while you wait, Sir? I can send the concierge over with the key when your room is ready.' He gave Dave a registration card to sign. 'Will you need car parking, Sir?'

'No car parking,' Dave replied. His car was still parked by the markets. He signed the registration card and swiped his credit card across the EFTPOS machine.

'Perhaps luggage to store, Sir?'

'No luggage,' Dave advised.

'Will you require more than one night, Sir?' *Will you stop with all the questions, mate?* Dave knew this would be the longest fifteen minutes of his life.

'Is there a chance you will be staying on, Sir?

'No!' Dave said bluntly. *But you can bet your boots on it—I would if I could.*

'Very well, Sir. Enjoy your beverage.'

Dave jammed his credit card back into his wallet, grabbed June's hand and made a beeline for the bar. June noted the frustration on his face—she chuckled to herself.

Dave pulled out two stools and they sat down.

'Margarita?' he offered. June gave it thought.

'I've always wanted to try one,' she said. 'Yes—please.'

'Two Margaritas, thanks,' Dave advised the female bartender as she approached them.

'Artisan, Sir?' she asked.

'Please,' Dave agreed. June's ears pricked. *Artisan?* He sensed her interest. 'House-infused white tequila, triple sec, fresh lime juice and Fleur de Sel.'

'Fleur de Sel?' June asked.

'Fancy salt,' Dave answered.

'You know your cocktails,' June said, impressed. Dave's tension gave way to a snort. 'What's so funny?' He pointed to a blackboard. June read it. *Today's Special—Artisan Margarita, House-Infused White Tequila, Triple Sec, Fresh Lime Juice, Fleur de Sel.* 'Oh,' she giggled. 'And here I was thinking you were pretty sharp.'

'But I am,' Dave insisted. 'Beer and wine, sharp.'

June watched on with interest as the woman created their drinks. She was immaculately presented with graceful hands and manicured nails. *You won't be giving suppositories any time soon with nails like that!* Her skills were showcased in the way she flawlessly hand-crafted their margaritas. *I can mix an iron infusion with less drama.*

June wondered what her stoic face had seen at her bar: the types of people and the reasons they were there. She'd not considered it before, but the role of a bartender just might be like that of a nurse—dealing with people and problems while endeavouring not to become personally involved.

'Have you ever considered what type of person would sit at a bar like this? June asked. Dave nodded no.

'Lovers, the lonely, people checking in, people checking out, those trembling with excitement and desire.' Their eyes met.

'Us, then,' Dave said with a wink. June responded with a knowing smile.

'And where they would come from—international travellers, domestic holidaymakers, local farmers and nurses on a promise.'

'Again—like us,' Dave grinned wickedly. The bartender placed the cocktails in front of them. Dave handed her cash.

'Keep the change,' he said. They both took a sip.

'Very nice,' June nodded and licked her lips. Dave froze, the movement of her tongue savouring the Margarita almost too much to bear with hypervigilant senses.

'You can't go wrong with a Margarita—Artisan or House,' he insisted. June continued her reflection.

'Just imagine how many tears have been shed at this bar alone,' she said. 'Tears of laughter and sorrow. The quarrels started and finished, apologies made and accepted, promises made and broken, hearts mended and shattered. I've never thought of it before—there are one million reasons someone might sit at a bar...'

Dave downed his margarita, always in awe of the different ways the male and female brains worked. Here he was, struggling to sit still, just trying to survive fifteen minutes that felt more like fifteen hours, waiting for a room. And here she was, babbling on about the ways of the world from the perspective of a small bar in a hotel lobby. He stood, pressed his mouth to hers, and kissed her with an intensity that left her speechless. Dave had seen the concierge headed toward him with the key. He put his hand out mid-kiss, and without June realising, took charge of the room key and slipped it in his pocket.

'And now it's my turn to talk, June Hall,' he said. June's head was spinning from the kiss. His mouth moved to her ear, and he whispered into it. 'Regarding this bar and these bar stools, there are two people here that like each other very much, have just acquired a room key, and are heading upstairs right now.' June released a long, slow breath.

'Have they now?' she said, her tone smoky and teasing. Dave quirked a smile, the confirmation clear in his eyes. He took her hand and tugged it. She slipped off the bar stool and her dangling feet connected with the floor.

Hand in hand, June carrying her handbag, Dave the cotton bag of boots, they became a number entering a hotel lift.

Chapter 37

Help Me Find My Hair Tie
Week 2—Saturday Afternoon Rocks On and On

Fumbling with the key, Dave opened the door, and they stumbled inside. The room was spacious and carried a faint scent of citrus and clean linen. They took turns freshening up—Dave went first. When June emerged from the bathroom—blonde ponytail swinging as she walked—she wore only a towel wrapped discreetly around her. She saw him out on the balcony. He wore only a towel slung low around his hips and beckoned her over.

'What a view,' she said, stepping out through open double doors and into the breeze. He turned to her with a mischievous grin.

'You mean me, or that?' He swept an arm toward the view.

'Both,' she replied with a soft smile. She admired him before shifting her eyes to the panorama beyond. The scenery was breathtaking, but so was he, just as he'd looked the first time she saw him in nothing but a towel. Now she knew what lay beneath the dark trail of hair that ran south from his navel—and it was a vision that lingered in her dreams. This time, she wasn't nervous.

'That's East Trinity,' he said, gesturing to the mountains on their right. 'Port Douglas is about an hour that way.' He pointed again, and together they stood, silently taking in the glittering sprawl of the harbour, marina, and city below. The sky was clear and the humidity high, but the breeze cooled her skin, and she appreciated it.

'Funny,' she murmured. 'There wasn't a breeze down at ground level.'

Dave moved in behind her, his arms wrapping firmly around her waist. He pressed a kiss to the curve of her neck, and she instinctively tilted her head back into him, eyes fluttering shut. His hands moved gently upward, smoothing over her shoulders and collarbone, and melting away all tension.

She reached behind her, tugged his towel loose, and flicked it playfully to the side—it landed in a heap across the sunlounge. With a mischievous grin, he returned the favour, whisking her towel away and letting it fall over a nearby chair. She turned to face him fully and then pulled out her hair tie. He stood and watched appreciatively as her blonde locks fell around her face, across her breasts and down her back. She handed him the hair tie. He took it, spun around, shot it back inside, hit the fan, and then watched it fall onto the bed. Now, not a stitch of fabric remained between them.

On the top floor of the hotel, in the open air of their private balcony—and later, between crisp, starched king sheets adorned with a single rose—Dave and June came together with aching intensity. Their need for one another was insatiable until, finally, breathless and tangled, they surrendered to the quiet stillness of each other.

Spooning, Dave's now calm breaths teased June's hair. She gazed dreamily out through the balustrade and watched reflections of sunlight dance across the harbour water, flickering like stars scattered across the sky. She'd never felt so perfectly content—until a quiet melancholy stirred. *All good things must come to an end.*

Their lovemaking had been fierce, tender, unforgettable. She was completely spent, body humming, nerves singing. Dave's hand began to wander again—slow and lazy—and she glanced at the bedside clock.

'I suppose we should be thinking about Alice now,' she said softly.

'Righto,' he groaned, flopping onto his back. 'If that's not a passion killer, I don't know what is.'

'We have to pick her up,' she said, rolling to face him. He reached over and gave her bottom a cheeky slap.

'Stop it,' she giggled, swatting his hand.

'If Gran knew what we were up to, she'd probably volunteer to stay in hospital another week,' he said with a laugh, gathering her close.

'It's after four—we need to find our way back to the car, pick her up, and head home. Plus, I've got animals to feed,' she added, though the truth was, she didn't want to leave. She'd stay the night if she could.

'There's no Winston. The pig's already fat, the dogs won't starve, the turkeys will roost, the chickens will head into the Penthouse on their own, and the mother turkey will either take her poults into the Schoolyard or put them underneath her on the ground,' he said. 'So, there you go—we can stay.' June burst out laughing.

'That's a terrible sales pitch, Mr. Andersen. And you're forgetting Mrs. Little—and Alice.'

'I can euthanise Mrs. Little,' he said with a deadpan face. June stared at him, horrified.

'And Alice?' she asked.

'I could always euthanise her too,' he joked, laughing as she smacked his chest.

'You're awful,' she said, though she was smiling.

'You're right. We do have to get going,' he sighed, his tone dropping to that of a boy being made to clean his room.

June disappeared into the bathroom. Dave sat up, grabbed a complimentary bottle of water from the minibar, and downed the lot. Then he pulled on his jeans, stepped out onto the balcony and stared at the world—but he saw nothing. His thoughts were many, but one bothered him the most—he would have to let this woman go. In just two weeks, she'd become a wonderful friend, a passionate lover, and the idea of not seeing her across the road at the Woodwards filled him with quiet dread. He had to be careful. The deeper he let himself fall, the harder it would be to say goodbye.

June stepped out, dressed and glowing. She wrapped her arms around him from behind.

'You took me to a hotel and seduced me, Mr. Andersen,' she said in mock reprimand.

'That I did, Miss. Hall. That I did.' He turned, looking into her eyes with quiet satisfaction. She smiled at his mussed hair. 'But sadly, the time right now is officially Alice o'clock.' He pressed a kiss to her forehead, held her a beat longer, then reluctantly let go to pull on his shirt.

'Help me find my hair tie?' she asked. Together, they searched the bed, underneath it and around it, but it was nowhere to be found. She gave up and left her hair loose. She tidied it with her fingers, but Dave just mussed it again, making her laugh. She ruffled his hair right back.

After gathering their things, they headed downstairs to return the key. The same receptionist from earlier was still on duty. He looked at Dave's ruffled hair and then glanced at June's messy locks. She offered him a wide, unapologetic smile. He clearly knew what they'd been up to—and neither of them cared one bit.

Hand in hand, they made their way back to the car, stopping for ice cream along the way.

At the hospital, Alice beamed when she saw June beside Dave. When the orderly wheeled Alice to the pickup area, June took charge of her bag, discharge paperwork, and care instructions while Dave fetched the car.

'I don't have to dress this daily, Alice,' June said, reading the notes and relaying the information to her. 'It says to keep the wound dry and attend outpatients here in ten days for suture removal—prior if you have concerns. Dave will bring you down, I'm sure.' Alice dipped her head, disappointed. So much effort and pain to stick a knife in her foot—and the plan failed. June wouldn't be coming to the house, and she wouldn't be attending the surgery taking Dave to June.

When Dave pulled up, June insisted Alice ride up front, and with his help, she was settled comfortably. June climbed into the back, directly behind Dave.

While Alice snored most of the way home, their eyes met silently and often via the rear-view mirror. Words weren't needed—the gleam in his blue eyes and the satisfied glow in hers said everything.

Chapter 38

Dave Will Walk You Home
Week 2—Saturday Evening

June did her evening animal rounds at Barrine Views in her new yellow gumboots. A quick shower and she'd head over to Dave's house for dinner and a chat with Alice. Everything looked good at the Woodwards with the chooks, Mrs. Little, the turkeys, the poults, and Wilbur. On her way out the door, she picked up Doc's torch. She'd walk tonight, and with daylight already fading, she'd need it on her walk home.

Dave met her at the door and greeted her with a passionate kiss.

'I saw you walking up the driveway,' he admitted. 'I watched you—I couldn't help it.'

'I could feel the heat from your eyes, Superman,' June said, jokingly.

'Come in.' Dave held the door open for her to walk through. 'Alice is in the lounge room with her foot up.' June made her way in.

'Here she is, the knife-wielding pavlova bandit,' she joked. Alice returned a guilty smile, and then they made small talk while Dave prepared dinner.

'Here you go, Gran,' Dave brought in a tray of food and placed it on Alice's tray table—she needed to keep her leg elevated.

'Thank you, my Dear boy. What would I do without you?' She smiled at her grandson, and then at June. She was treading on eggshells—June could tell, and imagined the scolding that Dave would've given her, knowing she was self-harming to set them up.

June wasn't very hungry after their hotel lunch, so she was pleased to see Dave had prepared them a light meal—cold meat and salad. It was perfect. She didn't need any wine either—she'd had enough at lunchtime—but accepted the small glass Dave offered her. It was a pleasant, dry Riesling and hit the spot. She kept a glass of cold water on the side.

'Do you want some help at Paddock-to-Plate again, tomorrow?' she asked. Dave looked at her and smiled.

'You don't have to do that. I'll manage,' he said.

'Do you have the coach coming in again?'

'Actually… yes I do.' He'd almost forgotten.

'Then you'll need help. I'll come at midday.'

'Do I have a choice?' Dave asked with a smile.

'Nope. You can't cook and serve at the same time,' June continued. 'You're going to have to hire someone after I leave.' *After you leave.* He hated hearing the words, but it was the reality of their friendship. He was staying and she was going.

After small talk over dinner and a hilarious game of Scrabble with Alice, June felt tired.

'It's 9:00 p.m., and I'm exhausted from all the sightseeing today,' June admitted. Dave's lip lifted in a partial and naughty grin. 'I think I'll head home.' Dave jumped up.

'I'll drive you,' he said.

'I'm okay to walk. It's a beautiful night,' she insisted, but before she could say anything further, Alice piped up.

'Dave will walk you home,' she said, and turned to Dave. 'Won't you Dave?' He stood up—he could do with some fresh air.

'Of course,' he nodded and reached down to help June out of the bean bag she'd been sitting in.

'Do I have a choice?' she asked, laughing.

'Absolutely not,' Alice said, grinning.

'Will you be alright here, Gran?' Dave asked.

'Right as rain, love. Right as rain.' Alice hadn't expected to see June at the house, but she had come, and she was glowing. Alice knew they'd been playing bed tennis again. *Game, set, match—marriage next!*

The stars in the sky amazed June on every night that wasn't cloudy, and she was excited to be able to point out both the Southern Cross and the Saucepan now.

'You're doing well,' Dave said.

'Thank you, Mr. Andersen. I'm a good student.' They stopped at the bottom of the stairs to the Woodwards' deck. She wanted to invite him in, to snuggle up to him naked all night, but she knew he needed to get back to Alice, and she needed to get some sleep. 'Well, goodnight,' she smiled. He pulled her close and kissed her, albeit briefly.

'Goodnight, June. I *really* enjoyed today.'

'Me too—it was a lovely day. Thank you for showing me around—goodnight.' Without hesitation, she turned and walked up the stairs and across the deck. She acknowledged the dogs, then disappeared inside. Dave watched the kitchen light come on, then finally turned to walk home. If it was this hard to say goodnight after one full day together, how would he say goodbye to her in two weeks, when she left to return to Adelaide?

From the glass door of the dining room, June watched the light from Dave's torch as he made his way down the Woodwards' driveway, across Arthur Willis Road, and then home on the opposite hill. When the light disappeared—a sign he'd gone inside—tears ran down her cheeks. Why did she feel she couldn't live without him? She had to leave in two weeks and needed to step back. She couldn't have a relationship from three thousand kilometres away—even the thought of it was absurd. She was angry at herself for letting her guard down, for becoming infatuated with him. From tomorrow, she promised herself, she'd pull back. Friends only—and no more hanky panky in hotel rooms.

Chapter 39

Nailing It

Week 3—Sunday Afternoon

Sunday's Paddock-to-Plate was much busier than the week before, and June wasn't surprised by the turnout. The sun had been out all day, and a beautiful breeze swept across the hills—it was perfect weather.

She was busy and happy about it—it limited her time with Dave. Dave had noted a lack of eye contact between them and put it down to the pace they were working. They'd served 126 meals in just two hours. After the final patrons left, they got straight into cleaning up and had the job done in no time at all.

'Fancy a swim in the creek?' Dave asked. 'Lovely day for it.' June thought about it—it was indeed a lovely day for a swim. She remembered her skinny dip last Sunday—watching the fish swim, enjoying the bird calls, and the way he bashfully covered his eyes on seeing her naked from the waist up.

Things had become complex now. *Are you chasing a skinny dip today, Dave Andersen?* She thought about the hotel, returning to Adelaide, and not getting hurt. *Don't make it any harder. Just pull back.*

'Not today,' she said. Disappointment crossed Dave's face.

'A few drinks back at your place, then?' he suggested. She shook her head to say no. He looked bewildered.

'I have a few things to do this afternoon—raincheck?' Dave paused, his face shifting—rejection, disappointment, understanding.

'Raincheck,' he agreed, nodding with a forced smile. He would miss her company.

Sunday afternoon saw June catch up on washing, cleaning, preparing for the working week and more animal rounds—starting with Wilbur's pen.

'There she blows!' June let out a squeal and then laughter, as water came gushing out of the hose faster than intended. She soaked herself—and consequently splattered manure and mud over both herself and Wilbur. She didn't mind the drenching, but the stench? That she could live without. Wilbur, meanwhile, was in hog heaven.

When June first arrived at Barrine Views, she gagged at the smell of all animal manure—Wilbur's, by far, affected her most. Now, she didn't bat an eyelid. Not that she'd learnt to like it, she'd just learnt to tolerate it.

Wilbur's pen was cleaned thoroughly and with great pride. June scrubbed his water trough, refilled it, scratched his ears more times than she could count—thanks to his continual headbutting for her affection—and even picked him some overripe vegetables going to waste in the vegetable patch. She'd never grown anything edible before and made a vow that one day, if she ever had a yard and space, she'd give it a go. Besides, if growing food were as fun and therapeutic as hanging out and talking to a blind pig, it would be right up her alley—Wilbur had been privy to her most intimate thoughts regarding Dave Andersen.

Her next task tugged at her heart—a chicken with a broken leg.

'You're a trooper, Mrs. Little,' she said softly, cradling the wounded chicken in her arms. She'd picked her up and brought her back to the house. 'We need to check your leg, see how it's healing and re-splint it.' The chicken blinked, unimpressed but obliging—a patient putting up with an overenthusiastic nurse. She'd been hobbling around but looking comfortable. The thought of her little feathered friend being in pain drove June to heal her. 'We're not calling helpful Mr. Andersen today. It's just you and me, and we've got this.'

In the kitchen, she wrapped her patient securely in the old towel—just as you would a baby—all the while talking calmly to her. She couldn't flap her wings, stand up, or move. June set her down on the bench next to the splints and bandages she'd prepared earlier. Gingerly, she removed the existing splint.

'Aw… look at that, Mrs. L. Your leg looks beautiful—and so straight.' June was thrilled, the chicken—not so much, although she didn't appear scared and tolerated the poking and prodding well. It was almost as if she understood that this human was trying to help her.

While pleased with the straightness of her leg, June knew it needed time to knit properly, and for the bone to gain strength. She took the two fresh padded splints and taped them in place, then rebandaged the leg.

'You're a pocket rocket, Mrs. Little,' she said. 'And you're going to be just fine. You'll have to wear this splint for a few more weeks, I'm afraid, but then there'll be no stopping you.'

June returned her to the Penthouse grounds. The chicken didn't fuss—she hobbled straight to the feeder and began happily pecking at the seed. June was chuffed; her splint was working beautifully. *And I did it myself.* It wasn't the bandaging that had daunted her—it was the idea of holding a flapping, live chicken while she did it. The towel trick had worked a treat—she was no longer scared to pick up a chicken, or any other bird for that matter.

June returned to the house. In the glass sliding door that led from the deck to the dining room, she caught her reflection and stopped. A woman with comical yellow boots, soggy, mud-splattered clothes and mussed hair looked back. She turned her head slightly. *Is that a feather?* She plucked it from her hair and tossed it over her shoulder. *You're not just surviving this locum and menagerie, June Hall. You're nailing it.*

She headed inside and cleaned up the mess. She'd have to redo Mrs. Little's splint again before she left, but after that, she'd hand the job over without worry. *Nurse Woodward will handle it. I've no qualms about that.*

Chapter 40

Penthrox

Week 3—Monday

Monday morning started with the nail bed ablation of a big toe—having any amount of toenail removed was painful. June fetched the dressing trolley, opened a sterile pack on top of it, and set everything up ready for Dr. Flint's procedure. She needed a syringe of local anaesthetic, mosquito forceps, scissors, phenol to destroy the nail bed and prevent regrowth, and a saline flush.

The patient was a burly bloke who boasted, "I can handle pain" and "I'm tough as nails". June caught the flicker of panic in his eyes when he spotted the syringe and needle containing the local anaesthetic. She discreetly grabbed an emesis bag and kept it close in case he vomited, then in a soft voice, she talked him into a state of calm.

'Anything on a digit is somewhat painful, Eric,' she advised him. She'd learnt long ago not to hold the hand of someone in pain. If she did, she risked a crush fracture to her petite hands, and she'd had close calls before. Her alternative was a flexible, plastic Barbie Doll. 'Hold this,' she said, pushing the doll into his hand and wrapping his fingers around it. He gave both June and the Barbie, a strange look. 'If you experience pain, think of someone you don't like and squeeze—works a treat.'

Dr. Flint arrived in the treatment room, scrubbed up, took a seat on the stool at the foot of the bed, and got down to business. After light-hearted small talk about the weather, he started inserting the needle into the top of Eric's toe. Eric let out an almighty scream that filled the surgery, and in a reflex action, kicked his foot in the air. Flinty—not a stranger to the procedure—automatically moved his head to the side and avoided a connection with Eric's foot. It was a move as sharp as a professional boxer dodging a jab. He stopped and looked hard at his patient.

'I have a few of these to put in, Eric,' he explained. 'They're all going to hurt. Are you sure you're up for this?' Eric nodded; his knuckles white as he squeezed Barbie.

'I was just taken by surprise, Doc,' he insisted. 'That's all—honest.' Dr. Flint tried inserting the anaesthetic needle a second time but got the same response. He had always been prepared to dodge a rogue foot during a toenail procedure.

'Holy cow!' Eric screamed. The toe folds around his ingrown nail were red and inflamed and there was no doubt he'd benefit from the procedure.

'Your thoughts, Nurse June?' Dr. Flint asked, looking at June for inspiration. June turned to Eric.

'I can offer you some pain relief, Eric, but there is a cost—around fifty dollars.' Eric was instantly sold on the idea.

'I'll have it—two of them,' he said. 'I don't care about the cost.' June noted the big country lad was more a grazing steer than a fighting bull.

'It's called a Penthrox Inhaler and contains a non-narcotic drug called Methoxyflurane, Eric. It comes in a little green whistle that you suck on. It only works as you suck, so you'll need to keep sucking.' Eric nodded.

'I can do that,' he insisted eagerly. He was happy to give it a try. June prepared the inhaler and handed it to him. Eric started sucking long and hard and Dr. Flint started anesthetising the toe. It worked like a charm, although Eric still insisted on holding June's Barbie doll in his free hand, for comfort. So, while Eric sucked, Dr. Flint cut, and Nurse June supported. Within minutes, Eric's troublesome big toenail had been removed. Phenol was applied to the nail bed, and then it was flushed with saline. June jumped in and dressed the toe.

'That was great!' he commented. 'I didn't feel a thing!'

'That's the idea, Eric. But now I need to take that from you,' June reached for the whistle.

'But I was enjoying it!' Eric pulled it away from her.

'You can't keep it, and you can't drive until we know you're safe too. I need to keep an eye on you for half an hour. Seeing the serious look on her face, he begrudgingly handed it over. In the sharps container it went. While June watched the time and her patient, they chatted freely about country life.

'You like it so far—our country up here?' Eric asked.

'Yes—well, at least I'm learning to,' June replied. 'The tropical environment is *very* different to Adelaide's Mediterranean climate.' She paused. 'My work is the same, of course—people are people—but home life is something else.'

'I hear Doc Woodward has a menagerie going on,' he said.

'Yes... he sure has,' June replied with a smile. Pictures were floating around in her head that would never leave her.

'You takin' care of things, yourself?' he asked.

'Trying to,' she said. 'I started with no idea about anything, but I think I've got a handle on it all, now.'

'Good for you,' Eric nodded. 'Don't like the big smoke, m'self—traffic, people, all of that. You thinkin' o' stayin' on?'

'No. I go home in just under two weeks.' June suddenly felt melancholy.

'I know your neighbour,' Eric explained. 'Good mate o' mine.'

'Which one?' June asked curiously. She only knew two, Alice and Dave.

'Dave—Dave Andersen. You met him?'

'Yes, I have,' June replied. Eric nodded.

'Sad story that,' he said.

'Sad story?' June asked, intrigued.

'Bought that place of his just before he got married—near town so his lady would be happy, but like most city chicks, Millbrook wasn't big enough for her. Left him with a whole lot o' debt and on his first anniversary too—bit mean 'ay. But he's doin' good now. Got that Paddock lunch thingy happenin' at the ol' slaughterhouse. Seems to be a hit, too. Nice bloke our Dave.'

'Oh,' June nodded. Dave had mentioned his wife, albeit briefly. He hadn't said he'd struggled with debt—not that it was any of her business. June wondered what his wife was like and why she *really* left an all-around champion like Dave Andersen. *Why would anyone leave a man like that?*

'Hmm,' she muttered.

'What's that?' Eric asked. June looked at him, surprised. Her thoughts had left the building.

'Oh, nothing—just clearing my throat,' she lied. Was she leaving him, too? She'd paused to consider it and her mind started racing.

No... no... you're not leaving him, June, you've just had sex with him—that's all—a harmless fling! That's not an affair or a relationship—it's just a fling-thing, a one-night stand-thing! Well, maybe a two-night-stand-thing?

She considered whether Dave had become infatuated with her, as she might have with him. She doubted it. *Men don't fall that hard. It's just sex to them.* She was just a silly, young woman caught up in moments of youthful passion. They'd only known each other for two weeks. It felt like harmless fun they were having, but had she led him on? After all, she'd made the first move and dragged him to her bedroom. She wondered how he might feel when she left. She didn't want to hurt him—that was the last thing she wanted to do. She felt confused. She glanced at the clock on the wall.

'Your half-hour is up, Eric,' she said.

'Permission to leave, Captain?' he asked.

'Yes—permission granted. You can leave. Keep your toe dry for a day or two, and if you have any problems, let us know,' she explained. Eric made his way to reception to pay his bill—his words lingering long after he left the room.

'June,' Coral's voice grabbed her attention. 'We've another caravan step injury.' She had a woman with her. June nodded. She never saw people injuring themselves on caravan steps in the city, but out here in the country, things were a whole lot different. She'd seen a leech on an eyeball, numerous ticks on numerous body locations, injuries from rusty bits and pieces around people's properties, non-venomous snake bites, fishhooks in fingers and more.

June asked her to sit on one of the beds, and Coral returned to her office.

'Before I do, Dear, can you look at my backside? I landed hard on it,' she said.

'Sure,' June agreed, pulling the curtain around. The woman lifted her dress, slid her knickers part-way down and exposed her right butt cheek. 'Oh... wow... you did fall hard!' She had a deep, black bruise that covered her entire cheek. 'We'll get Doc to sight that. Meanwhile, can I look at that calf wound of yours?' The woman lay down on her stomach. June donned a pair of gloves and removed the dressing that the patient had placed around it.

'Oh. Mmm. I'm going to give it a clean, is that okay?' June asked. The woman nodded. June fetched her dressing trolley and opened a dressing pack on the top, popped some saline into the tray and cleaned the wound. 'I think you might need a suture or three in that. It's not big, but it has a bit of depth to it.'

'Oh dear,' the woman remarked, sounding worried.

'I'm not concerned about it—it'll fix up nicely,' she reassured her.

'Well... that's good news, I suppose,' the woman replied.

June then prepared a suture tray ready for Dr. Lee-Anne, who arrived within minutes. The doctor dealt with the wound first, suturing it with June's assistance. June placed a dressing over the sutures, and the doctor viewed the bruise, giving it the okay.

'Silly me falling down a caravan step,' the patient said.

'Oh, you're not alone. It's a regular thing here,' Dr. Lee-Anne explained. 'It's very common for travellers to slip on caravan steps and injure themselves, particularly those with aging skin. The older van steps had quite square corners—they're unforgiving. But I see the newer van steps have rounder edges to them—my parents have just bought one. Perhaps that's why they rounded the steps—fewer accidents. But that could just be a coincidence.'

'Our van *is* an older model,' the woman said. 'The step has square, sharp edges. I'll be holding the door frame when I step down, in future.' With her wound sutured and her buttocks given the all-clear by the doctor, the woman left, and June tidied up.

The rest of the day flew by.

'See you tomorrow, June,' Coral called out. She was finishing up in the office.

'Thanks for your help today, Coral. See you tomorrow,' June said. Today she would go straight home. She no longer had to visit Alice and tend her wounds. *I'll cook up a storm, that's what I'll do—something with eggs.* She noted how black the sky was and how sticky everything felt—the air, her skin. *Humidity. Looks like we're in for rain.* She climbed into her car and drove out of town.

Less than ten minutes later, June pulled into the Woodwards' shed. It was about to pour down—she could both see it and feel it. She ran to the deck, threw her bag inside, changed her work shoes for her boots and raced out for a quick round with the animals.

All was well at Barrine Views, it seemed, and June returned with *more* eggs. She'd no sooner gone inside than an enormous bolt of lightning lit up the dark grey sky. Seconds later, thunder exploded right above the house, shaking the ground. She jumped and swore. Perhaps she wouldn't have a cook-up tonight. The likelihood of a power outage was high.

She scrambled some eggs, ate them with toast, washed them down with hot chocolate, and then sat on the couch to watch the storm. She wasn't keen on storms, but she'd survive— what other choice was there? *A man to snuggle up with would be nice right about now.* She sighed. It was time to fetch her big girl pants—and wear them!

The rain was intense, smashing down on the roof iron with the sound of a freight train. It was even heavier than the last deluge. *Surely, this roof is about to collapse on top of me.* For a moment, she wondered whether anything was sheltering from it—inside the roof space—and shuddered. *Put that thought out of your mind, girl, or you'll never sleep.*

It rained and rained, and then it rained some more—cats, dogs, sheep *and* horses, as Alice would say. June's thoughts were with the turkeys who roosted in the trees. They didn't have the comfort of a purpose-built house like the chickens did. Wilbur had cover, as did the mother and poults, but she wondered how Winston and the other cattle were fairing out in the middle of a paddock.

She didn't bother turning on the television—she wouldn't hear it with the rain belting down. She took a cup of tea and a country lifestyle magazine from the Woodwards' bookcase to bed and found herself engrossed in the stories. The relentless sound of thunderous rain and the persistent partying of celebrating frogs proved both meditative and wearying. She drifted off to sleep—magazine still on her chest—and dreamt of a rugged farmer.

Chapter 41

Need a Lift?

Week 3—Tuesday Morning, June

June woke to her phone's 6:00 a.m. alarm. If Russell Crow had crowed, she didn't hear him over the sound of rain. She wondered how it was possible for the rain this morning to be even heavier than it was last night. The tin roof on Barrine Views echoed, making the bucketing rain sound as though cats, dogs, sheep and horses were inside the buckets that fell!

With a stretch and a sigh, June sat on the edge of the bed and looked out the window. It was grey, the ground was soddened, and the "View" in "Barrine Views" was non-existent. She could smell the damp—she loved the smell of rain, but the mustiness of indoors was not as pleasant. *Ring, phone. Please ring. Let it be Coral. Make her close the surgery for the day—pleeease.*

It seemed so dark. *We're on top of the mountains—we must be inside the clouds.* She had to do her animal rounds whether she liked it or not. *Procrastination is getting you nowhere, June Hall.* She stood before she fell back on the pillow and never got up again. She'd do her rounds in her pyjamas and take the umbrella. Nobody was going to see her running around in short pink pyjamas and yellow gumboots out here, especially in this weather.

She headed to the Penthouse.

'Don't look at me like that,' she insisted, the chickens glaring at her as if *she'd* made it rain. Mrs. Little was staying dry in a nest box. June double-checked that she could reach food and water.

When she got to the turkeys, they were lined up at the fence, waiting patiently as always. She opened the gate for them, then took the lid off their bucket of soaked, cracked corn. Today, they'd eat breakfast on flat ground. She would not be going near any slippery slopes. She opened the Schoolyard but neither Mum nor the poults were interested in venturing out. She gave them some crumble.

Wilbur was the only one who didn't seem bothered by the rain. He was enjoying the extra mud.

Back inside, June took a long, hot shower and dressed in shorts and T-shirt. Today, she'd pack her work clothes and change at work—it was possible she'd get soaked running to and from her car.

She had half an hour to spare. She made her bed, hung her pyjamas to air and downed a bowl of muesli. Her clothes, shoes and socks went inside a plastic bag before going into her work bag. *Better to be safe, than wet!* She'd head off sockless and in her gumboots.

She backed her car out of the shed. The heavy rain made the Hyundai i30 sound like an empty can under a running tap. Down the drive and onto Arthur Willis Road, she made her way cautiously toward Millbrook and the surgery. She struggled to see out of the windscreen, even with the wipers on their fastest setting. Suddenly, she came across a raging torrent of water across the road and braked hard. She'd crossed this causeway many times, always glancing at the markers trying to fathom why they were there. She'd never imagined a creek could just pop up like this but wasn't surprised given the rainfall overnight. Staring at the water, wishing it away, she knew it was too deep to risk driving the small hire car through. She contemplated how she'd get to work. She could walk the rest of the way to Millbrook. It wasn't that far and if she got wet it didn't matter—she'd packed her work clothes and even spare underwear.

Preparing herself, she rolled her shorts up as far as she could and readied her umbrella. Out of the car, she pressed the umbrella button—it opened with a *whoosh*. She grabbed her bag, slung the long strap across her body, shut the door, locked the car and threw the keys in her pocket.

At the water's edge, she kicked her boots off—she'd carry them across. She began wading barefoot through the water - boots in one hand and umbrella in the other. It was thigh-deep, and the current was strong. She could feel the sheer force of the flowing water pushing at her. She knew she could *not* lose her balance. If she did, she'd be swept downstream. She gripped the ground with her toes and ensured each step was secure. Midway across the causeway, and as she became level with the marker posts, she noted the water level continually rising. Second thoughts overcame her. In hindsight, this was not the brightest idea she'd ever had, but she ventured on. She would not let the surgery down. She reached the other side with great relief, and thanks to her umbrella—mostly dry—all but the hems of her shorts and she had a change of clothes so it didn't matter.

Exiting the water, she pulled on her boots and started along the muddy road. She made it to an intersection before a light truck, approaching from her left, tooted its horn and stopped. The driver lowered his window enough to keep the rain at bay and called out. 'Need a lift, June?' It was Eric, yesterday's nail bed ablation.

'Yes, please,' June shouted.

'I have to make two deliveries on the way though, so you may be a few minutes late.' June struggled to hear him over the noise of the rain on her umbrella. 'Hop in.' He leant across and pushed the passenger side door open for her. She ran around the front of the truck, folded her umbrella, and climbed up the two steps into the cab. She shut the door, pulled her bag from around her, and put it in the footwell along with the dripping umbrella. She turned to Eric with a smile.

'I don't think I'll get there any quicker by walking, Eric. Thank you.' Eric started off.

'No, thank you for getting me through my toe op. Who'd have thought a toe could hurt that much.'

'How does it feel, today?' she asked.

'Bonza. Just bonza,' he insisted.

Chapter 42

Well, It's Not Your Fairy Godmother
Week 3—Tuesday Morning, Dave

Dave set off toward town with several errands to run. At the bottom of his driveway, he glanced toward Barrine Views—not that he could see it through the wall of water hammering his ute—and thought of June. A smile tugged at his mouth as he pictured hauling her up from the muddy slope and hosing her down in the garden. *No matter what's thrown at you, June Hall, you tackle it with humour and grace.* June would be at work now—not great weather for going out or staying in.

This farmer's everyday life had unexpectedly become a tug-of-war between feelings. Rain or shine, night or day—it was all better with June around, and he wanted that. But entrepreneurial, practical, hard-working Dave didn't have the time or need for pulled heartstrings.

A few kilometres up the road, Dave slowed his ute and came to a halt. Parked on the side of the road near the causeway was June's car. He eyed the torrent of water rushing across. The depth marker read one metre. Dave knew this creek—knew it rose by the minute, strong enough to move an unweighted vehicle at thirty centimetres. It dropped as quickly as it surged, but after the deluge overnight, it would keep rising for hours yet.

June? Panic gripped him. She wasn't with her car, and he hadn't seen her walking back to the Woodwards'. He knew what time she left for work and would've passed her if she'd been on foot. He picked up his phone, called her number, lowered his window slightly and listened. Over the noise of the rain, he could just make out ringing inside her car. *She doesn't have it with her!* He couldn't see her anywhere and grew concerned. *Why doesn't she have her phone on her—I've told her how important it is?* Had she forgotten it? Left it there, unwilling to get it wet? Had she gone to check the water and been swept away? His heart sank. He dialled the surgery. Coral answered.

'No, Dave, June's not here. It's not like her. She's always early.' June hadn't shown for work, and it was nearing eight-thirty. 'Thank you, Coral,' he said and ended the call. Had she tried to walk across the causeway? The volume of water Dave was seeing would be enough to drag someone as slight as June off their feet and downstream. She wouldn't understand the force it had—she wasn't from the tropics. He turned off the ute's engine and made a call—he had to. A deep male voice answered.

'Millbrook Emergency Services, this is John.' Dave reported June missing at the Arthur Willis Road causeway. When he ended the call, he put on his hat and jumped out of his ute. He was already wearing his Driza-Bone coat. In the pouring rain, he peered through the window of her car—nothing. Then he started walking the north side creek bank in search of her. He called and called and heard nothing but the sound of rushing creek water and rain on his leather hat and coat.

It took about twenty minutes for help to arrive, and it came in the form of a fire truck with three volunteers on board. The men got out of the cab. They couldn't be missed in their fluoro raincoats and hats. Dave ran back to the causeway and stood on his side—the north side. The volunteers stood on the south side. One telephoned Dave.

'Dave, you're speaking with John. Tell me what's happening.' He had Dave's number from his earlier call for help. Dave struggled to hear him over the noise, but thought he recognised his voice.

'John Richards?' Dave asked.

'Yes, Dave. Sorry, we're catching up in these circumstances.'

'Ditto. Her name's June Hall. This is her hire car,' Dave said. 'I think she's tried to walk across. I rang her work—Millbrook Surgery, she's a locum nurse and hasn't made it to work. I'm worried she's been swept downstream. She's not from here. I haven't found signs of anything on this side.'

'How long ago would she have crossed?' John asked.

'She starts at eight—sometimes earlier,' Dave continued. 'Within the last hour.' The firemen talked briefly among themselves, then John put the phone back to his ear.

'You and I will follow the creek, Dave. The others are heading downstream to see if they can find anything.' Dave knew what he meant—to look for a body. *Dear God, please don't let it be.* Dave wasn't a religious man, but he didn't see the harm in asking for whatever help he could get.

Dave resumed his search along the north bank, while John moved parallel to him on the south side. June was petite, not strong, and he didn't know whether she could swim or not. When he'd seen her in the rock pool after Paddock-to-Plate, it had only been in waist-deep water. That was no indication of her water skills. He hadn't given it a thought until now.

With every heartbeat, fear and worry churned in Dave's gut, leaving him more nauseated by the minute.

They'd searched about three hundred metres of the creek's edge when Dave's phone rang. He pulled it from his coat pocket. *Millbrook Surgery… they'll be looking for June—what will I tell them?* He answered it on the third ring, holding it to his ear, under his hat, and out of the rain.

'Dave Andersen,' he answered, cautiously.

'Dave, it's June. You called….' She was going to say, "the surgery, looking for me," but instead, she got cut off by a suddenly excited Dave.

'June! June—is that *really* you?' It was her voice. A wave of relief washed over him. June was surprised at his tone.

'Well, it's not your fairy Godmother,' she said, confused.

'I'm at the causeway,' Dave explained. 'We're all looking for you.' Now she was even more confused.

'Why?' she asked.

'I thought you'd tried to walk across the causeway and been swept away.'

'I did walk across it, but I didn't get swept away. Eric, the delivery driver, picked me up. He was heading to Millbrook. He had deliveries on the way but dropped me off after them—I was late for work, but better that than never, as they say.'

June could hear the initial panic in Dave's voice fade. *You were worried about me, Mr. Andersen.*

'I'm fine—better than fine,' she said, trying to reassure him. Dave could've listened to her voice all day.

The thought of June drowning had shaken him. Had he doubted her ability to cross the causeway alone? Had he failed to trust her judgment about whether it was safe? Or had he simply panicked, knowing how fast the creek could rise? Maybe it wasn't fear or logic at all—maybe he just cared so deeply he couldn't bear the thought of losing her. He covered the phone with his hand, drew in a slow, steadying breath, and let it go.

'It's all good,' he yelled across the creek. 'She's at the surgery.' He was uncertain as to whether he'd been heard, so he gave a thumbs up. John nodded and returned the gesture. He understood.

'I've got to go, Dave. I have patients waiting. I'll talk to you soon.' She hung up the phone. *He thought I'd drowned. The realisation surprised her.* She returned to the treatment room, too busy to overthink Dave's conversation.

Dave watched John call through to his colleagues before they both made their way back along the creek and to the causeway. With a wave of thanks, Dave jumped in his ute to return home—the errands could wait. He knew the fire truck would be back at any moment for John—he'd call and thank them later. He turned on the radio and listened to the news. The weather report was for easing rain. Dave would have to give it a good few hours before he could drive into town, but the timing would be right to pick June up at five. She'd need a lift back to her car.

Chapter 43

Unwritten Rule Number 236
Week 3—Saturday morning

It was Saturday morning. Week three of June's locum had come to an end. Like the two before it, the week had flown. June had not seen Dave since he'd given her a lift back to her car the afternoon of the causeway fiasco.

She completed her animal rounds like a seasoned professional, then took time out to stand on the Woodwards' deck, soak up the sun and enjoy the views—she wouldn't have them for much longer. It had taken days for the ground to even start to dry up after the drenching they'd had early in the week. She now knew why they called Tropical North Queensland the "wet tropics," and the seasons, "wet" and "silly". *This humidity and damp would drive anyone barmy.*

'Lazy lot,' June said, eyeing the four dogs stretched out on the deck. It was hot, but they were enjoying a few minutes in the sun—just like she was.

'You're getting rounder by the minute, Tank,' she commented. The black Staffy gave a wag of her tail. June hoped she'd wait until after she left to give birth to her puppies. According to the vet's home visit notes left in the letterbox, that would be the case. She didn't need any more chaos in her life. Besides, she'd never delivered puppies and didn't want to have to call on Dave again. He'd done enough for her, and she still felt bad about the causeway episode. She never envisaged he'd call the emergency services. However, she'd learnt another "country lesson" from the experience—the dangers of both walking and driving through creeks and causeways. She wouldn't do it again.

Reflecting on the week, she had once again learnt a lot. Every day of every week was different at both the Woodwards' home, Barrine Views, and at their business, Millbrook Surgery. She loved the buzz in the treatment room and her patients were almost all happy-go-lucky people who were content with their lot in life. They weren't in a hurry like her city patients, and they weren't worried about time constraints, traffic lights, or parking fines. The whole surgery had an all-around friendly, yet professional, vibe to it.

The sound of a motorbike rattled in the distance. She could see Dave out in one of his paddocks, on his ATV. He appeared to be checking troughs or maybe fences. It made her think of Winston. He looked her way and even from a distance, spotted her on the deck, and waved. She waved back, then watched as he rode down the hill toward Arthur Willis Road and stopped at a gate. He dismounted the ATV, opened the gate, then jumped back on and drove through the opening. Once through, he dismounted again to close the gate. *No wonder you're fit, Dave Andersen.* It was a strict rule in the country—one she quickly learnt—to ensure that if you opened a gate, you closed it securely after you.

Dave rode along Arthur Willis Road and ventured up the driveway to Barrine Views. He pulled up, killed the engine and removed his helmet. *Even with helmet-hair, you're a picture.*

'Good morning, Miss. Hall,' he smiled. June reflected on last weekend and the Saturday they'd spent together, the hotel, the boots, lunch, Alice… Goosebumps tickled her, even standing in the sun.

'Good morning, Mr. Andersen,' she smiled. Her smile made Dave's day. He watched her as she stood on the deck, her long, blonde hair blowing gently in the mild breeze. Her shorts and t-shirt hugging her curves. He wanted so badly to hold her.

'Come for a ride,' he said, invitingly.

'Can't,' she declined. 'Don't have a helmet.'

Dave stepped off the ATV and lifted the lid of a box that was mounted on the back. He pulled out a helmet and held it out toward her.

'Voilá, Miss. Hall. I always come prepared.' June laughed.

'That you do, Mr. Andersen. That you do. Give me a minute.' She ran inside, threw on socks in the bedroom, downed half a glass of water in the kitchen, snatched up her sunglasses from the dining room table, and slipped into her chicken boots on the way to the ATV. She took the helmet from him and put it on her head. It was a little big but better than nothing. She fiddled with the strap.

'It's a bit tricky, that strap.' Dave reached for it, fiddled with it, and fastened it. They were eye to eye—June had missed their closeness. His eyes seemed bluer every time she saw him. She caught Dave's eye.

'Everything alright, Green Eyes?' he asked.

'Everything's fine, Blue Eyes,' she smiled.

'When you climb on, you'd better hang on tight—around my waist, it can get a little bumpy out there.' Dave threw his leg over the bike and seated himself comfortably, then it was June's turn. She stepped onto the rear passenger footrest and threw her leg over the seat between Dave and the utility box on the back. Dave gave her a moment. 'All set?' he asked.

'All set,' she answered. He started the engine. She wrapped her arms around his waist and held on tightly, just as he'd asked. He felt so good; warm, strong, and trustworthy. He felt like… home? Yes—home, and she didn't mind a bit. Her arms around him had made him draw a shaky breath—he hoped she didn't notice.

They set off down the driveway of Barrine Views and up the driveway of Dave's Place opposite. Dave stopped at a gate just beyond his house.

'Those not in the driver's seat, get the gate,' he explained.

'Oh… Okay….' June climbed off the ATV.

'It's the unwritten rule number 236, just after rule number 235, "do not walk through flooded causeways," and before rule number 237, "do not park under fruiting trees". Rule number 234 is "always keep your phone on you,"' he said, grinning mischievously. Her head was spinning with the barrage of rules.

'Well,' she sighed, remaining straight-faced. 'Perhaps if the rules were written—instead of remaining unwritten—people would be warned!' Dave laughed. He loved her quick wit and the banter between them.

While opening the gate, she admitted to herself that there was indeed a lot to learn about country life, and if she was going to learn more, she'd better get moving. She only had one week left in Millbrook.

After closing the gate, June got back on the bike. Dave rode fast, yet cautiously, across the paddocks—the ground bumpy and boggy after the rain. They splashed through puddles and succumbed to ruts, but the ATV handled it all without missing a beat. June lost count of how many times her bottom left the seat. They reached a hill and went, up, up and up some more until Dave brought the ATV to a standstill and turned off the engine.

'Hop off. I want to show you the view behind us,' he said. June jumped off the bike, and Dave followed. She turned around.

'Wow... now that's a view,' she remarked. The view was outstanding, and the greens were so vivid from the rain. Dave stood next to her and took her right hand in his left. She drew a sharp breath; it felt nice. With his right arm free, he gestured and pointed at landmark after landmark. He explained where the two crater lakes were, towns, and every interesting thing that ever was. June was in awe. 'It's truly beautiful, Dave.' There was silence around them, yet it wasn't silent at all. Cicadas buzzed and crickets trilled both near and far, cows mooed in distant paddocks, and birds sang—their calls unfamiliar to her. She listened intently. One bird sounded like a high-pitched whip, another like a child's squeaky swing. 'Thank you for bringing me here,' she said.

'The pleasure's mine,' he replied, and on that note, he turned to her, leant down, and kissed her long and hard. She was a drug, and he was addicted. The kiss took her breath away. 'I enjoy your company, June,' he said, pulling back.

'I gathered that,' she answered, slightly giddy from the kiss. A fire inside her that had smouldered all week had just had fuel poured over it. She ached for him so deeply it physically pained her. She needed to cool down—there were no hotel rooms out here.

'Plans tonight?' Dave asked, staring at the horizon north. *Don't do it, Andersen.*

'None,' June replied, staring south. He thought for a moment. *Don't say what you want to say—it'll only lead to trouble—don't do it!* But a lack of control where June was concerned came over him. He turned his head to her, and instinctively she turned to meet his gaze.

'Dinner and a movie at yours?' he suggested and then paused. 'Do the Woodwards' have Netflix?'

'Yes, they do,' she nodded.

'I'll bring dinner,' he offered.

'No, don't. I've been itching to use their country kitchen and have a cook-up. I've got the stuff to cook Thai, that's if you like Thai?'

'I love Thai—in fact, I love food.' Dave licked his lips in anticipation, and June stared. *Please don't do that.* She recalled the places those lips had kissed across her body. *Why are you impossible to refuse?*

'I'd better take you back,' he said, not looking happy about it. 'Alice will be wondering where I am.' He didn't look keen to go home.

'Alice would be thrilled to know you were with a woman,' June said.

'True, but I'd best not get her hopes up. She knows where we stand in our relationship. Friends—that's all.' He let go of her hand. June thought about what he'd said. *Friends with benefits.* She liked being his friend, but her body craved more. She blamed the country air. *Adelaide, roll out the red carpet, I'll be back in a week.*

Chapter 44

I Need a Guinea Pig
Week 3—Saturday Night

Dave arrived at 6:30 p.m.. June was unaware—too busy cooking. The dogs' barking alerted her, followed by the sound of his footsteps across the deck.

'Come on in,' she yelled. Dave appeared through the sliding door, a grin on his face and a bottle of wine in each hand.

'It smells amazing in here. I didn't think I was hungry, but suddenly, I'm ravenous.'

'Glad to hear it,' June said as she juggled pots, pans and dishes all over the kitchen. 'I've cooked enough for an army.' She glanced his way briefly, smiled, and returned to her busyness.

Dave put a bottle of white wine in the fridge and a bottle of red on the table.

'Didn't know which one you'd prefer with Thai,' he said. 'So, I brought both colours—red and white.'

'Thanks, Dave—I'm just about done.'

'What have we got?' he asked, trying to sneak a peek.

'Moo Satay, Som Tum and Khao Pad,' she replied. Dave roared with laughter.

'Moo and cow pads? Sounds like something from my paddock.' June turned and slapped him with the tea towel.

'This has less moo than your paddock.'

'I'm sure it does,' he chuckled. 'Can I pour you a glass of wine to go with your moo, Madam chef?' he asked.

'A white to start, thanks.' June put the last of her cooking dishes into the dishwasher. She'd pre-prepared everything. The Som Tum was in the fridge in a bowl. She'd even managed to pick a green papaya for it, fresh from one of the trees close to the house. The Moo Satay and Khao Pad were on serving dishes in the oven. She wiped the bench; everything was ready to serve when they felt like eating.

'Shall we take our drinks outside and enjoy the view for a bit? Dinner's ready to dish up anytime.' She turned the oven down to warm.

'Yeah, that'd be nice.' Dave poured two glasses of white wine and handed one to June. She took it and raised the glass.

'To the new friends I've made, and the new things I've experienced.' They clinked their glasses. Dave's face was unreadable.

'To new friends,' he added.

The temperature was twenty-six degrees according to the thermometer on the deck—a perfect tropical evening. Dave sat on the top step, and June joined him.

'Guess I'll be bringing Winston back soon,' he said softly.

'Don't rush,' she insisted with a pleading smile. 'Cleaning the dogs' muddy paw prints off the deck is enough without Winston's bowels joining the party.' Dave agreed with a nod.

'Daisy's looking bigger than last week,' he noted.

'Yes, she is. The vet doesn't think she'll go into labour until her due date or sometime after that. Especially being her first litter.' June lifted her free hand and crossed her fingers. 'I have my fingers and toes crossed he's right.'

'That's good news for you,' he said. 'Gets you off the hook.'

'Indeed,' she nodded.

Dave sipped his wine and gazed out at the paddocks and patches of rainforest that were Barrine at dusk. He was pleased with the way his place looked from the Woodwards. Until June had arrived, he'd only really come and gone, never stayed to enjoy the view.

'Guess you're looking forward to your return to Adelaide?' he said.

'Sure, but I've enjoyed the change. I've never lived so close to nature in my life, and I must say, it's been an eye-opener.'

She raised her eyebrows in fun. 'And that's the understatement of the year.'

'Have you enjoyed it?' he asked curiously.

'Not at first,' she admitted. 'But it's grown on me, and I got to taste the best eggs I've ever tasted in my life.' Dave agreed with her.

'Yeah, those caged, shop-bought ones are pale and have no taste in comparison.' *Eggs? Really?* He didn't want to talk about eggs. He didn't want to talk, full stop. He wanted to kiss her, and that was all he wanted to do. It took a whole load of self-control not to make a move. *Don't ruin a good friendship, Andersen.*

June looked at the sky. It wasn't quite dark, but stars were appearing.

'Southern Cross,' she said, pointing to it.

'Sure is… funny thought though… we may be thousands of kilometres away from each other next week and yet be looking at the Southern Cross at the same time.' When he realised how permanent that sounded, sadness slapped him across the face. *Thousands of kilometres away.* Reality told him that even a friendship was a stupid idea.

Next week is one week away—she wouldn't worry about that now. Dave Andersen would be a fleeting memory. She stepped back into the friend zone.

'Ready to eat?' she asked. He turned to face her.

'Absolutely.' He stood, took her hand to help her up, and they made their way into the kitchen.

'Can you please grab the bowl of Som Tum—that's green papaya salad—from the fridge? I'll get the hot stuff.' Dave opened the fridge, took out the bowl and carried it to the table. He noted June had gone to a lot of trouble with their place settings—glasses, nice crockery, cutlery, and flowers to the side. He recognised the flowers from the Woodwards' garden. June took the hot dishes from the oven and placed them, one at a time, on the table. All three delicious-looking dishes now sat between them. She added serving spoons.

'Help yourself,' she insisted. 'Guests first. Besides, I've never made Som Tum fresh before—I need a guinea pig!'

'I'm game,' Dave said, keenly.

Over dinner, they talked about plans for their futures. Dave wanted to grow high-quality beef and be renowned for it. He also wanted his Paddock-to-Plate venture to become busy enough to employ staff, which would allow him to concentrate on the business side of things. June would continue in her line of work but had no other real plans. She'd considered travel but decided she was more of a homebody. She admitted she'd like children at some stage, and Dave agreed that he would too.

The evening passed with banter and conversation flowing.

'What about our movie?' she asked.

'To be honest, I haven't felt the need to swap our conversation for a movie,' Dave replied. 'You're great company, June.'

'As are you, Dave Andersen.' Dave made a move to collect the dishes. June put her hand on his to stop him. He looked at her. 'The dishes can wait till morning,' she insisted. 'Come, sit on the couch with me—it's more comfortable.' He followed her, sat beside her, and then suddenly had nothing to talk about. The silence was momentarily awkward.

She placed her hand on his knee. Anticipation shot through him like a boot from an electric fence. She leant over and kissed him. It wasn't a passionate kiss—just a gentle pressing of the lips, and then she pulled away. He remained stilled.

'Thank you again for everything you've helped me with while I've been here,' she said.

'You're welcome,' he replied. His body felt like a taut wire ready to snap. *And your hand is still on my knee!*

'I mean it—cleaning my poopy car, removing the python from my dash—and the monsters in the roof space.'

Dave dug deep and mustered a caring smile, fighting off the one that betrayed how much he missed her already.

'All in a day's work,' he said, his smile still fixed.

'You took punches for me, helped me splint Mrs. Little's leg, and saved me from the causeway I didn't need saving from. Not to mention, buying me a hamper and kick-arse boots, feeding me, hauling me up from the turkey mudslide, delivering the Schoolyard, taking Winston for respite—you've done everything for me. So many things.' She paused. 'You've *really* made my stay here extra special. I haven't felt like I've been on a locum job, it's been more like a holiday abroad.'

Dave gave a nod, teeth clenched behind his smile. *Your hand is still on my knee.*

'I guess when you put it like that,' he said, her sweet kiss lingering on his lips. 'It's been a hoot.' She was irresistible, and that was her problem—or was it *his* problem? His lips itched, wanting to devour hers. Then he spoke out, awkward with his words.

'Thanks for everything, June—for helping with Alice, the pavs, the food… for being here. This community needs nurses like you. You're important—valued. Even the menagerie knows it,' he said.

June drew a breath in and smiled gently. Her eyes softened, sparked with grace. She was ready to speak her heart. *Dave, I'm thinking about staying in the area so we can explore this thing between us…* But he kept talking.

'I need to go home right now, June,' he said directly and clearly. She was taken aback. His caring smile became an expressionless face. He stood up. She followed suit. He took hold of her hands. She stilled.

'I can't do *this* anymore,' he said.

This? June was silent. Confused. *What are you saying?*

'I can't be *this* close to you, June Hall. It's killing me,' he said. His stare was steely—no softness, no surrender. His body wanted to hold her so badly—skin on skin again—but his heart had other ideas. He cleared his throat and swallowed hard. Undoubtedly, he'd miss her when she returned home, but if he stayed tonight, he risked more than that—he risked heartbreak.

June Hall had swept him off his feet in a way he'd never experienced—not even with his wife. He needed to go home and stay there. It was the only way. Her emerald-green eyes, as pure as truth, pleaded with him.

'We can go to the bedroom, if that's what you want?' she whispered. Her soft words boomed in his ears—his senses *always* hypervigilant around *her*. His body moved in close, but his heart took control—it would not be broken again. Without another word, he pulled his hands from hers, walked out through the sliding door, hurried across the deck and down the stairs, jumped into his ute, and left Barrine Views for what he intended to be the last time.

June was left wanting—rejected. Her chest ached with the hollow burn of heartache. The grief of lost love clawed at her throat. *Don't cry, June Hall, you're a grown woman.* Threatening tears stung her eyes; every moment she held them, a betrayal of her feelings. She latched the door for the night, ignored the mess, made a beeline for her bed, and fell onto it—tears and loneliness her only company.

Chapter 45

Shame vs Commitment

Week 4—Sunday Lunch through Friday Afternoon

'I didn't expect to see you,' Dave said, surprised when June walked in just before midday. They'd made plans last week—she was rostered on for the lunch shift at Paddock-to-Plate. The fact that he left abruptly last night changed nothing in her eyes.

Dave was still trying to work out why he'd walked out the way he did—so abruptly and dramatically—after she'd cooked him a wonderful dinner. It wasn't her—it was his will that was the problem. Shame forced him to lower his head.

June walked past him, dropped her bag in the kitchen, took an apron off the hook and put it on. He was right behind her. She turned to him.

'When I commit to something, I don't walk away. A commitment is a commitment—so I am here,' she said, her face neutral. A nod confirmed his appreciation and respect. *And that's a kick in the balls—Andersen. Well earned.*

Without another word, they got to work. Patrons pulled into the car park, just as the clock struck midday. Paddock-to-Plate was once again a hit, and June enjoyed the busyness. Dave wondered how he'd manage without her—he needed to hire someone pronto.

When the lunch guests had left and the place was cleaned up, Dave threw out an icebreaker, his voice laced with awkwardness.

'Swim?' he asked. 'Nice day for it.' Without hesitation, June declined, using preparation for the week ahead as her excuse. She was weaning herself from him; one memory, one habit, one hope at a time.

Monday came, and in addition to the usual workload at the surgery, a skin specialist from Cairns was visiting, performing skin checks. He stayed for both Monday and Tuesday and worked at one end of the treatment room. When it was necessary for questionable spots to be removed, June assisted with the procedures, which kept her on her toes. She'd done a small amount of skin work back home in Adelaide, but the tough skin of the northerners was something else, particularly on some of the old farmers who'd spent their lives outdoors and in the tropical sun. Some of the lesions removed resembled pieces of boot leather. June loved the surgical side of nursing and thought she'd like to do more in the future.

Finally, after a week of goodbyes, thank you goodies brought in by patients, and hugs from all who'd worked with her, Friday afternoon came—the day of June's departure—and, for her, it was bittersweet.

She finished work at 3:00 p.m., her flight was at 8:00 p.m.. She needed to do a last-minute check of the animals at Barrine Views, shower and change, collect the suitcase and carry-on bag she had mostly packed, and drive down the winding Gillies Range to the Cairns airport. She'd allowed plenty of time for it, preferring to be early rather than late.

All week, she'd avoided Dave Andersen. She hated goodbyes, and despite his rejection, still felt something for him—infatuation, possibly, but she knew a long-distance relationship wouldn't work. She'd move on, but she'd always reflect on their time together fondly. No goodbye was warranted.

Chapter 46

Yes—It's Squeaking
Week 4—Friday Late Afternoon

June parked her car as close to the deck as possible. Grabbing her handbag, she jumped out, climbed the stairs two steps at a time, and stopped at the top.

'Oh, shit!' she blurted. Daisy was on one of the dog beds, giving birth. '*Nooo,* you're not meant to do that yet,' she cried. She raced to the dog's side and dropped to her knees. *What am I going to do?* 'Oh, crap!'

She needed to leave soon. One reliable farmer instantly crossed her mind. *Dave!* Fumbling with her bag, she pulled out her phone, followed her finger to her contacts list, and pressed "Bunnings Boy".

'This is Dave,' he answered.

'Dave! Oh, Dave… thank goodness you've answered! It's Tank…'

'Is she alright?' he asked in a worried tone.

'I don't know… she's giving birth—like… NOW!'

'You're shittin' me? I'll be straight over…' Dave hung up. June slipped her phone into her pocket. Within minutes, he was by her side. 'How many so far?'

'Only one,' she said. 'Just this minute.'

'Is it breathing?' he asked.

'Yes—it's squeaking,' she replied.

'That's good… no, that's *great!* Do the Woodwards have any old towels?' he asked.

'Yes. There are some in the laundry,' she said, glancing at him. 'I used one for Mrs. Little—they're *definitely* old.' She stood, ready to help him with whatever he needed.

'Great! Grab them,' he said. June ran to the laundry, took the pile of old towels that were stacked up on the shelf and returned. A second pup had been born. 'We need to take each pup and rub it vigorously with a towel to get it breathing properly.' He handed June the newest pup. Adrenaline surged through her. She was nervous, but excited.

'Daisy will be alright, won't she?' June asked, her voice shaky. Dave smiled—she hadn't called the dog Tank.

'Calm down,' he said gently. 'This *is* nature—it's normal. You should try calving!' He focused on Daisy, though a pleasant memory of time spent in a hotel room crept into his head, forcing a cheeky, one-sided grin.

'Penny for your thoughts?' she asked curiously.

'This stuff *is* what our bits are made for,' he replied. 'They're not just for pleasure, you know.' She returned a guilty smile. There had been much pleasure in their time together. However, his light-hearted, titillating—yet practical words did nothing to lessen her worry for Daisy. *How could I have done this without you?*

'You've helped deliver pups before?' she said.

'Many times,' Dave replied. 'I'm not just a pretty face, you know.' He glanced at his watch. 'What time's your flight?'

'Eight—I need to be there by seven.' June passed the puppy to him, and he put it next to Daisy's teat alongside the firstborn. *You weren't going to say goodbye.* Dave felt a pang of sadness.

'Okay—then you've time to call Keith,' he said. June nodded, headed for the kitchen where she'd left the vet's card, pulled her phone from her pocket and dialled his number.

'Keith, it's June Hall—house-sitter at the Woodwards. Tank—I mean, Daisy the Staffy—is giving birth. Now!' Keith noted the urgency in June's voice.

'That's perfectly fine, June. She isn't far off her due date. Nature has a way of doing what it wants, when it wants, and if Daisy's time is now, it's now.' *Why is everyone so calm about this?* 'Are you alone, June?' he asked.

'No—I have Dave Andersen with me,' she explained.

'Ah… no problem then.' He sounded reassured. 'I'm not far from finishing up here at the clinic. I'll come straight over after I've seen my last patient.' *Your last patient? Why not now, for heaven's sake?* She took two calming breaths.

'Well… alright, then, I suppose,' she accepted his offer. 'We'll see you soon.' She was surprised. In her mind, Daisy being in labour with her first litter was an emergency. She ended the call and returned to the dog's side.

'Here, take this one for me,' Dave said, handing June the third puppy to be born. She took the tiny black creature and rubbed it vigorously with a towel.

'Four puppies, June,' Dave said excitedly as the fourth pup entered the world. His enthusiasm helped keep her grounded. 'Five!' he cried out. 'And they're all fit and well.' In a very short time, they were looking at seven tiny, squeaking, little black puppies. Each one had been rubbed down and was now suckling happily or nosing around to find a teat. Daisy looked proudly at her litter, licking them in a motherly fashion, however, Dave had a sneaking feeling she was *not* finished delivering yet. He glanced at his watch again. 'You'd better get going—you don't want to miss your flight.'

'Oh, yes—my flight… I almost forgot about it in all the excitement.' She felt a pang of sadness to have to leave Barrine Views. 'But what about the puppies—and pythons?' The puppies would be mere morsels to a python.

'Keith will most likely take them back to the surgery for the night to keep an eye on Mum. If he can't, I can always take them to my place or stay here.' A hollow feeling overcame him as he recalled the last time he'd stayed the night—he'd never see June Hall again beyond this moment. June reflected, too, on his words. *Stay here? Yes, you've done that.* She sighed. She'd missed him so badly all week that it physically hurt.

'The Woodwards return in the morning,' she said. 'It'd only be for one night.' She'd be happy knowing that Daisy and the puppies were in Dave's safe hands. Dave nodded. 'Okay, then… I'll get moving.' She had to, time was getting on. She hurriedly showered, finished packing, double-checked the house was as she'd found it, and was back on the deck in seven minutes, bags in tow. 'I'll need an update,' she insisted. 'Message me. If I don't get it before I fly, I will when the plane lands.' Dave gave her a warm smile, nodded and agreed. He made himself busy palpating Daisy's abdomen, checking for unborn puppies—Keith would bring his portable X-ray machine as well. Dave knew the process.

'I'll check the other animals after I finish here—make sure all's well—and also in the morning.'

'Yes! The animal rounds!' She'd forgotten about the other animals. *Dave Andersen to my rescue again!* A wave of sadness washed over her, and suddenly she felt as if her feet had been glued to the deck timber. She didn't want to leave. She'd never see Mrs. Little, walk without her splint, the turkey poults grow and leave the Schoolyard, or get to pat Wilbur again and share her thoughts on Dave Andersen with him. But they'd all go on just fine without her—even Dave. Dave stood.

'I'll get your suitcase,' he said, but she grabbed the handle.

'I've got it,' she insisted. With her handbag slung around her and a carry-on bag in tow, she dragged the suitcase down the stairs and to the rear of her car. She threw both bags into the boot. When she turned, Dave was standing there—his eyes void of their shine.

'Guess this is goodbye, Miss. Hall,' he said with a heavy heart.

'Guess it is, Mr. Andersen.' Dave leant down and gave her a peck on the cheek.

'Feel free to return any time,' he said. 'There's always room at my house, and Alice would love to have you stay.' June nodded.

'It's a long way,' she said.

'That it is,' Dave agreed. He looked longingly at her. He was taking a mental snapshot to remember her by.

'Thank you for the offer, anyway,' she said. She was not going to cry. *Big girl pants, June Hall.* This was just another locum job; there'd be plenty more. She pecked him on the cheek, pushed past him before he could respond, jumped into the driver's seat and started the car. She left the window up and, with a wave, turned and drove down the driveway, watching him fade into a distant figure in the rearview mirror. As she turned onto Arthur Willis Road, she glanced toward Dave's place and thought of Alice. She'd become fond of the meddlesome grandmother. Tears welled.

She needed to take her mind off Dave Andersen, permanently. *Think about the puppies.* She wondered whether Daisy would give birth to more. She tried to focus on the thought, over and over, but no matter how hard she tried, her thoughts kept jumping back to Dave. Everything reminded her of him—cattle in the paddock, the Millbrook pub, even the twisting bends of the Gillies Range Road. *Argh.* She'd miss him, there was no doubt about that. He'd become a very special friend who was not only good company but made her heart flutter and her body ache. He'd rejected her, but she'd live with it. Home was calling, life moves on.

Some loud music would clear her head—on went the radio, and bend by bend, she descended the Gilles Range Road.

Chapter 47

How Was Your Trip?
Back Home—Friday Night

The baggage claim carousel at Adelaide Airport was busy. *Is this usual for midnight on a Friday night, or is there something happening in town?* She'd come via Sydney, and the plane had appeared fully booked.

The steady stream of suitcases looping past her heavy eyes was almost hypnotic. *Mine is always the last bag out.* She waited patiently.

Around her, people pushed past each other to grab their bags—no eye contact, no conversation. Even manners, it seemed, had gone to bed. She was exhausted and figured the impatient people were just as tired as she was. *Being tired is no excuse for not using manners.*

The more June looked around, the more she noticed that most people were dressed as dark as the night outside the terminal windows. So much black. She recalled Tropical Fridays at Millbrook Surgery and how much effort the staff made to look bright and cheery—and she'd loved it. Her heart sank at the thought; she'd become fond of the happy staff who approached each day with a smile. *Nobody around me is smiling.*

Finally, her suitcase appeared—one of the last. The crowd had thinned. With her carry-on balanced precariously on top of her suitcase, she headed for the taxi rank and waited in line.

Cloaked in night, everyone appeared machine-like—a sea of expressionless faces. Only the flicker of eyes caught in the glow of mobile phones gave away their humanity. If she squinted, the glows shone like stars. She remembered how brilliant the stars had appeared above Barrine Views and glanced up into the night sky. They were still there, though not as dazzling—just as Dave had said—muted by light pollution. She wondered if he was looking at the stars tonight, too. No, he'd be asleep.

'Miss—you after a taxi?' a man yelled from a vehicle, drawing her attention. She'd been one million kilometres away, lost in the Southern Cross and the Saucepan. She stepped forward, surprised it was already her turn, and gave a nod.

The taxi driver jumped out and lifted the boot. June hoisted her bags in with little help from him. She slid into the back seat, gave him her address, and stared out the window—too tired for conversation. While the driver studied the road, she studied lights and their sources—streets, houses, cars, traffic, buildings, even planes nearing the airport. She'd never noticed light pollution before. *So many lights, so many people… such a lonely world.*

Reaching her unit complex, she trudged up the stairs, dragging her cases behind her: *ergh-clunk-clunk, argh-clunk-clunk*—audible as she heaved. *Why didn't I answer a "flatmate required" ad that boasted a lift?*

She opened the door, struggled through the threshold, and locked it behind her. *The Woodwards never locked their door. Nor did Dave.*

'Welcome back—how was it?' Her flatmate, Elizabeth, called out. She was on the couch being spooned by a man June didn't recognise—both were glued to a movie and munching their way through an oversized packet of Twisties.

'Interesting—and very different,' June replied.

'Any man-candy?' Elizabeth asked. She made no effort to look at June or introduce her man friend.

'No. Just work,' June lied.

'Oh,' Elizabeth said. Her eyes moved from the television to the bottom of the Twisties packet in search of crumbs. June was disappointed but not surprised by her flatmate's lack of interest. She'd been away for the entire month of March, and "Oh" was the end of their conversation. June glared at the back of Elizabeth's head. *Why have I never noticed how rude you are before tonight?*

'I'm going to unpack,' June said. No reply. She made a beeline for her room and closed the door behind her. *She was home.*

Her room was just as she'd left it—bed made with fresh sheets and envelope corners. Very minimalist. Most of her belongings fit into two cases. Besides work, this was where she spent her time.

She sat on her bed. The view out the window was pointless, day or night—just another unit block.

She remembered the landscape of the north—undulating green, cattle grazing, rainforest pockets, acreage, farm lots, and, of course, Dave's place. *Argh, Dave's place.* Alice. Foreign muck. A stolen kiss in the kitchen. Towels on hips. *My messages!* She'd forgotten to check her messages. There was a text from Dave.

June, 9 healthy puppies—8 black, and 1 that belongs to the milkman. Proud mum, Daisy, is doing well. Keith took them for the night. Animal rounds done. Hope you had a good flight home. Dave.

Clutching her phone to her chest for comfort, she fell asleep on the top of her bed and stayed there until morning.

Chapter 48

She'd Have Herself a Motto
Back to Work—A Reality Check

June's weekend went quickly. Reading and a long walk helped pass the hours, and then it was Monday and time for work. Her next job was in the city centre. She caught the bus.

At the first stop, a man boarded and sat beside her.

'Nice morning,' he said, and made himself comfortable.

'Indeed,' she replied. He wore a sharp suit and had a modern hairstyle. She figured he probably had a corporate job. His conversation didn't continue—his ringing phone saw to that—but she wasn't fussed. She glanced sideways at him. He was rather handsome and maybe a little older than her. She wondered if he could wrangle a python, handle a steer, or help birth puppies? Could he rescue a woman from a mudslide, help splint a chicken's leg or make love like no one else existed? She doubted it.

Finally, the bus reached the city. June got off at her stop and was swallowed by the crowd, another face among many. She made her way to the Medical Centre, where she would spend the next two weeks working. She didn't know why, but her usual interest in new surgeries just wasn't with her this morning.

The staff greeted her pleasantly but formally, explained the layout of the building, and then escorted her to the staff room, where she put her bag away. A table and chairs sat in the middle of the room, but there were no signs of home-grown fruits or home-baked goodies.

The treatment room at this surgery was staffed with two nurses. With one away, June would work alongside one of the surgery's permanent nurses.

'Good morning, I'm June, your locum nurse,' she said, introducing herself to the surgery nurse. June stood in the doorway of the treatment room office.

'Meg,' she replied, her eyes remaining fixed on her computer screen. 'Done practice nursing before?'

'Lots,' June answered.

'Thank goodness. We usually get a locum with no idea,' she muttered. 'So, I won't have to double-check all your work then, 'ey?' June considered her far from welcoming. 'You're registered on the computer,' she continued. 'And you have a list of patients.' She handed her a piece of paper. 'Here's your login and password. Use the computer at the far end. Need anything— ask.' June gave a nod, not that she saw it. *It's going to be a long two weeks.*

Her first patient was booked in for a simple set of vital signs. He'd been having panic attacks and appeared quite on edge. She wanted to talk to him and discuss relaxation techniques, but her screen lit up—her next patient was waiting. She reluctantly sent the man back to the waiting room, feeling she'd robbed him of helpful information.

The next patient was booked for an iron infusion. June escorted the woman into the treatment room and, while she set up around her, began explaining the procedure.

'This is not my first iron infusion!' she snapped. 'I know all about it.' The woman was more interested in browsing Instagram than talking with a nurse. It made June feel faceless and servant-like.

Morning teatime arrived. June headed to the bathroom and then to the kettle. She needed a strong cup of coffee. The tearoom appeared more of a thoroughfare than a quiet place to relax, and everyone coming and going seemed to be on a mission—nobody stopped for tea or a chat. She realised she was still in "country mode". She needed to put her head down and bum up and get the job done.

The next few hours were filled with mothers who were experts on the National Immunisation Program. They were argumentative, knew everything, and needed her for nothing more than drawing up the vaccines and physically injecting them into their children. *Why do parents always want to argue the pros and cons of immunisations with me? Like I developed them! And as if the whole idea of immunisation is some kind of government conspiracy! If they'd lost six of eleven kids to disease two hundred years ago, they'd be begging for vaccines.*

Later in the day, she dealt with a patient who insisted their wound be dressed as per "Dr. Google" and not according to "best practice" and the "doctor's instructions". After that, a businessman refused her request to obtain a set of vital signs, and a weight and measure check as booked. June then received a complaint from the doctor—she hadn't done her work. He was uninterested in hearing her side of the story. *Damned if you do, and damned if you don't.* She didn't have the energy to argue.

Two weeks passed, and June Hall was glad to see the back of the surgery; however, her next two-week locum was equally as horrid. On her final day, as she walked to the bus stop to go home, she began to question herself—was she losing patience and her ability to be empathetic? She figured, perhaps she'd just had enough of working in doctors' surgeries, a role she'd always loved. *I should look around, consider a surgical, medical or community role.* Deep in thought, she stopped dead in her tracks. The man walking behind her managed to step aside, but his briefcase swung and hit her calf.

'Ouch,' she said aloud and glanced at him.

'Best watch where you're going, Love,' he said and kept walking. *Arsehole!*

She'd stopped outside a newsagency and moved toward the window. Perhaps she'd be better off working permanently somewhere—a place she could embrace as her own space and not simply as a temporary fill-in for someone else. That would do it—that would reboot her career. She did something she never did—bought a newspaper before boarding the bus home. She'd look in the employment section and online—see what was on offer, and she'd have herself a motto. *Embrace a place as my own space!*

Sitting on her bed with a toasted cheese sandwich and a cup of chicken noodle soup for dinner, June Hall turned the pages of the paper until she found what she was looking for—employment. There were many career options available to her with her nursing credentials—hospital work, primary health, aged care, emergency room, orthopaedics and more. Turning the page, one job caught her eye, and she tore it out.

Practice Nurse wanted for our friendly surgery.
Rural and remote experience preferred.
Accommodation provided & excellent remuneration.
All applications to Dr. Woodward,
Millbrook Surgery, Millbrook, TNQ.

She wanted somewhere friendly, she'd recently gained one month's experience working rurally, she needed accommodation away from Elizabeth, and what they'd paid her before was good. The phone number was supplied—a mobile number. She also remembered Dr. Flint talking about the need for a second practice nurse, but Millbrook was a long way away from her family and friends. She gave it more thought. Her friends she rarely saw—work fixed that, both hers and theirs. And her family? Well, they were in the city, not far from her, but she spoke to them more on Messenger than she did face-to-face, and she could do that from anywhere. Besides, their get-togethers these days were few and far between—everybody worked—and Adelaide to Cairns was less than a three-hour journey if you caught a direct flight.

…and then there was Dave. She looked at herself in the mirror and spoke aloud.

'If you move, it needs to be because it's the right thing to do and not for any other reason—including Bunnings Boys.' She thought of Coral, Lisa and Angelica—they'd been so accommodating and friendly. Drs. Flint, Lee-Anne and Anna were fun to work with but also super professional. She imagined Dr. Woodward would be knowledgeable—everyone had spoken so highly of him—and she still had a lot to learn about rural practice.

'Haaa…' she let out a sigh—and then there was Mrs. Woodward. She'd be working side-by-side with her. They hadn't met, but June figured her organisational skills were second to none, and she loved nothing better than being organised. She felt sure they'd get on well.

'Mmmph…' she exhaled long and slow as if deflating. Of course, there was also Dave and Alice—she missed them both. *Friends, of course—Dave included.*

She read the advert again. *Damn it—you need a change and so does your career. Rural and remote is a great way to further your experience and skillset. You've tasted it and you loved it. And… you can drive—have a holiday on the way up. Give it a year, study online, and the world is your oyster after that—brilliant idea!*

She called the number, which happened to be Dr. Woodward's mobile, and discussed the role. After a thirty-minute discussion, she was offered the position without a probationary period—Doc considered that her month already worked sufficed. Everyone had talked highly of her, and that was all he needed. She sent a resignation text to her agency, packed everything she owned into three suitcases and two boxes, and left the next day. Within a fortnight, she'd driven across New South Wales, seen the coast of Queensland, and was back in the Tropical North.

Chapter 49

I've Relocated "The Beast"
The New Position—Monday through Friday

'I'm sure you'll be keen to get settled after your mammoth drive from Adelaide, June,' Dr. Woodward said. 'I've relocated "The Beast," so you have undercover parking in the shed.'

'Which "beast"—Winston or the ride-on mower?' June asked jokingly.

'Both,' Doc replied, laughing. 'Both "beasts" have been relocated to Dave's place. He has plenty of shed space and offered to house the mower. He also offered to take Winston off my hands—that "beast" is now living in his paddock permanently.' The Woodwards had finally realised the steer was much too big a pet for them.

June gave a thought to Winston. *You're going to eat him, then. Can't say I'll miss grey custard! Listen to yourself, June— you're thinking like a farmer!*

Thank you for my parking space—and thinking of me,' she replied excitedly. They were standing on the small deck at the front of the tiny home. Doc put the key in the door and opened it.

'It might be small, but it's cosy and functional,' he said. 'I hope you feel right at home.' The kindness in his tone was not lost on her—his welcome felt real. *True country hospitality— privacy, views, a deck—what more could a girl ask for?*

She'd been keen to see the inside of the tiny home and had even had the key during her house-sit, but she wasn't one to snoop—so she hadn't.

'I love it!' she said with a smile that hit the doctor in the heart. The accommodation boasted natural light, was modern, had a full kitchen, a bed loft, and was surprisingly roomy for a studio design. *Bingo… an air-conditioner!*

Doc informed her that the turkey poults had all grown well and were now roosting, albeit lower than the adults. Dave had retrieved the Schoolyard and had come up with a plan to revegetate the slope that led down to the papaya plantation. Mrs. Little was getting around just fine without her splint, and nine six-week-old puppies were tearing around the main deck exploring everything there was to explore and chewing everything there was to chew. Dave was adopting the odd-coloured pup—the one he'd called *the milkman's*—a male he'd already named "Moo". He'd take it at eight weeks of age. *I'll get a dog one day.*

She wondered how it was that a city girl, who'd had nothing to do with animals, could fall so in love with the wildlife of Tropical North Queensland and the domestic animals on the Woodwards' property? *Except pythons… and rats!* Anything long that slithered or had fur and ate engine wires, she'd gladly leave for someone else to handle.

***

June loved her first day back in the treatment room at Millbrook Surgery and knew she'd work well—and happily—beside Mary Woodward. Mary had excellent organisational and time management skills—qualities June hoped would rub off on her. She was gentle, caring, and exceptionally funny. June had never experienced humour like it—nurses' humour, with a wealth of experience thrown into the mix. As an older nurse, Mary had seen her share of terrible and heartbreaking things, and insisted it was humour that had helped her through it all. *You so need to laugh more, June Hall.*

***

Friday afternoon came—the end of June's first week as a permanent employee of Millbrook Surgery. She had five minutes to herself and took time out to make a cup of coffee. As she carried it back to her desk, she thought about Dave and visiting Paddock-to-Plate on Sunday to surprise him. She could hardly wait.

Before she got to sit down, her computer screen lit up. Her next patient was waiting. On her way past reception, Angelica spoke.

'How's your first week been, June?'

'Fabulous, thank you,' she said with a wink and a wave. In the waiting room, she called out. 'Linda.' A tall, attractive woman around her age stood up and smiled—she had perfect teeth. 'Hello Linda, I'm June. Would you mind coming with me to the treatment room? You haven't visited us for a while, and I just want to ensure your details are up to date. Dr. Woodward has also asked me to do a set of vital signs on you—it won't take long.'

'Certainly,' she replied. She carried herself with elegance—in her looks, her voice, and the way she presented. June felt like a short frump beside her, dressed in scrubs and Crocs. Linda followed her into the treatment room.

June checked her patient's date of birth and address before proceeding—Arthur Willis Road.

'Oh, I live on Arthur Willis Road—perhaps we're neighbours,' June said with a smile.

'Perhaps,' Linda replied, her disinterest evident. *186 seems familiar.* June didn't know why. She weighed her patient, took a set of observations, and then noted them in the woman's file.

'All done. Is there anything else I can help you with before you see the doctor?' she asked.

'Yes—a pregnancy test,' the woman explained.

'Oh—certainly. I'd love to help with that. Have you been trying for long?'

'No, not long,' she smiled. *How are your teeth so white?* June subconsciously ran her tongue across a chip in her tooth—she'd kill for teeth like that. She noted Linda's brown eyes—dark, mysterious and captivating. She was a beautiful woman indeed with perfect, long, dark hair that shone under the fluorescent light of the treatment room. *What I'd give to have your elegance.*

June provided Linda with a urine specimen jar and sent her to the bathroom. She took a pregnancy test from the cupboard and prepared it. When Linda returned, June gloved up and conducted the pregnancy test.

'Oh, it's two red lines,' June said excitedly.

'I'm pregnant, aren't I?' Linda asked. She didn't seem overly excited, but June knew that everyone received news like that differently. *You'll be excited when it sinks in.* She was happy for her patient.

'Yes, the urine test is positive, but the doctor may also require a blood test to be certain.'

'That's okay. It's very early days,' Linda explained. 'Oh, can you change my mobile number? I have a new one.'

'Of course,' June said happily. She de-gloved and washed her hands, then jumped back on her computer and updated the phone number as Linda called it out. She ran her eyes over the other details on file just in case she needed to update anything else.

Next of Kin… Dave Andersen.

Relationship… Husband. *Good Lord, you're Loopy Linda!*

'186—that's Dave's place,' June blurted.

'That's right,' Linda said with her flawless smile. 'Dave is my husband.'

June swallowed hard. She was speechless. *You're pregnant. It only just happened. Pregnant to Dave… who's jumped from your bed to mine and back again!* She felt sick. *But he told me that you left him—he said it to my face!*

This was one "beast" June Hall hadn't imagined relocating to Dave's place.

Chapter 50

The Words We Don't Speak
Friday Through Sunday

Nurse Woodward had knocked off at 3:00 p.m., just missing June's "Loopy Linda" experience. June was grateful. She shut down the treatment room and prepared to go home—it had been extremely hard to be polite to her last few patients, but she'd done it like the true professional she was.

The weekend was knocking at the door. She would *not* be going to Paddock-to-Plate on Sunday—or any other day—despite the girls from work talking about it. She would be staying as far away from Dave Andersen as possible. *Scumbag.*

The time they'd spent together, and their lovemaking, had been nothing but a lie. The date of Linda's pregnancy was the truth. Dave was seeing them both simultaneously—her for fun and Linda for breeding! *Dirtbag.*

Where had Linda been while he was fooling around with her? *Shopping? Sailing? Having her hair done? Getting her fancy teeth done?* June didn't know, and she couldn't and wouldn't guess. *Care factor—zero!*

When June knocked off, she snuck out the back door and drove home. To say she was furious was an understatement. Tonight, she would hibernate, read her book, and eat chocolate for dinner. Tomorrow she'd expand her diet and eat chocolate for breakfast, lunch, dinner and supper too!

***

It was Sunday morning, and June had cabin fever. She imagined zits welling under the skin on her face from all the chocolate she'd eaten. She needed fresh air. She dressed in old shorts and t-shirt, and a pair of chicken boots and made her way up to the main house. She needed something to take her mind off Lying Dave and his Loopy wife. As much as she loved her tiny home, it looked straight across the valley to Dave Andersen's property—even more so than the main house at Barrine Views. Doc had fetched The Beast from Dave's—she'd seen him riding back to Barrine Views. If the house yard needed mowing, she would do it. It was time to tackle The Beast.

At the top of the deck stairs, June stepped over the makeshift fence that kept the puppies in—she recalled the Winston chain. It was still there, coiled to the side. *Surely, they're not thinking of another steer.* She headed for the sliding door—a slow process with nine puppies to fuss over.

'Yoo-hoo,' she called out. Mary Woodward came to the door. She looked at June, a picture bent over fighting off nine puppies who were hell bent on chewing her boots.

''Give them a centimetre and they take a kilometre,' she said. June stood back up. 'You look like a woman on a mission, June,' Mary said with a smile.

'I see Doc has fetched The Beast. Would you mind if I mowed?' June gestured toward the lawn that surrounded the house and driveway. 'I need some outdoor time.'

'Oh, okay.' Mary turned and called out to Doc, who was in the kitchen. He poked his head around the corner. June smiled at his milk moustache. 'Can you fetch the keys to the ride-on for June, Dear?' Mary asked. 'She wants to do the mowing.'

'Of course!' Doc agreed, jovially. He turned to get the key from the key hanger on the wall. 'I'd be a madman to refuse a volunteer mowing my lawns.' He thought for a moment. 'Are you sure you want to do it? Don't you have something better to do?'

'Not really,' June replied.

'Do you know how to drive the thing?' he asked.

'Nope,' June said. Doc looked bemused.

'Well, a crash course then, hey?' he said.

'Best way to learn,' June smiled. 'Get thrown in the deep end.' Mary nodded in agreement.

Doc and June made their way out to The Beast. June sat upon it, and Doc explained how to use it. It was simple—no gears, push forward to go forward, pull backward to go backward. No brakes—if you lift your foot off the accelerator, it stops. On off button. Done.

She took the keys from Doc and started it.

'The puppies won't get out, will they?' she asked. 'I'd hate to run over one.'

'I'll make sure they don't, June.'

'Promise,' she said.

'Promise,' he replied. 'It's all fuelled up and good to go.'

June reversed, took off, and started around the house yard. The chickens moved out of her way before she even got close to them—they weren't fans. Within a few laps of the yard, she was mowing like an expert. Doc gave her the thumbs up and went inside.

With the house yard mowed, she decided to tackle the long slope of the driveway. Up and down, she went, her concentration so intense she didn't notice Dave coming down his driveway opposite. June on the ride-on, and Dave in his car, reached the bottom of their driveways simultaneously and looked up to see one another. Dave looked surprised and gave a hearty wave out of his window, but all June could see was the beautiful woman in the passenger seat beside him. *You're with your pregnant wife, Linda!*

June exaggerated each syllable as she mouthed *arsehole* across the road, her lips slow and deliberate so there was no mistaking her message. No sound needed, her message landed loud and clear. *If I were game to take my hands off this mower, you'd be getting "the bird," too!*

As Dave drove off along Arthur Willis Road, June turned the mower around for its last run up the driveway. She'd finished the mowing and was glad. Her focus was no longer on it; it was once again on how Dave Andersen could blatantly lie to her. He was clearly still married, and his wife was indeed pregnant. *How naïve you are, June Hall? A silly little girl fantasising about happy ever afters.*

She drove the mower to the house and parked it alongside the hose, just as Doc had requested. She knew that once the engine cooled, he'd be cleaning it and fussing over it—he kept it like new. Hopping off and stretching, she decided a walk around the property would clear her mind. She never tired of the Woodwards' garden.

Just before midday, as she sat on her couch flicking through one of Dr. Woodward's medical journals, a car made its way casually up the driveway and stopped outside her tiny home. She jumped up and opened the door. The car windows wound down, and she could see who it was.

'Surprise!' Voices in unison announced the arrival of the girls from work.

'You can't spend your life locked away at Barrine Views,' Coral said. 'We're going to lunch at Paddock-to-Plate and you're coming with us.'

'And if I say no?' June said. Her hands on her hips and her scowl a giveaway that she'd planned to *never* go there again.

'You can say no, but if you do,' Lisa explained with a serious face June never knew she had. 'We're going to drag you kicking and screaming and then force-feed you hamburgers!' Their cheesy smiles and infectious giggles made her defiance useless.

'Honestly, you lot are impossible.' June glared at them and they laughed even harder. A grin she fought pulled at the corners of her mouth.

'You're one of us now,' Angelica added. 'Don't let the team down!' June's love of people overcame her. She'd felt part of the Millbrook Surgery team since her first day, nearly 11 weeks earlier. 'Okay, give me five minutes to change.' She didn't want to see Dave or his wife, but she couldn't explain that to the girls—privacy issues, both theirs and hers.

She washed her face, brushed her hair, and then swapped her old shorts and t-shirt for a dress. She grabbed her bag, slipped on her sandals, made her way out the door, and jumped into the back of Coral's car.

'Has anyone ever called you lot pushy?' she asked.

'Many times,' they all replied.

Coral headed down the driveway of Barrine Views and out onto Arthur Willis Road. Despite it being on her side of the car, June refused to look toward Dave's place. Within minutes, they were turning into the crowded car park of Third Creek Paddock-to-Plate.

Dave was as busy as ever. He stood at the barbeque cooking for the crowd. June noted he'd taken her advice and set the salads, rolls, sauces, and cutlery up next to him. The girls joined the queue for food, pushing June in front of them.

June tried to act oblivious to the goings on but watched closely as Dave took payments on his Square Terminal, cooked the meats, and dished them up. Twice, there was a delay as he ran to the cold room to fetch more meat and salad. June could see he was managing, albeit in a frantic sort of way. The beer and wine fridge was closed—he'd never manage to serve alcoholic drinks, as well as all the other things he was doing. It was a shame with the current crowd—a loss of revenue, and everybody looked thirsty with money to spend.

June had to admit it, but Dave Andersen was doing what he did best, giving the moment one hundred per cent. He'd done that with their lovemaking—given one hundred per cent. Or was it fifty per cent—half to her and half to Loopy Linda?

With that thought, realisation and anger that had been smouldering inside her, reignited on the spot, and quickly exploded into a flaming volcano, but where there's fire, there's fantasy—vivid fantasy. She could do that now—fantasise—he'd taught her. With scorn in her eyes, she built herself a picture of revenge:

...she took his sharp carving knife—pavlova and the blood of Alice's foot still fresh on the blade—and cut the fly of his jeans wide open. She relieved him of his dim-sims and tossed them on

the hotplate. Then, she cut off his beef bayonet, shoved it on a skewer and grilled it!

Suddenly, she felt a wave of calm wash over her. *Okay, June Hall, now you've got that off your chest, move on!*

She wanted to despise him, but instead, felt empathy for him as he struggled to keep up with the crowd. That's who she was—empathetic to the core, but she would not be helping today, not while his so-called "wife", Linda, sat in the corner doing nothing but looking gorgeous. *What kind of wife doesn't lift a finger to help?*

Having waited patiently in the lineup—the girls right behind her—June finally reached the barbeque. Dave dished up half of her meal, before realising she was standing in front of him. He froze momentarily—a steak in his tongs.

'Um… oh… hello, June—I see you're back. I was surprised,' he said in a genuine tone. *Not as surprised as I was to find your pregnant wife has moved back in!*

'Did you accept the position at the surgery?' he asked. She nodded. 'Good on you,' he said, finally putting the steak on her plate. She cleared her throat.

'I thought I'd give the country way of life a bit more of a go,' she explained, trying to sound unaffected by him. She refused to look into the eyes she knew too well; eyes that had driven her wild only weeks before and eyes she now considered gouging out with her suture removal kit.

Dave stopped and looked over the top of June and toward the road. All guests at Paddock-to-Plate followed suit. An ambulance roared past with lights flashing and sirens wailing. It was headed in the direction of the Woodwards and Dave's Place. June knew there were more properties beyond theirs—she didn't see reason to panic. She used the distraction to move sideways to the salad. When Dave looked back, it was Coral that now stood in front of him, her plate held out ready. He glanced toward June, but she was not looking at him. She'd dished up her salad, taken a roll and cutlery and was headed toward an empty table.

Dave continued his cooking, hiding his worry from his patrons. His thoughts were of Alice. She was fine when he left the house and had promised she'd never self-harm again. He pushed the thoughts from his mind. Alice was a woman who upheld a promise, and Dave knew that. He dished up Coral's meat, then Lisa and Angelica's. The women helped themselves to salad before joining June at the table, away from the main crowd. They could see both the paddock and the crowd within.

The girls' table was made of solid-but-rustic, recycled doors—Coral fell in love with it. June wondered if the doors had hung in the original slaughterhouse. She wouldn't ask.

They were almost through their meal when June looked toward Dave. The line had stilled—he was talking on his mobile. When the call ended, he appeared to scan the crowd, then his eyes fell upon her. He made a beeline for her.

'June… Can I talk to you for a second?' he asked. His look was worrisome. June stood up, and they stepped just out of earshot of the table.

'Doc just called. Seems Alice has had a turn of some sort. The ambulance is there now. They're going to take her to the hospital in Atherton. She's asked if we can accompany her, you and I—but I can't,' he said, gesturing to the crowd around him. 'Will you, June, accompany her? Please?' June made the mistake of looking into his worried eyes. She nodded.

'Okay,' she agreed.

'The ambulance will collect you on the way past. They won't be long. Thank you so much.' He gave her a quick hug and then returned to the line-up at his barbeque. *What a nerve,* June thought. *He's already told them I'm coming!*

June explained the situation, excused herself from the table, and left the ladies to finish their meals. She headed to the roadside to await the ambulance. *How do I get myself into these situations?* She could hear the siren getting louder as the ambulance approached. She knew lights and sirens were used only for time-critical cases, and they were using them for Alice. She started to wonder if the elderly woman was alright.

The ambulance pulled up, and the rear door flung open.

'You can sit in here with Alice and me, or take the front seat—stat,' the paramedic offered. June wanted to know what was going on—she jumped in the back, closed the door behind her, took the seat next to Alice and fastened her seatbelt. The vehicle raced on. June took Alice's hand in hers—the grandmother was pale. A nasal cannula supplying oxygen sat across her face, and a portable ECG machine was connected to her chest to monitor her heart. June studied the monitors.

'Acute myocardial infarction, we believe,' the paramedic explained. She was seated face to face with June. June nodded—she understood it was a heart attack—and focused on Alice.

'Hello, darling, June,' Alice said. June noted the struggle in both her voice and her breathing. 'It's so nice to see you.' Her smile was genuine. 'How's Dave managing today?' June didn't want to worry her.

'He's managing fine,' she answered.

'Fiddlesticks,' Alice gave a one-sided smirk. 'Loopy won't help… not enough brain for a headache—that one.'

'It's just the bar he can't manage,' June insisted. She patted the back of Alice's hand to comfort her.

'Don't let Loopy put you off, Dave,' Alice said, referring to Linda. 'Came for the last of her things…. *cough, cough*.'

'Shhh, Alice, best you concentrate on your breathing,' the paramedic insisted.

'Don't shoosh me. I'll shut up when I'm dead.' The paramedic ignored her. Alice turned her attention to June, her words continuing between ragged breaths.

'I told David… *hhhnn—hahh*… throw the drongo and her things in a heap and light the begger… he doesn't listen… I'll throw the match…' She squeezed June's hand. Her voice was shaky.

'Perhaps you shouldn't talk,' June urged. 'Alice—concentrate on your breathing.' Alice nodded no.

'He picked her up from the airport, Friday… taking her back tomorrow… not soon enough. He doesn't love her… it's just Dave… he treats everyone well, whether they deserve it or not… and she deserves Jack Shit!'

Alice stopped and breathed as deeply as she could, though it pained her. She squeezed June's hand tightly. She was giving it her all. June responded by gently stroking her knuckles intuitively. But Alice was far from finished.

'Loopy told me this morning she's pregnant… to Deadhead—Dave's worst best mate. They ran off together… on my David's first wedding anniversary…' Air rattled in her chest.

'He did us one helluva favour taking Loopy off our hands!' she laughed—and coughed. 'Problem with this world—we let the dumb breed!'

'Rest, Alice—please,' June insisted, watching as she breathed in and out, concentrating on every breath, but the meddlesome Gran had things to say, and she'd darn-well say them. Barely audible through exhaustion, she spoke softly.

'My David loves you, June.' June nodded. She moved in closer. 'When you've lived as long as I have… you learn stuff—lots of stuff… There's everyday-love, and there's once-in-a-lifetime love.'

'Breath, Alice, please,' June pleaded with her to rest. She was growing concerned, but the stubborn woman would not stop.

'Linda and Dave's love was everyday-love and that shit's everywhere—lust, infatuation, stupidity. Now she's pregnant to Deadhead, hopefully her "forever" because as sure as God made little green apples, we don't want her back!' June smiled. Even in the face of a heart attack, the grandmother remained loyal, fearless and jovial.

Alice's breaths were fading to sighs. She clutched her chest with one hand, refusing to let June's hand go. Her voice was ever so slight.

'Dearest June… once-in-a-lifetime love doesn't come from saying the soppy "love" word… hell no… that rare kind of love is the divine connecting of two souls… ….. It's the butterflies inside us and the excitement and joy we experience just thinking about the one we love... ... . It's the pain in our hearts when we're separated, for minutes or years, and...'

Alice's eyes fell shut; her body could not keep up with her will.

'Rest, Alice—*please*,' June pleaded. Alice took a few moments to breathe.

'I haven't finished...' She opened her eyes and met June's gaze with quiet resolve.

'It's the desire to be together physically... and simply wanting to be together for no reason at all. But most of all... ... it's in the eyes. Both you and Dave have eyes for one another... ... like my Frank—God rest his soul—and I had for one another.' She stopped and took a few breaths.

'You and my David are each other's once-in-a-lifetime, June—you can't let that go!' Overwhelmed with emotion, tears welled in June's eyes, rolled down her cheeks and fell onto her dress. Alice was right—Dave was all of that to her.

'Now I've finished, Dear,' she said. 'I'll rest.'

Alice's breaths came unevenly. Softening. Feather-light. Faltering. Life slowly slipped away from the Andersen family matriarch, and her eyes shut—they'd seen enough of this world.

Her hand fell limp in June's. June clutched it tighter, willing life to remain. But Alice's chest stayed still. Her breathing had ceased. The ECG flat-lined, its alarm piercing the silence inside the ambulance.

June let go of Alice's hand and scrambled to find a pulse—anywhere—there wasn't one. The grandmother's heart had stopped. She looked past the paramedic in front of her and toward the driver and screamed out.

'Stop the ambulance!' They were just minutes from the hospital.

'We can't,' advised the paramedic seated with June. She spoke calmly. The driver switched off the lights and sirens but kept driving.

'Stop, I said!' June screamed again. 'Please—we need to bring her back!' She released her seatbelt, leant forward, and prepared herself to start compressions. The paramedic next to her moved forward, grabbed her hands, and stopped her. June glared at her, infuriated, but the paramedic stood her ground and would not let go. She looked directly into June's eyes.

'Mrs. Andersen has a DNR—do not resuscitate,' she said, calmly.

'I know what a bloody DNR is!' June screamed at her. 'But I don't want her to die!' The paramedic released her hands and then held June by the shoulders. She let her vent until flooding tears replaced her rage.

'June,' the paramedic said softly. 'Alice would only come with us in the ambulance if we agreed to her DNR. We spoke with Dr. Woodward. It's at the surgery, and a copy is at the hospital.'

'Oh—no—no—no,' June picked up Alice's lifeless hand and pressed it to her face. Tears continued, trailing over the now-dead woman's hand. 'Oh Alice,' she sobbed. The paramedic rubbed June's shoulder and let her grieve. As they pulled up outside the ED, June's sobs slowed. The paramedic spoke.

'June, Alice told us she'd had enough of this fast-paced world. She said she was ready to be with her husband. I asked her why. She said it was because the pain deep in her heart, the pain of being separated from him, was no longer bearable. I didn't believe for a moment that she'd pass today, but she has, and we must honour her wishes.'

'He was her once-in-a-lifetime love,' June voiced softly. She turned to the paramedic and nodded gratefully.

Epilogue

June sat red-eyed in the hospital lounge, waiting patiently for Dave. He had still been at Paddock-to-Plate, tied to the barbeque, when the hospital doctor notified him of Alice's passing.

'Dave said he's on his way,' the doctor had advised her. 'Said, the ladies from the Millbrook Surgery were taking over.' His words had tugged at her heart. Her new family had her back—and Dave's as well. She knew they'd tackle everything they could, cooking, cleaning and closing. Later, she'd find out they'd put Loopy Linda to work at the kitchen sink. They had her over a barrel—she couldn't refuse them. It was either wash dishes and get a ride home or walk a country road in heels.

With both hands wrapped around the extra-strong mug of coffee the nurses had brought her, she gathered her thoughts. She wondered how Dave would cope with the news. He and Alice were as close as grandson and grandmother could be. She stared at the liquid in her mug. The coffee was undrinkable, but it gave her something to hold on to and stare into.

Her ears pricked, and she looked up. It was the sound of work boots running... thud—thud—thud—thud. Dave appeared in the doorway of the hospital lounge. Without taking her eyes off him, she put her mug down on the small table beside her. He came to her, stood before her and looked down at her.

Her beautiful, strong Dave looked so wounded.

'They told me you were there at the end,' he said softly. June nodded.

'She loved you so much, Dave,' June told him.

'I know,' he attempted a smile. 'She told me every day without fail.'

'She didn't want to be resuscitated, Dave.' June's eyes pleaded for forgiveness. 'There was nothing I could do.' A tear escaped her eye and started down her cheek. He stopped it in its tracks with the back of his finger, then leant forward and put his hands upon her shoulders.

'I was aware of the DNR, June. It's okay. I don't blame anyone for her passing. It was her time, and she went her way,' he said. June gave a nod. 'I am, however, so very grateful that you were with her and she didn't pass alone. She thought the sun shone out of you, June, and she was right. She was always right.' June tried to smile. 'I am sorry you had to go through this.'

'I'm a nurse,' she said proudly. 'You think I'd be more used to it.'

'You don't get used to loss—ever, June.' His voice was low, broken. He gazed forlornly into the emerald-green eyes that haunted him—always there, waiting behind every blink. 'When you left the Woodwards', my heart was shattered, and I knew it would never mend. Alice knew it, too. I wanted to be with you so much, June. To waste time on the deck step with you, to stare at the stars with you, to hold hands with you and to make love to you.

'I didn't want to own you, so I said nothing that would stop you leaving and doing what makes you happy. I let you go because I love you, June Hall.' He stopped, drew a breath and released it through pouted lips.

You love me, Dave Andersen!

'Gran said, I was always running. I needed to stop, listen, and truly see the beautiful things in front of me—every single day. Now you're back, I'd love to see you again—every single day. That's if you'll let me. And, of course, if you want to see me too!' He quietened. It was June's turn to talk.

'Alice certainly spoke some wise words. She said that love is the pain we feel deep in our hearts when we are separated. I've been in pain since you walked out on me that night. I would love to have you in my life again, David Andersen.'

Alice's words rang out in June's head as if she were standing next to her, whispering them in her ear, "and most of all, it's in the eyes". June stood, reached up and kissed him on the cheek. He could taste the salt from her tears. As she pulled back, their eyes locked. *"Most of all, it's in the eyes".* Alice was right. The pain of loss in his sapphire-blue eyes broke her heart—and somehow, in the same breath, mended her soul. She was home.

With his arm tenderly wrapped around her, they made their way through the hospital and to the car park. Tonight, June's tiny home would be the beginning of something immeasurable—the rest of their lives.

The End.

Spinner, my favourite chook, and the
inspiration for Mrs. Little. Spinner
overcame a broken leg and went on to
become a great mother. We named her
Spinner because she was blind in one eye
and spun in circles a lot.

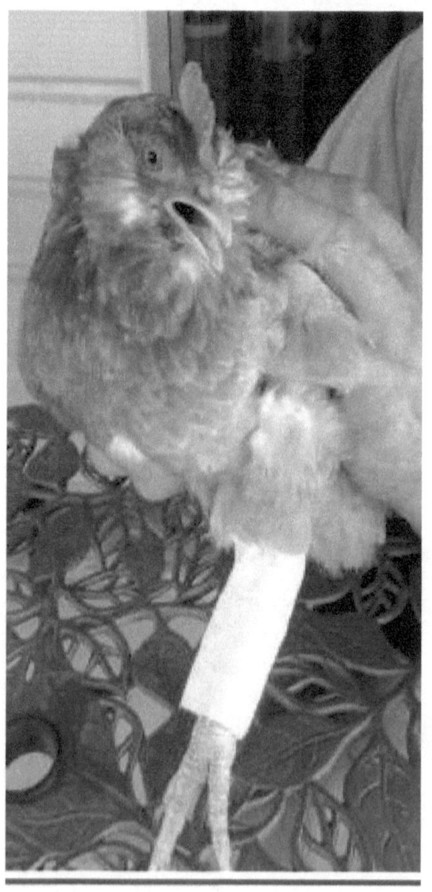

My turkey hen with her poults. Their lesson for the day—what happens when a cane toad doesn't make it across the driveway.

Afterword

Thanks for reading *June's March*. I hope you enjoyed my novel.

I wrote this novel in 2023—quite hurriedly—keen to finish it and dedicate it to a terminally ill friend for her birthday. After she passed, I wanted to spend more time on it, do a rewrite, and further develop my characters, hence *June's March* © 2025 was written from my home in Moonta Bay, SA.

Inspiration was not a problem for either the setting or the story. I've lived on acreage in the tropical north and done plenty of animal wrangling. I was house-sitting on another friend's property during the initial writing of the novel with four weeks to fill.

On the first day, I sat on the timber deck surrounded by four dogs, a pet steer—Nox, wandering chickens, and guinea fowl, and just soaked up the atmosphere. The Atherton Tablelands is quite a remarkable and beautiful place, with outstanding wildlife. Many of the menagerie goings-on have been my own experiences in one way, shape or form.

On the second day, before I began to write, I had to shovel Nox's manure (grey custard) off the deck. I didn't realise I'd be doing it every morning thereafter—much to my horror, a "Winston chain" (the chain in the novel that keeps pet steer, Winston, off the deck) didn't exist to keep him away.

On the hills that surrounded me were scattered farmhouses framed by cattle in lush green paddocks. Many quirky homes sat at the end of long, steep driveways stretching up from unsealed roads that passed their properties. These properties gave me the inspiration for Dave's place and Dave as a character. By the end of the book, I was kind of wishing Dave was my neighbour—what eye candy he'd be!

As for June, she is purely fictitious, however, I did work for several years as a rural practice nurse—a wonderful experience never short of characters.

I've owned turkeys, a blind pig, chickens (and yes, I mended a broken leg on one who went on to become a mother), many dogs, a cow, horses, and I've grown (and continue to grow) many things.

June's March is a work of fiction, however, the Gillies Highway, Cairns, Rusty's Markets, Kuranda Range Road (an informally named section of the Kennedy Highway), the Atherton Tablelands and the Palmerston Highway all exist. The town of Millbrook, the surgery, Dave's place, Barrine Views, the pub, Harbour Hotel, and the characters are all from my imagination. Any similarities are purely coincidental. However, I did slide down a muddy turkey run, and I did have to call for help by yelling at the top of my lungs to draw my husband's attention. He threw me a rope, hauled me up, and hosed the mud and manure off me—Ah… my Dave!

I have written and edited this book myself, and I imagine it's not perfect. Any errors in language, facts, or figures are mine, though I've done my best to be accurate. I admit I am not perfect, if I were, I'd have nothing to strive for!

Special thanks go to Judith, Marina and Sherrie for proofreading for me. Your interest, help and direction have helped me no end. Thanks also to my patient husband, Marty, who held the fort while I created this book and all my surgery patients who read the first version and showered me with encouragement to keep writing. Also, a shout out to Bunnings (who I swear my husband keeps afloat) for allowing me to use "Bunnings Boy" throughout the book.

I hope you'll join me again when big brother Justin gets his chance at love.

Strive on, Heather Jane Hill 2025

Meet the Author

Heather Jane Hill is an Australian writer who divides her time between Tropical North Queensland and South Australia's Yorke Peninsula, where she lives with her husband and two much-loved staffies. A proud country girl, art enthusiast, nurse, and former tour guide, she draws endless inspiration from the rhythms of everyday life, the beauty of the natural world, and the complexities of human nature. After honing her skills writing for the tourism industry, she leapt into independent publishing, creating works across multiple genres, including novels, poetry, young adult fiction, and children's picture books. *June's March,* her heartfelt debut romance novel, marks the beginning of a new chapter in her writing journey and is a story close to her heart.

Other Titles by Heather Jane Hill

Adult Poetry

Gettin' Poetic Down Under

Kids' Poetry

The Baker's Dozen—
13 Critter Poems from Northern Australia

Kids' Rhyming Story Books

The Quickest Quokka's Quest

They Seymour Big-Cloud Strut

The Termi'rific Haircut